AN
IMPROBABLE
SEASON

ROSALYN EVES

FARRAR STRAUS GIROUX
NEW YORK

Farrar Straus Giroux Books for Young Readers
An imprint of Macmillan Publishing Group, LLC
120 Broadway, New York, NY 10271 • fiercereads.com

Our books may be purchased in bulk for promotional, educational, or business use. Please
contact your local bookseller or the Macmillan Corporate and Premium Sales Department at
(800) 221-7945 ext. 5442 or by email at MacmillanSpecialMarkets@macmillan.com.

Library of Congress Cataloging-in-Publication Data
Names: Eves, Rosalyn, author.
Title: An improbable season / Rosalyn Eves.
Description: First edition. | New York : Farrar Straus Giroux Books for Young Readers,
2023. | Audience: Ages 12–18. | Audience: Grades 10–12. | Summary: In 1817
England, teenagers Thalia, Charis, and Kallie navigate a London Season gone awry.
Identifiers: LCCN 2022005891 | ISBN 9780374390181 (hardback)
Subjects: CYAC: Balls (Parties)—Fiction. | London (England)—History—19th
century—Fiction. | Great Britain—History—1789–1820—Fiction. | LCGFT:
Novels of manners. | Romance fiction. | Novels.
Classification: LCC PZ7.1.E963 Im 2023 | DDC [Fic]—dc23
LC record available at https://lccn.loc.gov/2022005891

First edition, 2023
Book design by Michelle Gengaro-Kokmen
Printed in the United States of America

ISBN 978-0-374-39018-1

1 3 5 7 9 10 8 6 4 2

To my parents, Bruce and Patti,
for introducing me to reading—and to Regencies

AN
IMPROBABLE
SEASON

CHAPTER ONE

Away to London Town

(Thalia)

To market, to market, one girl as a bride,
Home again, home again, lord by her side
To market to market, I'll be no man's wife
I'll write poems instead and make my own life.

— *Thalia Aubrey*

Oxfordshire, late February 1817

Charis Elphinstone was missing.

To one unacquainted with Charis, this might be alarming, even shocking. But Thalia Aubrey, tasked with finding the cousin she had known since infancy, was neither alarmed nor shocked. She was, truth be told, rather put out. She settled her bonnet on her golden curls and set off toward the gardens in a huff, her half boots crunching across the gravel rather more loudly than was ladylike.

On an ordinary day, Charis's disappearance would not be so remarkable. Charis quite often went missing, only to turn up hours later with dirt on her hem and a smudge on her nose, having heard the siren call of some rare bird. But it was beyond anything for Charis to disappear on *this* morning, which was to take Thalia, her sister Kalliope, and Charis to London, for the London Season that paralleled the sitting of Parliament, running from late winter until June. A Season that, for Thalia, had already been delayed a year due to Mama's illness last spring.

"Charis, where are you?" Thalia muttered, more to herself than anything, leaving the road and crossing the dead lawn. Spring was still just a hopeful thought in Oxfordshire: Most of the bushes were dormant, and what few leaves clung brown and determined to their branches bore the hint of last night's frost. The frost was a good sign: Uncle John said it would mean clear, hard roads and a quicker arrival at their destination.

But what good were frost and clear roads if Charis would not appear?

Thalia cleared the corner of the house and spotted the hedges that surrounded the garden. She didn't think Charis would have picked this morning, of all mornings, to thread her way through the maze, but one never knew. Perhaps she'd spotted some new insect among the twisting paths. But surely it was too early in the year for bugs?

The windows of Elphinstone manor winked at Thalia in the morning light. Her aunt and uncle's manor house had often proved a sanctuary for her, when her father's crowded parsonage had become too much, though its vastness didn't feel very sanctuary-like at the moment, since Charis might be hiding anywhere.

"Thalia!"

She turned to find Adam Hetherbridge bearing down on her.

Though Thalia was uncommonly tall for a young lady, Adam was a few inches taller still than she, with sandy hair and blue eyes that were bright behind gold-rimmed spectacles.

Thalia returned his smile. "You've come to send us off?" Adam had begun as their neighbor, and then her brother Frederick's friend, but something had shifted last spring, when Adam graduated from Oxford while Freddy continued to slog away at his studies. Adam intended to go into the church, but while he waited to become eligible for a suitable living, he continued his studies with Thalia's father. His near-daily visits to the vicarage inevitably turned into near-daily visits with Thalia, where they argued amicably about history and books and philosophy and anything else that caught their interest.

"Yes. Good thing for me that Charis went missing, or I'd have missed you entirely!"

Thalia made a face and twitched a blond curl over her shoulder. "I'm glad her disappearance is lucky for someone." She entered the maze, Adam at her side. "But you needn't have bothered—you'll join us yourself in a few days."

Adam had not meant to come for the Season at all, but his father insisted he acquire some social polish before burying himself in a country parish. Even then Adam might have resisted, but Thalia overheard her own father telling Adam it would ease his mind to have a "stable influence" in town with his daughters (never mind that their aunt and uncle would accompany them). Perforce, Adam agreed to stay with a cousin in London once he had finished up some work for Thalia's father. "True enough. But I told Frederick I'd see you off in his stead."

"Did Freddy ask you to?" That seemed most unlike her brother, who could not reliably be depended upon to remember anything that did not closely concern himself. Thalia highly doubted he'd sent word from Oxford.

Adam hesitated for a minute, thwacking a loose branch out of their path. "Not exactly. But I'm sure he meant to."

"What you mean is, you would have done so, had you any siblings. Because you are a prince among men."

"That's rating me rather too highly," Adam said modestly. "Say rather . . . a marquis."

As a marquis was still several degrees higher in the social order than a vicar's daughter and an aspiring vicar, Thalia laughed, and led Adam into the center of the maze. She had walked it so frequently now that she might have traversed it with her eyes closed and come to no harm. She called out to Charis again when they reached the center, but without much hope of an answer.

"And what shall you do first, when you reach London, Miss Aubrey?" Adam asked.

"Oh, so I'm Miss Aubrey now? I was Thalia a moment ago."

"I'm giving you practice in responding to your proper name," Adam said. "I can call you Toodles, if you'd rather."

Thalia made a face at the childhood nickname and turned a corner round a hedge. "Don't you dare."

"You're avoiding my question."

"I'm not avoiding it." Thalia reflected for a moment. "First, I imagine we shall eat, then sleep. Then I shall find Hatchards bookstore, if Aunt Harmonia does not make me go shopping."

"I'm glad to see you have your priorities in order," Adam said. "I'm always skeptical of enterprises requiring new clothes."

Thalia laughed. "Don't tell Kalli that. She has her heart set on a new wardrobe."

They emerged from the maze. No Charis.

"Has anyone checked the greenhouses?" Adam asked, indicating the glass structure some distance to their right.

"Uncle John was dispatched to look there," Thalia said, starting across the broad stretch of grass reaching to a small, wooded area. "Though knowing Charis, she's halfway through the wood by now, and once we find her, she'll be covered in mud, and we'll all have to wait while she changes clothes. Mama sent the children to look through the house with Aunt Harmonia, or we'd no doubt be looking for them too at this point."

"What do you think Charis is after this time?" Adam asked.

"Heaven only knows. Perhaps she heard a birdsong she wished to identify. Or a gardener found some fox scat that she wished to inspect." Though if that were the case, wouldn't the gardener have reported seeing her?

"And she's to make her debut with you? What on earth will Charis do in London?"

Thalia shrugged. "She'll dance with young men, promptly forget their names, and wish the entire time that she was at some lecture at the Royal Academy of Sciences." Aunt Harmonia had wanted Charis to debut last spring, when she and Thalia were both seventeen, but Charis had refused to do so without her cousins, and now they were all to come out to society together. Being "out" meant one was officially of marriageable age and allowed to attend balls and society events.

Thalia wondered if Charis was regretting her rash promise to debut with her cousins. Perhaps she was hiding. But Charis's parents could afford to send her to any number of Seasons, so it was not likely to matter if Charis did not take this Season. Or any Season, for that matter.

It was different for Thalia and Kalli, whose straitened circumstances meant they needed to establish themselves. Mama hoped they would both find husbands, but—

"And you?" Adam asked.

"Well, I shan't be wishing I was at a scientific lecture," Thalia said, and Adam laughed. She liked his laugh, the way his eyes lit and his freckled cheeks crinkled. "I enjoy dancing, thank goodness for small favors. But I don't mean to go to London to find myself a husband. I'm going to find the intellectual heart of the city, the salons with the brightest ideas, and soak it all in. It will be better even than a library. And then I'll get a publisher for my poems, and I won't need a man to support me."

"Take care that you don't become a bluestocking," Adam teased. "Your family and friends have reputations to uphold."

"If being a bluestocking is the worst that is said of me, Mama will be relieved. And it's not like that reputation could harm *you*," Thalia said. Adam had his own reputation for being "bookish," though it was unfair that a penchant for scholarship was accounted an advantage in a man and a disadvantage in a woman.

As they neared the wood that edged Uncle John's property, Thalia caught a glimpse of something blue.

"There she is," she said, tugging Adam forward.

A moment later, Charis herself marched out of the wood, her hair hanging loose down her back, wearing an old blue dress that she reserved for field excursions. As Charis was rather ample and the dress several years old, the fabric strained at the bodice and hung short enough that Thalia could see the top of Charis's old boots and a good few inches of wool stocking.

Charis had spotted them. "Hallo!" She gave a friendly wave. "What brings you both out this way? Isn't it a glorious morning? There was a mandarin duck on the pond, floating snug as you please."

Thalia took a deep breath. Charis had not been hiding—she had simply forgotten what day it was.

Charis drew closer and took in Thalia's navy traveling dress. Guilt stole pinkly across her wide, freckled cheeks. "Oh no. London. Mama even sent a maid up to remind me, and I only meant to steal away for a few moments because I'd heard a call that I thought might be a hoopoe, but of course it wasn't, and then the duck drove it entirely out of my head." Her pink cheeks paled. "Is Mama very angry?"

Thalia considered this. "I'd say resigned, rather." As Aunt Harmonia—Lady Elphinstone—had no other children to lavish her maternal ambitions on, Charis was the sole (if often disappointing) vehicle for her societal dreams. Her ambitions were not dimmed by Charis's reluctance to share them, though they were frequently thwarted.

"Oh, worse and worse! I'd rather face her angry than despairing." Charis picked up her skirts and began to run across the field, her sturdy legs pounding and her wavy auburn hair bouncing along her shoulders. Thalia and Adam followed more sedately.

Thalia's parents were waiting for them in the courtyard, along

9

with Thalia's sister Kalli, who practically bounced with enthusiasm, her dark curls quivering about her face. The two youngest Aubrey children were darting about the carriages, but Antheia, who at fourteen was too young for a Season, was sulking beside their mother.

"Thank goodness Charis has been found," Thalia's mama said. "Have you everything you need for London?"

"Yes, Mama," Thalia said, checking to see that her and Kalli's trunks were securely lashed behind one of the carriages.

"I've brought you something," her father said, handing her a neat leatherbound book. The pages inside were blank. "I hope you'll fill it with poetry and keep me updated on your progress."

"Be sure to attend church regularly and listen to your aunt. She knows all the eligible gentlemen," her mama said. She pressed a quick, distracted kiss to Thalia's cheek before dashing away to rescue her youngest son from one of the horses, calling back over her shoulder, "And write us every week!"

Thalia's father tugged her to him in a firm hug. "I'm depending on you to be a help to your aunt and uncle. You're my sensible child, and I trust you'll watch over Kalliope in my absence and keep her from trouble."

"Of course, Papa." Thalia swallowed a tart response: *I thought Adam was to be the "stable influence."* She would not say, even to her father, that she hoped London would allow her to be a little reckless and irresponsible for once.

"Come on, Thalia!" Kalli said, giving one last hug to their sister Antheia, who was now sniffing damply. "Aunt Harmonia has given us our own carriage. She says it's because we won't want to listen to our uncle snoring, but *I* think it's because she means to sleep alongside Uncle John."

Adam helped Kalli into the carriage, then held his hand out to Thalia. As she took his hand, Adam surprised her by brushing his lips against her cheek. "Safe journey, Toodles, and don't forget me."

Her skin tingling where his lips had been, Thalia tried to ignore the heat rising in her face—and Kalli hooting in most unladylike fashion inside the carriage. She pretended she did not see the significant look her mother gave her father. Adam was like a brother to her—the oldest friend she had, outside of Kalli and Charis. She struggled for a quip, something to make the moment light. "I doubt I am in danger of forgetting you in less than a se'nnight."

Adam laughed, and Thalia settled herself beside Kalli.

Within minutes, Charis presented herself meekly in the courtyard. Her cheeks bore the bright red of the freshly scrubbed. Adam helped her into the carriage as well. "Go take London by storm."

"If by storm you mean hurricane," Charis said gloomily, "then I rather think I shall."

Thalia had a sudden image of an auburn-haired whirlwind wreaking havoc on the unsuspecting city. A line of poetry began to take shape in her head: *The whirling wind that wrecked the world was merely woman, scorned.* Hmm. No. Charis was hardly scornful.

Adam laughed again. "Have a little faith in yourself, Charis." He shut the carriage door and stepped back, waving at them.

The youngest Aubrey children shouted, banging on the carriage until Thalia's mother pulled them back.

The carriage lurched forward. Kalli's fingers closed around

Thalia's, cold despite the blanket she'd pulled over them both. "London," Kalli breathed.

Charis, sitting on the seat facing the Aubrey sisters, peered through the window and waved. Thalia kept her face forward, toward the road that would carry them away from the only world she'd ever known.

"London," Thalia agreed, echoing her sister.

And she meant to make the most of it.

CHAPTER TWO

On the Joy of Parties

(Kalli)

One cannot have too large a party.
A large party secures its own amusement.

—the author of Emma,
found in Kalliope Aubrey's commonplace book

As the last of her siblings' voices faded away behind them, Kalliope Aubrey pressed her hand against a curious fluttering in her stomach. She could not tell if she wanted to laugh—or to cry. She was on her way to London, as she'd dreamed since she discovered that going to London was a thing that young women did when they were deemed grown-up.

Kalli had been away from home before. She'd gone to Bath at fifteen with a great-aunt, but they'd only taken the waters, as her aunt had believed her too young for any of the famous balls and assemblies. And she had been to Oxford, and to Warwick Castle. She'd even been as far as Banbury for market day.

But to London, to the center of the social universe? All seventeen years of her life seemed to be building toward this. Miss Kalliope Aubrey loved her family more than she loved anything, but parties were a close second. Certainly she loved parties more than she loved the church her father served, though she tried not to think of this often, as it made her feel rather guilty. But then, even the Bible had descriptions of parties, so it could not be *too* wicked of her.

And what was London—more particularly the London *Season*—but a party on such scale as Kalli had only dreamed of?

Yet as her sister Thalia faced firmly ahead and her cousin Charis waved wildly behind them, Kalli was not filled with the bounding enthusiasm she'd expected. She wanted to turn the carriage around and snatch up her mother and father—and yes, even the children—and bring them with her. If only she didn't have to leave parts of her heart behind her, then London would be perfect.

Kalli sniffed once, and when Charis handed over a clean, if wrinkled, handkerchief, told herself she was being ridiculous. London would be delightful, she was sure of it, and she meant to enjoy every minute of it, from the clothes to the concerts to the eligible suitors. She watched the familiar fields flick past them and listened to the clip-clop of the horses' hooves on the packed-dirt roads, determinedly shoring up her spirits. When the head groom blew his horn as they approached the toll road, she did not even have to force herself to smile.

"Do you think we shall have beaux right away?" Kalli asked, cutting into Charis's observations about the mating habits of the trumpeter swan, to Thalia's obvious relief. Kalli sent her sister a covert smile. Though the two sisters looked nothing alike—Thalia was tall and fair, with nearly black eyes, while Kalli was short and dark-haired, with blue eyes and skin that tanned easily in the sun—they were only thirteen months apart and had been best friends for Kalli's entire life. If Kalli did not always understand Thalia's love of ideas, and Thalia did not always understand Kalli's love of people, they did, at least, genuinely love each other.

"I predict that you shall," Charis said. "You love everyone and so everyone, as a result, cannot help but love you in return. And Thalia is so lovely, I'm sure she will have suitors too." She sighed. "As for me, if Mama can scare up anyone to court me, it will only be for my money and that I will not like at all." She brightened. "I mean to approach the Season as a kind of experiment, make careful observations about the rituals of high society, and draw my own conclusions to amuse myself."

"Only if you share them with us," Thalia said.

Privately, Kalli was less interested in Charis's observations of the *haut ton* than in her own experiences, but she added comforting murmurs to Thalia's. After a moment, the conversation veered off into a discussion of the scientific and artistic luminaries Charis and Thalia hoped to meet, most of whom Kalli had never heard of, reinforcing her secret conviction that smart people did not necessarily make up the *smart* set she hoped to join. Which was just as well, because intelligent people were often so earnest that they failed to be any fun. Kalli ignored their conversation and turned to her own speculations instead. *Did* the Prince Regent's corsets creak as they were said to? And would Aunt Harmonia be able to acquire invitations to Almack's Assembly Rooms, as she had promised?

She pulled a copy of *La Belle Assemblée* from her traveling bag and imagined what dresses she might order. She knew that most of this order would have to remain imaginary, as the daughter of a clergyman with a large family had to be moderate in her wishes, but this did not daunt her. At least, it did not daunt her *much*. Aunt Harmonia had offered to make a gift of her wardrobe, and perhaps she could be persuaded to indulge a favored niece more than Mama might judge suitable.

And a modish wardrobe was a necessity, if Kalli were to shine in society as she hoped. She meant to have friends and suitors—and perhaps, if she was very lucky, a husband at the end of it. Mama needed one of them to marry well, and Thalia was too caught up in her books to be practical.

But there was no reason practicality could not also be *fun*. After all, it was possible to marry for love *and* money.

They spent one night on the road at a small but tidy inn, and Kalli did not think about Mama and Papa and the children above half a dozen times. Then, before Kalli would have believed it possible, they were on the road again and pulling into the outskirts of London. The packed dirt gave way to cobblestones, the farms to close-crowded houses and shops. Kalli admired the increasingly fine buildings as they passed, the hawkers filling the air with advertisements for their wares. She even secretly enjoyed the crush of traffic that delayed their arrival at their new home, because it gave her more time to look at everything and offered indisputable evidence that they had arrived in London.

Kalli had hoped to attend a ball that very evening, but Aunt Harmonia forbade it. "We will not appear in public looking like country bumpkins, and we must refresh our wardrobes before we venture out," she said. But then she rather spoiled the grand effect of her words by adding, "Besides, London is still rather thin of company, and it would not do to appear desperate."

So Kalli cultivated patience as best she could. Over the next several days, they visited more shops than she could have imagined: the finest (and, she suspected, the most expensive) of milliners, haberdasheries, modistes, and more.

As soon as their new riding dresses arrived, the girls were allowed to ride sedately in Hyde Park with a groom. They ambled down Rotten Row and alongside the Serpentine, and Kalli eyed the young gentlemen who passed them and tipped their hats, and wished she had been introduced to someone, anyone, as it was not polite for a young lady to greet a young man with whom she was not yet acquainted.

A week after their arrival, Lady Elphinstone initiated morning calls to select members of the *ton*. She introduced the girls to her friends and their daughters, and then, when they had not disgraced themselves with their behavior, to select patronesses of Almack's, whose approval was required before any Elphinstone or Aubrey could enter that elite dancing hall.

Kalli could hardly breathe as she curtsied before Lady Sally Jersey, a pretty brown-haired woman with a ready smile. As Lady Jersey began to talk, a nearly nonstop flow of words that betrayed the source of her teasing nickname, Silence, Kalli relaxed. The woman was not so intimidating as Kalli had feared. Thalia was her usual charming self, and even Charis appeared to advantage, confining her comments to short, unobjectionable remarks on the weather (and *not*, thankfully, the mating habits of any creature, swan or otherwise).

Another patroness of Almack's, Princess Esterhazy, arrived at Lady Jersey's just as the Elphinstone and Aubrey party were taking their leave and was everything gracious. She seized Kalli's and

Thalia's hands and drew them together. "But you two are sisters? What a charming contrast you present. I predict that you shall set the *ton* on its ears."

Kalli wished her mama could have heard the praise, but she stored it away to send to her in her next letter home. She ignored the pinch of homesickness at the thought of her mother and focused instead on what it meant that she and her sister were to have vouchers to Almack's—one of the most exclusive events of the social season.

Kalli's contentment with the day's outing carried her through dinner and several hands of whist with the elder Elphinstones and Charis, while Thalia scribbled lines of poetry onto some scraps of paper. It wasn't until she'd retired to her own room and was faithfully recounting the day's activities in her diary, determined not to miss any of the joys of her first Season, that Kalli realized something dreadful: For all their visiting, she had not met a single eligible gentleman.

The next morning brought another round of visits, the first to Mrs. Salisbury, an old schoolmate of Aunt Harmonia's. A footman led them to a salon tastefully decorated in pale gold and green, and Mrs. Salisbury rose languidly from her seat to embrace her old friend. The two older women drew into a window embrasure and began chatting, leaving the young women to entertain Mrs. Salisbury's two daughters, the eldest of whom was married to a Lord Stanthorpe and had brought a small child with her.

Charis and Thalia were drawn into conversation with the younger

Miss Anne Salisbury, a pretty girl with Titian hair who was just embarking on her second Season. But Kalli saw the round, rosy cheeks of the little boy on the floor and could not resist sitting down beside him. She adored babies. Aunt Harmonia gave her a sharp look, but as no one was present beside the two families, she did not say anything.

Kalli held her hands over her eyes and then removed them, and just as her siblings had done as babies, the little boy giggled. His mama smiled down at Kalli.

"Do you like children, Miss Kalliope?" Lady Stanthorpe asked. Like her mother and sister, she had red-gold curls and bright blue eyes.

"Kalli, please—and yes, I love them! They're such funny things, aren't they? I help my mama with my younger siblings, and sometimes, when women in the parish have been quite sick, Mama and I have helped with their little ones."

"And soon, perhaps, you'll have your own?" Lady Stanthorpe raised her eyebrows slyly.

Kalli blushed. "Not too soon, I hope. I am in no rush to be wed—though I am eager for the Season!"

"Have you been to any parties yet?"

"No. Aunt Harmonia would not let us go until our clothes were ready, but we are to go to the Gardiners' evening party tomorrow night."

The baby crawled over to Kalli and patted her knee until she scooped him up. He was warm and smelled of milk. He tried to stand on her legs, and she grasped his fat hands and helped him upright.

"The evening party should be rather good: Mrs. Gardiner always has the best refreshments, and her daughters are both extraordinary on the pianoforte." Lady Stanthorpe added, "I think my brother Henry might be sweet on the elder Miss Gardiner."

As if her words were a summons, a young man entered the salon then, tapping a riding crop against glossy top boots. Though not above medium height, his curly ginger hair was arranged in a fashionable Brutus cut and his countenance was open and smiling.

"We were just speaking of you, Henry," Lady Stanthorpe said, her smile deepening to reveal a shallow dimple. She patted the settee beside her.

The young man turned toward them just as the baby in Kalli's lap erupted, milky white liquid spilling across the shoulder of her dress and dripping down her arm.

Kalli's face ignited. Mr. Salisbury—if it was, indeed, Lady Stanthorpe's brother—was quite possibly the handsomest man she had met in London. And here she was, sitting on the floor covered in baby vomit.

Lady Stanthorpe flew out of the settee and picked up her child, handing him off to a nearby nursemaid before following them both from the room.

"Oh, Kalliope." Aunt Harmonia sighed, as if it was Kalli's fault that babies often spit up.

Thalia stood, but Mr. Salisbury was faster, reaching Kalli's side with an easy stride before bending to offer her a hand. His grip was firm, and he hauled her up as though she weighed nothing. Kalli might wish that *she* were more graceful, but there was nothing to criticize in Mr. Salisbury's bow, or the handkerchief he handed her as she sank onto the settee Lady Stanthorpe had just vacated. She wiped off her arm and dabbed at her sleeve.

"That benighted child has done that to me more times than I can count," Mr. Salisbury said, sitting beside Kalli and making the cushion beneath Kalli shift with his weight. "And always on my finest waistcoat, as if he has an unerring sense for what he might best spoil."

She caught her breath, more conscious than she wanted to be of his immaculately clad thigh only inches from her own. Could he smell the sourness of the baby spit on her? But then, Mr. Salisbury seemed remarkably cheerful, and the fact that the baby had done the same to him *more times than he could count* suggested that he was much less put out than he pretended.

"So," Mr. Salisbury said, a light that she mistrusted coming into his eyes, "you and my sister were speaking of me before my nephew so regrettably interrupted?"

Kalli flushed again. Though being caught speaking about a handsome young man was considerably less embarrassing than being covered in baby vomit, it was not precisely agreeable either. "We were talking of the Gardiner party tomorrow night, and your sister said that you—" *Were fond of the oldest Gardiner girl.* No. She could not say that to a man she'd just met. "That you were fond of dancing."

From a neighboring couch, Miss Salisbury said, "Do you think there will be dancing? Mrs. Gardiner usually discourages her parties from becoming romps."

Mr. Salisbury's eyes—brown with flecks of green and gold around the pupils—still rested on Kalli's face. "If they do," he said, "I would be honored if you would dance with me, Miss Kalliope."

"Oh! I was not . . ." She broke off in some confusion, realizing too late that he must have thought she was fishing for an invitation, but if she protested that she had not intended him to ask her to dance, she might seem ungracious.

Mr. Salisbury grinned, showing the same slight dimple his sister had, and turned to Thalia and Charis. "I'd be happy to dance with your sisters as well, once we're introduced."

Aunt Harmonia hastened over to make the introductions, and added, "Thalia and Kalliope are sisters. Charis is my daughter, their cousin."

Mr. Salisbury turned back to Kalli. "Kalliope is not a common name. I believe it is Greek? Is your father a scholar then?"

This time, Kalli managed to return his smile. "Papa is a clergyman. He is a great reader, but I should not call him a scholar. The fault for our names lies at Mama's door. Her father *was* a scholar. She is Sophronia, her sister Harmonia, and between the two of them they decided that they would continue the tradition of Greek virtues and graces in their daughters. Thalia and Charis you've met, and my younger sisters at home are Urania and Antheia."

Thalia added, "Only our parents rather got our names mixed, as Kalli is our comic one and I am of a more poetic turn of mind."

Kalli knew Thalia only meant to help her through the conversation, but she wondered if Thalia realized the small, sniping sting of her words. To imply that Thalia was serious and poetic, and Kalli was—a joke.

"Yes," she said, trying to shrug off the sting. "I'm the witty one. I mean—not witty precisely, as it would be quite vain to claim that of myself, only I make people laugh . . ." Kalli trailed off in dismay. She was babbling again.

"One's name can rather be a burden," Henry said, kindly disregarding Kalli's incoherence. "Only look at me—'Henry' is supposed to suggest a noble leader, and I, alas, am hardly that. Tragically misnamed."

Like Charis, Kalli thought. Aunt Harmonia had named her after one of the Graces, as if anyone could live up to such a name.

"It might have been worse," Mr. Salisbury continued. "You might have been Euterpe or Terpsichore."

Kalli laughed. "A dire fate indeed! When I have children, they shall have plain, ordinary names that they can make their own, however they like."

Mr. Salisbury's grin deepened, and those wide, appealing eyes remained fixed on her face.

"Not that I think of having children, much, because of course I am not married yet, and one hopes to be married before having children—" *Stop talking*, Kalli told herself fiercely. Between her blunder about the dance and now this, Mr. Salisbury must think she was angling for a proposal. Which she was not. At least, not *yet*. She scarcely knew the man. All her fine-tuned social senses seemed to have deserted her.

And she *did* still smell strongly of sour milk.

As Aunt Harmonia walked past her toward the window, Kalli tugged at her sleeve. "May we leave soon?" she whispered, gesturing at her soiled arm. She knew she was being rude, but the combination of her spoiled gown and Mr. Salisbury's proximity was nearly unbearable.

"In a moment, my dear. I must say goodbye to Mrs. Salisbury first."

While Kalli's aunt talked to her friend, Mr. Salisbury made one last attempt to engage her in conversation. "How are you liking London, Miss Kalliope?"

Good heavens, *why* was the man trying so hard? Could he not see that she wished to leave? Or barring that, to be politely ignored?

"It's very fine." There, that was unobjectionable.

Mr. Salisbury waited a long moment, clearly expecting her to elaborate. When she did not, he said, "And what do you find so fine about London?"

You, darted into Kalli's head. No, that would never do. She grasped for something else to say. "Lady's hats. And . . . er, sunshine."

Confusion deepened the furrow on Mr. Salisbury's brow, and Kalli shrank into her seat. Likely he now thought her stupid as well as unpolished. *Lady's hats? Sunshine?* Kalli's fourteen-year-old sister Antheia could have answered more elegantly than that.

From her seat near the settee, Thalia pressed her lips together. Kalli recognized that expression: Her sister was trying desperately not to laugh. At *her*.

Could they not leave already?

At last, Aunt Harmonia finished speaking with Mrs. Salisbury. Kalli had never been so grateful to leave new acquaintances. She sprang to her feet, curtsied to her hostess, and was making a dash toward the door when someone caught her hand.

It was Mr. Salisbury. "It was a pleasure to meet you, Miss Kalliope."

"The pleasure was all yours," Kalli said.

At Thalia's snorted laugh, Kalli reviewed her words. Her face burned. "I mean *mine*. The pleasure was all *mine*." Then she grasped what was left of her shredded dignity and shot through the doorway of the salon and down the stairs to the front door. She pulled her spencer on over her wet sleeve and went out to wait by the carriage.

As they settled into the vehicle, Thalia said, "You seemed quite struck by Mr. Salisbury, Kalli."

Aunt Harmonia brightened. "Oh, he is a lovely young man! He would do very well for you, Kalliope."

Mr. Salisbury would not touch me with a ten-foot pole, Kalli thought. She had to dissuade her aunt before she tried to engineer any more uncomfortable encounters. "Oh, please, do not go matchmaking, Aunt. I've only just arrived. Mr. Salisbury is well enough, I suppose, but I do not believe we should suit."

Thalia watched her with a widening smile, as though she knew Kalli was lying. Kalli looked away, fixing her gaze out the window, and folded her arms across her chest, though the tight stitching of her spencer made this difficult. She wished she were not too old to scratch her sister. Or to indulge in a good childish sulk.

Start the way you mean to finish, Mama always said.

Kalli sighed. If that were true, her conquest of the *ton* was off to a lamentable start.

CHAPTER THREE

Everyone (but Me) Loves a Rake

(Charis)

It is now very generally known to astronomers, that, for several years past, Dr. Brinkley, with the eight feet circle of the Observatory at Dublin, has constantly observed a periodical deviation of several fixed stars from their mean places; which strongly indicates the existence of an annual parallax in those stars.

—John Pond,
Philosophical Transactions of the Royal Society *[Charis's note: The London Season, aka the annual societal parallax, where everyone's role seems to shift because of a change in vantage point.]*

From her vantage point in the Gardiners' entrance hall, Charis watched her papa disappear into the cloakroom, half buried under a mountain of cloaks. Charis wished she could go with him: She'd rather like to disappear into a room lined with coats, to smell the wool and ermine and wrap herself in warmth and quiet instead of standing, exposed, beneath the well-lit chandelier in the midst of the other guests slowly streaming up the stairs to greet the hosts before crowding into the great salon.

Her mama leaned over and gently pinched her upper arm. "Stand straight, Charis, you're slouching."

How one could slouch with a wooden busk down the front of one's stays, Charis couldn't fathom. Nevertheless, she tried to straighten further and rubbed the spot her mama had pinched, scrubbing at the few inches of skin revealed between her short sleeves and the long gloves she wore. Kalli and Thalia were similarly attired, but neither seemed cold or self-conscious. Charis's more ample bust, pushed up by the stays she usually tried to avoid, spilled out over the top of her gown. Though Mama insisted the décolletage was perfectly appropriate for a young lady, Charis was showing far more freckled skin than she was comfortable with. She tugged her neckline up, but Mama caught her at it and shook her head.

This was why she preferred scientific study to social appearances. At least she knew she had nothing to apologize for when it came to her brain. But she lacked the social graces Mama expected of her, and there were far too many ruffles on this confounded skirt.

Charis's glance fell on Kalli again. With her hands clasped and her lips slightly parted, Kalli looked like a child on Christmas morning. Charis squared her shoulders. Well. She wouldn't be the one to ruin Kalli's enjoyment of her first party of the Season. Charis would suffer through the evening without uttering a single complaint and would entertain herself by planning the research she would conduct when the Season was over.

Far too soon, Papa returned, and they mounted the stairs. Charis curtsied to Mr. and Mrs. Gardiner and followed her mother and cousins into the crowded salon. Kalli gripped her hand.

Charis saw that beneath her eagerness, Kalli was also nervous, her skin a shade paler than usual. Behind them, another family had just come into the room—that young man who had so rattled Kalli the other day, accompanied by his sisters. What was their name again? San . . . no, Salisbury. That was it. Mr. Salisbury's eyes landed on Kalli and his face lit up. In return, Kalli smiled tremulously—and clutched Charis's arm tighter than ever.

The Salisburys approached, made small talk, and passed on. Kalli's grip on Charis loosened.

"You've never been so discomposed by a man before," Charis observed.

Kalli sighed. "I know. Pray, let us not speak of this anymore. It's demoralizing."

Mama and Thalia had been drawn into a conversation with an acquaintance, but Charis was determined not to be drawn in as well. Mama had impressed upon Charis that she must not move around social events without an escort, but surely she and Kalli could chaperone each other? Charis edged toward the refreshment table, tugging Kalli in her wake. Food never judged her for feeling awkward in company, and it would give her something to do with her hands and her time.

Papa stepped in front of her, followed by a dark-haired man. The stranger was dressed rather severely, in a white shirt and matching waistcoat, and a black jacket that set off his tanned skin. None of the color that the pinks of the *ton* seemed to adore, but Charis had some vague memory of Kalli explaining that truly sophisticated men eschewed color in their clothes.

Papa said, "Mr. Leveson, may I present my daughter and her cousin? Charis Elphinstone and Kalliope Aubrey."

Kalli made an odd, constricted noise. When Charis glanced at her, Kalli's eyes were wide. She must have recognized the name, but as it was not a name that appeared regularly in any of the scientific journals Charis followed, Charis had no idea why.

Mr. Leveson inclined his head while Kalli and Charis curtsied.

Papa continued, "Mr. Leveson's father was an acquaintance of mine before he passed some years back. A regular nabob, they say— found his fortune and his wife in India."

Mr. Leveson pressed his lips together and his glance drifted off over Charis's head. He clearly wished her father at perdition, though whether that was because he was bored with the company or disliked having his business told to strangers, she could not tell. Either way, she could feel herself pokering up. How *dare* this man be so dismissive of her father? He knew nothing of them and seemed utterly uninterested in learning.

"Are you very rich, Mr. Leveson? Like your father?" she asked, widening her eyes and hoping she looked innocent rather than possessed. "That must be very pleasant for you, if it absolves you from having to be polite."

Kalli gasped, and Papa's brows drew together. But her words had the gratifying effect of bringing Mr. Leveson's eyes snapping back to her face.

"And why should I make the effort to be polite," he asked, "when your father introduces me by telling you where I am from and my father's income?"

"Is it not common, when introducing company, to explain something of their context—where they are from, what their occupation is? An introduction presumes the possibility of a longer acquaintance, and in such cases, it may be helpful to know something of the person one is introduced to. In this case, I am glad of the context, and your response, because it tells me that this is not an acquaintance I wish to pursue. Good day, Mr. Leveson."

She started to turn away, when his voice slapped across her. "How very convenient for you, Miss Elphinstone."

Frowning, she turned back. "I'm afraid I don't follow."

"Using your moral high ground as a shield for your prejudice. Quite convenient."

"My *what*?" She stepped toward him, dimly aware of Kalli making an aborted grab for her arm. "You, sir, are the one who dismissed us as uninteresting as soon as you'd met us. No doubt because my father is not important or wealthy enough for you, and I am no diamond of the first water."

The smile that flickered across his lips was distinctly unpleasant. "Was it not upon meeting me and learning that I am Anglo-Indian that you decided you were offended? Far better to profess disdain for my behavior than confess yourself prejudiced by my race. You would not be the first Englishwoman to make such claims."

Charis took a deep breath and selected her words with care. "I do not object to your race, which no one can choose, but to your manners, which you *do* choose. And since this conversation is giving neither of us pleasure, I choose to end it. Good day, Mr. Leveson."

With a steadiness she did not entirely feel, Charis slid her arm through her father's and took Kalli's hand and dragged them both away from Mr. Leveson.

"Charis!" her father said, when they were out of earshot. "How could you speak so to Mr. Leveson?"

"He was rude," Charis said, beginning to feel embarrassed now that her outrage was fading. She never had been able to hold on to her anger long. Mr. Leveson *had* been rude, but her own behavior scarce bore examination, and that vexed her more than his rudeness. *Had* she been prejudiced against him upon learning that his mother was Indian? She did not think so, but as a scientist, she would have to examine her reaction more closely.

"Charis, do you know who that is?" Kalli asked. "Mr. Leveson is a nonpareil. He is young, but already his taste in fashion is admired everywhere. The new Beau Brummell, they call him. Even the Prince Regent speaks highly of him. Offend him, and you might as well not show your face in society."

Guilt poked her in the stomach. After all Mama's efforts, she would *not* be pleased if Charis had ruined her prospects on their first evening in public. On the other hand . . . "Good," Charis said. "If I am ruined, then Mama cannot expect me to make meaningless polite conversation, and I can go back home."

Papa patted her hand. "I am sure it will not come to that. I will speak to Mr. Leveson and apologize for my own words and explain that you were only defending me."

"I wish you would not, Papa. *He* should apologize, not you."

But Papa would not listen. He wove back through the crowd, directly to Mr. Leveson, and began speaking. However, Mr. Leveson did not appear to attend to her father. His eyes were fixed on Charis, and the expression on his face sent shivers all through her.

She turned away. Detestable man. Let him ruin her, if he could. She would not care a whit for him, or his actions, or anything he might say.

Charis stalked to the refreshment table, forgetting her intention to stay with Kalli. She spent a few pleasurable minutes surveying her options, before selecting a delicately molded chocolate. As the sweet dissolved on her tongue, she felt marginally more cheerful. She stole a second chocolate.

"Miss Elphinstone?"

She nearly choked on her chocolate in surprise. Turning around, she felt heat stealing up her face, all the way to her ears and the crown of her head.

Mr. Leveson stood before her, holding out a glass of lemonade, and smiling. Charis's heart fluttered oddly. It was decidedly unfair for him to be so good-looking. If life were just, one's face would reflect one's heart, and a girl would know which men were to be avoided only by looking at them. After all, animals often signaled venom through colors or rattles or other means. Why not people?

Charis looked past Mr. Leveson, searching for Kalli or her father—someone to rescue her from this conversation. But Kalli was talking to Mr. Salisbury, and her father only smiled encouragingly at her from several feet away.

Charis took the proffered lemonade. She wanted desperately to drain it, to avoid having to speak with Mr. Leveson, but she was rather afraid that if she tried, Mr. Leveson would say something reprehensible, and shock would make her snort the lemonade through

her nose and spend the rest of the evening in a cloud of humiliation, her nose burning. (She wished that her knowledge of both the
humiliation and burning nose were purely theoretical, but alas, they
were not.)

Mr. Leveson stood for a moment, inspecting her. His eyes trailed
from the crown of her head (was her hair out of place already?) to
the pale pink dress Mama had insisted she wear. A slight moue of
distaste twisted his lips, and temper curled its fists in her stomach.
She wondered what he objected to more—the dress's excessive frills,
or her. How dare this man try to make her feel small?

After a long silence, Mr. Leveson said, "Your father said you had
something you wished to say to me?"

Charis pressed her lips together. Papa wished her to apologize, no
doubt. Well, she would not do it. She would die first. "I have already
said everything I wish to say to you, sir." She sipped very cautiously
at her lemonade and propriety forced her to add, "Thank you for
the refreshment."

"Most properly done," he said approvingly. "But tell me, *did* you
set out to insult me deliberately? If not for my race, perhaps for my
status? There are some who deem it their moral duty to snub men
and women of fashion, as though the fineness of our dress connotes
a poverty of soul."

Charis opened her eyes innocently. "Are you a man of fashion? I
confess, I had never heard of you before tonight."

He gave a shout of laughter. The sound fizzed all through her body
in a delightful rush, though Charis ruthlessly suppressed her urge to
smile.

"Oh, very good, Miss Elphinstone," he said. "Will you accept my apology for my earlier rudeness, and let us begin our acquaintance-ship anew?"

Charis hesitated. There was something rather appealing about Mr. Leveson, when he was not being rude, and she was rather lacking for friends in London. But there was also the not-insignificant fact that he had brought out the very worst in her within minutes of their meeting.

Mr. Leveson smiled at her. "Come now. Most people find me unobjectionable. I'm told my friendship can even lend a certain cachet to one's reputation."

That settled it. If there was one thing Charis could not abide—well, actually, there were many things she found irritating, but unalloyed conceit was high on her list. "I'm afraid that is impossible, sir."

A distinct coolness slid down his face, wiping away any softness. "No? Pray tell, why?"

"I dislike wealthy, handsome men on principle." Charis regretted the words almost as soon as they'd escaped her lips. She needed to end this conversation and get far, far away from Mr. Leveson.

"Oh, so you do find me handsome? Very generous of you." His eyes glinted. "Curious principles you have—many in the *ton* set appearance and wealth as their highest priorities."

Charis *had* meant to end the conversation. But she couldn't help responding, "Then those people are fools. Why should one set good looks—something attributable to luck and inheritance as much as any actual effort—at such a high premium? Looks fade, money might be lost, but an amiable character can be relied upon for life." She forced herself to meet his mocking gaze. "And unfortunately, you, and others like you, have become so accustomed to being fawned upon for attributes to which you can claim no credit that you have neglected that which might bring you and your future wife most happiness—cultivating your character." It occurred to her that he might already be married, in which case she had just insulted him *and* his wife. Ah, well. She had set out to trim his pride and she would not back down now.

Gasps sounded around her. They had drawn an audience. She could not bring herself to look at her father, to see his disapproving face among the ranks of their auditors.

But Mr. Leveson did not seem furious, or even offended. Indeed, a tiny curl played around the edges of his lips (rather finely shaped—not that Charis meant to take notice of them). "You have favored me with a blunt assessment of my character. Allow me to return the favor. You pride yourself on being a woman of sense, of *character*, even. Perhaps because you have not been favored with both wits *and* beauty, you believe it is not possible for anyone to be so gifted. But trust me, Miss Elphinstone, that many of those in the *ton* are more than their pretty faces, and you would be wise not to make assumptions on so shallow a basis."

Then, casually, as though he had not just eviscerated her with his words, Mr. Leveson selected a chocolate, popped it in his mouth, inclined his head at Charis, and walked off. The gasps around them turned into snickers, their audience laughing at her comeuppance. At *her*.

Charis blinked again. Mr. Leveson's response was no more than she had invited with her own bluntness, but it sent shame waving through her. The room felt at once too hot and too close. She needed air. Her vision blurring, Charis set down her glass and blundered to the French doors that opened onto a garden. She would not give Mr. Leveson—or anyone else—the satisfaction of seeing her cry.

CHAPTER FOUR

Mad, Bad, and Dangerous to Know

(Thalia)

You are now
In London, that great sea, whose ebb and flow
At once is deaf and loud, and on the shore
Vomits its wrecks, and still howls on for more.
Yet in its depth what treasures!

— *Percy Bysshe Shelley*

London was not at all what Thalia had expected.

Her first true event of the Season, her first opportunity to meet and mingle with the greatest minds of British society, and the only thing anyone talked about was their supper, the weather, and the monstrously indecent gown Lady What's-Her-Name was wearing, as if she thought herself some twenty years younger. (Though Thalia had seen the lady, and she was quite sure Aunt Harmonia would say such a gown was decidedly unsuitable for a *young* lady. Thalia herself admired the woman's bravery in wearing what she liked.)

She'd talked to several of her aunt's acquaintances and met a few new faces, but they had been uniformly unsatisfactory. Even the poet she had been introduced to had failed her—he had only said some nonsense about her face and offered her a lemonade.

In short, Thalia was bored.

It was with considerable relief that she caught sight of Adam Hetherbridge's tall frame and sandy head, and waved to him. At least with Adam she should have *some* reasonable conversation.

"Are you enjoying your first crush?" Adam asked, navigating around a cluster of older women. "The Gardiners should be proud of themselves. There's scarce room to move in here."

"Oh, please don't talk to me of the party. Or of food. Or weather," Thalia begged, glancing beside her. Aunt Harmonia was deep in conversation with an acquaintance and would not chide her for speaking ill of the party. "I have heard nothing else tonight. Tell me something you are studying. Talk to me of ideas."

"My poor Toodles," Adam said, laughing at her. "Did you think the crème de la crème of London spent their time discussing actual ideas?"

"Someone must. Somewhere."

"Assuredly. But seldom on a dance floor, and even less frequently to unmarried young ladies. Once you are a fashionable young matron, now—"

"But what an impossible conundrum. I must marry to find anyone to talk sense, but how can I marry if no one will talk sense to me? I might find myself saddled with a fool."

"I cannot imagine any such dire fate for you. Your wits are obvious to anyone who meets you, and only a great fool would propose marriage to someone so much more intelligent than he, and a great fool you would spot at once, so you are safe."

"I don't think you've ever said anything so pretty to me before, Adam."

"Then you'd best savor it." He studied her, smiling a little. "Shall I fetch you some lemonade?"

"No," she said, a trifle despairingly. "I was already offered lemonade by a poet."

"You truly are in a dire way, if a *poet* could offer you nothing better than that," Adam said. "What would you like to speak about? I've been reading of Queen Elizabeth and the troops at Tilbury again. Do you remember reading her speech with me years ago?"

"How could I forget? We argued over it, and you did not speak to me again for two days." Thalia had always admired the queen, who had held her own with the greatest wits of her age—Edmund Spenser, William Shakespeare, Sir Philip Sidney, and Mary Sidney—*and* maintained a throne independent of any king. "You thought she was foolish to draw attention to her femininity, when she said, 'I know I have the body of a weak, feeble woman; but I have the heart and stomach of a king.'"

"And you argued that many of her soldiers would already think her weak for being a woman, so why not acknowledge it and emphasize the more important part—that her courage was as good as any man's."

"She called herself a prince," Thalia said. "She reminded them that she was their king before God, and they had a duty to obey her."

"But she was not a king—she was a queen."

"Does the title matter or the office itself? She was still the sovereign ruler of England."

"And a woman," Adam said.

"Do you think she was less, because of that?" Thalia asked, the old familiar fire of the argument lighting in her. "I would say, rather, that she had to be smarter and stronger because she knew she would be underestimated."

"Are you speaking of Elizabeth or of yourself?" Adam asked.

Thalia flushed. Adam would never know what it was like to be a young woman in society, underestimated because of her sex and because she was young and pretty. But she didn't want to talk to Adam of that, so she said, "You were wrong then, and you are wrong now."

Adam grinned at her. "If I admit that I was—and am—wrong, will you admit that you are no longer bored?"

Reluctantly, she returned his grin. "Very well, I am no longer bored. But what does it say about me, that I prefer a good argument with you to mingling in society?"

"That you have excellent taste." Adam looked around the room, frowning slightly. "Dash it all, the place is far too crowded to see anyone. I'm going to hunt out some old Oxford chums to introduce you to, if I can find them. I can't promise they will argue with you as well as I do, but I don't think they will bore you."

Thalia watched him go with some regret. Her aunt was deep in conversation and Thalia had no desire to join in, but nor could she leave her aunt's side. A young woman was not supposed to wander alone at such parties. She stood awkwardly for a moment, trying to decide how to smile so that no one looking at her would pity her for having no one to speak to.

A gentle tap on her arm caused her to turn. A man stood beside her—tall, nearly as tall as Adam, with a face so ridiculously and exquisitely chiseled beneath dark hair that Thalia could only stare. It was as if one of the Renaissance masters—Michelangelo or Donatello—had conjured his face from their sketches.

"I beg your pardon," the vision said in a low voice. "I know it is not at all the thing to speak when we haven't been introduced, but I could not help hearing your conversation. I admired your spirited argument and found myself deeply curious to know your name."

Thalia hesitated. Something in her was strongly drawn to this man (and it was not simply that he was the best-looking man she had ever met). But she knew what Aunt Harmonia would say of her speaking to a man to whom she had not been introduced.

Aunt Harmonia, however, was whispering behind her fan and not paying the least attention to Thalia. Whatever gossip she was sharing must be good.

The man continued. "You look a sensible girl—far too sensible to be swayed by a ridiculous custom. After all, what are introductions at a party like this? Presumably, everyone attending has been invited by our hosts, so what objection can there be to our knowing one another? To imply we ought not speak without introductions is an insult to both our hosts' taste and our own judgment."

Thalia straightened, responding to the smile lurking about the man's dark eyes. She had not much thought of it before, but he was quite right. It was not as though she were speaking to a stranger off the street.

"Thalia Aubrey," she said, extending one gloved hand.

"James Darby," he said, taking it in a firm grip—neither too strong nor too limp. Something sparked up Thalia's arm at his touch.

"Are you from London, Mr. Darby?"

"I was born in Florence, but I have attended school here in England, and my uncle, who has been my guardian since my father died, has an estate in Sussex. So not a Londoner, though I am by now quite familiar with the city. And yourself? I would guess that you are *not* from London, or you would identify my accent at once as not having the true London air."

"I am from Oxfordshire," she admitted. "Are you a student of accents then, Mr. Darby?"

"Ah, my old stomping grounds! In fact, Miss Aubrey, I am a student of nearly everything, and have been since my time at Oxford. Languages, behaviors, natural philosophy. My uncle would prefer I devote myself to one course of study, but I find it impossible to limit myself when the world itself is so engaging."

"How dull the world would seem if we were confined to only one branch of ideas! I find that very often ideas feed off one another: The study of nature might inspire a poet, and the poet's words might inspire the philosopher."

Mr. Darby smiled down at her. "You'll find yourself in good company here. There are any number of us who prefer debates to dancing, poetry to posturing. Have you read Percy Shelley's most recent poem, 'Hymn to Intellectual Beauty'? It came out only this past January."

Thalia shook her head. She knew of Percy Shelley, of course—he had rather scandalized polite society when he ran off with Mary Wollstonecraft's daughter, Mary Godwin, to Europe. But she was not up-to-date on poetry and literature, as Papa did not subscribe to any literary magazines.

"It's rather magnificent," Mr. Darby said. "I think you'd like it. In this poem Shelley argues that beauty gives meaning to an otherwise godless world:

> *"Thy light alone like mist o'er mountains driven,*
> *Or music by the night-wind sent*
> *Through strings of some still instrument,*
> *Or moonlight on a midnight stream,*
> *Gives grace and truth to life's unquiet dream."*

Thalia did not respond at once, when Mr. Darby finished his quotation. He had a good voice for poetry—low, and clear, and the distant images of his words caught at her heart. But as a vicar's daughter, she couldn't accede to them completely. "Do you believe this?" she asked. "That beauty alone gives truth to 'life's unquiet dream'?"

"Don't all beautiful things bring their own truth to the world?" he said. "Surely our world is big enough to accommodate truths other than God."

Their conversation danced very near heresy, and Thalia found it more thrilling than she ought to have. But entertaining an idea or possibility wasn't the same as adopting a belief, she told herself, and besides, she was enjoying herself.

"Thalia," Adam called out, returning at last with a short, stocky man in his wake. "Let me introduce my friend—" He broke off, seeing Mr. Darby at her side. He gave a short bow. "Darby."

Mr. Darby returned the slight bow. "Hetherbridge."

"Thalia, may I speak with you?" Adam asked. Without waiting

for her response, he took her by the elbow and led her away, leaving both his friend and Mr. Darby in the crowd behind them.

Thalia yanked her arm back. "There's no call to be so rude. What do you have to say to me that can't be said in front of Mr. Darby?"

"Did your aunt introduce you to that man?"

Thalia didn't answer. She didn't want to lie to Adam, but she wasn't about to tell Adam that she'd introduced herself and have him lecture her on manners.

"Let me guess. He introduced himself and suggested that introductions were an outdated relic in polite society."

Thalia felt a little jolt of surprise that Adam had read Mr. Darby so well. "Do you know him?"

"He was at Oxford a bit ahead of me. I know him well enough to know that he is *not* someone you should know, Thalia. He's friends with Byron and Shelley and others of that crowd, and the same might be said of him that Caroline Lamb said of Byron: 'he's mad, bad, and dangerous to know.'"

Thalia stared at Adam. She'd never known him to be so dismissive of someone else. "You're jealous."

Adam pinched the bridge of his nose. "Of Darby? Don't be ridiculous. I just don't want to see you hurt."

"I can handle myself, thank you very much. And I'm hardly in any danger in a public venue, in company with my aunt, uncle, sister, cousin, and a nosier-than-needed neighbor. I find him amusing, that's all. We were talking of poetry, if you must know."

"I can talk to you of poetry, too," Adam said, though Thalia knew there were few things that he found more tedious than rhyme schemes.

"There once was a tulip named Darby
Inveigled himself with Miss Aubrey.
His words, they were slippery,
Concealed well his frippery,
And diddled her mind with things tawdry."

Adam finished with a flourish broad enough to draw stares from the surrounding guests. Even Aunt Harmonia seemed to notice at last, gazing at them with a strained expression.

Several competing emotions wrestled for supremacy in Thalia's breast. At the forefront was a desire to laugh, followed closely by indignation at Adam's presumption. She refused to be dictated to by someone she'd known as long as Adam, someone so downright *conventional* as her parsonage-bound friend.

She clapped mockingly. "Forget the church, you ought to be a poet. You put even Wordsworth to shame." After a beat, she added, "Though you may want to work on your rhymes. Darby and tawdry? Really, Adam."

Adam was blushing now. "All right, that was ridiculous. I acknowledge as much. But truly, you should avoid that man, and if you won't listen to me, at least heed my poetry." He winced at the unintentional rhyme. "Right. I heard that. I'll stop now."

Adam led her back to his friend and Mr. Darby and introduced them all. The friend was nice enough, but in Mr. Darby's presence he faded to such a nonentity that she struggled to remember his name. The four of them had a pleasant conversation about history, though it lacked the stimulating thrill of her tête-à-tête with Mr. Darby. And then, when Thalia thought Adam and his friend must leave to seek newer acquaintances, they stayed on. Mr. Darby did not leave either, and it occurred to Thalia that the two men were each seeking to outstay the other in her company.

At length, Adam's friend bowed and drifted on, and Thalia took matters into her own hands.

"Adam, I'm parched. Won't you fetch me some ratafia?"

Adam, far from obliging her, only stared. "But you never drink the stuff. And besides, didn't you just have lemonade?"

She smiled, baring more teeth than might be considered seemly. "It's not polite to turn down a lady's request."

"I'm sure Mr. Darby would be pleased to fetch a drink for you."

"I'd be—" Mr. Darby began.

"No, he wouldn't," Thalia cut across. "I asked you, Adam, and if you continue to begrudge me, I shall take it as a personal affront."

Adam glowered at her. "Fine." He stalked toward the refreshments, resentment stiffening every line of his body.

Thalia snuck a glance at Aunt Harmonia again, who was watching Adam instead of Thalia. With a boldness that sent a thrill through her, Thalia grabbed Mr. Darby's hand and pulled him into the crowd away from both Aunt Harmonia and Adam. She knew she might get a lecture for it later—from both her aunt and from Adam—but really, a lady might walk with an escort in a public gathering without attracting any scandal, so long as they kept moving.

"Miss Aubrey?" Mr. Darby asked.

"Shh. If we hope to lose the prosy parson, we've got to move quickly." If she felt a qualm at so abusing Adam to Mr. Darby, it was forgotten as Mr. Darby laughed and allowed himself to be led.

The evening, Thalia thought, was proving unexpectedly delicious.

CHAPTER FIVE

Indiscretions in the Garden

(Kalli)

A deviation from propriety, scarcely ever escapes punishment.
— *Regina Maria Roche, found in Kalliope Aubrey's commonplace book*

Vicarious embarrassment rose in a wave through Kalli. While Uncle John went to soothe Mr. Leveson, and Charis headed for the refreshments with a determination usually reserved for her natural studies, Kalli wanted only to melt into the floor. For Charis to say such things to a gentleman of Mr. Leveson's standing! And for him to say such cutting things in return. Kalli wished she could say she didn't believe it possible of Charis, but, in truth, Charis could be disastrously frank.

With a sigh, Kalli set off after Charis. Aunt Harmonia would want them to stay together, and perhaps Kalli could prevent another such disastrous encounter.

"Miss Aubrey!"

Kalli had not quite reached Charis when Henry—that is, Mr. Salisbury—approached her through the crowd, his sister Anne following close behind. Both Salisbury siblings beamed at Kalli, and she stopped to greet them. She sniffed her sleeve surreptitiously. She smelled of lavender and rose water—*much* better than the sour milk Mr. Salisbury had found her doused in last time.

"You look lovely," Miss Salisbury said.

Privately, Kalli had thought she looked rather elegant in a seafoam-green gown with a pale blue underdress—like some sort of mythical sea creature. But it was nice to have that belief confirmed by someone who was not related to her.

"And how are you finding your first London event?" Mr. Salisbury asked.

Rather uncomfortable, thanks to Charis and Mr. Leveson, Kalli thought. She said, "There are so many people here! I know scarcely anyone aside from my family."

"Oh, I remember that feeling well. It can be so uncomfortable to wander about a room full of strangers," Anne Salisbury said. "But take heart—I predict that before long, you'll know as many people as Henry and I."

"And wish that you did not know half of them," Henry grumbled.

Kalli laughed, suddenly feeling much lighter. "I am sure that will not be the case. I find most people to be likable, once I get to know them."

"Impossible. I'm sure it's the other way around," Mr. Salisbury said.

"She does appear to like *you*, Henry," Anne said. "Is that simply because she does not yet know you?"

Mr. Salisbury grinned. "I must be the exception to my rule. Society ladies adore me. My presence has frequently been said to elevate a mere party into a true spectacle."

"Because you frequently make a spectacle of yourself," his sister said with mock-severity, and then both Salisbury siblings laughed.

Envy pinged through Kalli at this camaraderie. She missed bantering with her siblings at home. She loved Thalia, but Thalia was often so serious it was hard to tease her as Anne teased Mr. Salisbury. If Thalia was in a *mood*, then the teasing would only offend her.

"I say, why does Mr. Leveson look as though he's bitten into a lemon?" Mr. Salisbury asked abruptly.

Kalli's good mood evaporated. She had been so diverted by their conversation that she had forgotten to watch Charis. She turned back in the direction of her cousin to find that Mr. Leveson had left Uncle John and was making his way—good heavens—toward Charis again.

Kalli should probably do something. She should join Charis, try to soften Mr. Leveson's irritation and Charis's unholy frankness.

Her feet seemed glued to the floor. "I'm afraid my cousin was quite uncivil to him," Kalli said.

"Uncivil?" Miss Salisbury echoed. "To Mr. Leveson? I wonder he did not slay her where she stood."

"That may yet happen," Kalli said, watching her cousin flush a mottled pink and white as Mr. Leveson spoke to her. She really ought to go to her.

"Does your cousin need assistance?" Mr. Salisbury asked, his earlier teasing expression smoothed serious.

Probably. Kalli sighed, "I do not think she would thank you for trying to protect her. Charis likes to fight her own battles." She turned back to the Salisburys. She could not watch Charis bring disaster on her head again.

Mr. Salisbury studied her closely for a moment, then said,

"Properly giving offense is an art form, as I should know." He launched into a story about a recent excursion to an artist's gallery. "Saw a painting of Helen, launching a thousand ships, that looked rather like my aunt Agatha. And so I said—she had a face that has been known to frighten small children. If she launched any ships, it was only because they were fleeing away from her."

Kalli smiled reluctantly.

Anne leaned in and said, "What Henry hasn't said is that the artist was right behind him as he spoke."

"And he heard you? The poor man!" Kalli said.

"Nothing poor about it," Mr. Salisbury said. "I felt compelled to purchase one of the blasted paintings, and I'll tell you it cost me a pretty sum."

Kalli laughed. Had Mr. Salisbury done this on purpose—seen her discomfort and tried to distract her with a story? Or was it only that he could never be serious for more than two moments at a time?

Her laughter was picked up by the crowd around them. It rippled out and then returned, swelling louder, and Kalli realized it could not be from Mr. Salisbury's story. Oh no. She whirled back to her cousin to see Mr. Leveson heading away from the refreshment table (looking abominably pleased with himself) and Charis fleeing toward the doors. She looked on the verge of tears.

"Is your cousin all right?" Miss Salisbury asked, concern drawing her reddish-gold eyebrows together.

"I don't know," Kalli said. "Excuse me, I must go to her."

This time, it took no effort to move her feet, to push through the crowd surging between herself and the door. Kalli's anxiety over Charis spurred her forward. By the time she reached the balcony outside, Charis had already disappeared. But which way had she gone? Two curving stairways swept away from the balcony, ending on either side of a stone square. Gardens branched off in all directions, densely decorated with hedges and rosebushes.

Kalli thought she caught a glimpse of pink near a tall hedge. Charis? Clattering down the stairs, she called after her cousin, but Charis didn't answer.

The muffled sound of sobbing drifted through the hedge. Kalli trotted along it, following the greenery as it curved toward a massive stone wall, but she couldn't see an opening. She reached the wall and retraced her steps, listening hard. Voices floated down from the terrace, and she heard what she rather suspected was a couple being indiscreet, but the sobbing had stopped.

Parting the hedge with her gloved hands, Kalli squinted into the gloom. She wished the lanterns that sparkled so brightly near the house were lit near the walls as well. She couldn't see anything of her cousin. Maybe she should let Charis sort herself out and go back to the house. If Charis *was* in the thicket somewhere, she'd gotten herself in and could get herself out.

No—Kalli couldn't do that. It wouldn't be proper to let Charis wander around the gardens alone, but more importantly, it wouldn't be kind to let her do so when she was so upset.

She walked along the hedge a few more paces. "Charis?"

The faintest sniff answered her. There was something heartbroken in the sound, in its softness, as though someone had muffled it lest they be heard and mocked for it.

Kalli's heart twisted. She wouldn't let someone she loved weep alone.

With renewed determination, she peered through the bushes again. The sound had *seemed* to come from behind the wall of shrubbery, but it was hard to tell for certain. *There*. Kalli was nearly certain that flash of pale fabric was pink. Well, if Charis had made it through the hedge, she could too.

"I'm coming, Charis!" Squaring her shoulders, Kalli pushed her way into the hedge, picking a spot where the branches looked sparser and easier to breach.

Bare branches scratched at her face and snagged at her gown. She shoved in deeper—and stopped. She couldn't find a way through the branches that barred her way and trapped her skirts. She groaned and tried to move back the way she'd come. But she was stuck fast. Her sleeve was so soundly tangled that she could not move her shoulder, and her delicate, filmy skirts were caught fast as well. Something sharp poked into her backside.

Confound it all.

"Charis!" she called in a loud half whisper, not daring to speak louder lest someone else find her in this predicament. "Charis!"

No answer. *Had* Charis really disappeared into this thicket or had Kalli only imagined it? She tried to wiggle free, and only succeeded in trapping herself more surely.

Kalli swore, a choice selection of words she'd picked up from her brother Frederick. Aunt Harmonia would have a swooning fit simply knowing Kalli *knew* these words, much less used them.

The tap of approaching footsteps halted abruptly. "Is someone there?"

Kalli froze. She could *not* be caught in such a humiliating position. For several long moments, she did not so much as breathe, but then a gust of wind shivered through the hedge and a trio of twigs tickled her nose.

A tremendous sneeze burst from her.

"There *is* someone there."

The branches near her face parted, and Kalli found herself staring into Adam Hetherbridge's wide-eyed face, moonlight reflecting off his round glasses. She sagged with relief, so happy to see a familiar face she could kiss him. Adam might mock her for her predicament, but he would never expose her to shame before London society.

That is, she didn't *really* want to kiss him. It was only gratitude making her giddy.

A sudden memory came to her. Once, as a small child, she'd been playing hide-and-seek with Thalia and Charis and Frederick and Adam. She had hidden so well, beneath a large flowering bush, that no one had been able to find her. But then the others had been distracted by something—she could not remember what—and had forgotten to come find her. It was Adam who remembered first, Adam who had parted the bush at the sound of her crying to find her tearstained and shaking, Adam who had helped her out and carried her home on his back.

For months afterward, she had thought Adam was the most splendid person in existence. But then, of course, he'd become Thalia's particular friend, and Kalli had quietly folded away her hero worship. Funny—she'd nearly forgotten that.

"Kalli? What on earth are you doing here?"

She sighed. "Looking for Charis."

"And Charis is . . . hiding in a hedge? That seems extreme, even for her."

"I thought I saw her. I must have been mistaken."

Adam began running light hands along the branches, trying to disentangle them from the delicate silk of her dress. Kalli winced at the ragged sound of tearing.

"My hair is caught too," she said, and then Adam's gloved fingers traveled along her neck to the dark curls piled high on her head. His fingers were gentle against her scalp and sent a curious thrill through her. A few deft moves, and her head was free.

After several long minutes of work, with Adam blocking some of the shrub with his own body, she was mostly released. Whatever had wound around her short puffed sleeve was proving uncooperative.

"You'll simply have to pull free," Adam said. "I'll hold the branches back as much as I'm able."

With effort, Kalli wrenched herself out of the hedge. She had never been so happy to stand on a cobbled trail before, the uneven stones pressing into the dirty and scratched soles of her slippers. Her poor sleeve hung torn and useless below her shoulder. She hoped Aunt Harmonia's abigail could fix it.

Adam took her arm and she was struck anew by his height—she did not even reach his shoulder. "We'll have to get you back into the house without being seen. If you can get to the ladies' room, there might be thread and scissors to repair your sleeve. I'll find Thalia to fetch your wrap, in case it can't be mended."

Kalli shook her head. "The damage is too great to be fixed in a few minutes." She considered for a moment. "I think I'd better go home. I don't want anyone to see me like this."

"Then I'll find your aunt and uncle and secure a quiet place for you to wait for the carriage."

"Thank you." Kalli tried to smile up at Adam, but her lips trembled. She would *not* cry. A shiver coursed through her.

Adam shrugged off his tailcoat and was just handing it to Kalli when a sniff interrupted them. It was a very eloquent sniff, managing to convey both annoyance and censure at once. Adam, in his shirtsleeves and waistcoat, and Kalli, her torn sleeve sagging off her shoulder, whirled to meet it. A bit of twig tumbled from Kalli's hair to land at her feet.

Kalli's horrified gaze fixed on the equally shocked gaze of the woman facing them. Wearing the kind of silken headdress sometimes favored by matrons, Mrs. Drummond-Burrell was not only one of the patronesses at Almack's, she was often said to be the most exacting of them. Her eyes darted from Kalli's untidy hair to her ripped and rumpled clothing to Adam's shirtsleeves. It was not difficult to guess what conclusions she was drawing: that Kalli and Adam had been scandalously kissing in the garden.

"I beg your pardon," Mrs. Drummond-Burrell said in glacial tones. She swung around, her long skirts swishing behind her.

"Oh Lord," Adam muttered.

Kalli blinked hard. Of all the people to discover them—those vouchers to Almack's that Aunt Harmonia had been at such pains to acquire would surely be revoked. And what would people say of her? Of Adam?

Social rules dictated that young, unmarried women were never to be alone with a gentleman—except in a public place, where they were moving (such as walking in a park or riding in an open carriage). Those rules supposedly existed to prevent intimacy before marriage, and the merest suspicion that such rules had been violated with so much as a single illicit kiss could send a young woman back to the countryside in disgrace, as gossip about her flew through the *ton* and doors were closed to her.

Kalli had to fix this.

She started after the famous patroness. "Mrs. Drummond-Burrell? Please, it's not what you think."

The great lady stopped, turned her head. A statue might have been more yielding. "As we have not been introduced, you can have nothing to say to me. As your behavior is demonstrably wanton, I can assure you we never *shall* be introduced." She resumed her walk.

"I was trying to find my cousin! She was upset, and I thought she was crying in the hedge," Kalli said, her voice rising in desperation.

Mrs. Drummond-Burrell did not acknowledge her. Her back ramrod straight, the lady continued her slow march toward the house.

Adam tried to hand Kalli his coat again, but she pushed it back at him, as though by repudiating the coat she could repudiate what had just happened. Gooseflesh prickled her arms. Her heart squeezed small in her chest. Already, she could hear the scandal spread, from Mrs. Drummond-Burrell to Lady Jersey, who could not help but talk.

But perhaps Mrs. Drummond-Burrell would not know who she was? It was dark in the gardens, after all, and as the lady had noted, they had not yet been introduced.

Kalli shivered again.

Adam frowned at her. "Come, you're freezing. Are you sure you don't want my coat? At the least, it will help cover your dress."

"But people will talk—" Kalli faltered.

"People will talk regardless of what we do," Adam said. "And wouldn't you rather be comfortable?"

Kalli let herself be persuaded to take the coat. It *was* blessedly warm, and she felt fractionally better, as though the coat were armor against the fears starting to crowd her mind. And it smelled nice, like paper and ink and something a little musky that was pure Adam. Wearing it felt like a reassuring hug.

They were nearly to the house when Kalli found herself being hailed.

"Miss Kalliope? Is that you?"

Dismayed, Kalli turned toward the voice. One of Aunt Harmonia's friends—a plump, middle-aged widow whose name Kalli couldn't remember—was waving at her as she hurried over. "Kalliope, my dear, have you been in the gardens this whole time? Perhaps you have seen—oh, it's quite shocking, perhaps I shouldn't tell you." But the woman's eyes were bright and eager, and the story came pouring out. "Mrs. Drummond-Burrell was walking in the gardens just now, and she caught a young couple quite *in flagrante*. Imagine being so lost to all propriety as to be seen embracing in the pathways. Well!" Her last exclamation was both offended and pleased, as though this scandal was a bonbon to savor.

Kalli did not know what *in flagrante* meant, but she caught a glimpse of Adam's face, stiff and stony, and her heart quailed. Whatever it was, it was bad. Had the woman come into the gardens hoping to catch the couple in question, to add to her stock of gossip?

Adam put his hand on her back protectively and tried to shepherd her away from the woman. "If you'll excuse us, ma'am, Miss Aubrey is not feeling well, and I must get her to her aunt."

The woman blinked, her gaze sharpening as she registered, finally, Kalli's untidy hair and Adam's coat about her. "Oh, Miss Kalliope . . ." she breathed, her tone bright with delighted understanding. "Of course. I shall fetch your aunt for you, shall I?"

And spread gossip all along the way, you vicious harpy, Kalli thought. But what choice did she have? If the woman did not go, she might elect to stay with Kalli while Adam went, and Kalli did not think she could bear the woman's prying questions masked as false sympathy.

"Thank you," Adam said, and the woman darted back toward the house. He helped Kalli to a bench and sat down beside her.

All she had wanted was to enjoy her first party, to help Charis. How was it fair that something innocent and generous was being reimagined as something sordid? The back of her throat prickled and she wrapped her arms tight around her torso to keep her tears at bay.

Beside her, Adam tentatively put one arm around her. Kalli stiffened for a moment, then relaxed into him. She was already suspected of embracing Adam far more intimately than this, so how could this hurt? She needed the comfort. She tried not to notice how nice he felt, how nice he smelled. It was only a brotherly hug, such as Frederick would have given her.

"It will be all right, Kalli," Adam said.

Kalli did not believe him.

A chill breeze lifted Kalli's tangled hair from her face. For the first time since coming to London, she wished she had never left home.

CHAPTER SIX

A Matter of Principle

(Charis)

Strongly impressed with the conviction that every attempt to elucidate any part of natural history, will meet with a favorable reception, I have ventured to submit to the notice of the Royal Society, a few observations relative to the mode of propagation, &c. of the *Hirudo vulgaris*.

—James Rawlins Johnson, Philosophical Transactions of the Royal Society *[Charis's note:* Are leeches required to engage in courtship before "propagation"? Or are such rituals reserved for more complex species? *]*

No one in the carriage was acting at all like themselves, Charis observed. Kalli was curled in the corner beside Thalia, as though if she kept shrinking, she might vanish entirely. Thalia's arm was tight about her sister, and she kept murmuring comfortingly to Kalli. But every once in a while, Thalia's words trailed off, and her eyes went soft with some memory. Across from Charis, Mama sat with arms folded, her lips pressed grimly together. Even Papa was not nodding off as he usually did after social events but was watching Charis's mama with a frown.

And Charis . . . she could hardly bear to think of how dysregulated her behavior had been. First her quarrel with Mr. Leveson, then her tears in the garden.

Did London society affect everyone so?

At least she should not have to speak with Mr. Leveson again. After her performance that evening, no doubt he would be more than happy to avoid her for the remainder of the Season. Following her flight from the ballroom, Charis had found a stone bench hidden away at the back of the garden, behind a hedge that snaked around almost like a maze. Once her tears had dried and her cheeks had cooled, she had begun to feel rather embarrassed about her flight. She had snuck back into the ballroom, hoping no one had marked her absence.

Charis had known something was wrong the instant she returned. She could not immediately find her parents, but she had caught whispers of Kalli's name, paired with "scandalous," though she could not imagine what Kalli could have done. Kalli had been looking forward to her debut for years—she would not endanger her position in society on the first official night of her Season. Then Charis's father had found her and told her Kalli was feeling unwell, and they must leave at once.

Charis turned to Thalia beside her. "What happened?"

Kalli released a single, sharp sob, and Thalia shook her head at Charis and bent to her sister.

"Mama?" Charis asked.

"Hush," her mama said. "Now is not the time, Charis."

Not the time for *what*? When would it be time? Charis wished that the rules that governed society and human interactions would follow the same orderly logic as the rules that governed the natural universe. Some rules her mother articulated for her: A young lady should never be alone in public in London, nor should she venture down St. James's Street, where many of the masculine clubs were. Such rules Charis could understand, though she did not understand the *why* of them. But she did not understand why they could not talk about whatever had obviously upset Kalli.

By the time they reached home, Charis was itching to go to her room and find the densest scientific book their scanty London library offered, to drive away the lingering unpleasantness from the evening. However, she could not in good conscience do so while Kalli was still so distressed. While Mama and Papa went into her papa's study to confer about something, she followed Kalli and Thalia up the stairs to the hallway outside their rooms. Kalli had stopped weeping, but her sniffing tugged at Charis.

"Kalli, are you all right?"

"It's kind of you to ask *now*," Kalli said.

Charis's face scrunched in confusion. "I did try to ask earlier."

"But you were not so concerned when you ran pell-mell for the garden in tears. You did not think that someone might follow you."

Why could people not say what they meant? "Did someone follow me?" Enlightenment dawned slowly. "Did you follow me?"

"Yes and got caught in a hedge for my pains. Adam Hetherbridge had to rescue me and then Mrs. Drummond-Burrell found us, and she thought . . . and oh, everything is a disaster."

Charis remembered her own misery in the dark corner of the garden, and guilt washed over her. She'd been so engrossed in her own feelings that she'd missed the drama playing out not far from her. Worse, Kalli had tumbled into trouble for *her* sake. "You didn't have to follow me."

"You were *crying*," Thalia said. "Of course Kalli followed you. You might as well have raised a flag in front of a bull. She cannot resist responding to distress."

"I'm sorry," Charis said, setting her hand tentatively on Kalli's arm. She rarely knew what to do with strong emotions—hers, or anyone else's. It was so much easier to *think* through things than to *feel* them.

Kalli shook her hand off. "If you had not quarreled with Mr. Leveson, none of this would have happened!"

Charis blinked at the surprising leap of logic.

"This is not Charis's fault," Thalia said soothingly. "Any more than it is yours. You only meant to help Charis, and Charis meant to defend Uncle John." Charis wondered what, exactly, Thalia had heard from Papa. Or, more alarmingly, from Mama. "The fault is clearly with Mrs. Drummond-Burrell for spreading unfounded gossip."

"Yes," Charis said, a little more eagerly than warranted. "Let's blame Mrs. Drummond-Burrell. Death to tyrants!"

Kalli gave a watery laugh. "Do not try to make me feel better."

"Very well, we shall not," Thalia said. "Come, let me tuck you into bed. No doubt things will be clearer in the morning."

Charis watched the sisters disappear into Kalli's room and tried not to feel relieved that Thalia was shouldering the brunt of Kalli's emotional distress. She went into her own room and lit a brace of candles at her desk, then settled into her chair and began paging through the latest copy of *Philosophical Transactions of the Royal Society*. Within minutes, she was engrossed, the humiliations and discomforts of the evening sloughing off her like the outgrown skin of a snake.

One article caught her attention: a response to the French naturalist Lamarck's newest volume on the natural history of invertebrates. The text of the article had been delivered before the society in February, just before the Elphinstones' arrival in London, by someone styling himself *L.M.* The reviewer was overall warm in his praise of Lamarck's idea that species change gradually over time, always toward greater complexity, though he cautioned against Lamarck's reliance on alchemical principles and favored the newer chemistry used by Lavoisier.

Charis read through the article a second time, muttering to herself. She had read Lamarck's book and agreed neither with the alchemical principles he relied on nor his basic thesis. Why must he assume that species' change was always increasingly complex? Yes, generally that seemed to be the case, but one had only to look at linguistics, at the way English grammar had simplified since Old English, to see that nature often favored efficiency. Efficiency did not have to mean complexity. Van Leeuwenhoek had discovered all kinds of animalcules that thrive despite being simple organisms.

Ideas sparking for a point-by-point rebuttal of L.M.'s response, Charis began scribbling some notes in a book she kept by her bedside. She wrote until her candles guttered out, until she had forgotten about Kalli, and Mr. Leveson, and, indeed, London itself.

Charis hoped to spend the morning cloistered in her room, finishing a rough outline of the letter she'd begun in response to L.M. She had never quite seen herself as a scientist on the same scale as the men whose words peppered the pages of the journals—she hadn't the same education, for one, and she was a woman. But one must start somewhere. Perhaps, if her rebuttal was sound enough, she might be brave enough to submit her letter (under an appropriately ambiguous pseudonym that would conceal her gender, of course).

But at breakfast all her plans dissolved like sugar in water. Kalli's pretty face was wan and miserable, and she poked at her food instead of eating it. Morning had evidently not brought clarity. Then Mama came down to announce, with color high in her cheeks and steel in her tone, that they were to spend the morning in the drawing room receiving visitors.

Charis's dismay at Kalli's unhappiness turned to confusion: Mama was treating the receiving of guests like an act of defiance. But who, or what, Mama intended to defy, Charis could not guess.

When they were settled in the drawing room, Charis apologized again. She was not certain she understood why the previous evening's episode had been so very dreadful, so she focused on the part that she did understand.

"I'm sorry, Kalli," Charis said. "It should have been me in that hedge, not you."

"It's not your fault," Kalli said, but her voice lacked conviction.

Thalia shook her head impatiently. "It doesn't matter who it was. It's all a silly misunderstanding. Kalli did nothing wrong."

But Mama said, "It's not so simple. Ours is a society that places a good deal of weight on appearances. And this—well, it does look very bad. But your uncle and I have been talking, and we'll figure out a way to come about yet."

"So Kalli might be wicked, but so long as she hides it from the *ton*, she is acceptable?" Thalia asked. "If society is so shallow, why should we care for their good opinion?"

Mama sighed. "I brought you girls to London in the hopes that you might find an eligible marriage partner. Your mama is depending upon me. And while yes, sometimes society may be shallow, their good opinion matters. If the *ton* believes Kalli's reputation is compromised, not only will Kalli be shut out from society, but you and Charis may be seen as tainted as well. You will not be able to meet the right sort of men if you are not allowed to attend the right sort of parties."

Charis frowned. What did "the right sort" mean, anyway? Men of wealth? Lineage? If she were to marry—which she thought unlikely—she would want a kind man with some semblance of wit.

"But that's ridiculous," Thalia said. "We are not creatures to be bought and sold at market to the highest bidder—we are women with hearts and minds and wills and deserve to be valued on our own merits, and not merely for our appearance or our reputation."

"I think perhaps my sister has given you more freedom to speak your mind at home than is good for you. I hope you do not speak so freely in company!" Mama said. "What do you propose we do, Thalia? Challenge all of society? We do not have such power. Not even your uncle, with a seat in Parliament, could do as much."

"I do not want to challenge society," Kalli said in a small voice. "I only wanted to be accepted, to go to parties and have beaux and dance."

Mama patted her hand. "And so you shall, dear heart. We shall receive callers together and show everyone that we are not ashamed of you."

Thalia gave an unladylike snort. Charis wondered if it would seem coldhearted of her to read her scientific journal. Despite her genuine concern for Kalli, she found all the society talk trying. But when she tried to reach for the journal, her mama caught her eye and shook her head. Charis dropped her hands back into her lap.

Then they waited.

After an hour, Kalli said, "No one is coming. I am ruined."

"It is early yet," Mama said.

"If people cannot see your value despite a silly rumor, then they are not true friends." Thalia crossed her arms across her chest.

They waited some more. This time, Charis's mama did not stop her when she slipped her journal into her lap and began to read.

After breaking for a light luncheon, Kalli begged to be excused to her room. "I am fatigued, Aunt Harmonia, and feel a headache coming on."

While Mama fussed over Kalli, Charis and Thalia returned to the drawing room on Mama's orders. Thalia went at once to the writing table and picked up a quill, and Charis resumed reading, pausing occasionally to scribble a note in the margins of the journal.

At length, Thalia laughed and swiveled around in her chair. "Well, aren't we a pair? I don't believe this is what your mama had in mind when she sent us to wait for callers. We're supposed to sit quietly and decoratively, sewing or embroidering. Now I've ink stains on my fingers and you—what is that you're working on?"

"A letter. I think. For the *Philosophical Transactions*."

"Oh!" Thalia sounded surprised. "I did not know you meant to publish."

"Well, scientists must, at some point, if they wish to share their ideas. I had not meant to do so this Season, but I read a ridiculous article that merits a response, and I might as well be the one to write it." Charis shrugged. Somehow, she could not bear it if Thalia were to ridicule the idea. Easier to pretend it meant nothing to her.

Thalia did not reply at once, so Charis asked, "What are you working on? Another poem?"

"Yes, but the words won't come as I'd like them to." Thalia scrunched up her face, which made Charis laugh, and it was at that moment that the drawing room door opened.

"Mr. Leveson," Dillsworth announced.

Charis dropped her magazine. She stared, horrified, at the tall, elegant figure that emerged from the doorway behind her parents' butler.

As Thalia dropped a polite curtsy, Charis stood and blurted, "What are you doing here?" She wished, nearly as soon as the words had left her, that she had bitten her tongue.

A smile played around Mr. Leveson's well-shaped lips. "I believe it to be customary to call on new acquaintances?"

"I rather thought you'd see me in h—ah, perdition before you'd see me at home," Charis said. Drat it. What was it about this man that robbed her of all her tact? Not that she had much to begin with. Belatedly, she fumbled an awkward curtsy and added, "sir."

Mr. Leveson eyed her with amusement. "Nothing quite so dire is necessary, I assure you."

Thalia stepped in. "Won't you be seated, Mr. Leveson?"

Mr. Leveson sat on the couch beside Charis, and Charis

immediately withdrew to a nearby chair. She did not care that Thalia stared at her with wide eyes, or that Mr. Leveson smirked. She would not be trapped in such close proximity to him. Charis picked up her scientific journal, but her pleasure in the ideas was lost. She contented herself with writing in the margin: *The existence of the fashionable London gentleman, with nothing on his mind but fashion and horses, proves my point: Sometimes the change in creatures over time regresses rather than progresses.*

Having thus routed Mr. Leveson in her mind, Charis sat silent while Thalia carried on a creditable conversation, speaking of the gloomy weather and Mr. Leveson's childhood memories of India, of his mother's family, who had been in Gujarat for generations.

As the conversation continued, guilt pricked at her. Papa would want her to apologize, and indeed, her own conscience acknowledged she had not been entirely fair to Mr. Leveson. When the conversation faltered, she jumped in: "I feel I must apologize for some of the things I said to you last evening. Even if they were true, I ought not to have said them to your face."

"I'd far rather you say them to my face than behind my back," Mr. Leveson said. "But I will take your apology and meet it in kind—I'm afraid I was rather more blunt than I meant to be."

Charis shook her head. "You said nothing that wasn't true. I *was* rather prone to prejudge you, and I should not have. That said, you are under no obligation to cultivate my company, or that of my family, when it clearly gives you so little pleasure."

"My friends will tell you I do nothing that gives me no pleasure, so you may rest assured on that count."

What could he possibly mean by that? That this visit brought him pleasure?

Mr. Leveson's gaze lingered on her face, before dropping down to the floor. Charis followed his glance, and saw that in her rush to move, her skirts had rucked up a bit, leaving an inch or two of stockinged ankle exposed. This was another of those social rules she did not fully understand—how was it permissible for a young lady to expose part of her bosom in a ballroom, but to display one's ankles, even if covered by a stocking, was utterly indecent?

But Mr. Leveson didn't seem to be dismayed or disgusted. As a point of fact, he was smiling a fraction.

Heat rose in Charis's cheeks, and she tucked her feet more securely beneath her skirt.

"Shall we start over?" Mr. Leveson asked, bringing his gaze back up to hers. "I will forget the regrettable things you've said, if you will forget what I have said. Then we will proceed to have an unobjectionable conversation on the weather, and I shall compliment you on . . ." He cast another glance over her and frowned a little. Charis felt herself going rigid again. "On your charming dress."

The pale lemon day dress she wore was à la mode and clean enough—there were no visible ink spots on it. It was not, however, the most flattering color: Charis's auburn hair and freckled skin looked best in rich colors, golds and russets and greens and umbers. But Mama said such colors were wholly unsuited to very young ladies, and so Charis bit her tongue and did not argue.

"It might be charming on someone else," Charis said. "It's a lovely dress, but the color is all wrong for me, and I cannot convince Mama I should not wear ruffles."

"No one should wear ruffles," Mr. Leveson said. "But I believe the proper response to a compliment is 'thank you.'"

Thalia pressed her lips together, as though she were holding back a laugh.

"Even if the compliment is a lie?" Drat it, she had just agreed to be inoffensive. "I meant, thank you," Charis said, earning a grin from Mr. Leveson. "I suppose I ought to also thank you for the pleasure of your visit?"

"Is that your unsubtle method for dismissing me?" His grin deepened.

Yes, she thought. "Of course not."

"Then I will not stay much longer. In truth, I came mostly to stanch the flood of rumors," Leveson said. "I cannot abide rumor-mongering and the most unfortunate speculations are flying this morning in regards to Miss Kalliope Aubrey. I thought my visit might downplay their effects."

Charis stole another glance at Thalia, who no longer looked as if she wished to laugh.

"Why did you suppose your visit might allay rumors?" Thalia's voice was dangerously quiet.

"If it was known that I visited you, the *ton* might not give so much credence to rumors. If I do not shun you, not all of polite society will, no matter what Mrs. Drummond-Burrell has said."

"So you felt sorry for us?" Thalia asked.

Charis stiffened. The man had a downright petrifying effect on her posture. "I'd rather not be patronized, thank you all the same."

The line of Mr. Leveson's mouth tightened. It really was a very fine mouth. A thrill shot through Charis at the anger sparking in his eyes. "Would you rather I lied to you, told you pretty truths that flattered you? It was not pity that drove me here, but compassion."

"My sister has done nothing wrong," Thalia said.

Mr. Leveson nodded at her, his eyes softening. "It is not my belief that you need. You have that already. But as my presence appears to pain your cousin, I will take my leave."

As soon as the door shut behind him, Thalia turned to her. "Charis—I had no idea you'd made such a conquest."

"If by conquest, you mean confounded nuisance, then yes." Charis sighed. She *had* meant to be civil. She picked up her journal once more and flipped it open to the offending article. Thinking about her response had eased her frustration with Mr. Leveson the night before—maybe it could do so again.

"Charis—" Thalia began.

An unwonted hesitation in Thalia's voice drew Charis's attention back to her. She looked up.

"I think I owe you an apology too," Thalia said.

"For what? *You* haven't insulted or patronized me today."

"No, but I have been a poor cousin and a worse friend. When you told me of your letter, I ought to have said something. Congratulated you or encouraged you. But my first thought was a jealous one, because writing has always been *my* skill, the talent that defines me. I am the poet, you are the scientist, and Kalli is the domestic one. If you are a scientist *and* a writer, then what am I?"

"Still the poet, I hope," Charis said. "I've no gift for poetry at all. Anyway, even if I were also a poet, that wouldn't make you any less one. Surely we can both do great and good things in the world without making each other smaller?"

Thalia stood and rushed across the floor to hug Charis. "I do love you, Charis. Can you forgive me?"

"So long as you do not talk to me of conquests ever again."

CHAPTER SEVEN

Disaster Descending

(Thalia)

When Shelley writes of London, he claims a seething sea,
Whose waves recede revealing lost treasures unsurpassed.
But noisy swells and wreckage shall not discourage me:
In claiming here my birthright, I'll find my voice at last.

—*Thalia Aubrey*

Thalia took refuge in her anger. She glared out the window of the green drawing room, scowling at the rain-slicked streets and passersby with their umbrellas and turned-up coats. In truth, she wasn't angry at the hapless pedestrians or the weather, but anger was simpler than the other feelings tangling inside her.

She was furious at society, which seemed hell-bent on holding Kalli accountable for something she had not done. She was frustrated with Aunt Harmonia, who seemed to think submission to society's ridiculous rules was the only acceptable path forward. And she was angry with herself, because she could think of no meaningful way to help Kalli, as her father had asked of her, and that felt like failure.

Thalia had woken that morning with a sparkling sense of

anticipation, hoping Mr. Darby would call. But the morning and afternoon had worn on, bringing no callers save Mr. Leveson and a few of her aunt's friends, making Thalia feel foolish for hoping, which only made her more irritable. What did it matter if he was the first man in London with whom she'd had a sensible conversation? If he would not seek her out, surely there were other intelligent men and women in the city—though it would be rather hard to find them if no one came calling and Aunt Harmonia refused to let the girls leave the house while the scandal hung over them.

She had been jealous of Charis for wanting to be published, when she should have been supportive. Now she felt guilty, an irritant layered upon irritants, making her downright stabby.

And where was Adam? He ought to have been the first to appear, to help them figure out a plan for facing down this scandal. His absence felt more like an abscess—a painful spot on her tooth that she could not stop her tongue from probing.

Altogether, it was much easier to be angry.

"Miserable old vultures," Thalia said, when the last of Aunt Harmonia's friends had departed. She was certain they had come only to gloat and feed off Kalli's misery.

"Thalia!" Aunt Harmonia said half-heartedly, but she did not disagree.

"Rather an insult to vultures," Charis observed, not looking up from her reading.

Kalli, who had come down to the drawing room late in the afternoon at Aunt Harmonia's insistence, said, "I shall have to go home and live with Mama and Papa forever."

"Surely it's not so dire," Thalia said, trying to quash a flicker of impatience. It was Kalli's nature to weep at distress; it was Thalia's to be stubborn and contrary. It wasn't Kalli's fault she was not Thalia. "Perhaps if you wrote a letter to Mrs. Drummond-Burrell explaining everything?" Action was surely better than hand-wringing.

"No!" Kalli said. "I tried to explain that night—she thought it a great impertinence. A letter now would surely make things worse."

A maid came into the room, carrying a small stack of folded cards on a silver salver. Aunt Harmonia thanked her and began flicking through the cards. She opened one, and all the color drained from her face. She opened a second, and then a third, her hands trembling.

"Aunt?" Thalia asked. "What is it?"

"A letter from Lady Jersey," Aunt Harmonia said. "Rescinding Kalli's voucher to Almack's. Other cards too, uninviting us to several social events. They are not so bluntly worded, of course, but the import is the same."

Kalli buried her face in her hands.

"Well, if Kalli is not invited to Almack's, I won't go either," Thalia said.

"Nor I," said Charis.

"Please don't injure yourselves on my account," Kalli said. "I must bear the weight of my own mistake."

Thalia wondered if Kalli was secretly enjoying the drama. "I'm sure it will all blow over in a matter of days, as soon as the gossips have something else to worry about. If you'd like, I'm sure I can find something outrageous to do or say."

"Pray, do not," Aunt Harmonia begged. "One disgraced niece

is far more than my nerves can bear. Dear Kalli, please do not fret yourself so. We shall come about, you'll see." She directed a pointed stare at both Thalia and Charis. "So long as you two comport yourselves appropriately and do not add to the damage."

Mr. James Darby came at last on the afternoon of the third day after the Gardiners' party, following a morning rain and even fewer callers. Aunt Harmonia had not even allowed them out for church the day before. Thalia received him and his bouquet of bloodred hothouse roses with cool grace, determined not to show any sign of her hurt at his delay.

Mr. Darby offered her a rueful smile. "I owe you an apology, Miss Aubrey. My delay in calling must have seemed a discourtesy on my part. Truth is, I meant to call much sooner, but business affairs interfered, and I could not get free of them until today. But you have been on my mind every spare minute since we met."

"You're very kind, Mr. Darby." Thalia tried to squash a fluttering sensation in her stomach as she took the flowers and handed them to a hovering maid to find a vase and water. She invited Mr. Darby to join her on the sofa. Aunt Harmonia and Charis were discussing something in one corner, and Kalli was upstairs with a headache.

"It's good to see you again, Miss Aubrey."

"And you, Mr. Darby." Thalia hesitated. She did not know Mr. Darby well, nor did she know what he already knew of Kalli's situation. Still, she liked Mr. Darby and would gladly know him better—and she did not believe friendships could be founded on prevarications and secrets. She leaned closer to Mr. Darby and lowered her voice, sure Aunt Harmonia would not like what she was about to ask. "Will you be frank with me?"

His eyes lit with amusement. "That depends on what you ask of me."

"What do people say of my sister?" Perhaps if she knew what the gossip was, she might know better how to act, how to protect Kalli.

The amusement flickered out. Mr. Darby cast a quick glance at Aunt Harmonia. "I'd rather not say. It's not exactly flattering."

"Do you think my maiden sensibilities so fragile? I'm made of stouter stuff than that."

"Very well." He sighed. "Does your uncle take the paper? It may be easier to show you."

Thalia swallowed. If Kalli's situation had made the paper, things were bad indeed. "I believe it's in the library. I'll fetch it at once."

She excused herself and hurried down the corridor. The library was empty, and she snatched up the paper, carrying it by her fingertips as though it might spontaneously combust.

Mr. Darby took it from her and opened the paper to the society section. He pointed to a small square of text.

Thalia read in silence.

> **A recent party at the home of Mr. G— was enlivened by the apprehension of a young couple very nearly *in flagrante delicto* in the garden. The identity of the young man (dare we call him**

a gentleman?) is unknown, but the young lady, Miss A—, is said to be a vicar's daughter, though she doubtless did not learn such behavior at home.

Thalia was nearly shaking by the time she had finished. Of all the arrant *nonsense*—"If I were a man, I would challenge someone to a duel over this slander."

"If you were a man, we might not have met, and I would certainly not have brought you flowers, so I cannot say I'm sorry," Mr. Darby said, setting the paper aside, his fingers brushing hers. "Come, don't let yourself be troubled by this. Such trifling exaggerations say more of the writer's outmoded morality than your sister's."

So Thalia had thought, until Mr. Darby said the same. "That may be true. But can you not see how unfair this is? This rag does not care about the identity of the unknown gentleman, but only for my sister's disgrace. Such rumors hurt her more because she is female and of modest means. A man in a compromising position has little to fear. Even a woman—if she is an heiress—might weather the scandal. Look at the Prince Regent," Thalia said. "He is allowed to indulge in extravagances that would ruin a woman's reputation."

"And yet Prinny himself has his critics," Mr. Darby said.

"But such critics would not hesitate to allow him to their parties, did he show the slightest inclination in coming."

"You're right, of course. It's damned unfair that society allows a gentleman freedoms that are not extended to ladies. But such conventions won't change unless *we* change them. Let a lady act as she pleases, without regard for anyone's opinion but her own."

"Why is it on the ladies to change society's opinions? Haven't men some responsibility as well? If it costs women more to act as they please, then shouldn't some of that burden be shared?" After three days of feeling trapped by Aunt Harmonia's well-intended caution, this rapid-fire exchange felt liberating. Thalia's skin buzzed with electricity.

Mr. Darby started to answer, but Dillsworth's voice carried over him. "Mr. Adam Hetherbridge."

Thalia rose to greet Adam, her conversation with Mr. Darby forgotten in the rush of relief sweeping through her. Adam was here, and somehow the entire mess with Kalli no longer seemed so impossible. "Where have you been?" she whispered, taking his hand in greeting.

"Busy," Adam said. He could not quite meet her eye. He swept his gaze around the room, with only the briefest hiccup when he spotted Mr. Darby. "Where's Kalli?"

"We needed you," Thalia said.

This time Adam did meet her eyes. There was a look there she couldn't quite read: something firm and . . . resigned? She thought she knew all of Adam's moods. "I know. I'm sorry I couldn't be here sooner, but there were a few things I had to do first. I really must speak with Kalli."

Aunt Harmonia sent the maid to summon Kalli, adjuring her to be sure that Miss Kalliope was presentable.

Adam refused to sit, though Thalia invited him to do so, and she returned to her seat by Mr. Darby. Mr. Darby tried to draw her back into their discussion, but Thalia's heart was no longer in it. Where had Adam been? Why was he behaving so oddly? Was it this business with Kalli? And if so, why hadn't he at least written? He must have known how his absence in a time like this would hurt them.

Kalli appeared at last, and if her hair was not so neat as it usually was, it would not discredit her either. She didn't seem surprised to see Adam, so the maid must have warned her. She came a few steps into the room and stopped, not quite looking at anyone.

"Can I speak with you?" Adam asked.

When Kalli didn't move, he added, "In private?"

Kalli nodded, looking nearly as unhappy as Adam. The two disappeared from the room.

No.

Everything inside Thalia seemed to go cold. She could think of only one reason why Adam would insist on privacy with Kalli, and only one reason why Aunt Harmonia would allow it.

He meant to propose.

But of all the daft notions—this couldn't be the only solution to Kalli's predicament. Thalia was quite sure Kalli's dreams for her future did not include Adam, and Adam could not want to marry Kalli. Adam needed a wife who would encourage his studies and challenge his ideas. Kalli needed someone who would cosset her and give her a comfortable home. They would both be miserable.

Mr. Darby asked Thalia a question, and she answered at random, her imagination following her sister from the room.

After several moments, Aunt Harmonia slipped out. When she returned, it was with a cat's smile: smug and self-satisfied. Neither Kalli nor Adam came back.

Thalia frowned, unease curdling in her stomach.

"Are you well, Miss Aubrey?" Mr. Darby asked, studying her with some concern.

Thalia had nearly forgotten that he was there. "I'm well enough," she said. "But I'm afraid my sister is not. Pray excuse me, I must see to her."

Mr. Darby did not press her to stay, for which she was grateful, but she could feel his eyes on her as she left the room.

Everything would be all right, Thalia told herself as she hurried up the stairs to look for Kalli. Likely she had misread the situation, and Adam was only bringing some private news to Kalli.

Why then, did she feel this heavy weight in her gut, as though some disaster was about to descend?

CHAPTER EIGHT

Admitting Impediments

(Kalli)

A married state, if entered into from proper motives of esteem and affection, is certainly the happiest; it will make you most respectable in the world, and the most useful members of society.

—The Female Instructor, *found in Kalliope Aubrey's commonplace book*

Kalli followed Adam into the smaller rose salon, a tight, awkwardly placed room with only one narrow window and dim light and consequently not much used by the family. She walked across the room to the window and looked down at the mews behind their town house.

Adam remained in the center of the room. She could feel his eyes on her back. She knew what he meant to ask her, knew what her answer must be, and wished to delay both as long as possible. She rubbed her arms, her skin prickling beneath the muslin of her day dress. Why was there no fire in here?

"Kalli," Adam said, then stopped.

The silence swelled between them, a pregnant thing. Though perhaps, Kalli thought, wincing inwardly, *pregnant* was not the best descriptor given her current predicament.

Kalli turned, finally. She could not put off the inevitable, and Adam would not leave until he had spoken with her. Adam was nothing if not faithful.

"Adam," she said, echoing him. His face was pale and drawn, as though he had not slept much more than she had these past few days.

Adam stepped toward her and took her hands. His grip was warm against her chilled fingers.

"Kalliope Aubrey, will you do me the honor of becoming my wife?"

Adam didn't release her fingers, and she was glad of that. His question was not unexpected, but still the room seemed to sway around her, and his hands steadied her.

"I know this is not what you wanted." He was too much a gentleman to say this was not what *he* wanted, but Kalli knew it. Adam wanted Thalia, had always wanted Thalia. "And I'm sorry I could not be here sooner, but your aunt and uncle thought it best if I asked your father, formally, for your hand."

Kalli swallowed and pulled her hands back. Adam had spoken to her father. The iron bars of a trap seemed to be closing around her. "You do me great honor," she said, stalling, trying to think.

She had hoped, this Season or the next, to "marry well," to find a man of wealth and position who she could love, someone who made her heart sing, who looked at her the way Papa, still, after all these years, looked at Mama. Mr. Salisbury's dimpled smile flashed across her mind, and her heart twisted.

She did not want to marry because rumor had forced her into it. She did not want to marry someone who meant to become a vicar, like her father, who had neither wealth nor position to offer his children. She did not want to marry Adam, a man in love with her own sister.

Adam shook his head. "It's not the honor you deserve. I'm sorry. I know it isn't fair. But I want to do the right thing by you. I hope you know that I have always esteemed you greatly, that I dearly love your family, and I will do everything I can to make you happy."

Esteemed you greatly. Hardly the declaration of love Kalli had longed to hear.

"But Thalia . . ."

Adam's face took on that shuttered look that meant Kalli had said too much. "Thalia was never going to care for me that way. You and I both know it."

That was probably true. Adam was comfortable and familiar—not nearly exciting enough for Thalia. "I could go home. Retire to the country for a year or two before coming back." Kalli could hear the desperation in her own voice.

"I'm afraid not, my dear." Aunt Harmonia had slipped into the room in time to hear this last. She crossed the room to stand by Kalli and slipped her arm around her niece's waist. "Mrs. Drummond-Burrell has significant social power and a long memory. Whatever the truth of your situation—and I believe you—it's not the truth that matters. It's what appears to be the truth, what people choose to believe. Only look at poor Miss Thompson. Rumor got about that she'd kissed Lord Ainsley's youngest son, and when he didn't offer for her, no one else would have her.

"I think you would do well to accept Mr. Hetherbridge. He's a nice young man, of good family, and I'm inclined to believe he could make you as happy as you might reasonably hope to be."

"I will do my best," Adam said.

Aunt Harmonia squeezed Kalli gently. "I'm afraid you have two options. If you wish to be accepted by polite society, you must be married, though your engagement will be enough to silence critics. If marrying Mr. Hetherbridge is truly distasteful for you, then you must return home. Perhaps you could find someone in the country ignorant of London news and scandal who might still have you."

Kalli pulled away from her aunt and wrapped her arms around her chest. She did not want to give up her London Season, not as it had just begun.

Even less did she want to go home, to marry some ignorant fool who "might still have her."

Aunt Harmonia added, "And it's not just about you, you know. Your reputation will influence what people think of Thalia. Of Charis. Already our vouchers for Almack's have been rescinded, as have other invitations."

Kalli swallowed. She felt as though she were choking. Her own ignominy she could endure. But how could she ask the same of two of the people she loved best in the world? And when word got back to their friends in Oxfordshire, her disgrace would hurt Papa and Mama too. It might even affect Antheia's Season, though that was still at least three years away. Far better to sacrifice her own happiness than that of those she loved.

She released a long breath on a sigh. "Very well. Since it seems I have no other choice, I accept."

Her aunt reached for her hand and patted it. "Good girl. You'll have greater independence as a married woman, to go where you wish. You'll like that. And you know, marriage isn't really about romance. A good, comfortable friendship is often much better than a wild love affair."

Kalli felt herself flushing. She didn't want to think about Adam and "wild love affairs." Or the sort of intimacy marriage would require. It all felt wrong, somehow.

But Adam, who had stared fixedly at the floor while her aunt talked, was now looking at her, a faint gleam of humor in his eyes. "Thank you. You've made me the happiest of men."

"Please don't tease me," Kalli said. Tears pricked the backs of her eyes and she only wanted to escape before they betrayed her. "I've said yes, haven't I?"

"I wasn't—" Adam began, but Kalli was gone from the room before she could hear whatever new, kind lie Adam meant to offer her.

Kalli was lying on her bed, staring at the ceiling while hot tears stole down her cheeks, when someone scratched at the door. She knew it was Thalia before the door opened: No one else would think to check on her so soon. Aunt Harmonia was too pleased about the engagement, and Charis, bless her, would not notice for a little time yet that Kalli had gone missing.

The bed shifted under Thalia's weight, and then Thalia's gentle fingers wiped the tears from Kalli's cheeks.

"Congratulate me, if you please. I'm to be married," Kalli said. The words were bitter on her tongue.

"So, Adam did propose?"

Thalia's voice changed when she said Adam's name, and Kalli felt a deep, very unsisterly satisfaction. She'd always thought Thalia had a tendency to take Adam for granted. It served her right to find that now Adam was no longer to be her faithful squire in all things. Kalli burrowed deeper under her blanket.

"He has. And I've said yes. Aunt Harmonia said it was the only way to silence the slander against me."

"So you would marry him to save your good name? Kalli, you don't love him."

Was Thalia's concern for Kalli—or for Adam?

"And what choice do I have? It is this, or bury myself in the country."

"Why should you care so much what people think? Why not simply stay here and defy their judgment? What is the worst they can do—not invite you to their parties? You shouldn't care for that."

But that was precisely the problem. Kalli did care for that. She wanted to be part of society, not looking on wistfully from the fringes. She wanted Aunt Harmonia's approbation, and Mama's and Papa's. She wanted to keep her family safe, untouched by a scandal she had brought on them.

"I'm not so brave as you," Kalli said, turning onto her side so she wouldn't have to see the scorn darkening Thalia's eyes. "As a married woman, I shall have more freedom to go where I want, do what I wish." She was parroting Aunt Harmonia, a line she was not sure she believed herself, but it was better than letting Thalia see how pathetic she was.

"And so you'd trap Adam into a *lifetime* of marriage, simply because you're afraid? Because you want to keep going to a few silly parties?"

Kalli sat up then and looked at her sister. She was marrying Adam as much to protect Thalia and Charis as to save herself, but she wouldn't tell Thalia that, not if Thalia was determined to think the worst of her. "Adam asked me of his own free will—no one forced him to do it—and I accepted. There. If it disappoints you, you might console yourself with the thought that you might have married Adam yourself, anytime these past eighteen months, if you'd given him any kind of encouragement. You didn't, and now he's engaged to me, and don't pretend that you're upset with me over my so-called cowardice when it's your wounded pride that stings you as much as anything, because Adam isn't yours for the asking anymore."

Thalia pulled back, her cheeks flushed. "Don't be hateful, Kalliope Aubrey. I'm only trying to help."

Thalia got up from the bed and stalked out, letting the door bang shut behind her. Kalli pulled her knees up to her chest and cried in earnest, wondering what demon had provoked her to attack her sister, when what she really wanted was for Thalia to stay, to put her arms around her, and tell her comforting lies: that everything would turn out well, that Adam would come to love Kalli more than he did Thalia, that they would all be happy.

CHAPTER NINE

An Inconvenient Arrangement

(Charis)

The present provision for forming a nest out of its own secretions, in an animal of so high an order as the class Aves, strikes us with astonishment, since birds in all other countries find substances of some kind or other out of which they form their nests.

— *Sir Everard Home*, Philosophical Transactions of the Royal Society *[Charis's note:* In other words, the Java swallow builds its nest out of its own mucus. Would society brides be so eager to acquire their own homes if they had to do the same? Poor Kalli.*]*

The Elphinstones dined *en famille* with Thalia and Kalli the night of Kalli's engagement.

Charis normally found her family a relief, as she did not have to worry so much about what she said or what she wore, but that night she would have welcomed an addition to their family party (even the odious Mr. Leveson). Papa brought out a special wine to celebrate Kalli's betrothal, but though he and Mama seemed well-pleased with the announcement, Kalli sat at the long dining table beside Charis's mama and trained her reddened eyes on her plate, saying nothing. Charis wasn't much versed in falling in love—she'd never felt the slightest *tendre* for any gentleman of her acquaintance—but she rather thought that a newly affianced young lady ought to smile more than she cried.

Across from Kalli, beside Charis, Thalia resolutely ignored her sister. She chattered brightly about any and every topic that was raised, but her voice had a clipped quality to it. All this talking *at* people instead of *to* them disconcerted Charis. Thalia and Kalli must have quarreled about something—but what?

When the last course was cleared and the ladies of the family had retired to the drawing room, Charis's mama tried to cheer Kalli up by talking to her of the shopping they'd do for her trousseau. Kalli tried to rally and show some interest in the patterns her aunt showed her, but then she hiccuped, and a new flood of tears sprang to her eyes.

Charis wondered why people came to cry—what particular chemicals or nerves triggered the release of tears, and why they were so salty, and if people ever ran out of tears, as they did blood if they were wounded too greatly. She caught herself, with a pang of guilt, remembering that she ought to be more concerned for Kalli than curious about bodily fluids. Sometimes she found it hard to hold on to personal and present details when the abstract was so much easier and more engrossing for her.

Charis started to join Kalli on the sofa, but Thalia intercepted her, drawing her to the pianoforte and asking her opinion of some new song she was learning.

Thalia played the first few measures, a bright, brisk tune. "Well, what do you think?"

Charis did not really understand music and could not reliably remember the difference between the most popular of modern composers. "Why aren't you speaking to Kalli?"

"I think the tune is well enough," Thalia said, adding a few more measures, "but it does get repetitive. Perhaps I should abandon it."

"Thalia. Did you hear me?"

"I did. But you did not answer my question, so I thought we were making a game of ignoring our questions."

Charis did not think Thalia believed any such thing. Thalia must know by now that Charis did not play games. "Are you still angry with me about the article I'm writing?"

Thalia's fingers came down in a jangling chord. "What? No, of course not! I thought we had settled that."

"So had I, but you seem irritable. I thought it was me."

Thalia began playing again, hitting the keys harder than was strictly necessary. "I am not upset with you, Charis."

"But with Kalli? Why?"

Thalia glared across the room at her sister and spoke with slow deliberation. "Because my sister has decided to ruin not only her own life, but that of someone I care about."

Beside Mama, Kalli flinched.

Charis frowned. "I thought Kalli was to be ruined if she did *not* marry. So she is damned if she does and damned if she does not?"

"Charis, don't swear," Mama said, looking up from her pattern book. "Mr. Hetherbridge is very good to do the right thing by our Kalli. I've had an announcement sent to the *Times* and it should appear directly. I imagine once word gets out, we'll find we are received again as we were before."

Charis could not see why an announcement in the paper would make Kalli's scandal acceptable, but Mama seemed confident in her pronouncement.

Kalli stood abruptly. "Pardon me, Aunt, but I believe I shall go to bed. I have a headache."

"Of course she does," Thalia muttered at the keys. But only a few moments after Kalli left the room, Thalia left too, claiming exhaustion.

Charis followed Thalia out before her mama could invite her to look at the pattern books. She hesitated before going into her room and knocked at Kalli's door.

"Go away, Thalia," Kalli said.

"It's me, Charis."

A beat of silence, then, "Please leave me be. I only want to sleep."

Charis obediently tiptoed away and knocked on Thalia's door. Thalia did not even respond. Charis returned to her own room, her duty to her cousins discharged, and pulled up the chair at her desk. She sharpened her quill, thought for a moment, and began to write.

It was not entirely the fault of L.M. that her frustration—with Kalli's situation, with her cousins' refusal to talk to each other—found its target in him and his review. As she wrote, she recalled the times that her tentative efforts at scientific research had been met with scorn because she happened to be born a woman. She remembered how easily Mr. Leveson had dismissed her, because society valued women who were young and lovely and innocent and heaven forbid you should lack any one of those qualities. She wrote on, her quill scoring deeply into the paper, until at last her frustration was spent and she dropped, exhausted, into her bed.

The announcement of Kalli's engagement appeared in the *Times* two days later, and with it came a flood of visitors that afternoon, signifying their tacit readmission to polite society. It seemed Mama was right: The engagement *had* fixed their social standing. The rescinded voucher was not immediately restored, but Mama spoke with Lady Jersey, who assured them that one would be forthcoming.

Kalli and Thalia were still not speaking to each other beyond what was required by politeness, but in the rush of people, their pointed silences were much less noticeable.

The flood of visitors brought Mr. Leveson with them, rather like some unwanted flotsam washed up on the beach. When Dillsworth announced him, Charis started as though pricked. She had been rather bored with the fashion discussion going on around her, and as her eyes flashed to his, she had the lowering suspicion that he knew precisely how bored she had been.

He strode across the room toward her, smiling. The woman sitting beside Charis, whom Charis had counted on for some protection from Mr. Leveson, chose that moment to abandon her entirely, leaving the seat open for Mr. Leveson. He sat beside Charis, his thigh just brushing hers. She took a deep breath, shifted aside two inches, and willed herself not to blush at the heat still washing through her from that slight contact. She stared down at her hands and saw, to her mortification, that her fingertips were streaked black with ink from the piece she'd been working on that morning. She curled her fingers into fists in her lap.

"And how are you, this fine morning?" Mr. Leveson asked.

"It is a lovely morning," Charis said.

"It is," Mr. Leveson agreed, his dark eyes dancing. "But I asked after *you*, not your opinion of the morning. Though I suppose, being a properly brought-up English young lady, you would agree the morning was fine, though it be pouring rain outside."

"If it were raining, I would not say it were fine," Charis said.

"And still you avoid my question."

"I had much rather talk about the weather," Charis said frankly.

Mr. Leveson laughed. "Very well. Then perhaps you will go out driving with me? That will give us ample time to discuss the weather."

Charis didn't answer at once. She suspected he was the sort of elegant whip who would find her ignorance about his carriage skills insulting.

Unfortunately, her mama passed by at just that inopportune moment.

"I've invited your daughter for a drive, Lady Elphinstone," Mr. Leveson said, with a wicked side glance at Charis. "Will you give us your blessing?"

"Such an honor, Mr. Leveson," Mama gushed, "I'm sure Charis would be delighted. And I'll not have to worry a whit about Charis in your company, as I know well you're a member of the Four-Horse club."

Charis had no idea what that signified. Kalli would know—Charis made a mental note to ask her later.

Mr. Leveson turned back to Charis and quirked his eyebrow. "*Are* you honored, Miss Elphinstone?"

"Should I be honored to be driven about as though I were a fig-ure in an exhibition?" Charis asked. "I'm told that the *ton* only go driving to be seen by others, in which case, I should rather say the honor is all yours."

Mama pinched Charis's arm, and Charis realized she had once again spoken where she should have kept her thoughts to herself. She added hastily, "That is to say, yes, I should be delighted to drive out with you."

Now he was openly grinning. "Something tells me your first answer was by far the more honest of the two."

"And yet much of society doesn't value honesty in such cases." Charis darted a glance at her mama, who was frowning. "Some might consider it uncivil."

"I value it," he said promptly. "So much so that I hope you will never lie to me."

Now, blast it, why had *that* comment made her blush?

"I can safely promise you, sir, that I will never lie to you."

"Charis is a very good girl," Mama put in. "She was properly brought up."

Charis bit her lip to keep herself from saying anything that might further mortify her mother.

"Excellent. Now that's settled, will you tell me, have you a dress in amber or some such similar shade—like fall leaves?"

Charis had no such dress. In fact, she had utterly failed to persuade her mama to buy just such a dress. Did Mama remember that?

Mama said, "Hmm. I don't believe she has anything in that particular hue, but she has a very pretty light blue, or a pale pink."

"That's a pity," Mr. Leveson said. "Russets and golds appear to much better advantage against the brown and cream of my carriage."

He rose then, preparing to take his leave. "I shall call for you Saturday."

Lady Elphinstone followed him to the door, repeating her thanks on Charis's behalf. Charis didn't move, but her thoughts followed him, even after he was gone. In any other man, she would think his question about the color of her dress was out of pride, wanting her to wear a gown that complemented his carriage. But despite his fine appearance, Mr. Leveson did not strike her as the sort of dandy who paraded about town in clothing calculated to match his equipage. And he had not seemed particularly top-lofty today.

She could only conclude he remembered her comment about her unfortunate dress on the occasion of his last visit. Most people, seeing her indifference to the set of her hair and efforts at polite conversation, assumed that she did not care what she wore. In fact, she *did* care, but since she was to have little say in such matters, it seemed better to feign indifference.

The fact that Mr. Leveson might have seen through all that was—she hesitated, trying to name the emotion fluttering around her breast—troubling.

And now she had to go driving with him. Whatever would she say to him, tête-à-tête, for the better part of an hour?

CHAPTER TEN

A Woman's Soul Lacks Sustenance

(Thalia)

Bewitching girls with melting looks
Should not trade ballrooms for their books.
They should converse with morning callers,
Instead of reading classic scholars.
Yet thus denied of sustenance,
A woman's soul lacks subsistence.
There's no romance in mere existence.

— Thalia Aubrey

On the third morning after Kalli's engagement, tired of her own thoughts and the false cheer that permeated the household, Thalia put on her walking dress, summoned Hannah, the maid she shared with Kalli, and took herself to Hatchards bookstore, on Piccadilly. The store, its bay windows overflowing with new books, began to work its magic almost as soon as Thalia walked in. She drew a deep breath—ink and paper was one of her favorite scents—and let some of the tension of the last three days melt away.

A bookseller offered to direct her to the newest novels, but Thalia waved him away. If she wanted novels, she might have stayed at home: Both Kalli and Aunt Harmonia generally had the latest from the circulating library, though Aunt Harmonia's taste leaned to gothic tales and Kalli's to contemporary stories, like *Mansfield Park*. Instead, leaving Hannah to inspect the novels, Thalia made her way to the part of the bookstore that displayed the poetry titles. She ran her fingers across the spines, marking familiar authors: Wordsworth, Byron, Coleridge, even *The Restoration of the Works of Art to Italy*, by "A Lady," believed to be the young Mrs. Hemans.

Remembering her conversation with Mr. Darby at the dance, she looked for Percy Bysshe Shelley. Ah! There he was. She pulled *Alastor; or, The Spirit of Solitude* from the shelf and began flipping through the pages, skimming phrases as she went until a stanza caught her.

> *We are as clouds that veil the midnight moon;*
> *How restlessly they speed, and gleam, and quiver,*
> *Streaking the darkness radiantly!—yet soon*
> *Night closes round, and they are lost forever:*

There was something in the words that stopped her breath—a melancholy, a quicksilver vision of the moon at night. *We are as clouds.* Ephemeral, transient, driven by something outside ourselves. Thalia opened her reticule to count the coins in her money purse. She did not have quite enough to purchase the new volume. She'd have to cajole some coins from Charis, who seldom spent all her pin money. Reluctantly, she moved to set the book back on the shelf.

A gloved hand intercepted the book. "Are you not pleased with the poetry?"

Thalia's heart quickened as she looked up. She knew that voice. "Mr. Darby! I did not expect to see you here."

"But where else should lovers of words congregate?" he asked, smiling. "Though truly, this is a happy coincidence. My sister, Emma, begged I escort her. I was not averse to the mission, but you've proved the adage that every good deed is rewarded."

"Surely some good deeds go unrewarded, as some vile ones go unpunished? At least in this life."

"And where else should they be rewarded or punished? In heaven? Come, Miss Aubrey, you are too clever to take refuge in a fairy tale."

Thalia hesitated before responding. She believed in the heaven her father preached. And yet she liked being thought of as clever, liked the interest sparking in Mr. Darby's brown eyes. She did not want him to think her naive. "Must a story be literally true to have truth in it?"

"Of course not, else the poets would find their words very much constrained. I'll wager this book of poetry has more truth in it than your father's Bible."

She shook her head, smiling a little. "I cannot allow that, until you tell me how you define truth. Plato would say that that which draws us toward good is truth—can you tell me that these poems motivate you to be good?"

"I do not believe in 'good' as it is dictated to us by moralizers," Mr. Darby said. "I believe that what brings us pleasure is good, and that what we valorize as virtue occurs when self-interest coincides with a socially accepted ideal of what is right."

Thalia loved this, the exchange of ideas, and witty repartee, the sense of being both challenged and challenging. There were so few people with whom she could indulge: Papa, when he was not otherwise busy; Charis, when she was not distracted; Adam, on questions of history and theology. Kalli avoided such debates, claiming laughingly that Thalia was too clever for her. And now Mr. Darby, this near-stranger whose mind felt curiously familiar to her, who took her seriously and did not guard his words in front of her because she was a woman, who did not think she needed to be sheltered from hard ideas or heretical ones.

"I believe you are a cynic, Mr. Darby," Thalia said, smiling to take any sting out of her words.

"Say rather, a realist," Mr. Darby said, taking up her right hand. She could feel the heat of his palm even through her glove, and her skin prickled all the way up her arm with awareness of his nearness. "I believe you told me that your father is a vicar? Tell me, is he not happier when preaching on a topic that interests him, knowing a good dinner awaits him at home afterward, than preaching when his heart is not in it? But people will call him a good man speaking well when he does the first and uninspired when he does the second."

"Is that Quintilian?" Thalia asked, pleased to have caught his reference.

Mr. Darby's smile broadened, and he did not release her hand. "You are as bright as you are beautiful, Miss Aubrey."

Thalia flushed and tugged her hand away. "For that compliment, I will tell you that you are right, both about my father, and about Shelley's poetry. What I read was lovely."

"But you won't buy it?" His dark eyes twinkled down at her. "Does your aunt disapprove of Shelley's morals?"

"I'm not afraid of my aunt," Thalia said. "Only I've already spent my pin money." Better to be thought poor in purse than poor in spirit or wit.

"That's easily remedied. Will you permit me to make a gift of it?"

Thalia hesitated again. She *did* rather desperately want the book, particularly now when it would give her an excuse to seek out Mr. Darby again, to ask his opinion of the poems once she had read them all. But while her aunt might not know enough of Shelley to disapprove of him, she *would* disapprove of a gift from a man to whom Thalia was not related.

"It's a trifling gift, I assure you. No one objects to a man's purchasing flowers for a young, unmarried woman—how could they object to something that improves her mind instead of her appearance?"

Thalia laughed. His argument was ridiculous—there was a great deal of difference between roses and a book with potentially scandalous content—but she liked him for making it. In any case, how was Aunt Harmonia, or anyone else, to know where the book had come from? Hannah wouldn't tell, not if Thalia asked her not to.

"Then thank you, I'll accept gladly."

She followed Mr. Darby to the counter, where a dark-haired young woman was just finishing a purchase. Thalia pretended to inspect the display of books in the nearby window while Mr. Darby completed his transaction. Hannah joined her at the display.

"Who's your young man, miss?" she asked.

Thalia shook her head. "He's not *my* anything. We met at the Gardiners' party, and he's been to call at the house."

Then Mr. Darby was before them, a brown-wrapped package in his hands. "Miss Aubrey, will you allow me to present my sister, Miss

Emma Darby?" The dark-haired young woman Thalia had seen at the register stood beside him.

"Pleased to meet you," Thalia said.

"And I, you," Miss Darby said, with a sly glance between Thalia and her brother. "I've heard so much about you."

Heat crept up Thalia's neck. What had Miss Darby heard?

"This is for you," Mr. Darby said, extending the package to Thalia. When Thalia stretched out her hand to take the book, Mr. Darby caught her hand in his and pressed a swift kiss to her gloved knuckles. She looked up to find Hannah gaping at her, and Emma smirking. Thalia drew her hand back, and Mr. Darby smiled at her, those lips that had just brushed her gloves turning up in a stunning curve. Thalia caught her breath. He really was unfairly beautiful.

After exchanging farewells, Thalia and Hannah left the bookstore.

"Not your gentleman, is he?" The maid's round, rosy face dimpled.

"You mustn't tell my aunt," Thalia said. "She'd take away the book if she knew."

"It's quite romantic, isn't it?"

Thalia let herself return Hannah's smile. "I suppose it is."

She was still glowing from the combined exhilaration of fresh air, fresh thoughts, and her encounter with Mr. Darby when she returned to the house and found Adam sitting beside Kalli in the salon, Aunt Harmonia looking on indulgently.

Thalia's good mood evaporated. She knew that it was her sisterly duty to support Kalli, that her parents would expect that of her, but she could not bring herself to do it. She was not entirely sure who she was most angry with: society, for having such ridiculous dual expectations of women and men; Kalli, for giving in so easily;

Adam, for letting himself be pressured into proposing. Their marriage would make them miserable.

Then again, perhaps they deserved that.

"Adam!" she said brightly. "I've not had the chance to congratulate you. I'm sure you and Kalli will suit very well."

Both Kalli and Adam eyed her warily. Good.

Thalia held up her book. "I've just been to Hatchards and acquired this book of Shelley's poetry. It came highly recommended by Mr. Darby, who was there with his sister." She watched Adam closely as she spoke and was gratified to see a muscle in his cheek clench in annoyance.

"I don't believe he's a good influence on you, Thalia," Adam said.

"Careful," Thalia said. "Or some might think you envied him."

She wished she hadn't spoken almost as soon as the words left her tongue. Adam's lips thinned into a grim line, and Kalli went pink with mortification. Irritated as she was with both of them, Thalia had only meant to nettle Adam, not hurt Kalli.

"Thalia!" Aunt Harmonia chided.

But Kalli had not apologized to Thalia, so Thalia would not apologize either.

Adam shifted closer to Kalli, taking her hand. "No man who has the honor of being betrothed to you could be jealous of someone else."

Kalli looked at him for a long, steady moment, then tugged her hand away. "Please don't patronize me, Adam," she said, as she rose from her seat and left the room.

"Pretty lies are still lies, Adam," Thalia said. "Kalli deserves better than that."

Adam looked at her levelly. "You don't have to be happy for us, but you could at least try not to make things worse." He stood and stuffed his hat on. "This isn't like you."

Then he left before she had a fair chance to respond.

"Thalia, what would your mother say?" Aunt Harmonia asked.

Thalia did not want to discuss what her mother would say. She could already hear her mother's gentle voice in her ears: *Dear heart, you can be angry, if you like, but you should not take it out on your sister. Kalli needs you.*

But Kalli didn't need her. Neither did Adam. They had each other now.

Thalia clutched her book to her and sped out of the drawing room, up the stairs, and to her room. She flung herself on her bed, opened the copy of Shelley's poems, and began to read. The words of poetry burned through her veins like the first shots fired of a brewing rebellion.

Thalia sat up. She went to her desk, pulled out a sheet of paper, and began to write. Furious words that scorched the page. Harrowing words that furrowed it. She wrote poems of women wronged, giving words to Penelope, who waited faithfully for a faithless husband; to Medea to speak back to Jason; for Hera to hurl at Zeus.

She wrote the words she wanted Kalli to say, but her sister would never speak.

CHAPTER ELEVEN

The Prospect of a Ball

(Kalli)

Young ladies who think of nothing but dress, public amusements, and forming what they call high connexions, are undoubtedly most easily managed, by the fear of what the world will say of them.

—*Maria Edgeworth, found in Kalliope Aubrey's commonplace book*

Kalli did not see Adam's expression when Thalia accused him of envying Mr. Darby: She was staring fixedly at her hands, at the nails she had so carefully buffed only a se'nnight before, in anticipation of her first night in society. A night that had led her here, sitting passively in a chair beside her affianced.

It still felt strange to call Adam that.

Her whole world had been upended, and in the aftermath, she was all at sea. She did not feel like herself: The girl who had liked a party better than almost anything else had vanished, and in her place was a sober thing who questioned her own judgment. She missed that other Kalli.

Adam took her hand and said, "No man who has the honor of being betrothed to you could be jealous of someone else."

They were kind words, but Adam did not mean them, could not

mean them, and that hurt most of all. Adam *was* jealous of Thalia's flirtation. Why wouldn't he be? Anyone could see that Thalia was dazzled by this Mr. Darby in a way she had never been dazzled before, particularly not by Adam.

A wave of shame followed her from the room. She was being childish. Adam was taking the engagement well, despite Thalia— and Kalli had spent days moping, as though marriage to a kind man were the worst kind of punishment she could imagine. Yet Kalli was only giving up the theoretical prospect of marrying the man she loved (why was it that Mr. Henry Salisbury's friendly face rose before her?), where Adam was giving up the very real-and-present prospect of Thalia.

At least he would get to keep Thalia in his life. Kalli would not get to keep even a semblance of such love, because she had never had it in the first place.

When Charis tapped at her door a short while later, Kalli turned her away. Then she stared up at the darkened ceiling until sleep pulled her under.

The next night, the Aubrey and Elphinstone party attended their first ball of the Season, thrown by Mrs. Salisbury. Kalli dressed with care, putting on a pale blue silk dress with a delicate lace overlay that just matched the shade of her eyes. The promise of the ball brought her no pleasure (a disappointment in itself, as anticipation was a good part of the joy in an evening out), but she knew there would be eyes on her, as a newly engaged woman narrowly escaped from scandal. She would not give anyone cause to think she regretted her choice.

She adjusted the pearls around her throat and stared at her reflection, wondering absently if Mr. Henry Salisbury would think her pretty. Her fingers froze. Mr. Salisbury wasn't hers to hope for anymore. What must he think of her? Did he believe the scandalous rumors bandied about?

Kalli tried not to think of Mr. Salisbury as they drove through the darkening streets of London. And so of course she found it hard to think of anything else. One moment she hoped she might avoid him for the whole of the evening rather than face the change in their relative situations; the next, she hoped he would see her and, perhaps, ask her to dance.

She tried not to think about Adam, either, who would doubtless ask her to dance and then haunt the floor behind Thalia.

The regal front doors of the Salisbury mansion, near Grosvenor Square, were thrown wide for the night's celebration. Footmen stood near the door holding braces of candles. Kalli let Uncle John's groom help her down from the carriage and followed her aunt and uncle into the hall. Her uncle took their cloaks to the cloakroom, then rejoined them as they mounted the steps to the ballroom, where the Salisbury family stood in line to receive their guests.

Anne Salisbury was radiant, her strawberry-blond curls piled neatly on her head and threaded through with a strand of pearls. She wore a pale ivory dress with green ribbons adorning the hem, and as Kalli approached, she drew her into a lavender-scented hug. "Oh, I'm so glad to see a friendly face! So many of these guests are friends of my mother—and my father before he passed—but I feel that you and I are destined to be friends. Many congratulations on your betrothal, by the way."

"Thank you. And congratulations to you, as well! You look lovely, and your party appears to be quite successful."

Anne grinned. "I should hope so. But I shall be happy to be quit of the receiving line and start dancing! I believe Henry was hoping to ask you to dance."

Mr. Salisbury leaned out around his mother. "Henry is quite capable of doing his own asking, thank you all the same." He smiled at Kalli, showing the same flash of dimple that Anne had and causing her insides to tumble about. "What say you then, Miss Kalliope Aubrey? Will I be acceptable for the first set?"

Kalli found her enthusiasm for the ball returned with a rush and dropped a curtsy. "Most acceptable." She could not quite suppress a flash of smugness—it would serve Adam right, to find her already engaged for the first dance when he had not bothered to ask her.

Kalli followed the rest of her party into the ballroom, where the announcement of their names blended into the noise of the crowd already gathered. Adam found them a few minutes later, bearing cups of lemonade for the ladies. His gaze flashed over all of them before settling on Kalli.

"Will you dance with me, Kalli?"

"I will, and gladly, but not the opening set. Those dances are already engaged."

A shadow passed across his face, so quickly she could not quite read it. "But I thought—never mind. I am aptly punished for my assumption. I should have secured you much sooner. Thalia, will you dance with me?"

Thalia, looking amused rather than offended, said, "I'm not sure how I feel at being so clearly your second choice, but as it happens, I am also engaged."

"Charis will dance with you, Mr. Hetherbridge," Aunt Harmonia said.

"I'd be honored," Adam said gallantly, turning to Charis.

But Charis, wearing a pale pink dress with four layers of flounces at the hem, protested. "Mama! I do not mean to dance tonight."

"Nonsense. Why would any young lady come to a ball without meaning to dance?"

"Because said young lady had no choice," Charis grumbled.

"If I promise not to step on your toes above a reasonable amount, would you dance with me?" Adam asked. "Really, you should take pity on me as I've already been twice rejected by your cousins."

At this, Charis laughed and agreed. "But only to save your reputation."

The Salisbury family joined the throng, and the first set began to form up. Mr. Henry Salisbury approached Kalli and led her to the head of the two lines taking shape, to stand just below Anne and her partner.

The dancing itself was delightful—exactly what Kalli had hoped for when she imagined balls in London. Mr. Salisbury moved with ease, leading her expertly through the formations. His gloved hand was sure and firm around hers. But more than that, he knew precisely how to elevate her enjoyment, by complimenting and teasing her by turns, offering lively commentary on the other members of their set, and generally allowing Kalli to forget any anxiety she might have felt on arriving that night. She suffered only a small qualm, his kindness suggesting he did not yet know of her engagement. But Anne had known. Surely her brother did as well.

As they passed down the center of the set, Kalli smiled at Charis and Adam. She did not recognize Thalia's partner, but Thalia smiled at her for the first time in days, and Kalli grinned back. For a brief moment, all was right with her world.

At the end of the dance, Mr. Salisbury obligingly led her back to her aunt and uncle, where Adam waited. Mr. Salisbury greeted Adam cordially enough, but there was a coolness in his voice that Kalli marked, that secretly thrilled her. Was it possible he was jealous of Adam?

She caught herself: She should not hope such things.

Adam came to claim his dance, his tall shadow falling across her, making her heart skip a beat. He looked down at her rather solemnly, studying her face, and a muscle tightened in his jaw.

Kalli touched her hair, frowning. "Is there something wrong with me?"

"No. You're—you look fine. Pretty."

Kalli flushed. Adam had never called her pretty before.

He did not say above three words to her as they danced, but continued to study her with that curious intensity, as though there were something puzzling about her. Kalli was almost glad when the dance was done, and Adam returned her to her aunt and a new string of partners.

Kalli threw herself into the whirl and energy of the dance, taking pleasure in the movement and graceful formality of the figures. Not even her partner treading twice on her toes could dampen her enjoyment.

It was not until just before supper that she had a chance to sit out, and then it was not because she lacked for partners but because she wished to catch her breath.

"Is this seat free?" An elegant woman in a dark burgundy gown indicated the open seat beside Kalli. When Kalli said it was, the woman seated herself, and Kalli recognized her as Lady Stanthorpe, Mr. Salisbury's older sister. As she no longer lived at home with the family, she had not been part of the hosting party that had received them.

"Miss Kalliope Aubrey, is it not?" At Kalli's nod, she smiled. "I believe I owe you an apology for my child spoiling your dress."

Kalli shook her head. "It was nothing. The dress was cleaned easily enough, and small children *do* spit up."

"Terrifically messy, aren't they?" Lady Stanthorpe asked cheerfully. "Well, my dear, how are you enjoying my mother's ball?"

"It's all rather marvelous," Kalli said, forgetting for a moment that showing so much enthusiasm was not quite the thing.

But Lady Stanthorpe only laughed. "I remember feeling just as you do at my first ball."

"Everyone has been so kind," Kalli said, and then wished she had bitten her tongue. Though gentlemen were ready enough to ask her tonight, they had not been so kind a week ago when the scandal broke over her and Adam. Would Lady Stanthorpe think her a fool to claim their kindness?

"I think it is not kindness," Lady Stanthorpe said. "You are rather charming. Certainly, my son found you so. Henry seems to think so too."

Kalli flushed. "Mr. Salisbury is very kind." She closed her eyes briefly. She sounded inane.

Lady Stanthorpe's smile widened. "So you have already said. And so I have already disputed. Setting aside Henry's particular motives, I'm glad to see him happy." She hesitated for a moment, then added, "Our mother is not always the easiest to live with, and Henry has sacrificed much of his own happiness to see Mama happy, and to care for Anne."

Kalli's heart twisted. She knew that feeling, perhaps too well. But her fleeting sense of closeness to Mr. Salisbury vanished as she remembered Adam. "We are friends, and nothing more. I am recently engaged, you see."

Lady Santhorpe studied her. "So I have heard. Will you think me greatly impertinent if I ask—is this a love match, or an arrangement of convenience?"

Kalli flushed. It *was* rather impertinent, but Lady Stanthorpe had kind eyes, as though she cared about Kalli's feelings and not merely the opportunity for gossip. "I am sure you heard the rumors. Mr. Hetherbridge and I care about each other very much, but . . ." She found she could not finish her thought, as though admitting theirs was not a love match would make it so.

"I see." Lady Stanthorpe was quiet for a while, watching the dancers move past them. "I am going to say something that you may find shocking, certainly something that your good aunt would not tell you. First, you are not married until you are married. Do not write Henry off too quickly. Second, even if you are married, society offers married women much more independence than single women. As an unwed woman, any hint of scandal can be ruinous. As a married woman, so long as you are discreet in your affairs, most of society will turn a blind eye on your actions. It is not the thing, you know, to appear too much in love with one's husband, or fiancé, for that matter." Her lips twisted with a kind of wry amusement.

Competing emotions warred in Kalli's breast: part of her was shocked at this casual view of marriage, so unlike the commitment espoused by her own parents. Another part of her was angry. The merest suggestion of dalliance as an unmarried lady had landed her in an engagement with Adam—but as a married woman she would be free to be unfaithful so long as no one knew? How was that fair, or just? "Why are you telling me this?"

"Because Henry likes you and, forgive me, I believe you return his interest. I do not ask you to break off your engagement—only to consider that there are other options available to you."

Kalli took a deep breath, trying to calm her thoughts. She did not think she could be unfaithful to Adam, but maybe . . . maybe it was not so bad if she enjoyed flirting with Mr. Salisbury. Lady Stanthorpe would not have suggested as much if it were bad manners, and she knew the practices of society much better than Kalli did. It was not as though Adam showed her similar attentions. She meant only to enjoy herself, and since neither her heart nor Adam's was engaged in their match, it could not hurt him.

Lady Stanthorpe waved her fan at Kalli. "As I thought. You're a sensible girl. Now run along—Henry is hovering, hoping to take you in to supper, and you'd best not disappoint him."

Kalli stood and looked over her shoulder to find that, indeed, Henry—Mr. Salisbury—was waiting a few paces away with a hopeful smile on his face. She hesitated for a moment. Perhaps she ought to go in to supper with Adam? But as she ran her eyes quickly over the assembled guests, she saw that Adam had Thalia's arm tucked close to him and was heading in the direction of the supper room. She felt a tiny, sharp pang that he had not so much as thought to ask her, but then she summoned her brightest smile and turned to Mr. Salisbury.

He said, "Will you do me the honor of letting me take you to supper, Miss Kalliope Aubrey?"

"Thank you, Mr. Salisbury. I'd be delighted. But please, call me Miss Kalli. Only my mother calls me Kalliope."

"I rather like Kalliope, the way it rolls off the tongue. Are you a poet, like your sister?" he asked, and Kalli remembered that they had spoken of Thalia's poetry when they first met.

She shook her head. "I can scarce carry a tune, let alone compose my own lines."

"Then we shall rub along quite well. I make it a point that one should not be too accomplished, as then people begin to expect things of you. Better to surprise others by meeting their low expectations than disappoint them by failing high ones." He grinned at her. He had a lovely grin, with a dimple beside it.

He held out his arm to her, and Kalli took it, feeling his warmth spread through her. "I do not believe, Mr. Salisbury, that you could disappoint me if you tried."

He raised his eyebrows at her. "Is that a challenge?"

Kalli laughed, feeling lighter than she had in days. Perhaps Mr. Salisbury had not heard of her engagement, after all. She would tell him, she decided. After supper.

But then during supper, he made her laugh again and he complimented her on her dress, and she found she could not bear to tell him and watch the warm light of his admiration fade from his face. She thought of what his sister had said, about how he deserved to be happy in his own right. Was it so very wicked to take happiness where one could find it? They were only talking, after all.

She caught Thalia and Adam watching her. Thalia looked irritable, and she could not quite read the expression on Adam's face. She turned back to Mr. Salisbury, a bigger and brighter smile stretching her cheeks.

She would tell Mr. Salisbury later, she decided. Or perhaps someone else would tell him. For now, Kalli wanted to enjoy this golden bubble of a moment a little longer.

CHAPTER TWELVE

Needs Must When the Devil Drives

(Charis)

They have a more austere and purely astringent taste than any other of the vegetable substances of that class I have met with, and they produce, when thrown into any of the red salts of iron, a pure black tint.

— *William Thomas Brande, from* Philosophical Transactions of the Royal Society
[Charis's note: "Austere and purely astringent" might well describe a gentleman I know — and how many scientific gentlemen have died from tasting unfamiliar substances in the name of science?]

Charis had never been particularly devout—at least not from the perspective of the Aubrey family. She preferred to find her religion out-of-doors, among trees and brooks, contemplating the arc of heaven overhead. Yet in the days leading up to her drive with Mr. Leveson, she had prayed faithfully, night after night, with a fervor that would have surprised both her cousins had they known of it.

She prayed for rain. She prayed for tempests. She prayed for storms that would drop hail on London the likes of which had never been seen before. She would have settled for a drizzle; even some late-winter fog clinging to the bricks and balustrades and making driving dangerous.

But the day of her anticipated drive with Mr. Leveson dawned clear and appallingly bright, in an otherwise chilly spring, the morning following the Salisburys' ball. Charis was undecided whether this was a sign of her own lack of faith or if God was laughing at her.

Mama offered to help her dress, but Charis asked Thalia and Kalli to help her instead. She needed to borrow some courage from her cousins, and she rather hoped that in coming to help her, they might be forced to speak to each other. After Mr. Leveson's comment about his carriage colors, Mama had surprised Charis by purchasing an amber-colored spencer for her to wear for the drive, to ward off chills. It was rather vexing to realize that it had taken a man's suggestion to make Mama hear what Charis had sought in vain to suggest to her.

Charis still feared Mama would insist on pairing the jacket with a rose-colored dress or something with an indecent number of frills. Charis did not hide from herself: She knew that the frills and lacy overdresses that looked so ethereal on her cousins rather made her look like an overstuffed fowl. Simple lines and rich, warm hues suited her much better. But Mama volunteered nothing other than the new jacket, and so Charis paired it with a simply cut ivory dress with brown piping and drew on a pair of fawn gloves.

Thalia helped her adjust the jacket while Kalli hovered beside them. "You look so pretty, Charis!" Kalli said.

Charis sat down at her dressing table and studied her appearance as her maid, Mary, pulled her hair into a loose knot at the back of her neck, the sides draped low on the forehead, but without the curls Mama favored. She studied her broad, freckled cheeks, her auburn hair, her full, pink lips. Her eyes were good, wide-set and a rather pretty brown, like dark sherry. She did look nice. For half a second she allowed herself to wonder if Mr. Leveson would think so too, before banishing the notion. It did not matter what he thought of her.

Instead, Charis observed, "Kalli, you seem happy this morning. Did your first ball live up to your expectations?"

Kalli started to answer, but Thalia cut in. "Clearly, she enjoyed herself, since she did not dance more than one set with her own betrothed."

"And how was I supposed to dance with Adam, when every time I turned around, he was with *you*?"

Charis groaned. She had invited the sisters to her room to help them reconcile, not to find new grievances. "Please, do not fight! I'm nervous enough about this wretched drive. I need you both to calm my nerves."

Kalli looked stricken, Thalia marginally more contrite. But they stopped sniping at each other, so that was something.

"Is Mr. Leveson so terrible?" Kalli asked. "Perhaps you can beg off, tell Aunt Harmonia you are not feeling well."

"He is not so odious, only he is provoking, and I am afraid I will not hold my tongue as I ought to," Charis said.

"If he provokes you into speaking your mind," Thalia said, "then he deserves whatever he gets."

"Precisely," Kalli agreed, and Charis saw the sisters exchange a glance and a very small smile over her head in the mirror.

Charis tied on a straw bonnet lined with brown satin and made her way downstairs with her cousins to find that Mr. Leveson had already arrived and was chatting easily with Mama. Mama frowned as she entered, and, under the cover of embracing her, whispered, "You're so severely dressed, Charis. Perhaps you'd best go back up and ask Mary for a lace fichu or some such to liven things up. Or some curls, at least, to peep out under your bonnet?"

Charis flushed uncomfortably, but Thalia squeezed her hand and said, "You look very fine, Charis. That color is just the thing for you, brings out your eyes."

Mr. Leveson surveyed her. "I must commend your taste, Lady Elphinstone. You've chosen just the shade to complement my equipage." His eyes twinkled at Charis, and she had to admire how masterfully he'd handled Mama. Lady Elphinstone would now believe that it was she, not Mr. Leveson, who had first hit on the idea of dressing Charis in autumnal colors.

A sharp stab of fear assailed her as she climbed into Mr. Leveson's carriage, a rather handsome light curricle with a high perch seat and only two wheels. Charis could not say whether it was the height from the ground (which was considerable) or the sudden realization that she was being given Mama's blessing to drive out *alone* with a man she hardly knew that gave her qualms. A man, moreover, that she did not like above half.

"Don't be afraid, Miss Elphinstone. I may not be as flashy a whip as some I might name, but I assure you I'm perfectly competent."

"Your competency was never in question," Charis said.

He grinned at her. "Only my manners? I promise to behave."

Drat it, now why had *that* sent a flicker of disappointment through her?

Thalia, Kalli, and Mama waved her off—for all the world as though Charis had achieved an important milestone worthy of celebration, and not a simple drive in the park.

They rode quietly for some time, with Mr. Leveson clucking at his horses and steering them around the worst of the traffic between the Elphinstone town house and Hyde Park. Charis found herself admiring the steady way he held the reins and the nice shape of his hands. She wondered how it was that humans had come to have hands so remarkably adapted to so many tasks. Uncle Edward would say God designed them so, of course, but as a vicar he had to say such—and how had God happened on just such a design? And why was it that watching a pair of well-shaped hands caused such a peculiar sensation in the pit of her stomach?

Mr. Leveson looked up to find her watching him. "Well?" he asked, in a tone that suggested he was waiting for her critique.

"You do that quite well. Was it very hard to learn?"

"What, no complaints? Come now, Miss Elphinstone, you disappoint me."

She straightened in the seat and ran her hand over the sleeves of her new spencer. Mr. Leveson had been right: the amber color was a nice accessory to the brown velvet seats of his carriage. "I believe in giving credit where credit is due, sir."

"Then I thank you for the compliment. And no, it was not particularly hard to learn to drive. Only required consistent practice, like mastery of anything one has a mind to."

He did seem like the type of annoying person who could master anything he set his mind to. Charis did not think she was the same type. Some things, like dancing, required an aptitude in addition to the willingness to practice.

"Do you drive?" Mr. Leveson asked. "Or ride? What is your preferred method of enjoying the natural world?"

"On foot," Charis said. "That is, I do not drive, and I can ride, though I am not a particularly elegant rider. But I prefer to walk, as there are things one misses when one moves through the world too quickly."

"Such as? Snowdrops and violets and bluebells, I'd wager."

"You would most certainly lose your wager. Why must men always assume women are only interested in flowers? I like flowers well enough, but I'm more interested in fauna than flora: in the different wrens and sparrows, kestrels and merlins and every sort of thing that flies."

"A naturalist, are you?" His eyes brightened with interest. "Do you make a study of anything in particular?"

Charis hesitated. Her mama had repeatedly impressed upon her the importance of not sharing her peculiar interests, as gentlemen did not like to hear a lady studied insects. But as she did not particularly care for Mr. Leveson's good opinion, and she did enjoy discussing her studies, she ignored that advice. "In fact, I do. Insects are my specialty. I mean to make a study of *Sphinx stellatarum*, more commonly known as the hummingbird sphinx, when I am home."

"A hawk moth? I admit, I did not take you for a serious scientist."

It was on the tip of her tongue to ask him why she surprised him: Because she was a woman? Because she was young? Because he thought she was plain and only pretty girls were allowed to be interesting? "I recall that you once lectured me for presuming to pre-judge someone based on their appearance. Was that mere hypocrisy?"

He grimaced. "Touché. You're right. I ought not have made assumptions about you. I meant only that young ladies are not typi-cally encouraged to take such things seriously. I do not doubt your capability—you strike me as someone who observes things closely."

"Now you flatter me. Are you trying to atone for your gaffe in insulting me? I observe carefully the things that interest me, but that is all. Mama finds me lamentably vague about social niceties."

"And what have you observed about me?" Mr. Leveson asked.

Charis's eyes went first to his face, to the long lashes framing dark eyes tucked beneath thick eyebrows. She followed the sharp line of his bronzed cheek to his firm jaw, and then to the absurdly beauti-ful lips that were curling a bit under her scrutiny. The barest hint of stubble shadowed his cheek in a way that made Charis's stomach clench. He was very beautiful, but she could hardly say that to him.

"That you are prompt, that whatever you do publicly you take care to do well—from your dress to your dancing to your driving. That while you are proud, you are capable of pleasing where you choose. And that you must know something of nature, because when I mentioned the hummingbird sphinx, you knew it was a hawk moth, though it has a most peculiar name."

"I see you have observed me most carefully," Mr. Leveson said, and that dancing light was back in his eyes. Too late, Charis realized what such close observation implied: *I observe carefully the things that interest me.* The wretch had set a trap for her, and she had walked right into it. "If I *am* proud, it is not of my appearance or my wealth, which were things given me by my parents, but of things I have cultivated. My mind, my skills, and any eloquence I may be said to possess."

He was quiet for a long moment. Then: "Do you know why 'whatever I do publicly I take care to do well'? Have you never wondered at that?"

Charis had not, particularly. "I suppose that you wish to be well thought of."

"Yes. It is a most curious thing: As an Anglo-Indian, the more exceptional I am, the more amicable society finds me." His mouth twisted.

Charis did not find his observation curious, she found it distressing—nearly as distressing as the self-mocking tone in his voice. She did not know what to say, only she wanted to erase the bitter look in his eyes. "Society finds you amicable?"

A flicker of a grin curled his lips. "Most astonishing, is it not?"

"Quite," Charis agreed, smiling at him in pleased relief.

They had entered the park, the trees just beginning to show the green promise of spring. She imagined that in a month or so the park would be glorious, a riot of living things, but just now it was rather sad and bare and gray.

"Shall I tell you what I have observed about you?" Mr. Leveson asked.

Charis could well imagine. She folded her arms across her chest and looked out at the park. "I would prefer you did not."

"Very well," he said equably, nodding to a gentleman walking along the footpath beside the road.

The gentleman, of middle age with a cinched-in waist (he must wear stays, as Prinny was said to do) and a rather florid waistcoat, stared at them as they passed. A noted whip like Mr. Leveson, who regularly drove in Hyde Park, could not occasion such shock, so it must be Charis, as his guest, that drew the man's surprise. No doubt Mr. Leveson typically drove out with diamonds of the first water, if he drove with ladies at all.

What *did* Mr. Leveson see when he watched her? Did he see what most people saw—a plump young woman with few social graces? Or did he see what Charis herself saw: a bright, capable woman with no patience for social games?

Charis sighed and uncrossed her arms. She turned back to Mr. Leveson, who was now watching the road before them and surveying the passing riders and carriages. "Curiosity is my besetting sin, I fear. What is it that you have observed about me?"

"There are far worse sins than curiosity." He held the reins easily in his right hand and rubbed his chin with his left. There was a tiny spot of plaster near where his jaw met his ear, as though he had cut himself shaving and forgotten to remove the plaster. The oversight seemed most unlike him, and Charis wondered if he had also been unsettled by the prospect of this drive.

"I think, Miss Elphinstone, that you are often underestimated, and that you like it that way. You let your mama dress you, though what I have seen of your taste suggests that you might turn yourself out creditably if given half a chance. You take on the role of insipid debutante in society, and yet you have a keen mind and a broad interest in the natural world. You can be bold, when ideas or the well-being of others are concerned, but you are not bold on your own behalf. I find these discrepancies both intriguing and perplexing."

For a moment, Charis forgot how to breathe. His words made her feel simultaneously seen and stripped bare. If he were not someone she found more attractive than was good for her, she might feel gratified by his insight. Instead, she felt vaguely threatened—possibly betrayed, though by whom or what she could not say.

Her cheeks grew warm. "I do not set out to be intriguing or perplexing. I do not play games, sir."

"I know it. That's part of what intrigues me."

The heat in her face deepened. Was he flirting with her? And for heaven's sake, *why*? They were still heading into the park, away from the gates. She calculated how much longer she should have to be in this carriage with this discomfiting man. Too long, she decided, and wondered if it would be horribly impolite to ask him to take her home now.

Probably it would. Perhaps she could merely jump from the carriage and take refuge in that stand of trees over there.

No. Even she could see the latter was ridiculous. The former, less so. She opened her mouth, but he disarmed her entirely by grinning at her. "You are wishing me at perdition just now, aren't you? I apologize. I didn't mean to make you uncomfortable—and I promised so faithfully at the beginning of this drive to behave. Let us talk of impersonal things, shall we? Tell me, what do you think of the role of the humors in nature?"

She eyed him suspiciously. Was he making fun of her? But he continued smiling in that odiously calm way, and, after all, she had plenty of thoughts on the subject. It would serve him right if she bored him.

"I think they are outdated and cannot sufficiently account for what we know of the natural world. Tell me, have you read Lavoisier?" Waving her hands in her enthusiasm, she plunged further into the topic. Mr. Leveson did not appear well-versed in Lavoisier, but he listened attentively and asked just the right questions, and when humors were exhausted, he was able to tell her of some recent presentations he had attended at the Royal Society.

"I wish I might have been with you. My one consolation when Mama told me I must come to London for the Season was believing that I might attend some of the professional lectures. There are so few occasions at home to interact with truly learned individuals. I may be from Oxfordshire, but we are seldom in Oxford itself. But now that Kalli has landed in her fix—even though it is all repaired—Mama says we must be extra cautious not to court censure and for me to attend would be to invite the very censure we must avoid." Charis sighed. "I would not mind the censure so much, if it meant I could be part of it all."

Mr. Leveson was quiet for a moment, watching her face instead of the road. "Would your mama object so very much if *I* were to invite you?" His smile flickered. "It is true that women do not generally attend the Royal Society, but I believe I could get permission from Sir Joseph Banks, who heads the society."

Everything in Charis lit up. "Could you?" She recalled what he had said earlier, about having to work hard to sustain society's approval because of his race. "It would not hurt your standing? Or offend the Royal Society?"

"I believe my standing—indeed, the society itself—could withstand your presence." When Charis continued to survey him doubtfully, he smiled down at her. "I have been at some pains to cultivate connections in the Royal Society, as it bolsters my renown as a gentleman of culture and intelligence. But I believe I have accrued enough goodwill to spend some on earning your admission."

"That would be beyond anything. I mean, I must ask Mama first." With that reflection, her joy dimmed. Mama had become so cautious, since Kalli. But she seemed to like Mr. Leveson, and if only she would say yes, it would make everything else Charis had to bear this Season bearable—even Mr. Leveson's company. "Perhaps Mama will agree if I remind her that it might benefit my reputation to be seen in your company."

"Are you roasting me, Miss Elphinstone?"

"Am I? I did not mean to." She reflected a moment, then added: "At least, not this time."

Mr. Leveson laughed, and something warm washed from the tip of Charis's toes to the crown of her head. She liked his laugh, the way his dark eyes crinkled at the corners, the way the whole shape of his face seemed to soften. She liked it very much indeed—and that reflection she did not like at all.

Even less did she like the realization, after Mr. Leveson had returned her home and secured Mama's permission for Charis to attend a lecture of the Royal Society, that Mr. Leveson's company had not proved so grim as she had feared.

In fact, rather the opposite.

CHAPTER THIRTEEN

Amour on Display

(Thalia)

Morning mists across the moor
Dappled shadows on the door
Children dancing 'cross the floor —
This I'd trade for one far shore

— Thalia Aubrey

Thalia moved restlessly through the room. Aunt Harmonia's sitting room was crowded with visitors, and yet, as she moved from conversation to conversation, all she heard discussed was the weather, the latest *on dit*, the new fashion for sleeves, and the weather again. Charis was usually her saving grace in moments like this, for while she was not fond of the philosophical discussions Thalia adored, her conversation was at least interesting.

But Charis was uncharacteristically mobbed. A group of young men surrounded her, talking animatedly. Thalia drifted closer, hope sparking, only to find the discussion centered on horse flesh. And while Charis cared little about hunting or racing, she did like horses themselves and was managing to hold her own. Laughter rippled through the little group, with Charis at its epicenter. She looked pleased, rather than mortified, which meant that somehow—impossibly—Charis was successfully entertaining a group of dandies.

Amused, Thalia moved on. She blamed Charis's unprecedented popularity on Mr. Leveson. Three days ago, he had taken Charis driving in the park, and two days ago, after Sunday services, the deluge had begun. Were she the betting sort, she would have put her money on Kalli being the one to hold court in the Elphinstone house. But Kalli sat, subdued, beside Aunt Harmonia, letting the latest court gossip wash over her as though it held no more interest than Charis's horses.

Thalia found herself at the window, staring fixedly at nothing, and started when Adam spoke her name. "Oh! I didn't see you come in."

He raised an eyebrow quizzically. "Rather in a brown study, aren't you?"

"It's nothing dire. Only somewhat bored." She glanced around the room, thick with high-society guests, and laughed at herself. "I'd no notion I was so hard to please."

Adam followed her gaze, wrinkling his nose. "Say, rather, that you hold yourself to higher standards. Where did Charis collect those rattles?"

"Mr. Leveson has taken her under his wing. Apparently, his attention is all one needs to become wildly popular."

Adam glanced at Kalli, beside Aunt Honoria. "It's a pity he didn't single Kalli out. She always did like to be the heart of the party." He turned back to Thalia. "Is Kalli all right? She does not seem to be quite herself, and she won't talk to me of anything but trifles."

Thalia sighed. "She won't talk to me either."

"You're mad at Kalli," Adam observed. "And at me too, I think. Why?"

Thalia countered with her own question. "Why did you propose to Kalli? Do you love her?"

"I care about her very much." Adam faltered, his gaze dropping to the carpet. "Your family has been like a second family to me. Your father has given me so much—his time, his counsel. I could not see this shadow of scandal hang over you and do nothing, especially when it was my fault. I wanted to protect Kalli—and I wanted to protect *you*." He looked up at her then, adjusting his spectacles over his blue eyes.

"Even if it meant ruining your future? And Kalli's?"

"I hardly think I'm ruining her future. Kalli has always wanted a home and children—I can give that to her. Besides, she could have said no."

Thalia threw her hands up in the air. "No, she could not have! When has Kalli ever sought something for herself at the expense of people she loves? The minute Aunt Harmonia told her that we would suffer for her scandal, Kalli could not have made any other decision."

"Are you mad because I . . . *forced* her?" Adam asked, wrinkling his eyebrows.

Thalia saw Aunt Harmonia looking at them and lowered her voice. "No. But I am angry that neither of you have the backbone to stand up to society, and because you will make each other miserable. Kalli is too gentle for you, and you are too oblivious for her."

"I'm not—"

"Yes, you are. You saw Kalli dancing with Mr. Salisbury at the ball and did not once think that maybe Kalli wanted you to ask her."

"I did ask her!"

"Yes, and then followed *me* around."

"Because Kalli seemed happier without my company." Adam's voice grew soft. "Are you afraid I'm taking Kalli away from you? I don't believe I could. Kalli will always love you."

"I'm not worried about that." Thalia blew out a breath. "But you—you have been my best friend for the past five years. Once you become Kalli's husband, then I must perforce take a second place in your life. I—I don't know how to do that."

"You don't have to lose me," Adam said.

Thalia only shook her head. Adam might not think so, but it would be a rare wife who would let Thalia stand between her and her husband, even if that wife were Kalli.

A maid approached her then, holding out a plain envelope with *Miss Thalia Aubrey* scrawled across it. Excusing herself to Adam, Thalia stepped away and opened the card.

Inside, a feminine hand had written:

> *My dearest Thalia, I am planning a visit to the British Museum on Thursday, the 20th of March, and would be very glad of your company, if you should like to join me. —Yours, Emma Darby.*

Thalia's heartbeat quickened. This was precisely what she needed to distract herself from Adam and Kalli. She had not yet been to the museum and was anxious to go—and there was a good chance that Mr. Darby would accompany his sister. At the very least, Thalia could learn more about him from Emma.

"Is that James Darby's sister?" Adam asked, reading over her shoulder.

Thalia folded the card and slid it into her pocket. "I don't believe you were invited."

"If James is going, then I am too. We can make a party of it. Kalli can come as well. It might cheer her up."

Thalia's vision of a secluded tête-à-tête with Mr. Darby died a swift and horrible death. "Kalli doesn't like museums, says she cannot abide the sight of dead things and soulless sculptures." Perhaps if Kalli did not go, Adam would feel obliged to stay behind with her.

"It would be good for her. Better than moldering in the sitting room with a bunch of rattles. Charis would like it too."

But Charis, as it turned out, could not accompany them to the museum, having accepted the invitation of one of those rattles to go driving. "I wish I could go," she said, rather wistfully. "It should be more interesting than—but I'm being ungracious."

So it was only Adam, Thalia, and Kalli who disembarked from the hackney carriage on Thursday afternoon before the famous museum, housed in Montagu House on Great Russell Street, in Bloomsbury. As they entered the large double doors to the atrium, Emma Darby hurried to greet them, followed closely by her brother.

Adam halted on the threshold. "Damn it." He eyed Thalia grumpily. "If you were hoping for a private tryst with that man, you're out of luck."

"What I choose to do is not any of your business, Adam."

"Yes, it is—as your friend and future brother-in-law, it's only natural that I take an interest in your well-being."

"Having an interest in my life does not give you the right to dictate my decisions," Thalia said, plastering a smile on her face as the Darby siblings drew up to them.

"You all look a bit flushed," Emma observed. "Is everything all right?"

"I'm afraid I have a bit of a headache," Kalli said.

"Here, I'll have one of the guides fetch you some watered wine. You'll be right as rain in a few moments." Mr. Darby caught the attention of a whiskered, middle-aged man standing near them, who went to find the requested item.

Adam leaned in to Kalli. "I am sorry you aren't feeling well. Do you want me to take you home?"

Please, Thalia thought.

"And I am sorry I'm not Thalia, but we must all bear our separate burdens."

Thalia cringed at the tactless comment and caught a flicker of shocked hurt on Adam's face.

Kalli made an obvious effort to smile. "I beg your pardon. I am rather out of sorts today."

The guide returned with a cup, which he offered to Kalli. Thalia hoped it would help: Kalli had a lamentable tendency to play the martyr when she felt wounded. The drink did, at least, seem to revive Kalli's spirits enough that she was able to join them as they bypassed the library on the lower level and proceeded up the broad staircase. On the upper level, they found rooms full of various specimens, including a few animals Thalia had never seen except in pictures: long-necked giraffes from Africa, a rhinoceros with a fierce horn.

"Charis would have loved this," Adam said, looking around.

"Do you think so?" Kalli asked. "Those poor animals. I shouldn't like being stuffed after my death for people to stare at."

"Nor I," said Emma Darby.

Mr. Darby caught Thalia's eye, smiling at her in apparent amusement. She returned the smile, a pleasant flutter of nerves starting low in her stomach.

As Kalli, Emma, and Adam moved through the doorway to the next room, Thalia lingered by a glass-encased display of iridescent beetles, winking in the light like so many jewels. Mr. Darby came to stand next to her, so close that his arm brushed hers. Thalia said, "I wonder what it is that gives their wings this color, and what purpose it can serve for them. It certainly draws the eye, which cannot help them hide from predators."

"True," Mr. Darby said. "But only think of what we learn from society. Those individuals who draw the eye most often *are* predators." He ran one gloved finger lightly up her forearm, leaving behind a pleasurable prickle against her skin. "You, Miss Aubrey, most definitely attract attention."

Thalia laughed. "Are you saying that *I* am a predator?"

"You are too well-bred to hunt your prey openly, but I think you have an inner hunger, an ambition and desire that only the most passionate of people possess."

She smiled, irrationally pleased that he had seen this about her. "And you?"

He took a step nearer. "Oh, I am most definitely a predator." His breath was warm against her ear, and she shivered.

"Thalia! Are you coming?" Adam stood in the doorway watching them, and Thalia reluctantly broke contact with Mr. Darby to follow the others.

As they moved through the next series of rooms, Thalia dawdled as often as she could, feigning an interest she did not truly feel so that Mr. Darby would stop with her. A few pieces of information she stored up to relay to Charis, but mostly her attention was caught by Mr. Darby, the way he watched her, the way his eyes danced when he teased her, the way he brushed a curl away from her cheek with gloved fingers. His light cologne tantalized her, a mix of lavender and citrus. She found herself wishing it was not the fashion to go gloved in public, because she wanted to know how his bare fingers would feel against her skin, and her entire body grew warm at the thought.

They followed the others up another flight of stairs to the gallery, where the most famous of the museum's collections were housed: the Elgin Marbles, so recently acquired from Greece, and the Rosetta Stone.

They passed an alcove filled only with a single sculpture, and Mr. Darby caught her hand and tugged her into the shadows cast by the headless woman in a flowing dress. He pressed a kiss to her knuckles, then a second kiss on the bit of wrist exposed between her glove and the long sleeve of her day dress, his breath scorching against her skin.

"Mr. Darby! Someone will see us." Despite her protest, Thalia did not pull away.

"Does that worry you? You've nothing to fear from your

friends—Emma has agreed to distract your sister and her escort as best she can."

Thalia took a slow breath, trying to calm her racing heart. Perhaps this was rather fast—Thalia had only known Mr. Darby—James—a few weeks. But everything about him felt right. They were well suited in temperament and wits, and when she was with him, she was the best version of herself. Bright, sparkling, funny. Not the small, pinched, irritated scold she manifested so often around Kalli and Adam lately. Thalia had never met anyone who made her feel as James did. She had watched Kalli tumble in and out of crushes during their girlhood and wondered if something was wrong with her because she did not blush at the mention of any young man's name, nor did she go out of her way to find ways to meet them in the village. She had never wanted any of them to touch her, let alone kiss her.

But she wanted Mr. Darby to touch her. She wanted him to kiss her.

She wanted to kiss *him*.

Mr. Darby ran a finger lightly across the line of her jaw and just skimmed her throat. Fire burned behind his touch.

"I might take you driving in the park, or invite you to go walking, but such enterprises are so public, and one feels on display the whole time, the target of every gossip and busybody one passes. I should rather spend a private evening in your company, among friends who won't talk. I know a lady who hosts salons in the style of Madame de Staël, full of poets and intellectuals and philosophers. I should very much like to take you there, to see you shine in the firmament for which you are best suited. None of these insipid ballrooms or dry museum halls. Would you come?"

136

"Of course I would," Thalia said, her imagination already sparking at the idea. But then reality intruded, and she added, "Though I do not think Aunt Harmonia would allow me to accompany a single man to such a place."

"I shall have Emma invite you and say that it is for an evening at home with a few select friends. It's true enough."

"She won't let me come alone," Thalia said.

"Then bring your cousin. She might even enjoy the company."

Charis—not Kalli. Mr. Darby had already observed that Charis was less likely to watch them closely, or report on them if she did.

Mr. Darby traced one finger along her arm, starting with her gloved finger and moving up her sleeve, dancing across her shoulder before resting on the sensitive skin of her neck, just above her collarbone. "Just say you'll come."

Thalia found it hard to breathe. "I'll come," she whispered.

His hand rose to cup her cheek, and Mr. Darby leaned toward her. He was so close now—Thalia could feel the heat rising from his body. At this proximity, his eyes were a deep russet brown, with flecks of copper in their depths. His breath smelled faintly of honey.

Thalia shut her eyes, her heartbeat pulsing at the base of her throat.

Something brushed her lips, so faint she could not tell if it was Mr. Darby's finger, or his mouth, and then someone coughed nearby, and a woman's voice rose in conversation.

She drew back, suddenly recalled to her very public surroundings. She opened her eyes to find Mr. Darby smiling down at her, the liquid look in his eyes making her whole body warm. He held out his arm to her, and she walked with him into the next room, at last, to see the Parthenon friezes and rejoin the others. Yet for all her outward placidity, she trembled inwardly. She stood balanced on a precipice, and though she could not see what was beyond it, the promise of something immense both thrilled her and terrified her.

CHAPTER FOURTEEN

Unbecoming Conduct

(Kalli)

Respect for right conduct is felt by every body.

—*from the author of* Emma, *found in Kalliope Aubrey's commonplace book*

Twelve.

That was the number of times now that Kalli had watched Adam slow his steps and cast an anxious glance down the museum gallery, waiting for Mr. Darby and Thalia to appear. Each time he paused, he added a layer to the pall hanging over Kalli.

It was bad enough that she had to marry a man who did not love her. But for Adam to be so public in his preference for Thalia only twisted that particular dagger farther into her heart. Did he realize how ridiculous he appeared, mooning over Thalia like some callow calfling just come to London for the first time? How pathetic he made Kalli appear? Not yet married and already she couldn't keep her husband-to-be's attention.

She had told him, "I am sorry I'm not Thalia," and though she regretted saying the words aloud, she had meant them. If she were braver, like Thalia, she might not be in this fix. If she were more like Thalia, Adam would not turn away from her so often.

The twelfth time, Adam did not merely stall, he turned back toward the archway through which they'd come. Emma Darby intercepted him, twining her arm through his and directing him to a nearby frieze and asking his opinion of the carving. Frustrated, Adam cast another glance toward the doorway, but he was too much a gentleman to simply shake Emma off.

But not too much a gentleman to ignore Kalli.

Picturing a lifetime of such slights was enough to make her wonder if being single and scandalous might be the better option after all. Kalli gave up on the friezes and wandered to a nearby window, surveying the long gardens that stretched out behind the museum. Maybe fresh air would do more for her spirits than watching Adam watch Thalia.

She headed back toward the doorway. As she passed Adam, he turned away from Miss Darby. "If you see Thalia, will you ask her to please join us?"

Something tight burned beneath Kalli's breastbone. "I am not looking for my sister. I am going outside to the garden, for air."

Kalli wasn't sure what Adam read in her face, but his expression changed, anxiety giving way to something softer. "Oh, lord. Kalli, I'm so sorry. I've been a lousy escort, haven't I?" The shamefaced look he cast her eased the tightness in her chest a fraction.

Miss Darby glanced from Kalli to Adam and moved down the exhibit hall. Kalli wasn't sure if her gesture stemmed from tact or discomfort, but she was grateful for it.

"I did begin to wonder if I had somehow offended you," she said, trying to keep her tone light. It wasn't Adam's fault that he loved Thalia—who could help it? "You haven't said six words to me this past half hour."

Adam said, "You haven't offended me. On the contrary, I think I've offended you with my inattention. Thalia told me I was too oblivious to make you happy."

"Thalia said that?" Perhaps Thalia *did* still care about Kalli's happiness.

"She did, and I'm afraid that she was right. I'm sorry. You deserve better than that." He paused, his eyes searching her face. "Is it only frustration with me that leads you to the gardens? Won't you stay inside a little longer?"

Adam could not quite restrain another glance at the doorway, and Kalli read his concern: *We should not leave Thalia and Mr. Darby alone so long.*

Though Kalli truly would have preferred the gardens to the museum halls, she reluctantly agreed with Adam. Mr. Darby struck her as one of those people who mistook their own intelligence for actual virtue. But Thalia liked him, and Kalli did not know how to tell Thalia that without it sounding like sour grapes, especially since Thalia was being courted as Kalli had longed to be.

So Kalli sighed and followed Adam and Emma deeper into the hall.

Pausing before a section of the frieze depicting men on horseback riding into battle, Adam met Kalli's eyes before striking a pose, raising his right hand as if holding a spear and bowing his legs as though on horseback. The resemblance to the frieze was obvious, though without an actual horse beneath him, Adam looked absurd.

"Whatever are you doing, Mr. Hetherbridge?" Emma Darby asked. "Do stop. People are beginning to stare at us."

But Adam only grinned and began to "ride" his invisible horse. Then, in a sonorous voice, as though he were the narrator in a play, he said, "The brave Grecian warrior, uh, Adonis, rode his trusty steed, uh, Horse, across the plains into battle. At the first sight of the enemy, he did not quail, but rode onward and did not turn away until he had passed the battlefield entirely and trotted directly for home."

The exaggerated expression of terror on Adam's face tickled Kalli, and she laughed out loud, drawing a stern look from the museum worker watching them. "I'm afraid your brave warrior is not very brave," she said.

"No," Adam agreed, dropping the pose. "But I hear tell he was quite beautiful. And clever."

"Yes," Kalli said, still smiling. "Only think of the cleverness required to name a horse, Horse."

"Oh, do leave off this ridiculous playing," Miss Darby begged. "James and Thalia are here, so we may move on."

Kalli whirled back to find the pair walking toward them; her sister's cheeks were flushed, and Mr. Darby wore a self-satisfied smirk. Adam swayed toward Thalia, and Kalli turned away abruptly, walking past the frieze to stand beside the statue of a maiden, her shoulders and legs carved as though she were in flight. Her arms, like her head, were missing. Something sharp and hot pressed against Kalli's chest as she studied the statue.

Adam spoke from just behind her. "That woman appears to have lost her head. What do you suppose she lost it over? A rival? A burnt cake?"

A thrill ran all the way through Kalli. Adam had followed *her* this time, not Thalia. "Doubtless a lover."

Adam shook his head and *tsked*. "Paramours are such pesky creatures."

Succumbing to an urge she didn't want to examine too closely, Kalli mimicked the statue's pose, throwing her shoulders back and tipping her chin up. "In a far village, Helen waited for the return of her lover from war. But alas, by the time Adonis returned, she had lost her head, her wits, and her arms, and she could neither embrace nor kiss her cowardly cavalier."

Adam grinned at her. "I'd say it's no more than Adonis deserved for running off like that. Though it's a pity for Helen. A pretty girl *should* be able to kiss whomever she wishes."

He glanced sidelong at Kalli, a warm light suffusing his expression. Kalli met his eyes for a moment, then dropped her gaze. Adam had told her she was pretty at the ball—did *he* want to kiss her?

"Do you think so?" she asked, trying to keep her voice light. "Wouldn't such promiscuous kissing be quite scandalous?"

"I did say 'should.' I don't recommend *you* try it."

She looked up again. Adam stood directly before her, bent down so his height was not quite so towering over hers. His face was only inches away. It struck her that Adam was rather nice-looking, even with his glasses. She liked his eyes, clear and direct, and the smattering of freckles on his nose. His lips, now that she studied them, were well-shaped. She could lift herself on her toes and press her lips to his. What would Adam say to that?

What would Thalia say? Kalli glanced behind her to see Thalia watching them from across the room, an arrested look on her face.

Was *Thalia* jealous? The thought made her irrationally happy. Kalli set her hands on the lapels of Adam's jacket. His chest was firm beneath her palms, and he drew in a quick, sharp breath, his sternum lifting under her hands. Kalli made a show of smoothing the starched lines of his cravat. She raised herself onto her toes, as if to whisper something to Adam, and he leaned down toward her, turning his head to receive her words better. His breathing had gone shallow.

Still conscious of Thalia's gaze on her, Kalli brushed her lips across Adam's cheek. The faint roughness where he had shaved gave way to smooth skin across his cheekbone, and something hot and liquid stirred in Kalli's stomach. This was a mistake. But she'd already committed herself to it. She murmured, "Why shouldn't I kiss whomever I'd like? Am I not pretty enough? Too tainted by scandal?"

She released his cravat and rocked back onto her heels to watch his expression. A muscle flickered along his narrow jaw, and at his side, his right hand clenched into a fist, then released, his fingers flexing out.

Adam's voice was a trifle unsteady as he answered her. He looked at a point above her head, and his pulse jumped in his throat. "I have already told you I think you are pretty, and since I am also implicated in your scandal, it would be hypocritical of me to object on those grounds." He drew a deep breath before dropping his gaze to meet hers. Light glinted from the rim of his glasses. "I am afraid my objection is purely selfish: So long as you are engaged to me, I don't think you should kiss anyone else."

Kalli's stomach flipped. She found it suddenly difficult to breathe, or to form the questions crowding through her head. What did Adam mean by that? Did he mean that he wanted to kiss her? Or merely that it would reflect poorly on him if his affianced began kissing other men? (A small corner of her brain observed, *That would serve him right.* Kalli quashed the thought.)

"Kalli—" Thalia drew up beside them, a note of caution in her voice.

Kalli met her sister's look, daring her to say something about Kalli's inappropriate behavior, when Thalia had been sneaking into alcoves with a man she hardly knew. Thalia seemed to realize the same thing, because she flushed and bit her lip.

Kalli could not look at Adam though. How could she have been so forward? Feeling rather flustered and unlike herself, she picked a direction at random and walked away. She stared at a new statue without seeing it until Adam joined her, adopting another pose and joking with her as though he had said nothing out of the ordinary.

Well. If his speech meant nothing to him, then she would take nothing from it.

By the time Thalia and the Darby siblings joined them, Kalli was laughing, her face as sunny as if Adam had never ignored her, as if she had never quarreled with Thalia—as if Adam had never made her stomach flip.

They returned home from the museum to find their aunt receiving callers in the drawing room. Dillsworth told them that Miss Elphinstone was in her room writing—an activity that he appeared to find quite dubious. Kalli went up to change her gown, and Thalia followed her.

Thalia told me I was too oblivious to make you happy. Adam's words floated through Kalli's head, so when Thalia came into Kalli's room just behind her, Kalli did not tell her to go away. Of course they had fought before, but never a quarrel that had dragged out for days and weeks like this. If Thalia was prepared to apologize, Kalli was more than ready to forgive her. She had missed Thalia.

Thalia settled onto Kalli's bedspread. "Kalli, you really ought to have a little more self-respect."

Kalli stared at her.

"I heard what you said to Adam, that you wished you were me. You have so much to offer the world—you're kind, caring, generous." Thalia looked at her earnestly. "You shouldn't downplay your gifts."

Kalli's mouth stretched thin. None of those gifts were qualities Thalia particularly cared to cultivate. But they were good enough for *Kalli*.

Thalia went on, "I don't want us to fight anymore. I want things to go back to the way they were before you and Adam got engaged. I know I've been angry, and hurt, but—I forgive you."

Kalli dropped into the chair by her dressing table with a huffing laugh. "*You* forgive *me*?" As though Kalli had invented this whole mess as a means to hurt Thalia.

"Yes," Thalia flared back, color rising in her cheeks. "I forgive you for being too weak to stand up for your own happiness, for being so soft that you let Adam trample all over you. And for trying to make me jealous."

"You just said that being kind, caring, and generous were my best qualities. What you call weakness, I see as caring for other people. And you *are* jealous, or you wouldn't bring it up."

"No, I'm not," Thalia snapped. "Is it kind to drag Adam down with you into your morass of misery?"

"Oh, that's good. Did you compose that especially for me?" Kalli took a deep breath. "What exactly do you think happiness looks like for me, Thalia?" Had her sister ever really listened to her?

Thalia waved her hand. "Oh, a life full of children, parties, and a doting husband."

Kalli flinched. Thalia was right, but her life's dreams sounded so meager in Thalia's mouth. What Kalli really wanted was love—to be surrounded by family and friends who cared about her. "Don't be so condescending. Just because I don't want to be a published author like you or scientist like Charis—just because I don't need everyone in the world to know my name—doesn't mean that what I want doesn't matter."

"I never said it didn't!"

"Oh, not in so many words. But you are always implying it, trying to comfort me by telling me I am kind, when you don't value kindness, you want brilliance. Telling me I need more self-respect when you do not respect me or my choices, not really." Kalli dug for the cruelest thing she could think to say. "You have been berating me for using scandal to force Adam into marriage, but this entire afternoon you have courted scandal yourself. Do you mean to force Mr. Darby to propose to you?"

Kalli met Thalia's gaze, taking a perverse pleasure in her sister's wide eyes, in the hurt stealing across her face. "You're a hypocrite, Thalia Aubrey."

Thalia sprang up from the bed, shaking now. "And you, Kalliope Aubrey, are a coward. At least I fight for what I want." She slammed her way out of the room.

Kalli picked up her diary, then set it down again. Usually writing soothed her, helped her make sense of the disorder of her day. But she could not write about the trip to the museum without thinking about how she and Adam had talked about kissing, and she could not write about her fight with Thalia without acknowledging that Thalia might be right—she was a coward.

So what, really, was there to say?

CHAPTER FIFTEEN

All the Crack

(Charis)

I observed two of the *Hirudo vulgaris* in *actu coitus*, and found them to copulate after the same manner as the common snail.

—*James Rawlins Johnson*, Philosophical Transactions of the Royal Society *[Charis's note: I suspect Mama would say leech copulation is* not *the proper subject for polite conversation. Must remember it.]*

Two weeks after Kalli's formal engagement, and one month after their arrival to town, the Elphinstones threw a debut ball for their daughter and their nieces.

From her position near the entrance to the ballroom, Charis fidgeted, pleating the skirt of her ivory gown with her fingers. It was a gorgeous gown, with green and copper leaves embroidered about the hem and sleeves and neckline, and it did not deserve the abuse it was currently receiving. But the alternative for Charis was to tear at her hair, and she couldn't risk ruining the delicate pile of curls with the pearls threaded through it.

Mama noticed the fidgeting and placed a quieting hand on her arm. Charis stopped—until Mama was engaged with greeting the first guests and no longer looking.

Charis had thought herself beyond caring for society's opinion. Yet here, at the start of the ball that marked her official introduction to society, long-buried self-doubt surfaced again. What if no one asked her to dance? Or even spoke to her? She did not mind so much for herself, but she could not bear to be humiliated before—she caught herself, unwilling to finish the name that sprang to mind—before her parents and cousins, before people she loved and admired.

On the heels of her self-doubt, a memory burbled up.

For Charis's thirteenth birthday, during an unusually mild April, Mama had invited all the neighboring gentry children between twelve and sixteen. The young people had gathered on the smooth, green lawns of Elphinstone manor to play games and sample some of their family cook's best recipes. The mood had been high and infectious, children laughing and running across the grounds. If the guests seemed more excited by the food and the company than by Charis, she had not minded. She was herself more interested in the food than the company.

Then her attention had been drawn away from the games by a flash of orange and black and white wing near the maze that she thought might be a hoopoe. Charis followed the flash to the maze, but whatever she had seen was gone. She stood still for a moment by the hedge, listening to the ringing voices across the lawn. She felt oddly separated from the others, as though the shimmering spring air were a solid barrier she could not cross.

Words floated over the shrubbery of the maze, two light female voices. Charis recognized one of them as a friend of Kalli's she had met a handful of times.

"I wish we had a maze at home," Kalli's friend said.

"I should settle for a house like this with all the money and servants," said the other, tittering as she spoke. "I should be a better ornament than the poor girl who does live here. They say she's wild for insects and other unnatural things. Did you see her? Such an awkward, freckled thing that she is, she looks like a maid trying to carry off her mistress's clothes."

Kalli's friend laughed at this, and then their conversation muted, their footsteps carrying them out of Charis's earshot.

Charis dropped down in the shadows beside the maze and wiped her flushed, sweaty cheeks on the ruffled flounce of her skirts. She didn't care what those girls thought. Mama would say they were just jealous.

But she didn't go back to the party. She was sure that someone—Kalli or Thalia, most likely—would wonder where she had gotten to during her own party and would come find her.

As she sat alone, certainty stole over Charis. She had suspected before that she was a little strange, but she had not known it for sure. Now she knew. She was odd, and she feared that oddness made her somehow fundamentally unlikable.

At length, Kalli crawled into the shadow of the maze beside her. "Are you all right?"

"Just tired," Charis said, which was true enough.

"Will you come join our game?" Kalli asked.

Charis nodded and struggled to her feet, which had gone to sleep beneath her. She threw herself into the rest of the birthday festivities. Anyone watching her would think she was enjoying herself.

But she had refused to let Mama throw any more parties for her, no matter how Mama had begged.

Until now. Staring at the long line of people waiting to greet her and her cousins, Charis felt all those old sensations surface. That sense of separateness, that hurt. She thought she had learned not to care what others thought. And she didn't, much. But at her own debut, in front of the people she cared most for in the world, she was not sure she could bear having that initial fear confirmed: that she was, at her core, unable to inspire love, or even liking, from strangers.

It was true that Mama and Papa and her cousins loved her, but they were family—they didn't have a choice. In scientific circles, she was likely to be one oddity among many, and if she could not be liked, she could at least be respected. But here—she had nothing to offer society that it valued, aside from her money and standing, and that belonged more truly to Papa than to her.

She took a deep breath. She was overthinking everything once again. It would be fine—and finished soon enough.

Kalli glanced at Charis and must have seen some of her nerves in her expression, because she sidled behind Mama and gave Charis a quick, careful hug. "Don't be anxious. You look lovely."

"I'm not anxious," Charis said.

"Liar," Kalli said, smiling at Charis to take the sting from her words.

"I'm terrified," Charis said.

"Of a ball?"

Of disapproval, Charis thought, but she didn't want to weigh Kalli down with her fears. She picked an innocuous one. "What if no one will dance with me?"

"Then they are great fools, and I will sit out with you, and we will mock them while we eat some of the chocolates and spun-sugar candies your mama has ordered."

"And if they do ask me to dance, and I forget the steps?"

"Then they will have had the honor of being stepped on by one of my favorite people in the world," Kalli said.

Charis laughed softly and pressed a kiss against her cousin's cheek. "Thank you," she whispered, then turned back to help her parents receive their guests.

Charis opened the ball with one of her father's cousins, and then she resigned herself to sitting out most of the dances following the first. Mr. Leveson had not shown up to claim a dance, a secret wish she did not realize she had until it failed to materialize.

To her shock, after the first dance finished, she found herself besieged by potential partners, some young men who had begun to frequent Mama's drawing room in the past week or so, others she had been introduced to only that evening. Between them, they engaged all the evening's dances.

Charis could not account for it, and did not try to, but felt a rush of gratitude and relief for the kindness of these young men (and, admittedly, a few older men), who ensured that on this night, at least, she did not have to feel out of place among society.

She soon discovered, however, that being sought-after was, in its way, as trying as being overlooked. She had little chance to rest between the energetic dances of each set, and found herself flushed, perspiring, and breathless, handed from one partner to the next. Her third partner trod on her toes, so she had sore feet to contend with as well.

Still, that initial flush of gratitude did not fade away, even as

Charis struggled to converse sensibly with each partner. Her stock of small talk generally extended only to remarks about the weather and the crush of people at the dance, after which, if her partner did not exert himself to guide the conversation, she resorted to spouting naturalist facts at random. Silence during the set made her nervous, and she felt compelled to fill it.

"Did you know that the female mantis often cannibalizes her partner while he is fertilizing her eggs?" Her partner goggled at her in shock. *Stop talking, Charis*, she told herself. But then she felt compelled to add: "I saw one eating a goldcrest once, though the bird was nearly its size."

But this statement, astonishingly, was not met as it might have been at an assembly at home, by blank stares or frowns. Instead, when she finished speaking, her partner burst out laughing.

Charis blushed, sure she was being laughed at.

"Oh, Miss Elphinstone, you are indeed a wit! A true original, just as Mr. Leveson said."

Though Charis deduced from this that she was not an object of mirth, but of admiration, it did not make her feel any better. On the contrary. Had these partners only sought her out because Mr. Leveson encouraged it? This was worse than being ignored—if she was going to be liked, she wanted it to be for her own sake, and not because someone else had set his seal of approval upon her.

Charis was filled with an overwhelming urge to test the limits of Mr. Leveson's credit. He was known as an arbiter of taste, but what if Charis were not so palatable as he had set about? Could she manage to discredit his supposedly flawless judgment?

For a brief moment, her courage failed her. What if her experiment only served to push her further outside of polite society? She would be that abandoned thirteen-year-old girl again.

No. She lifted her chin. She was not that girl anymore; she refused to care what people who did not care for her thought of her. And if Mr. Leveson wanted to make her a spectacle, then by Archimedes, she would *be* a spectacle.

Well, a conservative spectacle. She did not truly want to humiliate Mr. Leveson (or, heaven forbid, her parents), but it would not hurt him to have his pride taken down a notch (or three).

Birds, she thought. And flowers and butterflies. Surely those were unobjectionable conversational topics for a young woman?

Her next partner was quite young, nearly of an age with Charis herself, with skin still spotted with adolescent acne. She felt a pang of guilt at the sight of his guileless countenance but ruthlessly suppressed it. She did *not* want to be all the crack (as her cousin Frederick would say) simply because Mr. Leveson had dictated it should be so.

She bided her time carefully, waiting for the perfect moment in the conversation. As the figure of the set brought them together, her partner asked, "Do you have any hobbies, Miss Elphinstone?"

Charis turned wide eyes on her partner. "I quite enjoy gardening."

Please take the bait, she thought. She only needed him to open the conversation a little wider.

"What do you enjoy most about gardening?"

Perfect. "I rather enjoy fertilizing flowers. Did you know that flowers have sexual organs? Both male and female? The pistil, which holds the seeds for producing new flowers, receives pollen from the stamen of the male part of the flower." Rudolph Camerarius had first discovered this over a hundred years before, but Charis just managed to avoid adding this unnecessary tidbit.

Her partner missed two steps and almost brought them both down. Charis caught his arm and bit her lip to keep from laughing. She raised her eyes to find Mr. Leveson watching her a few places down in the dance and nearly stumbled herself. When had he arrived?

When the young man recovered, his face was nearly scarlet. "Miss Elphinstone, I—you—that is, dash it, you shouldn't say such things!"

She opened her eyes even wider. "But I was only speaking of flowers. I did not think there was anything so scandalous about that."

"Well, no, as a general rule there's not. But you shouldn't speak of"—he lowered his voice—"organs of an intimate nature, in public."

"I see," Charis said, struggling to keep her voice steady. The poor boy couldn't even bring himself to repeat the words Charis had used. "I do beg your pardon."

When the set finished, Charis's partner all but dashed her across the room to return her to her mother. Mr. Leveson was waiting beside Mama.

After the young man left, Mr. Leveson shook his head. "For shame, Miss Elphinstone, that child's not up to your weight."

Charis's mama gasped a little. "Mr. Leveson!"

Charis did not *think* Mr. Leveson meant to insult her. At least, not about her actual weight. Thanks to her cousin Frederick, she was better versed in boxing cant than she should have been, and knew the phrase had something to do with fighting someone equally matched. "I don't know what you mean," she said primly. "Perhaps if you used the King's English and not some vulgar slang, I might understand you."

"You can think circles around him, and you know it. You've embarrassed him for your own amusement."

And why was it that Mr. Leveson had singled her out, brought her into fashion, if not for his own amusement?

"Why are you here?" Charis asked. "Is it only to chide me?"

"I should think to a person of your intelligence, the answer should be obvious. I've come to ask you to dance."

He was abominably sure of himself, was he not? With considerable satisfaction, Charis said, "Thank you for the honor, but all of my sets are spoken for."

Mr. Leveson lifted his eyebrows. "And who is taking you in to the supper dance?"

Charis did not answer. It was none of his business anyway.

Mama poked her in the side. "I believe Lord Herbert has reserved the supper dance with Charis, Mr. Leveson."

"Ah. Well then, Miss Elphinstone, will you let me have Herbert's place to take you in to supper? Herbert won't mind. He owes me a favor anyway."

Charis folded her arms. "That dance belongs to Lord Herbert, who asked properly."

Mr. Leveson did not seem at all cast down. He merely bowed and walked away.

Within the half hour, a rather shamefaced Lord Herbert approached Charis. "Your pardon, Miss Elphinstone, but I find I can't take you in to the supper dance. I've forgotten a prior engagement."

"Does this prior engagement start with *L* and end with *son*?"

Charis asked. But Lord Herbert didn't answer, only shook his head, bowed, and backed away.

When Mr. Leveson showed up to claim his dance just before midnight, Charis had half a mind to refuse him. She only forbore because she didn't want to cause a scene that would upset Mama at her own come-out party.

Mr. Leveson extended his arm to her. "You see, I've arranged everything."

"Including my sudden popularity, I understand. Should I thank you for that?" She didn't take his arm.

He peered at her, frowning a little, his dark brows drawing together. "You're angry with me. Why?"

"If I'm to be liked, I'd prefer it was for myself alone, not your patronage."

"I think you overestimate my social power. My attention might have drawn the notice of others to you, but that's all. And notice is not the same thing as liking. If you weren't worthy of being liked, my attention on its own would have done nothing."

Charis pressed her lips together, unconvinced. She tried to ignore the sudden painful hope that flexed fragile wings deep inside her. She had long accepted that she was not to other people's taste. A soft voice whispered, *But what if you are wrong?*

Mr. Leveson huffed an exasperated sigh. "Why do you persist with this fiction that you are unlikable? You have abundant sense, a keen mind, and a ready tongue."

"You've just described a man," Charis said.

"And why shouldn't a woman possess such facilities as well as a man? No one meeting you could doubt either your wits—" His eyes dropped, fleetingly, to her décolletage, and when he wrenched his gaze up again, his cheeks were a shade darker. "Or your ample feminine charms."

Heat started in her throat, crept up her cheeks, and settled in her ears. The compliment both gratified her and frightened her, because what was she to do if that light in his eyes proved to be real admiration, and not just the satisfaction of intellectual sparring with a competent partner?

Mr. Leveson held out his arm again, and she took it, resisting a sudden urge to lay her cheek against the superfine cloth covering his shoulder. The muscles in his forearm flexed beneath her fingers. "Why is it you have no faith in your abilities?"

"I have plenty of confidence in my mind," Charis said. "It's my social skills that are lacking. This was abundantly borne in upon me as a child."

"I am not sure what you were told, but I find nothing lacking in your manners."

Charis blushed again, and was grateful when the supper dance started then, and she did not have to answer. Mr. Leveson let the topic drop as they danced, confining his conversation to impersonal observations about the dance. But there was nothing impersonal in the way Charis's stomach fluttered each time the dance brought them together; in the way her fingertips burned, even beneath her gloves, each time they touched; in the heat rising through her whole body when he set his hand against the small of her back.

Nor did Mr. Leveson allude to Charis's insecurities when he

escorted her to dinner after the dance, but only asked if she preferred thinly sliced ham, or beef, or both, and would she like some of this syllabub?

Charis would, as she had particularly requested Mama to include the dessert, with its cream and froth and hint of tangy lemon.

When they were seated at a table, they were quiet for a moment as they ate. Then Mr. Leveson said, "There's a promising lecture at the Royal Society this coming Thursday on ornithology. I'd like to escort you, if your mama is still willing."

Charis brightened. "I should like that very much."

"The lecture starts at noon. I'll call for you a half hour beforehand."

Charis tried to tell herself it was only the prospect of the lecture that sent an electric charge through her, as though her blood were fizzing beneath her skin, and not the idea of spending more time with Mr. Leveson. Whatever the cause, when Mr. Leveson returned her to her mama, she was in such charity with him that she abandoned her half-begun project of testing his credit.

Perhaps Mr. Leveson was right, she thought, listening to her next dance partner laugh at some observation she made. Perhaps she was more likable than she knew.

CHAPTER SIXTEEN

The Life of the Mind

(Thalia)

Snowflakes falling crystalline,
Upon the head of Clementine.
Enrobed in gowns diaphanous,
They twirl and whirl . . . disastrous? miraculous?
Drat.

— *Thalia Aubrey*

Thalia knew the moment James Darby showed up in the receiving line with his sister, Emma.

Unlike Kalli, Thalia had not spent the past couple of years dreaming of her come-out ball. Unlike Charis, she did not particularly dread it either. She watched Kalli and Charis whispering to each other, and a pang shot through her. Thalia had always imagined that for their debut ball, she and her sister would dress together, whispering and giggling. Instead, Kalli had hardly spoken to her, and Thalia had dressed in her room with only Hannah's company. It was not an auspicious start to the evening.

But then James stepped inside the double doors of the entrance hall, and electricity shocked through Thalia's body. (When had she stopped thinking of him as Mr. Darby?) Beside his sister, he appeared tall and elegant, a navy coat snug about his trim shoulders, the faintest dark shadow about his jaw. He was beautiful, like some exquisite Renaissance painting brought to life.

She had not expected him to come, as he had made little secret of how insipid he found most balls, and surprise nearly made her weak at the knees. Suddenly, Thalia was grateful that Aunt Harmonia had insisted on having a new dress made up for her, of the palest rose shading to garnet about the hem. The dress was studded through with small brilliants, so she caught the light as she moved. She knew she looked well, and now she had the added pleasure of seeing that knowledge reflected in James's face as he stopped before her. He lifted her hand to his lips (though he had only bowed to Kalli and Charis) and pressed a gentle kiss upon her knuckles that sent tingles flooding through her body.

Aunt Harmonia raised her eyebrows, and Thalia tugged her hand back.

"I hope I may engage you for a couple of dances," he said.

Thalia supposed she should make a show of hesitating, but what would be the point? She liked him and did not mind if he knew it. "I have an allemande and the Roger de Coverley free. The supper dance as well."

From the corner of her eye, she could see Aunt Harmonia trying to catch her attention, likely to tell her she was being too forward to suggest so many dances, but Thalia did not regret it. Was not the purpose of such dances—of the whole marriage mart—to find someone she might share her life with? Thalia did not want to find anyone besides James Darby.

"Are there no waltzes to be had?" James asked.

Thalia, regretful, shook her head. "No. My aunt deems them too scandalous, though they are danced at Almack's."

"Then I shall take the allemande and the supper dance," James said. He leaned in, and Thalia caught his familiar scent of lavender and citrus. "I would take all of them, but I don't wish to embarrass you or your family."

James and Emma moved on, and at length the receiving line dwindled, and Uncle John led them into the ballroom. Thanks to Charis's newfound popularity and Aunt Harmonia's reputation as a hostess (none of that watered-down punch for her parties, thank you very much), the party had achieved the requisite status of a "crush," with too many people crammed into the ballroom to move comfortably.

Thalia danced the first few sets with partners whom she promptly forgot. The third set, she danced with Adam. She expected him to say something snide about Mr. Darby's presence, but he said only, "You look well," then lapsed into silence, his steps in the dance mechanical.

"Penny for your thoughts?" Thalia asked, when the dance brought them together again.

Adam shook himself. "My apologies. I've been woolgathering. I had a letter from my father today, encouraging me to enjoy my time in London and to stay as long as I like, but I can't help feeling that he's hiding something from me. When I came up to London, my plan was to stay until your ball tonight and then return—you know my father still is not fully recovered, and I've my studies with your father besides. But then Kalli and I became engaged, and your aunt seems to expect I will stay."

"I don't see why you must, if you're worried about your father. Kalli has . . ." *Me,* Thalia thought, and caught herself. "Kalli has Charis as well as my aunt to call on if she requires. We will be quite all right if you need to return home. Kalli cannot expect you to dance constant attendance upon her as though . . ." *As though yours were a love match.*

"I still mean to do the right thing by her, even if our betrothal is a little unorthodox."

The dance drew them apart again. "But—?" Thalia asked, when they reunited.

"But my father's an ornery old man who sees pain as weakness and would not admit to needing me even if he could not get himself from the bedroom to the privy." Adam looked at her, abashed. "I beg your pardon."

"We have been friends too long for me to be embarrassed by your mention of a privy," Thalia said. "Does your father not have his man to help him?"

"Yes, but he cannot do everything my father needs, if my father is unwell."

"If it will give you peace of mind, you should go home. We can spare you for a couple of days."

Adam nodded, relief washing over his face. "You're right, thank you. I think I have been making this bigger in my head than it is. Will you watch out for Kalli for me?"

"I can try, but I do not believe Kalli wants me to watch out for her," Thalia said. They had not really spoken since their angry words after the museum. There had been so much bustle in the days leading up to tonight's ball that it had been easy to avoid each other.

The steps of the dance separated them then, pairing them with new partners for a measure before bringing them back together.

"You should make up with her," Adam said, picking up their conversation where they'd left off. "This distance hurts both of you."

"Will you be this blunt with all your parishioners?" Thalia asked.

"Only the ones I wish to see happy," Adam said. "Why haven't you talked to her?"

"I tried—and it ended in a quarrel between us." *Hypocrite*, Kalli had called her.

Adam smiled slightly. "Let me guess—you were feeling generous, and you went to Kalli in a spirit of forgiveness, and she threw it back in your face?"

At Thalia's expression, his smile widened. "I have known you for most of your life. I know how your moods work." Then he sighed. "Kalli doesn't want your forgiveness, Thalia. She wants you to apologize."

"Oh," Thalia said, thinking it over. "Is that what she wants from you too?"

"Probably." Adam sighed again.

"It would be easier if we weren't both so stubborn," Thalia said. "We get that from our mama."

Light flashed off Adam's spectacles as he looked at her. "Kalli isn't stubborn—she's kind and generous to a fault."

Thalia laughed. "And here you claim to know us! Kalli is stubborn like a rod of iron hidden in a feather bed. Soft and yielding most of the time, until you hit the hard core and then she cannot be budged. She's just not stubborn on her own behalf." If she were, they might not be in this predicament.

Adam looked faintly horrified.

Good, Thalia thought. Maybe there was some hope for him and Kalli after all.

Outside of her dance and conversation with Adam, the only part of the evening that felt real was the time she spent with James. They whirled through the elegant steps of the allemande, passing their hands overhead and turning each other about. It was possible to get dizzy, twirling so much, but Thalia rather enjoyed the sensation of seeing the room blur before her only to come to a stop with James's face in focus. Each time, he smiled at her, and each time, her stomach fluttered.

They talked of everything and nothing in the snatches of the dance that they were together: of poetry and philosophy and the curious way time passed in company, how time with a bore lagged and time with a congenial friend sped by.

"And time at a dance?" Thalia asked.

"Dancing with you passes quickest of all," James said, smiling down at her.

A few more dances followed that were hardly worth their notice, though Thalia partnered with Charis's Mr. Leveson and found him surprisingly conversable, despite his intimidating reputation.

By the time James came to claim the supper dance, Thalia was sick of the crowds and the ballroom. "It's so stuffy in here. Can we take a turn on the terrace?" She wanted whole conversations with him, not just bits and pieces caught above the notes of the music. She thought, maybe, she was ready to share her poetry with him.

"We'll miss the dance," James said. "And people might talk."

"Let them," Thalia said, and James laughed.

The late March evening was bracing after the warmth of the ballroom, as the pair strolled along the nearly deserted terrace, and Thalia found herself wishing for her shawl. Through the windows, they could see the dancers forming lines for the supper dance.

In the darkened space between the windows, James stopped to face her. He caught her hands in his and bent his face toward her. But though her pulse quickened, Thalia stepped back a pace.

Now, before she lost her courage. "I have something I want to share with you," she said.

"A kiss? I was rather hoping for that."

She shook her head. "Not a kiss—a poem. One of mine." Sharing her poetry felt even more intimate than the way James had touched her at the museum, than the kiss James hoped to give her now. "I have not shared my poetry with many people."

"Then I am honored," James said.

Thalia didn't think James would like her favorite of her poems, about the social expectation that young ladies be pretty rather than smart, so she began with one she'd written a couple of weeks before, about her longing for travel, for adventure often denied to young ladies of quality.

Thalia made her way through four short verses, her speed increasing as she went, fighting against the feeling that she was wasting her auditor's time. When she finished, she held her breath, her heart thumping in her chest, waiting for his response. The cold caught up with her, and she shivered.

"You're cold," James said, tugging her forward until she stood in the circle of his arms. She leaned into his embrace, letting his heat enfold her. She had been aware of his nearness during the dance—his warmth, his solidity—but this was different, perhaps because the embrace was more conscious, or because they were alone. Her nerves were almost painfully alert.

"What did you think of my poem?" Thalia asked, when her shivering abated.

"There were some lovely images. But I'd expect no less from your exquisite mind." James pressed a kiss against her temple, and electricity prickled through her, making it difficult to think. "You are quite intoxicating, Miss Aubrey—yourself, your wits, your words. May I call you Thalia?"

Using her given name was an intimacy reserved for the closest of family and friends—and lovers. "Yes," she said, trying his own name in turn, "James."

His name lay differently on her tongue than in her mind, even more intimate somehow.

James tightened his grip on her, and she melted against him, her hands sliding across the muscles in his chest, discernible even through the fine wool of his coat. Neither Mama nor Aunt Harmonia would approve of how close they were standing, but Thalia did not care. James was warm and present, and she wanted to lose herself in this moment. To anchor herself in her body instead of in the rushing thoughts of her mind.

"Thalia," James said, his voice low with emotion that sent sparks flickering through her belly.

She looked up, and he brought his lips down on hers. First the barest brush, as at the museum. Then the pressure of his lips grew firmer. He kissed the creases of her lips and then the center, teasing at her lips with his tongue. When she opened her mouth on a gasp, he slid his tongue into her, and something molten erupted in her stomach. The sparks along her fingertips kindled into fire, racing through her body.

Thalia had not expected kissing to feel like this. She had never been one to dream of physical pleasures—of holding hands, embracing, kissing. She had thought she preferred the more abstract pleasures of the mind. But this: this was like poetry given form in limbs and lips and heat.

The sound of the French doors opening onto the terrace recalled her to herself and she pulled away. She'd entirely forgotten the cold, and very nearly forgotten where she was. She wondered if her own lips looked as pink and swollen and, well, *kissed* as James's did.

"We should go back inside," she said.

"We should," James agreed, but made no movement toward the door. He nuzzled at her neck.

But for Thalia, the spell was broken. Her scattered thoughts began to come back to her. "You said the images in my poetry were lovely. Was the poem any good? I've been hoping to submit some of my work for publication before I leave London at the end of the Season."

James was silent for a long moment, stroking wisps of hair away from her face. He was silent so long that Thalia began to suspect what his answer was. She stepped away from him and looked down the terrace. She didn't want to see pity in his eyes.

Finally, he said, "I think your poems show talent—extraordinarily so for a girl in your situation, with no formal training, no access to the intelligentsia of London. But if all your poems are of the style you shared tonight, you may wish to wait until your writing has matured before seeking publication. Come to the salons with me, listen to other poets present their work, learn to refine your sense of meter and theme. You'll understand then what I mean."

Thalia wrapped her arms around her waist, her face hot with mortification. Perhaps her poems were not as good as she had believed—certainly James would know. And she was grateful to him, for pointing that out so kindly, when a publisher would surely not be so gentle. Only—for a moment, she wished she was not here, facing him in her embarrassment.

James caught her hands. "Don't be angry, Thalia. You asked for the truth, and I gave it to you. Would you rather I lied?"

Yes. She heard Kalli's voice again in her head. *Hypocrite.* Thalia forced herself to laugh, to cover her shame. "Of course not. But I really must get back. Aunt Harmonia will have noticed I'm missing."

"You might wish to visit the ladies' room before you return to the ballroom," James said, releasing her. "I will wait for you in the supper room."

Thalia patted at her hair, felt where a clump of curls had worked loose. "Yes, of course. Thank you." She escaped down the terrace and made her way to the small room that had been set aside for ladies in need of a minor dress repair, a quiet place to compose themselves, or a mirror to tidy their hair.

It was in the ladies' room that Aunt Harmonia found her, not five minutes later. Aunt Harmonia pursed her lips and surveyed Thalia closely, sweeping her eyes from the curls Thalia was trying to pin back into place to her still-flushed face.

"People are beginning to talk," Aunt Harmonia said. "Of you and Mr. Darby. If it were only idle gossip, I would let it pass. But I hear rumors about Mr. Darby too—he has rather a reputation as a rake and a man who constantly outpaces his income."

Well, thought Thalia, resisting the urge to touch her lips, that explained the expert kissing.

"He's an atheist besides, and you know your parents would not like that for you."

Thalia bristled. "My parents want me to be happy. Mama said as much to me before I left. I do not care for money, and, as for his reputation, people change." And his beliefs were his own, just as hers were. But Aunt Harmonia would not understand that subtlety.

"Hmm," Aunt Harmonia said, helping Thalia pin a final curl. "Just mind you do not let your heart get involved. This is not a man that your uncle and I can allow to court you in good conscience, and I'm very much afraid that your father would refuse his consent."

Thalia stood, pulling away from Aunt Harmonia though her hair was not entirely secure. "If Papa does such a thing, it will only be because you and Uncle have persuaded him to do so. He has not even met Ja—Mr. Darby! I'm sure he would like him if he could but meet him."

Nettled by her aunt's interference, Thalia stalked from the ladies' room. James came to meet her outside the supper room.

"Are you all right?" James asked. "You seem vexed."

"It's nothing, really." Thalia's irritation melted away in James's presence, and she began to see the humor in the situation. "Only my aunt tried to warn me off you. Said my father would not approve of us."

James laughed. "Parental disapproval is the spice of all good romances, did you not know? Don't let it worry you. Everything will come out right, you'll see."

All good romances—Thalia let the words thrill through her. She knew James liked her, but she had not dared let herself think beyond enjoying the moment. But he had called her by her given name and called this thing between them a romance. Maybe she could let herself hope for more.

Thalia released a slow breath. If her parents were truly opposed to her and James, it would distress her, but it would not sway her.

All shall be well, and all shall be well, and all manner of things shall be well. Thalia could not remember where she'd read the words, but they hummed through her as she took James's arm and followed him into the supper room, resolving not to let future worries poison her present moment. It was her debut, after all, and she was beside the man she was coming to love.

CHAPTER SEVENTEEN

Midnight Reconciliations

(Kalli)

Almost all absurdity of conduct arises from the imitation of those whom we cannot resemble.

—*Samuel Johnson, found in Kalliope Aubrey's commonplace book*

Kalliope Aubrey danced the first set of dances at her come-out ball with Adam Hetherbridge, the man she had promised to marry. Adam had been careful to ask for them as soon as the date for the dance had been set, so as not to repeat his mistake from the Gardiners' ball. But though he was kind and attentive, he did not allude to their conversation at the museum about kissing. He did not attempt to flirt with her. Trying to quell a vague sense of disappointment, Kalli moved through the figures of the dance with Adam and caught Mr. Salisbury watching her while he waited his turn down the line.

She flushed. In contrast to Adam, Mr. Salisbury, who was most definitely not her betrothed, had lit up at the sight of her as he came through the receiving line with his sisters. He had smiled his dimpled smile at her and had asked for as many dances as she could give him and seemed genuinely disappointed when she could give him neither the opening dance nor the supper dance, which she had promised to Adam.

Back home in Oxfordshire, when Kalli had imagined the triumph of her come-out ball, she had envisioned herself besieged by suitors. She had wanted to be sought-after, torn between one suitor and another.

She had not expected the whole ordeal to be so confusing—or painful.

Kalli looked away from Mr. Salisbury to find Adam watching her. "Are you happy?" he asked quietly.

"Why should I be unhappy? I have everything I am supposed to want."

Perhaps her smile showed too much of her canines because Adam blushed. "I know I'm not everything you want, but I do want you to be happy."

"And I am happy, so you have nothing to worry about." The dance took her away from Adam then, but she felt his eyes on her even as she spun across the room in the arms of another partner.

When they came back together, Adam didn't return to the topic. Instead, he said, "I like that color on you. Makes you look like a Melusine."

"Thank you." Kalli wore her favorite pale green gown, with a wash of lace about the hem that looked like sea-foam. She liked the dress because it made her feel pretty and a little bit dangerous, a rare combination for someone as short as she was. "Though take care that I don't catch you in my nets and drown you."

Adam laughed softly. "I suppose I should quake at the very idea, but I know you. You're far too warmhearted. When we were children rambling around the countryside, you used to cry if we came upon an animal in a trap."

Kalli leaned in close and whispered, "Sometimes I still do."

Adam whispered back, "I know. I helped you free one such creature, not three months since."

This close, she could smell the orange scent of the cologne he was wearing for the occasion. She could nearly count his heartbeats through the pulse in his throat, so close to her cheek. Her insides did not dip and swirl as they had in the museum, or as they did when she danced with Mr. Salisbury. But she felt safe with Adam. Comfortable. If it was not as exciting as the romance she'd dreamed of, it was not the worst way to start a marriage.

When the dance finished and Adam led her back to her aunt, where Mr. Salisbury was waiting to claim her, she waited for a beat for Adam to say something. To hold on to her hand a moment longer than necessary. But he only smiled at Mr. Salisbury and passed her over to him, as easily as though she were a handkerchief on loan.

The dance this time was two concentric circles, with the gentlemen on the inside and the ladies outside. Mr. Salisbury bowed, and Kalli curtsied, and when they stepped toward each other, he said, "You look lovely."

His compliment was more polished than Adam's, *I like that color on you*, but somehow Kalli didn't like it as well. The figures of the dance required the ladies and gentlemen to move away from each other, so they switched partners at regular intervals, and it was some time before Kalli and Mr. Salisbury came together again.

"Are you happy?" Mr. Salisbury asked, studying her.

Why did people keep asking her that? "Do I look unhappy?" She gave him her most dazzling smile.

It worked briefly. He shook his head, as though stunned, and then said, "I don't know. Are you?"

Kalli was about to tell him no, when she remembered what Lady Stanthorpe had said of him. "Your sister tells me that we are both alike, in that we put the happiness of people we care about above our own."

"Sometimes," he admitted, uncharacteristically solemn. "And you?"

"Yes," Kalli said. "Sometimes."

"Is that what you are doing now?"

Was he speaking about her engagement? Or something else? "I don't know. Maybe. Sometimes I don't know what I want."

He smiled down at her, his dimple faint. His eyes were so gentle it made something inside her ache. "How very curious. I find I often do not know what I want, but right now, I am feeling the most astonishing clarity."

Kalli blushed and did not know how to answer him.

Her next few partners were, thankfully, much less confusing than Adam or Mr. Salisbury. They complimented her dress and her dancing, swirled her across the room, and left her smiling when she returned to Aunt Harmonia.

When Adam came to lead her in to the supper dance, she was almost in charity with him. They did not talk much during the dance, and Kalli wondered if he was tired. It was nearly midnight, and she knew Adam to be an early riser.

After the dance, he took her to the supper room and secured her some ham and some syllabub, which he knew she liked, and found a quiet table for them to eat. Kalli saw Charis laughing with Mr. Leveson across the room. She did not see Thalia anywhere. Perhaps she had not come in yet.

Adam speared a bite of beef, lifted his fork, then set it down. "Kalli, there's something I have to tell you."

She caught her breath.

"I need to go home for a few days to check on my father. He says he is fine, but I am not so sanguine."

Kalli laughed a little in relief. "Of course you must go then. But you did not need to frighten me—I thought for sure you meant to say something awful." This was one of her favorite things about Adam, how he cared for the people he was close to.

"That wasn't the first thing I meant to say," Adam said.

Kalli folded her hands over the napkin in her lap. "Then tell me at once. Is it dreadful?"

He shook his head. "No. At least, I don't think so. I owe you an apology. I feel we've gotten off to a bad start with this engagement, and it's my fault. Well, mine and Thalia's. I've been attending to her more than I've been attending to you, and I should not have done so. Thalia will always be a dear friend, but you—"

He hesitated, and Kalli's heart leaped into her throat.

"I would like you and I to be good friends too."

He held his hand out to her and she took it, curling her gloved fingers over his, though her heart plummeted. *Friends.*

"Of course we are friends, Adam," she said, and then discovered a minuscule tear in her skirt that needed mending, so she wouldn't have to talk with Adam through the prickling in her throat. She stood swiftly and rushed from the supper room, passing Thalia and Mr. Darby in the hallway outside as she headed to the ladies' retiring room.

The last of the guests slowly drifted from the front hall. Kalli watched them go from a spot at the foot of the stairs. Her feet hurt, her eyes drooped at the late hour, but she was still smiling. Charis had gone upstairs a half hour before, and Thalia not long after, when Mr. Darby left. Uncle John had disappeared into his library with a glass of port, and Aunt Harmonia waved the remaining guests off at the door and then swept back into the ballroom to fetch a mislaid glove.

Kalli let out a long sigh. She didn't want the night to be over. It had not been perfect—her conversations with Adam still sat uneasily on her, and there was the look Mr. Salisbury had given her that she could not let herself dwell on. But the rest of the night had been glorious, filled with dancing and new friends and laughter. If she went upstairs, the spell of the ball would be broken.

Footsteps from the hall beside the stairs startled her from her reverie. It was Adam, pulling on an overcoat as he went.

"Adam! You're still here?"

"On my way out, as you see. Oh, you don't have to see me off," he said, as she came down the last stair toward him. "I'm practically family. No need to stand on ceremony."

Practically *her* family. The thought hung between them for a moment—she could see it in the heightened color in his cheeks, the way his eyes met hers, then fell away.

She drew to a halt before him, and he smiled down at her, some odd tension around his eyes softening. The rims of his glasses caught the light and threw it back to her. "Did you enjoy yourself then?"

Kalli twirled, ending before Adam with a flourishing curtsy. "It was rather wonderful."

"Except for that one fellow wearing spectacles," Adam said, his nose crinkling as he grinned at her. "His dancing was atrocious."

Kalli nudged him with her elbow. "You weren't *that* horrid."

"Oh, good. Only a little bit horrid then."

She shook her head. "Not horrid at all." She caught his hands in hers, a rush of affection swelling in her. "Thank you for coming tonight." Kalli lifted on her toes, intending to press a grateful kiss on his cheek.

But Adam, his attention caught by the sound of Aunt Harmonia coming back down the hall, turned his head at just the wrong moment. Instead of his cheek, Kalli's kiss fell on the corner of his lips. And instead of pulling back, Adam slid his mouth beneath hers, the movement so swift that their lips were brushing before Kalli fully realized what was happening. His mouth was soft—so soft—against hers, and her hands went up to his shoulders to steady her suddenly limp knees.

"Kalliope!" Aunt Harmonia called, and Kalli rocked back onto her feet, her face burning. She dropped her hands.

"I didn't—I mean—" Kalli broke off in confusion.

"It's all right," Adam said, smiling at her in a way that made the heat in her face increase. He leaned forward, and in a low voice added, "I rather liked it. Though your aim was off." He tapped one finger against the center of his lips. Had his movement to seal the kiss been intentional, or accidental?

Even the top of her head was hot now. Kalli couldn't meet Adam's eyes, so she watched her aunt approach them instead.

"It's late," Aunt Harmonia said, drawing even with them, her eyes on Kalli. "Let Mr. Hetherbridge go, Kalliope. You should be in bed, not courting further scandal. Even if you are affianced."

Another wave of embarrassment washed over Kalli. Did Aunt Harmonia really believe she was such a fool as to conduct a liaison in full view of the front door? If she *had* meant to kiss Adam like that, it would have been somewhere private. Her brain, obligingly, presented her with an image of a dark corner of the garden, stars glittering overhead, and Adam's lips warm on hers.

No, Kalli thought. That wasn't what she meant at all.

"It's my fault," Adam said, bowing to her aunt. "I was talking with Miss Kalliope and lost track of time."

"Hmm," said Aunt Harmonia doubtfully. "Well, say your good nights and then be off with you."

Kalli said good night, to both her aunt and Adam, and whirled around to flee up the stairs.

"Wait," Adam said, his voice low.

Kalli turned to find that Aunt Harmonia was setting off again, and Adam was facing her with a look of some intensity.

"Do you remember that summer when we were children, when I

caught cold in July? While Frederick and Thalia and Charis ran wild in the woods and fields, you came every day to see how I got on and brought me soups and jellies and flowers."

Of course Kalli remembered. She had still been in the lingering thrall of her hero worship. She had sat by his bed and read books to him, stumbling over the words occasionally, but Adam had never laughed at her as Thalia and Charis sometimes did. He had listened, and helped her when she asked, and told her stories in turn of the Greek heroes he had learned about in school. "What made you think of that tonight? That was so long ago."

"Because I saw you tonight, how even in the midst of a party thrown for you and your family, you paused to make sure others were enjoying themselves—that Charis was comfortable, that your aunt had the wrap she wanted, that the nervous young man who trod all over your skirt was not too embarrassed by what he'd done."

Kalli didn't know what to say. Her pulse was fluttering oddly in her throat.

"I know you think I don't see you, but I do. I just—I'm not good at this." He made a circling gesture between the two of them. "But I do see you. I needed you to know that." Adam climbed the steps between them and pressed a light kiss against her forehead.

"Good night," he whispered, and then danced back down the stairs and along the hall and out into the night.

Kalli stood watching him. She brushed her fingers against her forehead, then against her own lips, feeling the phantom echo of Adam's lips against her skin.

Kalli had meant to record her memories of the ball in her journal before tumbling into bed, but she heard the low murmur of Thalia's voice in Charis's room and wandered there instead.

Charis sat at her dressing table, clad only in her chemise, as her maid, Mary, took the last of the pins from her hair and then brushed and braided it. Thalia was already in her dressing gown, sitting on the end of Charis's bed and working her own hair into a plait over her shoulder.

"Well?" Charis asked, looking sideways at Kalli. "Was our debut ball everything you'd hoped for?"

Kalli dropped onto Charis's bed beside Thalia and covered her face with her fingers. *I kissed Adam*, she thought, struggling to remember the events of the ball before that grand moment of embarrassment. The dancing. Mr. Salisbury. "Everyone was so kind."

"Including Mr. Salisbury?" Thalia asked. Her tone was arch, but there was a mild bite underneath her words. Kalli heard what she meant: *What does Adam think of your flirtation with Mr. Salisbury?*

"Mr. Salisbury is an agreeable gentleman and a practiced flirt," Kalli said. "He doesn't mean anything by it." Except there was that look he had given her—was it possible he did not yet know she was engaged? She needed to tell him. "And how was your evening? You and Mr. Darby were absent rather a long time from the ballroom." It hardly seemed fair. Kalli had not so much as kissed Adam, and gossip had forced them into a betrothal. Thalia, she was fairly sure, had kissed Mr. Darby, and with no consequences, and now she meant to make Kalli feel guilty about flirting with Mr. Salisbury in front of Adam, when Thalia's flirtation hurt Adam far more than Kalli's ever could.

At the dressing table, Charis quietly dismissed her maid.

Thalia smiled maddeningly. "It was a lovely evening, wasn't it?"

Ooh, Kalli hated it when Thalia did that: said something provoking to Kalli but then refused to be drawn in herself, as though she held the moral high ground. "It must be nice to indulge yourself with no concern for how your actions reflect on others."

"Like flirting with someone you are not engaged to? I quite agree." Thalia's smile showed a glittery expanse of teeth.

"Oh, please don't argue," Charis begged. "Particularly not about flirts or lovers or any such nonsense. If you mean to argue, go to your own rooms and I will go to sleep at once."

Amused, despite herself, Kalli laughed. "Yes, lovers are rather nonsense, aren't they?"

"And gentlemen who flirt are worse," Charis said firmly. "One can have no dependence on what they say."

"I suppose it depends on the gentleman," Thalia said. "Do you mean Mr. Leveson?"

Misgiving plucked at Kalli. "Charis, you're not developing a *tendre* for him, are you?" It would not do at all for Charis to fall for one of the most refined gentlemen of their acquaintance. Charis deserved every happiness she could dream of, but a man like Mr. Leveson could only break her heart.

Charis said, "He is quite charming, but I'm in no danger, I assure you. He's a pleasant enough diversion for this Season, but I don't mean to be distracted from my work."

"But do you not think," Thalia asked, lying back against Charis's pillows, "that one can both fall in love *and* have work that engages one? Mrs. Hemans writes fine poetry, and she has husband and children."

"I am sure *you* could do both," Charis said. "I am not sure I am meant to. There are some women who are happiest single, who dote on nieces and nephews but do not need children of their own to fulfill them. I think perhaps I am one of those women."

Charis had turned away from them as she spoke and was examining her reflection closely in the mirror. Kalli and Thalia exchanged glances, and for once there was no animosity between them, only concern for the cousin they loved like a sister.

"Charis—do not be offended, dearest, but do you say that because you genuinely believe you would be happier alone, with your work, or because you believe no one would love you, and therefore it's safer to pretend disinterest? If it is the former, I shan't tease you about it, but if it's the latter—oh, Charis, you deserve love as much as anyone." Kalli's heart twinged as she spoke. Weren't her words as true for herself as for Charis? *Too late*, she thought.

Charis patted at her hair, still staring at her reflection. "There are all kinds of love that can fulfill one, and for me, I do not think romantic love is in the cards. I do not think I have ever been in love, and I am quite certain no one has ever fallen for me. I do not have those qualities that men of fashion want in a wife, and I should far rather remain single than marry a man who only wants me for my money, or my father's position."

"Any man of fashion would be lucky to have you," Thalia said fiercely, and Kalli could forgive her almost anything for that ferocity in Charis's defense. "You are smart, and funny, and loyal, and—"

"Please," Charis said, cutting her off. "Let us talk of something else."

Charis stood and walked to the bed, nudging Thalia toward Kalli so she could just fit herself into the space remaining. She lay back against the pillows, and after a brief hesitation where Kalli and Thalia exchanged another look, the sisters did the same. Charis pulled a blanket up over them, and for a long moment they curled together, as they had so many nights as children. Kalli wished she could turn the clock back to those moments, erase everything that had happened since they came to London, and start over again.

Charis broke the stillness. "If you could have anything you wanted, be anything you wanted, what would it be?"

"Mr. Darby," Thalia said.

"Are you in love with him?" Kalli asked. She tried her hardest to keep judgment from her voice—she hoped her sister would see this for what it was, an apology for her earlier shortness.

"I think I am beginning to be," Thalia said. "I had no idea how happy I could be in the presence of a man who understands me— who understands the joy and the pain of wrestling with ideas that are bigger than oneself."

"Has he declared himself?" Kalli asked.

"It is early days yet, but I think perhaps he will. Someday."

"Then I hope you are very happy." Kalli ruthlessly suppressed the grief stinging her throat. She did not mean to quarrel with Thalia now that they were finally speaking again. She wanted to be happy for Thalia, not so bitterly conscious that she could never have what Thalia had. Oh, she did not doubt that she and Adam would rub along together tolerably well; she even imagined that they might come to love each other in that comfortable, settled way that old married couples have. But it would not be the same—it would not be this all-consuming passion, this sense of finding someone who completed you.

She didn't want to talk about romance anymore. "And what of your writing? I thought you meant to be a poet."

Thalia was quiet for a moment. Then, "I am not so sure my scribbles will amount to much. In any case, some things are more important than poetry."

Kalli blinked, startled by the change in Thalia's ambitions. Time was, she'd talked of nothing but her dreams of being a writer. But before she could follow up her question, Charis asked, "What about you, Kalli? What do you want?"

For so long, she had been focused on her Season, on the fairy-tale happy ending that was supposed to follow, that she had not quite thought out what her life would look like afterward. "I've always liked helping Mama with the younger children," she said at last. "So I should like to be a mother. But more than that, I would like to make a difference in the world. I want to help people—to ease their suffering, make their lives a little more joyful."

"Then it is a good thing you're going to marry a clergyman," Thalia said.

Kalli had not much thought about what marrying Adam would mean, beyond not particularly wishing to. But in marrying Adam, she would be a vicar's wife. She could not preach, of course, but she could share his ministry. She would not mind the inability to preach—she found most sermons a bit tiresome, to be honest (even her father's), and imagined that writing them would be even more tiresome. But she would be glad of the rest of the work—hearing parishioners' stories (even their complaints), finding ways to help and ease and mend. A tiny hope unfurled inside her. Perhaps she could aspire to more from her life than to rub along tolerably well with her husband.

"And you, Charis?" Kalli asked, passing the conversation along to her cousin. She would ask Thalia about her poetry later.

"I should like my own laboratory," Charis said, surprising exactly no one. "And an assistant, to clean the lab for me and conduct my correspondence and write out my papers in a neat hand. And someone to cook and keep house. Someday I will present my own work to the Royal Society, though no women are presently allowed to do so, and I shall be invited to present across Europe: maybe even in America and Asia and Africa. I shall travel the world and know all of the most interesting people, none of whom will care how poorly I dance or embroider."

"I think that sounds delightful," Thalia said.

Privately, Kalli thought all that travel sounded exhausting. She would not mind a sedate tour of Europe, but going farther afield sounded like more adventure than she wanted. She liked best to be among the people and places she loved, and if she were going to go to new sites, she needed to be there long enough to make new friends to render the place perfectly agreeable.

Their conversation softened and shifted to other topics. Gradually, without entirely meaning to, first Charis dropped off, snoring lightly, and then Thalia. Kalli remained awake a little longer, thinking of the evening she had just spent, and when she finally drifted off, it was to a memory of dancing.

But in her memory, it was not Mr. Salisbury she danced with, it was Adam.

CHAPTER EIGHTEEN

Birds of a Feather

(Charis)

Since this notice has been printed, I have made a number of researches on flame;
and as they appear to me to throw some new lights on this important subject, and to
lead to some practical views connected with the useful arts, I shall without any farther
apology, present them to the Royal Society.

— *Sir Humphry Davy,*
Philosophical Transactions of the Royal Society
[Charis's note: Do you suppose he meant to throw "new lights" on flame
research intentionally? Also, pondering how I might convince Mama to allow me to
research combustibles.]

A slim letter was delivered to Charis as she ate breakfast the third
morning after their ball. The toast in her mouth crumbled to ash as
she recognized the return address. She thanked the footman who set
it by her plate and washed the remainder of her bread down with
some tea. Still holding the teacup, she stared at the letter, wondering
if she had the courage to open it.

Mama said, "Are you going to open the letter, Charis? Who is it
from?"

"Perhaps it's from Mr. Leveson," Kalli said, casting an amused glance at Thalia, who sat across the table from her.

Charis shook her head. "It's not from Mr. Leveson." The address belonged to Somerset House, where the Royal Society had its offices, and to which she had sent her rebuttal to L.M.'s article.

It would be a rejection, of course, something vague and polite that would still sting damnably.

Charis set down her teacup. "I'm afraid I'm not very hungry," she said, clutching the letter to her and escaping the breakfast room for the relative sanctuary of her own room.

She tried to slide the letter open with her thumb, and promptly cut herself on the edge of the paper. Sticking the bleeding appendage in her mouth, Charis rooted around on her desk for a letter opener. She eased the narrow blade beneath the seal. The letter sprang open.

Dear Mr. Elphinstone—for of course she'd signed the essay *C. Elphinstone*. No use including her name if her sex would be used against her. Charis took a deep breath.

We should be delighted to publish your rebuttal essay in our next issue of Philosophical Transactions.

There were other details that followed, but Charis hardly saw them.

Her work was going to be published.

In a *real* scientific organ. In the same journal that had published Caroline Herschel some thirty years earlier.

She hugged the letter to her bosom and squealed, falling back on her bed in a paroxysm of joy.

Her door opened. "Charis?" Kalli asked. "Are you all right?"

Charis waved the letter over her head. "I'm fine. Better than fine!

Ecstatic. Excellent. Superlative." She sat up. "I—am going to be a published author!"

Kalli came to the bedside and kissed her cheek. "That is wonderful news!"

"What's wonderful news?" Thalia asked, following her sister into the bedroom.

Charis hesitated only a moment. She remembered Thalia's admission that she was jealous of Charis's efforts to publish and thought of Thalia's strangely dismissive comments about her poems only a few nights earlier. But Thalia would want to know, so she pushed her misgivings away.

"The *Philosophical Transactions* is going to publish my article."

Thalia was perfectly still for a heartbeat. Then she threw her arms around Charis and hugged her. "Congratulations, dear heart. I am so proud of you."

Charis's pleasure in her news carried her all the way through the morning, up until the moment her mama followed her into her bedroom to supervise her wardrobe change for Charis's much anticipated visit to the Royal Society with Mr. Leveson.

"Mama, no," Charis said firmly. "I am *not* wearing the lavender sprigged muslin. I should look ill."

"But it's such a pretty dress."

"Yes. For someone else. Why don't you have it made over for Kalli? I am going to wear the cream muslin."

"But Mr. Leveson has already seen you in that!" Mama looked

horrified, as if Charis had suggested appearing outside in only her chemise. "If you want him to court you, you must appear to advantage."

Charis sighed. "Mr. Leveson is not now—or likely ever—going to court me. We are not going to a society event, Mama. We are going to a public scientific lecture. No one will care what dress I am wearing."

But Mama persisted until Charis agreed to wear her new green-and-white cotton print. Mary helped her dress and style her hair, and Charis had just enough time to kiss Mama's cheek and beg her to stop worrying before Mr. Leveson was announced below.

Mr. Leveson had brought a phaeton this time, a four-wheeled open carriage instead of the two-wheeled curricle, as Mama had insisted that Charis bring her maid with her, lest she be the sole woman in a room full of men. Mr. Leveson helped Mary climb in front to sit by the groom, then he helped Charis into the roomier back portion of the vehicle and swung himself up.

Mama, Thalia, and Kalli waved them off. Charis hoped Mr. Leveson had not seen her mother's eager expression.

The roads to the lecture hall were congested, and Charis worried they would be late to the meeting. However, as Mr. Leveson did not appear at all concerned, Charis tried to calm herself.

Mr. Leveson exerted himself to be pleasant, asking her stories of her childhood in Oxfordshire and telling her, in turn, about his sister and his mama, still in India following his father's death some years earlier. "Papa insisted that I be sent away to boarding school, to learn to be English, when I was seven."

"So young?" Charis asked, horrified. Her little cousin Edward, the youngest of the Aubrey brood, was six. She could not imagine his parents sending him across an ocean to school. "Was it very difficult?"

"It is a common practice among English families in India." He shook out the reins. "I was mocked rather mercilessly for my accent when I first arrived. One of the other boys often swiped at me with a handkerchief, to wipe the dirt off my skin, he claimed."

"Oh no." Charis clenched her hands in her lap. She wanted to hug Mr. Leveson, to comfort the boy he had been, but she did not know if he would welcome the embrace. "How could your mother have allowed you to go?"

His mouth thinned. "I am not certain that my father consulted my mother. It was important to him that I become a British gentleman. I proved to be a very quick study—it was the surest way to avoid bullying. And my mother had my sister to console her—my sister, you see, is darker-skinned than I am, and a girl besides, so Mama was free to raise her as she chose."

"You must have missed them terribly," Charis said. She tucked away the second part of what he had said, about his sister being less important to his father because of her gender and complexion, to think about later.

"Yes" was all Mr. Leveson said. He changed the topic. "I go back to visit my mother and sister as often as I can, and I still hope to persuade my mother to settle here, with me—though perhaps it's selfish of me to ask that of her. But I've my father's estate to look after and other business to keep me in England. It's possible, I've learned, to live with a heart divided in two, between the home I was born in and the home I've come to love."

"Your mother must be proud of you, of the man you've become," Charis said, and then blushed. But she did not take the words back—she had meant them, and she wanted, somehow, to ease the hard look in Mr. Leveson's face.

"I hope so, though sometimes even I do not know which parts of me are the man I am, which parts are pretense. Much of society runs on appearances, and perhaps I am no better. I am accepted, despite my parents' unconventional match, because my father had money, and that wealth afforded me a good education. At school I learned that being tolerably amusing and good at sport bought me greater acceptance among my peers, and so . . ." Mr. Leveson splayed his hands wide, gesturing rather self-deprecatingly at his person.

Charis had thought him arrogant because of his fine clothes and his reputation as a sportsman and arbiter of fashion. But what if those had not been a manifestation of his vanity, but something else? A means to blend in, to survive and thrive in an unfamiliar society.

"I have influential friends, and it does not hurt that my skin is light enough that I might pass for European, perhaps Italian. But all of this is fragile—it could change in a moment. Time was that one in three British men in India had a native wife or mistress, but those times are changing, and public sentiment with it." He shook his head, rather fiercely. "I do not know why I am telling you this. Pray, forget that I have said so much."

Charis was quiet for a long moment. She had never seen a hint of vulnerability in the perfectly polished Mr. Leveson. His admission cracked something wide in her, spilling a curious warmth through her chest, and she could not dismiss his words as he invited her to do. "A very sensible person once told me that I ought to see my popularity in society as evidence that I was worthy of being liked." She was paraphrasing his words badly, but she hoped he would understand what she meant.

Mr. Leveson grinned. "A very sensible person? I have been called many things, but I believe that might be a first."

"Let us hope, then, that it is not the last," Charis said.

The hall was nearly full when they arrived, only a minute or two before the lecture was set to start. They found a pair of seats near the back of the room beside a pillar, and Mr. Leveson apologized for the poor view. They garnered a few suspicious looks from the gentlemen sitting near them, and Charis realized she could not see any other women aside from herself and her maid.

"I should have planned better and collected you a half hour sooner," he said.

A half hour sooner, and Charis would have been standing in her shift. She pictured receiving Mr. Leveson so and stifled a giggle at the thought of Mama's horrified expression. She wondered if Mr. Leveson would be similarly horrified, and then blushed to catch herself thinking of such. It did not matter what Mr. Leveson would think of her in a state of undress—he would never see her so.

"Please don't apologize," Charis said. "This is by far the best treat anyone has given me during my stay in London, and I refuse to let anything spoil it."

A middle-aged man stood up to the podium at the front of the room, and the buzzing conversations around them fell silent. The man—Charis did not quite catch his name, she'd have to ask Mr. Leveson later—was reporting on the recent work of French scientist Louis Jean Pierre Vieillot and his investigations into ornithology.

Monsieur Vieillot was one of the few scientists who studied live birds, rather than preserved specimens, and he had encountered all sorts of fantastic species in his travels to the West Indies and the Americas.

The speaker held up painted images of the birds in question, and Charis settled into her seat with a happy sigh. This lecture was speaking the language of her heart.

Mr. Leveson glanced over with an amused smile. "Enjoying yourself?"

"Very much," she said, then added, "but do hush. I don't want to miss anything important!"

With a small chuckle—though Charis was not sure what she had said that was funny—he subsided. Beside her, Mary pulled out a small bag of knitting.

When the lecture was over, and Charis's head was pleasantly full and fizzing with new ideas, Mr. Leveson introduced her to a handful of his acquaintances. Despite the odd looks she'd been given by several of the men present, none of Mr. Leveson's friends seemed discomposed by her presence. Or if they were, they were too polite to say so.

Charis entered into their conversations with energy, despite Mary's grumbled complaints, and once or twice caught a flattering expression of surprise and interest at her questions and insights. But the most gratifying response was a murmured, "Well said, Miss Elphinstone," from Mr. Leveson. She looked up to find him watching her, with something in his expression that made her both hot and cold at once, and she lost the thread of the conversation.

She did not know many men like Mr. Leveson, who admired her

forthrightness and her curious mind instead of fearing it. Her uncle Edward Aubrey maybe, or Adam. Sometimes her papa, though he rarely understood her. But they had all known her practically from infancy, and they did not make her feel like this, like she was both grounded in her own body, attuned to every nerve ending, but also capable of flying. She thought again of that cracked sensation, of warmth. How she had wanted to ease Mr. Leveson's hurt.

Was this how Thalia felt when she was with Mr. Darby?

Charis marveled at the sensation, turning it over in her mind like she might a feather from an unidentified species of bird, found on one of her rambles.

"Miss Elphinstone?" Mr. Leveson asked, one eyebrow cocked at her in a way she found utterly charming. "You have a most peculiar expression on your face. I can't tell if it's inspiration or indigestion. Do you care to share?"

"It's nothing," she said quickly, trying to return to the conversation.

But it didn't feel like nothing. It felt rather like everything. Not that she was in danger of losing herself to this sensation, of abandoning all her interests just to savor what it felt like to be near this person who made her feel so alive. His presence in the world made everything else seem more interesting.

Charis had learned it was easiest to navigate society when one did not expect others to return one's interest or affection—she did not expect Mr. Leveson to feel about her as she did about him. That would be rather like expecting the sun to take notice of a planet in its far orbit. So the question became: What would she do about this feeling? In her experience of watching Kalli, fighting a *tendre* seldom worked—it only intensified one's awareness. But if she let it run its natural course, it would likely extinguish itself in a few weeks, or months. She did not think she would break her heart over Mr. Leveson.

So why not enjoy this sensation? Charis would savor what little time she had in his company, add some personal experience with romance and flirtation to her store of observations about love, and in a few decades, she could entertain her nieces with the story of how their aunt Charis once fell in love during her London Season.

Having decided to thus rationally dispose of her growing affection, Charis returned to the conversation. It took only a moment or two to catch the tenor, then to vigorously disagree with one poor gentleman, who, when he saw he was routed, abruptly remembered an appointment elsewhere.

"Remind me never to get on your bad side in an argument," Mr. Leveson said.

Charis laughed a little ruefully. "You've already *been* on the wrong side of my opinions, Mr. Leveson. You survived that well enough—I doubt I could do any worse!"

There was that light in his eyes again. Charis could not interpret it, but she told herself firmly that she was *not* to go inventing explanations for it. Her observations of Mr. Leveson were already compromised by her clearly biased preference for him.

"I have no doubt, Miss Elphinstone, that if you set your mind to it, you could turn the world upside down."

And on that note, Mr. Leveson decided it was time to return her and Mary to their home. The drive was delightful: a clear spring afternoon, birds singing overhead, and their conversation similarly full of birds—the ones they'd seen in their studies, the ones Monsieur Vieillot had studied, the ones that had yet to be discovered.

"In America," Mr. Leveson said, "there is a tiny bird called a hummingbird, named for wings that beat so fast they appear to hum. I'm told that in flight, their wings appear only as a blur."

"Like tiny flying jewels," Charis said. "I should love to see one."

"I'm sure someday you will," Mr. Leveson said, smiling at her in a way that made all her insides jangle together. It wasn't uncomfortable, precisely, only disconcerting.

Charis wanted suddenly to kiss him. She wanted to press her lips against those beautifully sculpted lines, to feel if his lips were warm against hers or cool, to see if his skin smelled different at such close range. She reminded herself that her maid was sitting in the same carriage (though facing ahead and not currently looking at her), and that the mere rumor of illicit kissing had forced Kalli into an engagement.

It didn't help. She still wanted to do it.

And when, after all, would she have such a chance again? She doubted that she would find another man she liked so well in London, and after London, she would be immersed in her studies. Perhaps if she promised him that she would not force his hand to an engagement? Surely Mr. Leveson would know better how to be discreet than Kalli and Adam.

"What are you thinking of so intently?" Mr. Leveson asked.

After checking to make sure that Mary was not attending, Charis leaned toward Mr. Leveson and said, "Will you kiss me?"

"What?" Mr. Leveson looked at her as though she'd lost her mind. Perhaps she had.

"I have never been kissed before," Charis explained, "and I should like to know what the sensation is like. People seem to enjoy it." She shrugged, belying the rapid beating of her heart.

A smile curled the corners of Mr. Leveson's lips. "This is a most unusual request, Miss Elphinstone."

"You needn't fear I mean to force you to marry me," Charis said hurriedly. "I promise I will not. I won't tell anyone, if you will promise that you will not either. I see this in the nature of an experiment."

"And what result are you hoping for, from this experiment?"

"I am not certain. Are you a good kisser? If so, then I expect I will enjoy it."

Mr. Leveson laughed. "How am I to answer that? You shall have to tell me yourself."

Heat flooded her face. She ignored it. "Then you will do it?"

He nodded. "I confess, I am rather . . . curious as well." There was a strange light in his eyes that Charis could not read.

This was a mistake. "Or perhaps we ought not. I mean, it's rather forward of me to ask."

"Oh, I think we ought, now that you have brought it up. What kind of scientist would you be if you did not follow a question to its logical conclusion?"

"Very true." Did she sound as breathless to Mr. Leveson as she sounded in her own ears?

They were pulling up to her parents' town house now, and Charis did not know what to do. How did one go about planning an assignation? Did one arrange a time or merely wait for opportunity?

Mr. Leveson helped Mary down from the phaeton, and then held out his hand for Charis. As soon as her feet were solidly on the ground, he looked up to his groom. "I believe I should like to stretch my legs for a moment. Miss Elphinstone has told me that there is an impressive specimen of *Flora implausibilum* in the neighborhood that I should like to see. Please wait here with the horses."

Charis scrunched her eyebrows at him. She had said no such thing, and she did not believe any such plant existed . . . *Oh.* Perhaps one *created* an opportunity for an assignation.

Mary hovered on the front steps. "Shall I come with you, miss?"

"Oh, no, I don't think that will be necessary. Tell Mama I will be back shortly. I am going to show Mr. Leveson a . . . plant." She could not remember what he had called it.

Mr. Leveson held out his arm, and she took it, for all the world as though this were an ordinary public stroll. Her heart beat so hard she wondered if he could hear it. They walked down the street, until they could no longer see the front of the Elphinstone house or Mr. Leveson's carriage. Mr. Leveson led her around a corner, and then swung her beneath a providentially early flowering cherry tree.

Pink blossoms fell around them like a veil as Mr. Leveson backed Charis against the trunk of the tree, the bark rough against her spine even through her spencer. The sweet scent made Charis dizzy—though perhaps that was only the look in Mr. Leveson's eyes as he advanced on her. She slid her tongue across her dry lips.

Mr. Leveson paused scarce inches from her. "Are you certain you want this?"

Charis nodded. She was fairly certain she would regret her impulse later, but in the moment she did not care.

Mr. Leveson bent his head toward her. His eyes fluttered shut, but Charis watched him until she could no longer focus on his features and then she closed her eyes as well. His lips brushed hers with a surprising gentleness, petal-soft against her skin. They were warm,

Charis noted, cataloguing the kiss, and then she pressed her lips against his and forgot to think anymore. Her whole world tipped.

When Mr. Leveson broke away, Charis would have fallen were it not for the cherry tree bracing her. She curled her hands into her skirts and tried to catch her breath. Nothing she had ever read (admittedly, the copulation habits of leeches did not give her much of a standard) had prepared her for the sensations coursing through her—the delightful tingling along her lips, the tickling awareness of him across her skin, the mingled smell of cherry blossoms and sandalwood sending heat down to her toes. No wonder her mama had warned her against kissing men.

"Was that satisfactory?" How did Mr. Leveson manage to sound so unmoved? No doubt he had practice at this, and of course his emotions were not engaged as Charis's were.

"Goodness," Charis said.

Mr. Leveson smirked at her. "It was rather good, wasn't it?"

A prickle of irritation restored Charis to herself. She said, rather airily, "I suppose it was adequate. Thank you for indulging my curiosity. I believe I had better return to my mother."

She ducked out from under the tree, ignoring the indignant sputter from Mr. Leveson behind her, and scanned the road to make sure no one was watching. Out of sight of onlookers (and Mr. Leveson), she waved her hands at her cheeks, trying to cool them. Mr. Leveson stepped out beside her, and though he offered her his arm, she did not take it. Her nerves still felt electric, and she was afraid if she touched him again, she might combust.

Or try to kiss him again.

"Are you all right?" Mr. Leveson asked, glancing sidelong at her.

"I am perfectly well," Charis lied. "Only I think we had better pretend this never happened."

"Very well. But before I drop the subject forever, may I ask you for a favor, in return for the one I've given you?"

He sounded oddly diffident, which made Charis's heart squeeze tight. "What favor?"

"I wonder if, perhaps, you might read something I've written of a scientific bent."

Charis had not known Mr. Leveson sustained more than a casual interest in science. But if he had written something, he must have researched it, and research implied a serious inclination. And if he had asked her to read it, he must value her judgment, as a friend and as a colleague—not just a ridiculous girl who had asked him to kiss her. Moreover, if she read it, he would no doubt wish for a response, and that would be an excuse to meet again.

To meet, she reminded herself. Not kiss. That was a one-time aberration. "Of course. I would be delighted!"

"I'll bring you a copy tomorrow. It appeared in the last issue of the *Philosophical Transactions*."

"But I—" Charis started to say that she already had a copy of that particular journal, then caught herself.

Wait.

She had read all the articles in that journal, had studied what she could of their authors. She could not think of one with Mr. Leveson's name.

Only L.M. had not given his—or her—full name. But—

She swallowed against a rising sense of panic.

L.M.

Leveson, M——. Charis tried to recall what she knew of his first name. Matthew? Mark?

No. She must be dreaming, anxiety and post-kissing fog making her rational mind scramble things. Mr. Leveson's name could as easily be Charles. "That would be lovely, thank you."

Mr. Leveson would come, he would show her the article in question, with a perfectly rational explanation for his nom de plume, and she would laugh to think she had been so mistaken.

"Tomorrow, then."

"Tomorrow," Charis agreed.

CHAPTER NINETEEN

Love's Philosophy

(Thalia)

What is all this sweet work worth,
If thou kiss not me?
— *Percy Bysshe Shelley*

There was only one thing spoiling Thalia's near-perfect enjoyment of her first salon—and that was Charis.

Which was rather a pity, because otherwise the salon encapsulated everything Thalia had hoped for from her London Season. Seated on a sofa in the center of the room, Thalia was surrounded by congenial company, just as James had promised: the finest wits, poets, and philosophers in London. Their conversation dazzled, dancing from one topic to the next, from philosophy to politics to poetry and back again. Thalia's cheeks ached from smiling, her throat from laughing and trying to talk over the eager buzz of the crowd.

But Charis, Thalia's designated chaperone for the evening, was decidedly undazzled. Unable to secure a seat near the sofa where Thalia sat, Charis had selected a single chair in a corner, her arms folded across her chest in an approach-me-not gesture. She had been joined, initially, by a couple of middle-aged women, but they had abandoned her shortly afterward—perhaps finding that Charis's knowledge of lyrics was not nearly as extensive as her grasp of Linnaeus's nomenclature.

Thalia's conscience pricked her. She turned to James. "Charis is unhappy. Perhaps I should join her." Though that would mean leaving the cozy circle of friends James had just introduced her to, and she was reluctant to do so.

"Are *you* unhappy?" James asked.

"Of course not. How could I be, here?"

"Your cousin will be fine. There is plenty of pleasant company, and it's good for a young woman to learn to be conversable in society."

Thalia frowned. She loved James, she did, but sometimes he was a little . . . unthinking . . . when it came to people who were not his immediate concern. Never with Thalia, but sometimes with others. "Charis isn't shy, precisely, but she's sometimes uncomfortable among strangers who don't share her interests. And she has been behaving oddly all afternoon, since returning from a Royal Society lecture."

James sighed. "Oh, all right. I'll send Barnaby in her direction. He's a harmless rattle, knows enough of science he might be able to entertain your cousin."

Thalia wasn't sure that Charis would find a "harmless rattle" amusing, so she watched with a pang of anxiety as a reedy young man peeled himself away from their knot of company and approached Charis. But within a few moments, the young man had Charis laughing. Thalia exhaled in relief.

James put a finger under her chin, turning her to face him. "Your concern for your cousin does you credit, but I did not bring you here

206

to worry. I mean for you to get drunk on ideas, to float home on a wave of inspiration."

A wave of inspiration. Something sparked inside her at the thought, a line of poetry dancing just out of reach. Thalia tamped down the spark. That was not the inspiration she was meant to find here. She forced herself to smile. "And what does intoxication by ideas look like? Shall I stumble home, clumsy on my feet, and wake with a head-ache as my brother Frederick does?"

"I'm sure you could never be so ungraceful. I hope to see your eyes sparkle and your cheeks flush. And I'd rather like to hear you laugh again."

They were both pulled into the broader conversation after that, skating from one idea to the next with a rapidity that left Thalia breathless. She glanced at Charis a time or two, but each time she found her cousin smiling, and eventually she stopped looking.

The conversation was still swirling energetically around them when James curled his fingers through Thalia's. "Come with me," he said in her ear, his voice low.

Thalia wondered who it was he meant to introduce her to this time, but James led her out of the salon into the dim hallway where a footman stood at attention near the door. From there, they found an alcove, partially screened from view by a heavy curtain. James pulled her to him, and Thalia's heart skittered in her chest.

She closed her eyes and lifted her face for James's kiss, but when it was not immediately forthcoming, her eyes flew open.

James was watching her. He traced one thumb down the curve of her cheek, across her lips. "Ah, Thalia, how is it you are so lovely?"

Thalia had never particularly cared for her appearance. She knew her features were fine enough—she'd been told so by everyone from village boys passing in the streets to her aunt's friends, discussing her openly on morning calls as though she were not sitting in the same room. She had always found her looks to be the least interesting thing about her, fairly pointless, except that they generally made people disposed to like her. A handful of times, her appearance had even seemed a detriment, a reason for people to take her less seriously, as though someone could not be both pretty and smart.

But now she was fiercely glad James thought she was pretty, glad she had this to offer to him, glad to kindle that light in his eyes. She meant, when she married, for it to be a marriage of equals: heart, mind, *and* body.

James pressed a kiss at her temple, and her blood began thrumming. *"See the mountains kiss high heaven / And the waves clasp one another."* He set another kiss lower, on her cheekbone, his hands rubbing small circles across her back. *"No sister-flower would be forgiven / If it disdained its brother."*

"'Love's Philosophy,'" Thalia murmured, recognizing the Shelley poem. The lines James had not said ran through her brain: *Nothing in the world is single; / All things by a law divine / In one spirit meet and mingle. / Why not I with thine?*

Two more kisses followed: on the bridge of her nose, the line of her jaw by her ear, where the puff of breath against her sensitive skin made her shiver. *"And the sunlight clasps the earth / And the moonbeams kiss the sea."*

James paused, and Thalia supplied the final line of the poem. *"What is all this sweet work worth / If thou kiss not me?"*

His kiss finally—*finally*—fell against her lips. Thalia met him eagerly, pressing up on her toes until they were exactly of a height. James's hands slid down her spine, coming to rest at the small of her back and tugging her against him. His chest rose and fell against hers with each breath, sparks flaring between them at every point of contact. His lips were warm and soft as they moved against hers. One kiss melted into two, then three, and then Thalia lost count as James deepened the kiss, his tongue teasing at her lips, his hands tracing patterns against her back. Her head swam.

At length, he pulled back, meeting her gaze. His brown eyes were nearly black with desire. "I want to be with you, Thalia. For the rest of my life. Run away with me." His breathing was ragged and erratic.

Thalia's heart leaped. He loved her. He wanted to marry her. But—"Surely there's no need for us to run away. Have you spoken to my father?"

"It's not your father's consent that interests me, but yours."

"I should like my family's approval," she began, but James pulled away from her with a short laugh. Where moments before she had been warm in his embrace, now she felt chilled.

"You think your family would approve of this? Of us?"

"Why shouldn't they?" Thalia asked, confused and a little hurt. "They may not be so unconventional as you, but they are good people, who only want my happiness."

"But you have told me yourself that your aunt disapproves."

"My aunt is not my parents. I cannot believe that they would disapprove if they were to meet you. Let us talk to them—then we can take our time planning our future together."

Did she imagine that James hesitated for a second, before taking her hands in his and kissing each hand in turn?

"Of course, you are right. But is it not rather my responsibility, as a would-be suitor, to write to your father? I shall do so at once and beg his blessing."

"I am sure he cannot fail to give it to you," Thalia said, her heart singing with happiness.

She took James's proffered arm, and they left the alcove, walking past the footman, who pinned his gaze elsewhere. Before they reached the door of the drawing room, James paused.

"Please don't say anything of this to your sister or anyone else. I want to make my case to your father, and if he gets wind of our intentions through some other source—say, your aunt—it might fatally prejudice him against me."

"My father is not so unreasonable—" Thalia began.

"Please," James said again, and the uncertainty in his voice caught at her.

"Very well," Thalia said. "If it will set your mind at ease, I promise to tell no one of our plans until you have spoken with my father."

James pushed open the door—and they nearly collided with Charis. Her color was high and mottled. "Oh! Where have you been?"

Thalia shook herself free of James. "Whatever is the matter?"

"That—that fribble!" Charis's voice trembled. With anger, Thalia thought, rather than tears. "He tried to kiss me! In front of the company! When I did not ask for it!"

When Thalia spotted "that fribble" among the crowd, the lanky man did not look in the least abashed. Indeed, when he saw Thalia watching him, he raised a glass to her.

Beside her, James laughed. "Ah, yes. Barnaby has been known to do such when he's in his cups. You ought to take it as a compliment, Miss Elphinstone. Barnaby only kisses pretty girls."

"It is no compliment, Mr. Darby," Charis said. "I neither wanted the kiss nor sought for it." She looked uncertainly at Thalia. "Am I compromised now that everyone knows he tried to kiss me? I should far rather die a spinster than wed a man of Mr. Barnaby's ilk."

Thalia's heart softened. She went to Charis and folded her arms about her. "I don't believe so, dearest." But she looked back at James for confirmation.

"Of course not!" James laughed again. "Why, Barnaby would be quite the polygamist, were that the case, the number of women he's kissed or attempted to kiss. We don't adhere to such strict society rules here. Reason, not respectability, is our watchword."

Thalia felt a brief sting of irritation with James, to be so dismissive of the concern that had nearly ruined Kalli. What might be seen as a joke in an inebriated young man was not nearly so funny for the young woman he'd accosted.

But then James redeemed himself by offering to take them home at once. In the carriage, Thalia sat beside Charis, who clutched her hand tightly, the only sign of lingering distress. Occasionally Thalia looked across at James, who met her look with such tenderness and longing that she found herself bubbling over with her good luck, and it was all she could do not to tell Charis her good news. Charis settled her head on Thalia's shoulder, and they passed the rest of the journey in silence.

The next day dawned gray and stormy. Thalia peered out her window at the rain pouring down and sighed, knowing that the wetness meant there was little chance of getting out-of-doors that day. She hoped the weather would not put James off from seeking her father's permission for their marriage.

After breakfast, she joined Kalli and Charis in the front salon to work on various artistic projects that had been neglected in the press of social engagements these last couple of weeks. Thalia attempted to capture Kalli's silhouette on black paper with white chalk, but Kalli, who was working on a shellwork pattern for the top of a small box, would not hold still.

It was not entirely Kalli's fault: Charis was supposed to be sorting threads for embroidery, but she was much more interested in Kalli's shells and kept jostling her.

"Charis!" Kalli said, as Charis plucked three bluish-gray shells out of her already worked design and set them together on the table. "I was using those."

"Oh, sorry," Charis said, pushing them back toward Kalli. "These are periwinkles, *Littorina littorea*, I believe. Quite common, but still lovely."

"They will look lovely in this pattern," Kalli agreed. "If you'll let me finish."

"Oh, do stop moving," Thalia said. "I've smudged your nose

again." She wondered what her sister would say if she knew Thalia's secret—that even now, a letter (or James himself) might be winging its way toward home, to ask their father for Thalia's hand. The secret seemed to swell, threatening to burst from her.

But she had promised James she would not tell.

"How is Adam faring?" she asked Kalli. Thalia had heard nothing from him since he went to visit his father. Would he be at the vicarage when James's letter arrived? She hoped not.

Kalli didn't answer at once. She pressed another shell into a spot of glue and held it there. Then she shook her head, her curls shifting almost imperceptibly. "I haven't heard anything since he left. I believe he hoped to be back before the end of the week, but perhaps the weather will slow his return."

"And your letter for the *Philosophical Transactions*, Charis? Do you know when it is to be published?"

"I don't have an exact date yet," Charis said. She picked up a shell from the table, held it to her ear, then set it down again. She glanced at Kalli, then Thalia.

"And what of your poetry?" Charis asked. "I haven't seen you write anything lately."

Thalia bounced her chalk in her palm before dropping it beside her sketch. "I have not written anything of note lately." In fact, she had written nothing. She had set her poetry aside to "ripen" as James suggested, but her well of ideas had not been filling, as she'd expected. Instead, her words had slowly leaked from her, shriveling up on her tongue. Even her inkstand had run dry.

Silence fell among them like the rain still pelting the window, isolating each young woman in her own thoughts. The half-finished sketch of Kalli looked lonely and abandoned, the chalk lifeless beside it. Thalia found she'd lost the taste for the work and pushed her chair back.

"Thalia?" Kalli asked, raising her head from her project.

"I'm going to my room," Thalia said.

"We can speak of something else," Kalli said. "You don't have to leave."

But Thalia couldn't stay.

In her room, she tried to bury herself in the book of Shelley's poetry that James had purchased for her, but the words would not stand still on the page. She tossed the book aside and paced in front of her window, staring out at the rain.

She missed James. That must be what had triggered this restless itch.

That, and the weather.

Everything would come right when the sun came back, when James returned.

CHAPTER TWENTY

All Adventures Come with a Cost

(Kalli)

O what a tangled web we weave,
When first we practice to deceive!

—*Marmion, by Sir Walter Scott,*
found in Kalliope Aubrey's commonplace book

A spate of rainy days gave way at last to sunshine.

Upon discovering the weather shift, Kalli practically tripped down the stairs. Aunt Harmonia could not beg off tonight's engagements as she had the past couple of nights, giving the weather and an impending cold as an excuse.

The cold had not come, the sun was back, and Kalli was aching to be out and about among people she was not related to. More to the point, she wanted to go driving in an open carriage.

She had high hopes of Adam, who had just returned to town and was among the first callers to arrive late that morning. He settled beside her on the settee, and she asked how his father was.

"He's not sick enough to stay in bed, and not well enough to be at his usual activities, though he tries. I imagine I'll need to go back again soon to see how he gets on. I've charged your father with writing me the instant his health changes." Adam smiled at her. "Your father's well, by the way. He and your mother send their love. Antheia asks that you send her back a length of lace, and the children want ices from Gunter's."

"And how, precisely, am I to transport ices all the way to Oxfordshire?" Kalli demanded, but she was smiling too. It was good to have this glimpse of home.

"I don't know, but Urania charged me to tell you that you must discharge this errand faithfully or she will 'perspire of a broken heart.'"

Kalli laughed. "Do you mean 'expire'?"

"I'm only reporting what she told me." His smile broadened.

"And how was your drive? Were the roads clear? It's such a glorious spring day—I imagine it must have been delightful to be out in it all. We have been dreadfully cooped up these last three days."

"The roads were a bit muddy, but otherwise fair. I confess I wasn't paying attention to the sunshine—I was focused on returning to town."

"But don't you agree that being out in the sunshine is glorious after rain? I am longing to be outside."

"Then I hope you are able to go out of doors soon," Adam said.

Sighing, Kalli leaned back against the cushions. Adam seemed oblivious to her hints. She supposed she could be more direct and ask Adam outright if he would take her driving, or go riding with her, but somehow it seemed indelicate to push herself on him when he'd only just returned to town, even if they were engaged.

When she did not volunteer anything else, Adam drifted off to sit by Thalia, who persuaded him to pose for a silhouette like the one she hadn't finished of Kalli. Within minutes, Thalia was laughing, and chiding Adam for making her laugh so—it was impossible to move the chalk in an even line when her shoulders shook.

Kalli closed her eyes. Maybe she could imagine herself out in the sunshine. If nothing better materialized before luncheon, she would drag Thalia or Charis with her on a walk.

The settee shifted beside her, and her eyes flew open to find Henry Salisbury smiling down at her.

"Sweet dreams?" he asked.

Kalli's cheeks grew warm. "I wasn't asleep."

"One doesn't have to be asleep to dream. Penny for your thoughts?"

"They're hardly worth so much. I was only thinking how lovely it is to have sunshine again."

"Indeed, it is," Mr. Salisbury agreed. "In fact, I had hoped I might persuade you to come driving with me."

Kalli sat up. "What a perfect proposition," she began. But perhaps Aunt Harmonia would frown on driving with a man who was not her affianced? "Let me just ask," Kalli finished, standing to approach her aunt, who sat beside Charis on the far side of the room.

Aunt Harmonia said only, "If Adam does not object, I can have no objection." However, she pressed her lips together in a way that suggested she had more she wanted to say but was withholding it before company.

Kalli wondered if she was ever to be her own person. First her parents, then her aunt acted as her guardian—and now, before she was even married, everyone seemed to defer to her future husband.

Adam turned away from Thalia's drawing, earning another rebuke from Thalia. "Kalli, do you wish to go driving?" There was a funny look in his eyes that she could not quite interpret. For a brief moment, she wanted him to say no, to stake some claim to her, to her company.

But she did desperately want to be free of the house. She nodded.

Adam turned back to the position he'd held for Thalia and waved his hand. "Then you should do as you wish."

Kalli waited for him to say something more, but there was nothing, so she excused herself from the room to change. She refused to allow her irritation over a trifle spoil her day, particularly now that she had achieved her aim and was going driving in the sunshine. Mr. Salisbury had a fine carriage and a matched set of bays and was pleasant company besides.

It was not long before Kalli had donned a dark rose three-quarter pelisse over her dress, her satin-lined bonnet tied beneath her chin, and returned to the drawing room. Mr. Salisbury's eyes kindled appreciatively when he saw her. Adam, who was inspecting Thalia's now-finished sketch, looked up and smiled at her, but his smile seemed a touch strained.

Kalli did not understand him. Sometimes—like at the museum, or after the Elphinstones' ball—there was a charged closeness between them that made her cautiously hopeful for their marriage. Other times, like just now, he behaved toward her like a polite stranger. The thought of decades of marriage living with such politeness made her heart cold.

But Mr. Salisbury was waiting for her. Kalli pushed her disquieting thoughts aside and took Henry's proffered arm. She followed him downstairs to where his phaeton waited outside, his groom at the heads of the horses.

"Has your man been waiting this whole time?" Kalli asked. "Were you so sure of a positive reception?"

He smiled at her, flashing that dimple that made her sternness soften. "Say rather, hopeful. Besides, there are three young ladies in residence here. I thought my odds were good that I could persuade one of you to come driving with me."

Kalli shook her head at him in mock severity. "I'm afraid that isn't very flattering to any of us, if any of us might do!"

"On the contrary—it speaks highly of you and your sister and cousin." Henry helped her into the open carriage but did not release her hand. "But I hoped you would be the one to come."

Her heart performed a tiny flip. Kalli told it sternly that it should not be flipping for anyone, except perhaps Adam. But then, Adam had done nothing lately to earn a flip, so perhaps her heart was simply out of practice.

Mr. Salisbury climbed into the vehicle beside her and, after dismissing his groom to walk home, set the horses in motion. Kalli pitied the man for the long walk ahead of him, but the phaeton could scarcely hold a third person. And after all, they would be driving in a public place, where there could be no possibility of scandal.

"Will you tell me," Mr. Salisbury said, "why your aunt asked Mr. Hetherbridge if I might take you driving? Does she always defer to your betrothed?"

So he knew about her engagement. Kalli supposed she ought to be glad. "I'm sorry. I should have told you myself."

"I don't have any right to know your business, much as I wish

I did," Mr. Salisbury said, smiling ruefully at her. "Will he be very angry that you've come driving with me?"

"He will not challenge you to a duel, if that's what you fear," Kalli said.

"I mean, will he be angry with *you*?"

Kalli gripped her gloved hands together in her lap. Adam did not appear to care one way or the other what she did. "No, he will not be angry with me."

Mr. Salisbury studied her for a long moment, and the compassion in his hazel eyes nearly undid her. "Tell me," she said, her voice a trifle high, "how are your sisters?"

If he saw her desperate change of topic for what it was, Mr. Salisbury said nothing. He responded easily, conveying his sisters' greetings to Kalli and relating a funny story of one of his friends who had, in his cups, mistaken his coat, hanging on a peg, for a young lady and delivered a rather impassioned proposal.

Relieved, Kalli laughed rather more than the story warranted and leaned back against the squabs, letting the warm spring wind wash over her face.

"You remind me of April," Mr. Salisbury said.

"Because I am cold and long-winded?" Kalli asked, teasing.

"Naturally." Mr. Salisbury smiled at her, his dimple popping back into existence. "Of course not—you are bright and sunny and surprising."

"Why, Mr. Salisbury, that is quite the prettiest thing you've said to me."

They had entered Hyde Park, but the roads ringing the park were thronged with other drivers who also appeared drawn by the sunshine.

"This won't do," Mr. Salisbury muttered, and as soon as he was able, he had driven them out of the park once more.

"Mr. Salisbury, where are we going?" It was one thing to drive with a man in a public park—it was another thing altogether to go to some unknown destination.

"Not far," Mr. Salisbury assured her. "But you'll like this."

Kalli settled back again, watching the streets of London spin past on one side and the green lawns and trees of the park on the other. Once they reached a great arterial road heading north, Kalli had the wild thought that perhaps he was trying to elope with her. But he had said their destination was not far? "Mr. Salisbury," she said, hoping her tone was light enough to sound teasing, "I cannot drive to Gretna Green with you."

"I don't believe my mathematics skills are so bad as all that—not even I would describe Gretna Green as 'not far.'"

Kalli relaxed again, until they reached a long, straight stretch of road with no other carriages on it.

"Perfect," Mr. Salisbury said, then lashed his reins forward with a triumphant, "Spring 'em!"

The horses sprang forward as if unleashed. Kalli shrieked and grabbed the side of the phaeton with one hand, and Mr. Salisbury's arm with the other. Contrary to what might be expected for a young lady so fond of parties, Kalli did not particularly like surprises. Or adventures, which was what surprises often turned out to be. She liked things familiar and comfortable and fun.

And *safe*.

Mr. Salisbury hollered too, but his voice sounded more joyful than terrified. Kalli struggled to catch her breath. She would not be one of those females who resorted to hysterics, though she could feel her throat starting to close up with fear. When she found her voice, she said, as calmly as she could, "Mr. Salisbury, please slow down!"

It took her three tries for him to hear her. The thought flashed through her head that Adam, who had known her since infancy, would never try to race with her in the carriage, particularly not a high-perch phaeton, nor spring a surprise like this on her.

At last Mr. Salisbury seemed to realize that she truly was terrified, not just mildly alarmed, and he pulled on the reins, slowing the horses to a trot. When Kalli could not seem to stop shaking, he scrounged below the seat and pulled out a carriage blanket for her.

"Dash it, I'm sorry, Miss Aubrey! I thought surely you'd like a little adventure in fresh air."

Her heart still thundered in her ears. She did not want Mr. Salisbury to think her cowardly or missish, but—"I don't like fast vehicles. I was in a carriage accident when I was a little girl. The groom fell asleep at his post and the horses ran away with us. I broke my arm." Mama, who had been with her, had luckily only been bruised, and angry with the groom. She had carried Kalli the rest of the way home, murmuring reassurances into her hair.

What Kalli would not give to have her mama with her now, to stroke her hair and murmur reassurances to her.

"I'm so sorry, Miss Aubrey. I would not have scared you for the world." Mr. Salisbury seemed truly contrite, so Kalli told him she was fine, though she was not—not entirely.

Mr. Salisbury turned the phaeton around, and they rode in silence for a while. Then he said, "I would not take you to Gretna Green unless you wanted me to. *Do* you want me to?"

He didn't look at her as he spoke, and somehow that made her heart twist more sharply. His diffidence meant he was in earnest, his attention like water on a parched garden.

She said, very gently, "I am engaged."

"And yet you do not seem happy. When you speak of your betrothed, you sound resigned—and a bit sad."

Kalli said nothing. What could she say? He was not wrong.

"If I am out of place, you have only to say something, and I will stop." Mr. Salisbury took a deep breath, and Kalli did not stop him. "I think I am falling in love with you. You are kind, and charming, and loving—I don't know if you see this, how those around you are drawn to your warmth, how your kindness makes them softer and kinder in response. I—haven't seen much of that in my life. My parents were all that was proper, but proper does not always make space for love."

Kalli remembered what his sister had told her, how Mr. Salisbury—Henry—sacrificed his own happiness for those around him. As she had. What did it cost him, now, to reach for something *he* desired? She wanted to hug him, and the boy he had been. She wanted to bottle up the admiration shining in his eyes when he glanced at her. She wanted so many things she could not have.

"Do you love that man? Mr. Hetherbridge? Does he love you? Tell me that yours is a love match, and I'll say nothing more."

Kalli looked down at her hands, clasped loosely now in her lap.

Henry's voice was fierce. "You can't say it, because it isn't true. Don't marry a man who can't love you, Kalliope Aubrey."

Something sharp seemed lodged in her throat. "I agreed to marry Mr. Hetherbridge to avert a scandal. Marrying you would only tumble me into another one."

"What should we care for that, if we were together? Anyway, the scandal would die down quick enough, once we were married. We could go abroad for our honeymoon—see Europe and Greece, Turkey and Egypt. By the time we'd returned, no one would care a whit."

Kalli turned her hands over, one atop the other. She thought of Adam as she'd seen him that morning: distant, polite, not caring that his affianced was riding off with another man. She thought of a lifetime of that distance. She thought of Henry, warm and waiting before her. He claimed to love her, as Adam surely did not.

Yet still she hesitated. "How can I hurt Adam like that?" She might escape the scandal with Henry, but Adam would have to weather it alone. She could not ask that of him—or of her family.

Henry looked forward at the road again. He had such a *nice* profile. "But you'd hurt me instead? You cannot get both of us out of this unscathed."

Kalli looked at the green of Hyde Park just appearing again. What should she say? Nothing in Mama's training had prepared her to field a proposal while engaged to another man.

"Dash it all—never mind. Hurt me if you like, hurt him too. Just don't hurt yourself to make one of us happy. Your own happiness should be the sole thing that matters in this equation."

If only it were that easy. Kalli did not think she could enjoy any happiness bought at the expense of those she loved.

Henry continued, "You needn't answer at once. I know you were not looking for an offer. Just—don't say no yet. Think about it. Answer me when you're ready—I won't pester you."

Kalli nodded, then realized Henry was watching the road still and could not see her. "All right. I will think about it. Now please, let us speak of something else."

So Henry did, chattering lightly about a hundred different topics until he had reached the Elphinstones' town house. He paused every so often, as if waiting for Kalli to add something, and when she did not, he picked up the conversation again himself. Everything was so *easy* with him.

Henry was perfect: charming and kind, a man who cared for his sisters and who attended to Kalli's moods. If he liked surprises and adventures more than she did, well, no couple was exactly alike. Her answer should be simple, but something held her back.

She just wished she knew what.

CHAPTER TWENTY-ONE

A Day of Reckoning

(Charis)

I found from repeated trials, that both the oppressed breathing and the collection of
phlegm, caused by the division of the eighth pair of nerves, may be prevented by
sending a stream of galvanism through the lungs.

—*A. P. Wilson Philip*, Philosophical Transactions of the Royal Society *[Charis's note:*
If the use of metal plates and electricity can stimulate the nerves in the lungs and
produce better breathing, perhaps the same ought to be used to treat love-sickness.]

Alone of the women of the Elphinstone household, Charis had been
glad of the rain. It had put off Mr. Leveson's threatened "tomorrow"
for the unveiling of his article. It had bought her first one day, then
two, then three. When the rain stopped and Kalli cheered, Charis
only sighed.

Today then.

Charis dressed with care, in a pale gold cotton dress with yel-
low flowers embroidered across the bodice. She walked down to
the morning room, her limbs stiff with terror, as though she were
waiting for her own execution. She thought of telling Mama she
was sick, but that would only induce fussing and some foul-tasting

draught. And Mr. Leveson wouldn't be put off forever. Better to get it over with at once.

A few of Mama's friends arrived. Then Adam, who sat by Kalli but did not appear to make either of them happy, as he abandoned her quickly for Thalia. Then Mr. Salisbury came and whisked Kalli away for a drive. Charis did not understand why Adam had given such quick approval—after Kalli left the room, he stared at the doorway with such a peculiar expression she thought he might be in pain.

Mr. Darby arrived next. Charis could see that he was rather put out to find Adam ensconced on the sofa beside Thalia, though he hid it swiftly. He snagged a single chair and scooted it closer to Thalia.

Where was Mr. Leveson? Was he delaying on purpose to punish her? Perhaps he had already discovered the existence of her article. Charis pulled a handkerchief from her pocket and began twisting it through her fingers. She listened absently to the conversations happening near her but took no part in them.

"Have you been to Vauxhall yet, Miss Aubrey?" Mr. Darby asked Thalia.

"Not yet. Should I like it?" Thalia said. Charis glanced over at her, glad that Thalia seemed cheerful today, unlike her curiously grim mood the other day.

"Isn't it a trifle . . . fast?" Mama asked.

"Oh, no," Mr. Darby assured her. "To be sure, the gardens are open to anyone who can pay the fee, so some undesirables may be present, but the highest of the *ton* don't disdain it, I assure you. I've seen parties of dukes and earls there, merry as you please."

"Sounds rather common," Adam said, a slight grin hovering

about his lips. He caught Charis's eye, and she couldn't help smiling back at him.

"I propose we make a party of it," Mr. Darby said. "You needn't come, if it bores you, Hetherbridge."

"He's only teasing, J—Mr. Darby," Thalia said. "When shall we go?"

"Wednesday next, perhaps?"

Just over a week away, Charis observed.

When Mama frowned, Mr. Darby added, "I should be delighted to make you all my guests. Surely nothing untoward can happen with you and your husband to lend us dignity, Lady Elphinstone."

Mama relented, and Mr. Darby and Thalia began to discuss the plans in more detail. Adam abandoned them to join Charis, and Mr. Darby took his spot with alacrity.

Settling into a chair beside Charis, Adam said, "Your family is popular today. I'm surprised none of your suitors are here besieging you."

"I suppose the novelty of my conversation has worn off," Charis said. Privately, she was rather grateful. Bad enough that she still had to brave the prospect of finding out that Mr. Leveson had written that article. Far worse to have witnesses to their encounter.

"Anyone who sees you only as a novelty does not deserve the pleasure of your company."

"Now, that was very pretty," Charis said. "Did you practice that?"

Adam laughed. "I don't, as a rule, practice compliments! I am not Mr. Collins, though I am to be a clergyman."

"Then alas, I'm afraid you'll never have the patronage of a great lady."

"That's a burden I am willing to bear."

Charis studied his smiling face. "Why did you let Kalli go driving with Mr. Salisbury?"

He shrugged. "She seemed eager to go—and I . . . I don't want our engagement to curb any enjoyment she might choose." His eyes went back to the door as they had when Kalli left.

"Kalli has been itching to get out-of-doors anytime these past three days. If you'd offered to take her riding or driving, she'd have just as gladly gone with you."

"Is that why she was going on about the weather? I thought she was trying to bore me into leaving her alone."

"Kalli isn't so ungracious," Charis said. "You should know that by now."

Adam sighed. "You're right, I do. I just want her to be happy."

Their conversation drifted to other topics, and then Adam took his leave, stopping to say goodbye to Thalia and Mama on his way from the room. He passed Mr. Leveson in the doorway.

Mr. Leveson.

All the blood in Charis's body seemed to stand still. She swallowed.

"Good afternoon, Mr. Leveson," she said. It was still afternoon, wasn't it?

"Good day, Miss Elphinstone," Mr. Leveson said, smiling as he sat down. "My apologies for not calling sooner."

"Oh, I did not expect you! The weather was rather dreadful." Why, oh why, had Charis never bothered to learn the art of small talk? She wished she had Kalli's ability to chatter about the weather for hours on end, instead of one concise observation. Now she had merely set Mr. Leveson up for his reveal.

And in fact, Mr. Leveson was reaching inside his coat to withdraw something that looked horridly like a paper-bound copy of the *Philosophical Transactions*. Charis wished she'd never read the plagued thing.

"I've brought something for you," he began, holding out the journal.

"Of course! Thank you!" Charis snatched the periodical as though it were a pan, hot from the oven, and stuffed it into her embroidery basket on the floor near her feet.

Mr. Leveson looked startled. "But I haven't yet shown you which article is mine."

"Oh! My apologies." Did she appear as silly as she felt? Charis fetched out the journal, knocking loose a skein of embroidery thread as she did so. She kicked the thread toward the basket and handed the journal back to Mr. Leveson.

She watched, with a sort of horrified fascination, as Mr. Leveson's long, elegant fingers flipped through the pages.

"Here," he said at last, his finger coming to rest beneath the title "On Lamarck's Natural History of Invertebrates." "Are you familiar with Lamarck's work?" Mr. Leveson asked. "Some flaws, but withal, an excellent system. I've written about his newest work."

"Some," Charis managed, her throat closing up, her eyes tracing over the initials beneath the title: *L.M.* She had been right. Oh, but this was terrible. She must write to the journal at once, insist that they stop publication of her letter. Not that she had said anything factually incorrect, only that she had been so clever, so biting in her rebuttal. It had not seemed to matter before, when the recipient was an anonymous, faceless writer. But now—she pictured Mr. Leveson's dark eyes widening with hurt, those lovely lips (that she had kissed!) twisting with distaste.

Was it such a great thing to be clever, if her cleverness came at the expense of someone else? Even had it not been Mr. Leveson on the receiving end, she should not have abused some unknown fellow scientist so. Criticism did not have to equal cruelty.

"Thank you," she said, setting the journal on a table beside her, her hands trembling only a little. "I'm flattered that you trust my opinion." There, that was not a lie. "Why did you not use your full name?" Had he but done that, all of this mess could have been avoided.

Mr. Leveson did not quite meet her eyes but plucked an invisible speck from his jacket sleeve. "There have been some rumbling complaints about gentlemen dilettantes in the Royal Society. I wanted my work to stand or fall on its own merits, not my father's name."

Charis's heart twisted. Worse and worse. She could not even fault him for his reasoning—she understood only too well what it was to be judged on something other than one's mind.

She swallowed.

Mr. Leveson nodded toward the journal. "I had hoped you might look it over now, that we could discuss it together."

Good heavens—did he expect her to read it in front of him? She could not. Her face would betray her. Charis thought quickly. "I'm afraid Mama would consider me most rude to ignore my guests in favor of reading"—never mind that she'd done it before—"and indeed, I should feel awkward to read it in front of you."

Mr. Leveson nodded acquiescence. "Then we shall have to talk of it another time. I look forward to it."

Their conversation shifted to an art exhibit that had newly opened. Mr. Leveson was pleasant and intelligent as always. Talking with him was a curious kind of torture. Even as she smiled and laughed and responded to his questions, her betrayal hummed a steady counterpoint in her pulse.

Perhaps Mr. Leveson could tell she was distracted, because after a few minutes of her answering at random, he said, "Are you all right, Miss Elphinstone?"

"Perfectly fine," she said. "Only I cannot seem to keep my mind on one topic for thirty seconds altogether. Perhaps I've been cooped up inside too long."

As soon as she spoke, she wished she'd bitten her tongue. Now Mr. Leveson would think she was seeking an invitation to go driving again. Or hinting for another kiss.

But Mr. Leveson said only, "Then I shan't keep you any longer."

Charis watched him cross the room, feeling wretched. She both wanted him to stay and wanted him to leave, and she had no idea what to do with such contrary feelings.

Mr. Darby stopped Mr. Leveson, extending an invitation to join their group at Vauxhall, and Charis's silly heart leaped when Mr. Leveson accepted. Why could her heart not understand what her mind knew, that there could be nothing between them? And next time they met could only bring pain, as Mr. Leveson would want to know what she thought of that dratted article.

He would hate her when he knew what she had done.

And oh, she did like him. He was not the arrogant, hateful man she had initially thought—though about one thing, she had not been wrong. He *was* proud, though his pride lay in his intelligence, in the ideas he cultivated, not in his wealth or possessions. And she was about to expose his one true point of pride—his scientific work—to public ridicule.

She had to retract that letter.

Snatching a few minutes later that day between afternoon callers and dressing for dinner, Charis scribbled a hasty note to the Royal Society, telling them she had rethought her response to the Lamarck article. *Should you be agreeable*, she wrote, *I am willing to make revisions to the essay and resubmit it. But it cannot go to press as it stands.*

A week passed with no response.

Mr. Leveson called again, and Charis put him off with a flimsy excuse that she had not had the time yet to read his article as it deserved. The hurt that flickered in his eyes was masked quickly, but Charis's guilt tormented her after he left.

At last, Charis summoned up her courage and her maid, Mary, and braved the Royal Society itself. The two women took a hackney carriage to the Strand, where they disembarked outside the sprawling neoclassical building that housed the society, as well as the Royal Academy of Arts and the Society of Antiquaries. They entered the large vestibule before heading into the east wing. There, Charis had to stop a passing gentleman to inquire where she might find the office of the *Philosophical Transactions*.

His directions led her to a study, the door partly ajar. Peering inside, she saw that the room was rather untidy, but more to the point, quite empty.

"What shall we do, miss?" Mary asked.

Charis sighed. "I suppose we ought to wait." She didn't want to wait—already, they were drawing unwelcome attention and glares from scientific men who seemed to feel their precincts were being sullied by the mere presence of females. But then she thought of how Mr. Leveson might feel upon publication of her letter, and the resulting wave of nausea was enough to convince her to stand her ground.

It was some twenty minutes before a rather thin gentleman of middle age approached her. "May I help you?" he asked, in chilly tones that suggested he would prefer her to leave.

"Yes," she said firmly. "I've come to inquire about a letter forthcoming in your new issue—a letter in response to L.M.'s work on Lamarck's natural history."

"Oh, yes," he said, smiling a little. "I recall that essay. What's your inquiry?"

"I should like to have the letter pulled. I've rethought some of the arguments and it must be rewritten before going to press—if it goes to press at all."

Two narrow eyebrows lifted. "You should like to have the letter pulled? My dear young lady, we don't publish at the whims of society misses."

Charis could feel her cheeks heating. "I'm afraid you misunderstand me. I am the author—C. Elphinstone—and I would like to have the letter taken out. I can no longer support my conclusions as written."

"I don't believe it," the man said. "No woman so young as yourself wrote that piece. It has the elegant, linear thinking of a man."

"And yet, I wrote it," Charis said, her heart sinking. Was she sabotaging any chance of being further published by the society, now they knew her identity? No matter—it had to be done. "Why should this be so unbelievable? Your journal has published a woman's writing before, with Caroline Herschel."

"Ah, yes. But few women attain to the level of Miss Herschel."

"I do not aspire to her level," Charis said, trying to hold on to her courage. "I merely desire that you will remove my letter from the next issue of your fine journal."

"My dear young lady, let me assure you that had I the power, I would assuredly remove your letter from my publication, as it was clearly a mistake to accept it. A letter by a woman! But that issue has already been delivered to the printers. It is out of my hands."

"But surely you—or Sir Joseph Banks," she said, appealing to the society president, "have the authority to stop them."

"It is out of my hands," he said again, turning away to busy himself with some papers on the desk, and with that cold comfort Charis had to be content.

But oh—how was she to face Mr. Leveson when the issue came out? It bore her name. Others might not make the connection, but she had no doubt that he would.

And he would despise her.

CHAPTER TWENTY-TWO

Vauxhall Gardens and Secret Assignations

(Thalia)

AWAY! the moor is dark beneath the moon,
  Rapid clouds have drank the last pale beam of even:
Away! the gathering winds will call the darkness soon,
  And profoundest midnight shroud the serene lights of heaven

— *Percy Bysshe Shelley, "Stanzas—April, 1814"*

The day of the promised trip to Vauxhall dawned clear and bright. Thalia chose to see this as a positive omen, and though her day was busy with morning callers and shopping and walks, her heart was not really in any of it. Her entire focus was on the evening, and when she might see James again.

It was not as though she *hadn't* seen James in the eight days since he had issued the invitation to the gardens. Indeed, nearly every day had brought him to the Elphinstones' town house. They had once gone riding together, and once strolled through a nearby garden. But all of this had been in the company of others, and Thalia felt starved for time alone with James. Surely, in a place like Vauxhall, they could steal a few moments apart.

They had not spoken much of their secret betrothal. Once, Thalia had asked James, "Have you heard from my father?"

And James, frowning slightly, had said, "Not yet. Be patient, love." Thalia had not asked again.

But tonight, she had every intention of finding a quiet corner to talk to James—and to kiss him—and get a more detailed answer from him.

When at last dusk began to fall, Thalia retired to her room, to dress herself with care for the night ahead. She put on a white gown threaded with silver, which would pick up the lights of the colored lanterns at the garden and shimmer under the moonlight. She allowed Hannah to curl and set her hair, leaving a few curls loose to caress her long throat. Her mirror told her that she looked pretty—she hoped James would see her so as well.

She was nearly finished with her toilette when Kalli joined her. "You look well," Kalli said.

So did Kalli, in a pale blue gown edged in white lace, and Thalia told her as much.

"Is Adam joining us this evening?" Thalia asked.

"I think so. He said he would, though I have not spoken to him much this last day or two." Kalli bit her lip and moved across the room to the window. "I used to think I knew Adam fairly well. But I feel I understand him less now that we are betrothed than I ever did."

Thalia studied her sister for a long moment. "I know I was angry with you when you first agreed to this betrothal. But all I really want for you is happiness, dearest. If Adam won't make you so, you shouldn't marry him—betrothal or not, scandal or not."

Kalli traced one gloved finger over her reflection in the window. "I want to do the right thing. But what if that is not enough for happiness?"

"Then don't do it," Thalia said. "Ask yourself: What is it that you want? Truly want?"

"What if what I want makes other people unhappy?"

"You have to live your life, not other people's. The unhappy consequences of your actions will stay with you far longer than people's disappointment."

Kalli nodded, but her gaze was far away.

"Is there something you want to tell me?" Thalia asked.

Kalli's gaze flashed back to her. "No, there's nothing to tell. Not yet, at any rate." So Kalli *was* keeping something from her. It made Thalia ache, to think of the loss of their childhood closeness, when they had told each other everything. But she was keeping secrets from Kalli too, so she did not press her sister.

Then Kalli said, "Try not to flirt so much with Mr. Darby in front of Adam. It pains him."

"I do not *flirt*," Thalia said with dignity.

"You do," Kalli said, smiling a little.

"I can't be responsible for everything Adam feels," Thalia said. "Perhaps you should flirt *more* with Adam. That would certainly distract him."

A curious expression flickered across Kalli's face, and disquiet slithered through Thalia. She never used to find it hard to read her sister.

"One does not flirt with Adam," Kalli said. "He takes everything so literally that delicate sallies are always in danger of being wildly misconstrued."

Thalia laughed. She had always found Adam's literalness to be part of his charm. "Well, he is not unintelligent. Perhaps he can be taught yet."

Twisting her gloved hands as she moved toward the door, Kalli said, "Perhaps. But I am not sure I am adept enough to teach him."

She was through the door and to the stairs before Thalia could rise and pull on her own gloves, and by the time Thalia caught up with her, James and his sister, Emma, were already waiting in the front hall.

James smiled at Thalia, that warm, private smile that always made her heart turn over. Mr. Leveson arrived a moment later, then Adam. Thalia glanced at Kalli, but Kalli was talking to their aunt and ignoring Adam's arrival. Charis was the last to arrive—she came flying into the room with one curl already sliding free of its placement above her ear, and a smudge of ink on her nose.

"Charis, dear," Aunt Harmonia said, walking quickly to her daughter and whispering to her.

Charis gulped, glanced once at Mr. Leveson, and backed out of the room. When she returned a few minutes later, the smudge was gone and the tip of her nose was very, very pink. She refused to look at Mr. Leveson.

They took two carriages to Whitehall, then loaded into the boat James had chartered. As they crossed the darkened river, lights from the far bank shimmered across its surface. Thalia shivered, despite the shawl she wore and the mild spring night. The evening seemed too perfect somehow: lovely and fairy-tale like, waiting for the curse to fall.

She shook herself. Such fancies were absurd.

James helped her alight from the boat, and they climbed the steps up the bank and crossed the street to the wide gates of Vauxhall, where James paid for their group, and they walked into the gardens.

If the lights on the river had promised a fairy tale, this was fairyland incarnate: colored lanterns gleamed along the Grand Walk, and in the distance, Thalia could see the intricate trim of some exquisite building. Orchestral notes floated through the dark air.

"I've arranged for dinner at nine, in a private box," James said, "but we've still some time before then. Perhaps we can explore the gardens first?"

The party was agreeable, and Uncle John led them along one of the sidewalks. They admired the lanterns and the carefully placed statues among the shrubberies, exchanging greetings with a handful of groups they recognized.

Thalia took James's arm and matched her steps with his. She had hoped for some privacy, but perhaps it was too early to look for that—and in any case, Aunt Harmonia kept casting glances behind her, as though she was afraid she'd lose Thalia if she did not keep an eye on her.

Dinner was a lovely affair, served to them in one of the many semi-private alcoves that lined the Grand Walk, part of the ornate Chinese pavilions. There were cold meats, the famous Vauxhall ham sliced so thin it was nearly translucent, and salad. For dessert, the waiters brought cheeses, custards, cheesecake, and pudding, along with arrack punch. As they ate, a whistle sounded and servants set to work lighting additional lanterns, so the whole realm glowed with light.

James leaned toward her. "You look like Titania herself come to grace mortals with her presence." In this light, the silver threads of her dress gleamed gold.

Thalia smiled, pleased.

After dinner, their party split up. Aunt Harmonia wanted to see the rotunda and the miniature castle. Naturally, Sir John accompanied her, and Mr. Leveson indicated he would join them. "Kalli, you'll stay with your sister?" Aunt Harmonia asked.

"I'll stay with Thalia," Charis volunteered. She'd been oddly quiet at dinner, exchanging only the barest minimum of words with Mr. Leveson, who sat beside her, and talking mostly to Kalli. Such incivility, though not entirely out of character for Charis, was odd given her general liking for the man.

Aunt Harmonia exchanged a glance with her husband. "Please come with us," she said. "I saw some species of flower I most particularly wanted you to identify."

With only one longing-filled backward glance, Charis dutifully trotted after her mama.

Thus, Thalia and James found themselves with a trio of chaperones: Emma, Kalli, and Adam. For some time, they simply meandered, following the Grand Walk and then branching off into one of the side gardens. Thalia wanted to see the "Dark Walks," known for their illicit trysts, but somehow walking through those romantic trails with Adam and Kalli and James's sister watching her robbed the prospect of its appeal.

Halfway down a path, Emma stumbled. She cried out in pain, and Adam was the first to reach her. He helped her to her feet, and she gasped as soon as her right foot touched the ground. Adam slipped his arm around her waist to support her, but she could scarcely seem to bear her weight on her good leg.

"Shall I fetch help?" James asked.

"Oh, no, I imagine I'll be right enough if Mr. Hetherbridge and Miss Kalliope Aubrey can but help me back to our supper box," Emma said. "I just need some rest. You two go on ahead."

"I can manage," Adam said. "Kalli, stay with Thalia."

Kalli stood mutinous in the path, not moving toward Thalia or toward Emma. "You are not my lord and master, to tell me what to do," she said.

Adam looked astonished. "I never meant—only Thalia shouldn't be alone with Mr. Darby. In Vauxhall of all places!"

"Do you doubt my brother's honor?" Emma asked.

Adam didn't answer her directly, but Thalia could see the answer in his face. Of course he did. "We know how viciously rumors circulate among the *ton*. I shouldn't like to see Thalia forced into an unhappy alliance because of a rumor."

Thalia looked at Kalli, who had gone white. Had Adam even thought about how she would take his speech?

Without a word, Kalli whirled away and began walking swiftly, almost running, down one of the darkened paths splintering away from theirs.

Adam, anchored to his spot by Emma's weight, stared after her, belated recognition dawning on his face. He swore softly, then called after Kalli's retreating figure. "Kalli, wait! I didn't mean—"

Thalia didn't wait to see what Adam did with Emma. She worked her arm free of James's and began hurrying after her sister. She hoped Adam would have sense enough to take Emma back to their supper box and wait. In Kalli's current mood, he'd likely do more harm than good if he tried to go after her now.

She hadn't gone far before she became aware of James, his longer stride bringing him easily to her side.

"Is your sister all right?" James asked.

"I don't know. Adam must have boulders for brains." Really, it was unlike Adam, who was normally such a sensible creature, to be so obtuse. Was he *trying* to drive Kalli away? Only that seemed unlike him too—his honor was too strong to let Kalli bear the stigma of scandal alone. Was he making a point, or only a muddle?

That puzzle would have to wait. For now, Thalia had to reach her sister.

Kalli seemed to follow the paths at random, taking first this left, then that right. She was moving faster than Thalia had expected, given her shorter legs, and Thalia was nearly breathless trying to keep up with her. "Kalli!" she called after her. "Please wait! Adam has gone back with Emma. It's just me."

But Kalli either didn't hear her or didn't wish to. She plunged deeper into the paths, where the lanterns were sparser. She looked spectral at this distance, a pale, ephemeral creature floating through the shadows.

Thalia paused to catch her breath, and James snagged her around the waist. "Thalia, wait, please—I've been trying all evening to have a word alone with you, but your family is deuced hard to shake."

"But Kalli—"

"Your sister will be fine for a moment. If she's anything like Emma, she'd rather have a good cry in private anyway, and won't thank you for witnessing her distress."

Thalia stopped trying to break free. James was right: Perhaps Kalli *did* need a few moments alone to compose herself.

James, as if sensing her weakening, pressed on. "She's hardly alone, here in the gardens, and we're within hailing distance should something befall her. Please, I beg you, hear me out."

She turned to fully face him. There was an urgency in his words, a tightness around his eyes, that she had not seen before. "What is it? Is something wrong?"

"I—no. Yes." James ran a distracted hand through his hair. "I must leave for Calais in the morning."

"To France?" Shock pushed away all thoughts of Kalli. "Why? And why so suddenly?"

James looked away, his cheeks reddening. "A misunderstanding and a mistake. A debt I contracted and thought I could pay, but my uncle, miserable pinchpenny that he is, will not advance me the money and so I must away to the continent until the whole affair blows over."

"A gaming debt?" Thalia asked. She knew from her brother Frederick that gaming debts were debts of honor and must be paid at once. A debt to one's tailor could be ignored for months without so much as a whiff of scandal. A gaming debt could not. "Is there not something you might sell or pawn?"

He shook his head again. "I've tried everything. Upon my word.

It's flight or debtor's prison. The sum I owe—is not a small one, and the man I owe it to says he will wait no longer."

"Surely your friends wouldn't see you so embarrassed?"

"I can't ask it of them. I had to borrow money from a friend just to cover the cost of tonight. To ask so much—no, I could not do it. In six months, I come into my majority and my own income, and I shall pay everything back. In the meantime, I must lie low."

Six months. Suddenly, the future yawned before Thalia, joyless and lonely. "I'll wait—"

"Don't wait. Come with me, now."

She'd always wanted to see Paris, and to see it with James would make everything richer, deeper, sharper. But—

"Surely if we wait a little longer, with my parents' blessing we can arrange a marriage and I can join you in France within the month."

A shadow flickered across James's face. He glanced away from Thalia, the muscles in his jaw working. When he looked back at her, his expression was heavy. "I had not wanted to tell you like this, but your father will not give his blessing to our marriage."

Disappointment flushed hot, then cold through Thalia. "Did he say why?"

"Not in so many words. I've no doubt your aunt has been feeding him lies in her letters."

Thalia did not think that sounded very like Aunt Harmonia, but she granted that her aunt did not particularly approve of James. "He doesn't know you, that's all. Perhaps if I spoke to him—"

"Thalia." James took her hands in his. "There is only one question that matters right now. Do you love me? I love you. Why should we wait to start a life together because your father is narrow-minded and the world conspires against us? Come away with me."

Thalia slid her fingers through James's. She wanted to say yes. But eloping was such a big step, a final step. And it was all happening so fast. Was she prepared to leave Kalli and Charis and Aunt Harmonia without a word, to subject them to such emotional distress? To go against her father's wishes?

James laughed softly. "Ah, my dear Thalia. Always so cautious. When will you let yourself live?"

Thalia bristled. She was not cautious—that was Kalli, and Charis. That was her mother. Thalia was the dreamer, the one with a heart for adventure. And if Kalli was upset with her, she'd come around soon enough, when she saw how happy Thalia was. Her parents would too. She thought of what she'd told Kalli, only that evening, that the unhappy consequences of one's own decision lasted far longer than others' disappointment.

"All right," she said. "I'll come with you." She waited for the flood of exhilaration to fill her, but all she felt was a leaden anxiety for Kalli. "But I've got to find my sister first."

"Good girl," James said, pressing a kiss against her forehead. "Find your sister. Tell her you've a headache, and I'm taking you home. We'll stop by your aunt's town house long enough to gather a few things, and by the time anyone discovers you are not in your bed, we'll be halfway to Dover."

Thalia nodded. She took a few steps away, then came back. She pressed a kiss to James's lips, putting all her love and longing and hope into it. James deepened the kiss, one hand coming up to cradle the nape of her neck, the other going to the small of her back and pressing her against him. For a moment she forgot everything: the lights of Vauxhall, Kalli, the elopement. There was only her, and James, and the fire springing up between them.

CHAPTER TWENTY-THREE

How Often Is Happiness Destroyed

(Kalli)

Why not seize the pleasure at once? How often is happiness destroyed by preparation, foolish preparation!

—*from the author of* Emma, *found in Kalliope Aubrey's commonplace book*

Kalli had no particular destination in mind as she ran, so long as it was away. Torn between tears and fury—she knew Adam did not *want* to marry her, but did he have to make his reluctance so public?—she scarcely saw where she stepped. She picked a path at random, and when another opened up, veered to the side. She passed a couple twined almost indecently together, just beyond the globe of light cast by one of the famed colored lanterns, and her first reaction was not revulsion but envy. What would it be like, to love and be so confident of a return? The phantom pressure of Adam's lips against her forehead, against her own lips, returned to her, and she rubbed her skin as though she could wipe away the memory.

Eventually, Thalia's calls to her stopped, and Kalli slowed from a run to a walk. Her slippers were surely ruined by now, and the lace hem of her pale blue dress was torn from where she had brushed too close to a tree and snagged the delicate fabric. She found an unoccupied bench and dropped into it, her thoughts spinning as she caught her breath.

She wished she knew what to make of Adam. When he had first proposed, they had both been quietly horrified at their fate. It was not that they disliked each other, only she had hoped to choose her husband, and Adam, she knew, was in love with Thalia. For all she knew, he still was—else why would he have lashed out so thoughtlessly at Kalli by insisting that Thalia not marry where she didn't choose?

But there had been moments where they seemed to understand each other perfectly, and she'd begun to hope maybe they could make a marriage work. And then he ignored her, let her go driving with Mr. Salisbury, who had proposed to her—

And that was another worry. How was she to answer Henry? She liked him well enough, and sometimes when he was near, she felt that delightful frisson of awareness. She enjoyed the feel of his arms around her as they danced. He said he loved her. Was that enough, for a marriage? She had to marry somebody or go home and weather the next few years—perhaps forever—in disgrace.

Would it be Henry, who loved her and made her laugh—even if sometimes he did not seem to understand that she did not want adventure and excitement, but only a comfortable life? Or Adam, who was kind and decent but in love with her sister? And, if what he had let slip earlier were true, he was more unhappy than she knew in their engagement.

Of those options, she rather thought it should be Henry. With Adam behaving as he had, she should have less compunction about breaking things off. He might be a trifle embarrassed, but he would get over it.

Only why did she not feel relieved to have come to a decision?

Because it was still uncertain, she told herself. Once her choice was public, once the worst of the shock was past, things would be better.

Perhaps Henry would agree to an elopement, so she could present everyone with a *fait accompli*, and they wouldn't have to endure so much speculation. No—she could not put the people she loved through that public embarrassment.

Kalli removed her gloves and wiped the tears from her cheeks with her fingertips. She took several long, slow breaths, then replaced the gloves. She had just begun to retrace her steps to find the others when Thalia burst into view.

Her sister rushed to her at once and threw her arms around her. "Are you all right, dearest? I'm sorry Adam is being so awful."

Kalli shrugged. "He's only trying to protect you, as he always does."

"Well, he should spend more time attending to you, and so I shall tell him."

"Please don't," Kalli said, pulling away from Thalia. Her sister's face was flushed, her eyes overbright. "Are you well?"

Thalia's flush deepened. "As a matter of fact, no, I am beginning to feel quite unwell. I have a headache and rushing after you has only made it worse. James has offered to take me home."

"I'll come with you," Kalli said. "I fear Vauxhall has been spoiled for me."

"Oh, there's surely no need for that," Thalia said. "Only think how anxious Aunt Harmonia will be if we both go home. Come, I'll walk you back to the others."

But Kalli insisted instead on walking Thalia to the main gate, where Mr. Darby was waiting for them. She watched him bundle her sister into a waiting carriage, then returned alone to the Grand Walk and made her way toward the supper box. Kalli rubbed the bare skin on her upper arms, feeling oddly exposed without an escort, but no one seemed to notice her.

As she walked, she began to feel more cheerful. The worst was over, now that she knew what to do. If she were no longer engaged to Adam, he would no longer have the power to hurt her with his inattention.

Kalli took her time, stopping to watch a juggler with his balls, and to admire a trio of dancers with bells sewn into their hems. When she reached the supper box, Emma and Adam were both there. Emma looked bored, and Adam was trying hard to make conversation, but it was rough going as Emma couldn't be bothered to return more than monosyllabic answers.

They both looked pleased at Kalli's appearance, which would have been gratifying, except she was fairly certain it was only the appearance of someone new that pleased them, rather than her specific self. Adam opened his mouth as if to speak, glanced at Emma, and shut it again.

Perhaps ten minutes later, the rest of their party returned, Sir

John and Aunt Harmonia leading the way, a drooping Charis following behind. Her skin looked patchy, as though she'd been crying—or trying hard not to cry.

Mr. Leveson was nowhere to be seen.

Rising from the table, Kalli went to Charis, who was pretending to be fascinated by the engraving along the wall separating their supper box from the next. "Where is Mr. Leveson?" Kalli asked quietly. If he had hurt Charis, Kalli would punch him in the nose, though as a rule she saved violence for a last resort.

"Gone home," Charis said.

"Did he say something to upset you?" Kalli asked, her hands tightening into fists. On second thought, Mr. Leveson was rather tall. Maybe she would punch him in the stomach.

Charis pressed her lips together and shook her head. She hiccupped. "Nothing I did not deserve."

Kalli lifted her arms to hug her cousin, but Charis stepped back. "If you are kind to me, I shall cry in earnest, and I had rather not do so in public."

Her arms dropped.

"But where are Thalia and Mr. Darby?" Aunt Harmonia asked, looking about her in alarm.

"Thalia had a headache, and Mr. Darby took her home," Kalli said.

Emma muttered something that did not sound at all ladylike.

"This has been rather a disaster of an evening, hasn't it?" Adam said. "Miss Darby injured her ankle. If you'll help me, Sir John, I can see her home."

Together, the two men helped Emma to the street (though Kalli could not help noticing that her limp was inconsistent—first her right leg, then her left). There, Adam hired a hackney carriage to take them back across the river. Uncle John hired a second cab, waiting farther down the street, to do the same for his party.

Aunt Harmonia insisted that Charis and Kalli accompany Adam and Emma, lest, heaven forbid, any one of the young women should be alone with Adam in a closed carriage for any length of time. Kalli had hoped to sit by Charis, but Charis slid into the cab beside Emma, leaving Kalli to sit beside Adam. She tried to shrink into the corner, so that no part of her would touch him, but the cab driver took a rather reckless corner and she slid almost into Adam's lap. His arms went around her reflexively, and Kalli relaxed into his warmth for a brief, painful moment before pulling away.

"Kalli," Adam said. "I didn't mean you—I'm not unhappy . . ." He trailed away, and Kalli looked across the cab to see Charis and Emma both watching them.

She didn't believe him, but she didn't want to start an argument with an audience, so she said shortly, "It's nothing. We can speak of it later." She needed to tell him about Henry, about her decision. *Tomorrow,* she thought. She was so tired tonight—best to wait until she had slept, until she had her wits about her.

When Adam climbed out to escort Emma to the door of her home, Kalli shifted across the cab to sit by Charis. "Will you tell me what happened tonight? With Mr. Leveson?"

"I can't," Charis said, her voice thick. "It will only make me cry, and Kalli, I *can't.*"

So Kalli simply slid her arm behind her cousin and laid her head on her shoulder. When Adam got back into the carriage, she could feel his gaze on her, but she closed her eyes and pretended to sleep until they returned home.

Aunt Harmonia was waiting for them on the landing outside their rooms in her dressing gown. "Charis, I hope you haven't offended Mr. Leveson with your missish behavior."

"Oh," said Charis, sagging against Kalli. "I hardly think I was missish. But I cannot think why it matters. I do not think we shall be seeing him again."

"Such a coup it should have been for you, to be Mrs. Leveson! I hadn't thought to see you settled so well."

"I wish you had not speculated so, Mama. I was never going to be Mrs. Leveson."

Aunt Harmonia must have seen something in Charis's face, for her tone changed. She pulled Charis to her in a hug and patted her back. "Don't you worry, Charis, it will all come out right." She pressed a kiss to her daughter's head, and blew one to Kalli, and then retreated to her own room.

"It won't come out right," Charis said softly.

Kalli helped Charis settle into bed, then crept from the room and scratched lightly at Thalia's neighboring door. When Thalia did not answer, Kalli opened the door a crack, and saw the mounded shape of her sister, asleep on the bed. She shut the door and went to her own bed.

Kalli woke, too early, with the beginnings of a headache brought on by crying the night before. She pulled aside the heavy curtain in her room, peering down on the narrow mews behind the house. The day was lowering, wisps of fog still clinging to the brick walls of the alleyway.

She remembered Thalia had been ill and crept down the hallway to her sister's room to see if she was feeling better. Kalli listened for a moment at the door, and when she heard no sounds of stirring, carefully opened the door. She only wanted to know that Thalia was resting peacefully.

The gray morning light drifted through a gap in the curtains, falling across Thalia's bed.

Kalli froze.

That shape under the bedclothes was nothing human.

Kalli slid into the bedroom and crossed the floor. Throwing back the coverlet, she found a pair of pillows and some clothes, pushed together to give the semblance of a sleeping body at a casual glance. A quick search of Thalia's dressing table and her wardrobe revealed missing toiletries and clothes—and a card with Kalli's name inked in Thalia's scrawling hand rested on the dressing table.

When had Thalia left? Where had she gone?

The *why* Kalli suspected she already knew. With trembling fingers, she opened the card.

My dearest Kalli, please do not blame me harshly
when you read this. I have gone to become the happiest
woman in England (cliché though that sentiment may
be, it is what I feel at this moment). James has business
that takes him from London, and I shall accompany

him. We shall be married in France. I know Papa
disapproves of this match, but I hope when he sees how
happy I am, he can find it in his heart to forgive me.
Please break the news gently to Aunt Harmonia.

Love, Thalia

Kalli read the letter twice. Then a third time.

Thalia was not the sort of woman to lie, but Kalli could not seem to wrap her mind around the truth of the letter. Thalia had eloped with James Darby. But why? Thalia wrote that Papa disapproved of the match, but Kalli could hardly credit it. Had James spoken to Papa and been refused permission to pay his addresses? It seemed most unlike Papa. He cared more for their happiness than their status, and if Thalia truly loved James, Papa would not stand in her way.

Perhaps Thalia found the idea of eloping romantic. But how could she, when it would occasion such distress for her family and friends?

Kalli took Thalia's letter downstairs, her fingers cold. The pounding in her head grew as she walked. The dining room was empty—the servants had not yet set out breakfast. Kalli sent a maid up to see if her aunt or uncle were awake, and a few minutes later, Aunt Harmonia came into the room, yawning, still in her dressing gown.

"What is it, my dear?"

Kalli held out the card. Aunt Harmonia began reading absently, then her entire body stiffened. She looked up at Kalli, then set the letter on the table without a word and left the room.

Kalli waited. Her limbs felt heavy. While some corner of her mind spun in a panic—what ought they to do? Should they go after

Thalia?—the rest of her was curiously calm. This moment felt inevitable, as though nothing she might do could change it.

The door opened again—but it was not Aunt Harmonia, or even Uncle John. Instead it was Adam, and Kalli flushed, remembering that she had not dressed, but only flung a dressing gown around her nightdress, and her hair was still in its nighttime braid.

"Adam!" Something in her chest ached at the familiar sight of him. She thought, *I have to tell him about Thalia and Mr. Darby. And about Henry.*

"I'm sorry to come so early, but it couldn't wait," Adam said, looking steadily at her, his blue eyes intent behind his spectacles. "I was up most of the night thinking. You didn't let me apologize last night, for my behavior, and I've been wretched. I was thoughtless and inconsiderate, and I hurt you, which I never meant—"

"Adam," Kalli said again. She could not bear the way he looked at her, as though he were focused on her with everything in him, as though she were the only thing that mattered in that moment. Whatever that look meant, she was about to ruin it. She pushed the card toward him.

He picked it up. Read it.

"Has anyone gone after them?" Adam stared at the card and didn't raise his eyes to Kalli. She fought an overwhelming desire to go to him, to put her arms around him and let him enfold her in his arms, to find mutual comfort in physical touch.

"We've only just found out."

"I must—"

Uncle John came into the room then, followed closely by Aunt Harmonia.

"Sir." Adam bowed. "I fear I am persona non grata at present, to intrude on what must be a difficult family matter. But I beg you will allow me to presume upon my longtime friendship with this family and my betrothal to Kalliope to let me go after them. With luck, I can trace them and bring them back to London. If they still intend to go through with this marriage, let them do so surrounded by friends and family and free from scandal."

Uncle John listened intently. "I will come with you."

"No, John," Aunt Harmonia said. "Only be reasonable. Such a journey would be misery on your joints—you should only slow him down. Thank you, Adam, that is a kind offer, and we would be grateful to accept."

Aunt Harmonia and Uncle John followed Adam into the hall to discuss possible directions of flight. Kalli watched them go—not one of them turned back to look at her. As was only right, she told herself. It was Thalia they should be concerned about now.

She couldn't move. A narrow beam of sunlight found its way through the clouds and the windowpanes to trace a line across the edge of the table. She wanted to cry, though it was not distress at Thalia's disappearance that made her eyes prickle, that led her to suck at the roof of her mouth to keep from tearing up. Or at least, it was not *only* distress about Thalia.

She had realized something when Adam had appeared unexpectedly in the doorway.

At his appearance, at the sight of his friendly, familiar face, a deep calm had settled over her—a sense of safety and security she had always associated with home. With her parents and siblings, with a world where she had never questioned that she was loved, that she was valued. Never mind that Thalia was missing, that scandal was about to fall across their family.

Adam was there, and all was right in the world.

When had this happened, this sense that Adam was her home?

Or had it always been there, an outgrowth of her childish hero worship that she had hid from herself when she thought he was Thalia's?

Kalli had realized she loved him in the same moment she gave him Thalia's card, in the same moment his focused attention turned from her to Thalia. As it always had. As it likely always would. Now she ran her fingers across the smooth wooden surface of the table, splaying them wide like the blades of a fan.

There were two things she knew for certain.

She could not marry Henry.

Not when she loved someone else. If her own feelings were unengaged, perhaps she could agree to the marriage in good conscience. But knowing Henry offered her his heart—or thought he did—she could not accept a marriage where she could not offer the same in turn. Maybe in a year, or five. But not now.

She could not marry Adam either, not when he still cared for Thalia. A small, selfish part of her whispered: *Why not? At least he would be mine.* But the rational part of her recognized she would only be inviting pain. How could she spend her life watching the man she loved always light up at someone else's approach? Better to be single, better to throw herself into helping Papa with his parish, helping Mama with the children.

Better to let Adam find happiness with someone he truly loved.

Aunt Harmonia bustled back into the room, sighing. "Someone must write and tell your parents."

"Let me," Kalli said. She wanted suddenly, more than anything, to be home. To hug her mama, to sit at the desk in Papa's study and listen to him talk about his work. "Better yet, let me go home and break the news in person."

"Perhaps that will be best. I'll rouse Charis. She can go with you. I daresay she'd benefit from a couple of days away from London, the way things are going."

Kalli went back upstairs, to gather a few things together for the journey.

But before she went to her wardrobe, she sat down at her desk.

She had two letters to write. One to Henry Salisbury.

And one to Adam.

CHAPTER TWENTY-FOUR

Constant and Painful Exertion

(Charis)

In the *Lumbricus terrestris* there is no heart, and the organs of aeration are not external, but consist of small lateral cells with an external opening.

—*Sir Everard Home,* Philosophical Transactions of the Royal Society *[Charis's note:* If *Homo sapiens* had no heart, could he still experience heartbreak?*]*

The carriage rattled over a rut in the road, bumping the scientific journal from Charis's lap and nearly sending her flying into Kalli, in the seat facing hers.

"Are you all right?" Kalli asked.

"I'm fine," Charis said. "And you?"

"Fine," Kalli said.

They were neither of them very good liars. But at present Charis was content to let the lie rest. She did not want to talk about her own concerns any more than Kalli appeared to. She settled back into her seat and slid the journal into her bag. Why had she thought she might find it comforting? Though it was not the *Philosophical Transactions of the Royal Society*, every page, every carefully argued scientific treatise, reminded her of the disaster she had made of her own life.

She had never expected Mr. Leveson to fall in love with her, as she had fallen for him. But she had hoped to keep him as a friend, someone whose conversation and insights made her own life richer. Now she'd spoiled even that.

Trees flashed past the carriage road, but Charis hardly saw them. She saw instead the trees lining the Grand Walk at Vauxhall. She saw Mr. Leveson's face, flushed with anger. She relived every moment of that terrible night.

He had been quiet and stern at dinner in the gardens, and Charis, sensing his mood but not fully understanding (or perhaps fearing to let herself understand), had been quiet in turn. She'd never spent a more unpleasant half hour in his company, and she included in that tally their furious initial encounter.

After dinner, they had joined her parents to visit the rotunda. Looking back now, Charis couldn't even remember what that structure was like. All she remembered was that, as her mother walked around and exclaimed, Mr. Leveson put his hand on her arm.

"May I speak with you in private?" he had asked. There was no glimmer of a smile in his eyes.

Heart contracting, Charis had followed him a short distance down one of the secluded paths—far enough from the rotunda to offer privacy, but near enough to be safe from scandal. She could still see her mother.

Mr. Leveson reached inside his coat and brought out a sheaf of papers. "Do you care to explain this?"

Charis took the papers he extended to her, and all the tangled, half-wrought sentences on her tongue evaporated. There, in damning black-and-white, were the words she'd written in a fury of passion, after Kalli's scandal had burst. Her critique of L.M.

"Where did you get this?" she asked, knowing as soon as the question left her lips that it was the wrong one.

"A friend of mine brought me a copy of the printing proofs. Wanted to know what I made of this. What I'd done to earn such scorn."

Charis could not seem to swallow. The papers in her hands shook, the words blurring as she stared at them. In a small voice, she asked, "And what did you make of this?"

"That I had been properly swindled. I recognized your turn of phrase almost at once—even without the 'C. Elphinstone,' I should have known your words. Did it amuse you, to court my interest while mocking me behind my back?"

"I never meant—I didn't know it was you. Not when I wrote it."

But Mr. Leveson was in a white fury—if he saw any justice in her defense, he didn't acknowledge it. "And afterward? When I showed you my article? You might have warned me."

"I wanted to—" Charis started, then stopped. Why hadn't she? Because she had been afraid of precisely this kind of exchange. "I tried to stop the printing, but they only laughed at me."

"And you didn't think that I might have had greater success?"

A powerful hope gripped her. "Could you?"

Mr. Leveson seized the papers from her, flung them on the ground. "Had you told me at the outset, yes. But it's too late now. The pages have gone to press, there's no way to remove this article without delaying the whole journal. The society will not stay its hand to save my dignity."

A beat of quiet hung between them.

Charis stared at the crumpled pages. They looked very like a wounded dove she'd found once in the woods behind her home. She wished she were back there, caring for an injured creature she had some hope of healing. Not here. Not when she had no notion how to heal this jagged breach between herself and Mr. Leveson.

"Do you know what you've done, Charis?"

Surprise tugged her eyes up to his. He'd never called her by her Christian name before. The bittersweetness of it tore at her. His eyes were dark, intent, wounded, and she flinched away from the raw pain she saw reflected there.

"Do you know how hard I have fought to be accepted by English high society, by her scientific minds? I'd hoped to become a fellow of the Royal Society. Now I'm likely only to be ridiculous."

"I'm sorry," Charis said. *Sorry, sorry, sorry.* The words echoed in her ears. Perhaps she should etch them on her arms, so each stinging prick of the needle would underscore her guilt. "I shouldn't have been so scathing. I should have told you—"

"You shouldn't have written the damn thing," he said.

A tiny spark of anger flared to life in her. She had been wrong to write incautiously, wrong to hurt him by keeping the news from him. But wrong to write at all? She had been told her whole life that she was wrong—the wrong kind of woman, the wrong kind of scientist. To be told as much by this man, this man whom she had begun to love, proved more than she could endure.

"But isn't truth better than silence? Should I have let your statements stand when they weren't correct? Isn't natural philosophy about the challenging of ideas in the quest to understand the world?"

"Brava," Mr. Leveson said, clapping his hands. "That hurt indignation is the perfect touch to a compelling act. An onlooker might even believe that you are the injured party here."

"No," Charis said. "You do not get to make this all my fault. I will own my failings—I wrote in a fury, proud of my cleverness. But the core of those arguments is sound. They—I—deserve to be heard."

"And you think when men of the society read your words, they will celebrate you when they discover you a woman? Most men will not thank a woman for showing them up. Your very naivety betrays how very ill-suited you are for the world of science."

Charis's skin prickled with heat. "I thought you were my friend. I thought you valued the give-and-take of ideas, just as I did. But you have proven to me that you are no more than the 'most men' you disparage. I suppose it's as well that you show me this now, before I—" She clamped her lips shut. *Before I fall in love with you.*

"I'm not sure you understand how friendship works, Miss Elphinstone." His fury was fading, and now he was merely disdainful. "But I will agree that it's as well we know the true measure of one another now, before any lasting harm is done. I trust you can find your way back to your parents? I find I haven't the taste for company just now."

Charis heard the unspoken message—*I haven't the taste for* your *company*—and nodded. The initial rush of her own anger had blown through her, and now she only felt tired and chilled. Tears pricked at the backs of her eyes, and she blinked hard, unwilling to gratify Mr. Leveson by crying. She found her way to her parents in a daze.

Now, remembering that mix of anger, humiliation, and despair, tears pricked her eyes again. Mr. Leveson had been so cold, so unyielding, and she had liked him so very much. She sniffed and peered out the carriage window, beginning to recognize familiar landmarks.

It was better this way, she told herself. Mr. Leveson had revealed himself as the arrogant man she had known at first, and she was well rid of him. Her brief foray into romance had ended disastrously, but she would know better next time to avoid all affairs of the heart. Better to keep others at a distance, where they could not hurt her.

But just as Charis ordered her thoughts to her satisfaction, other memories intruded. The laughing half glance he would send her in company when someone said something ridiculous. The way he encouraged her ideas when they drove out together, the pleasure he'd taken in her frank speaking at the society lecture. The kiss that had turned her entire world sideways. Even supposing she could find another person she liked, she might be spoiled for kissing forever.

Drat the man anyway. He'd be so much easier to get over if all of him was repugnant.

"What shall I tell my parents?" Kalli asked, cutting through Charis's thoughts.

Of course. Thalia. A wave of shame washed through Charis. How had she become so absorbed in her own pain that she'd forgotten Kalli's? Her family's? She pushed thoughts of Mr. Leveson far away and began discussing with Kalli how best to break the news of Thalia's elopement.

They drove through the small village they'd always called home, and Charis felt a curious sense of time slowing and warping around her. Hadn't she done this a hundred times before? But surely that other girl was someone else, someone who had not been to London for the Season and had her heart crushed.

"Will Adam bring news here, do you think?" Charis asked. "If he finds her or—"

"I don't know," Kalli said, staring out the window. A posting house flashed by. She looked back at Charis. "I left a letter for him. Breaking off our engagement. I mean to stay here, at home. I won't be going back for the close of the Season."

"You—" Charis pressed her lips together, thought. "Because of Thalia?"

Kalli nodded. Her lower lip quivered, and a single sob escaped her. "I love him, Charis. I didn't know I did, but I do, and he's gone after Thalia, and I *can't* marry him."

And somehow, this jumble made perfect sense to Charis, who slid across the carriage to sit by Kalli, and gathered her younger cousin in her arms while Kalli cried. If a few hot tears of her own dripped onto Kalli's brown curls, no one else was there to mark it.

By the time they rattled across the cobblestone drive of the vicarage in the late afternoon, both young women had wiped away all traces of their tears. The two youngest Aubrey children, six-year-old Edward and eight-year-old Urania, were already on the lawn awaiting the new arrivals. They must have heard the carriage wheels on the drive.

When Kalli alighted, her younger siblings swarmed over her, giving her hugs and kisses before passing more of the same to Charis. She disentangled herself gently: Edward was particularly sticky about the mouth, as though he'd been eating jam from the jar again. Then the children ran back into the house to announce them.

Mrs. Sophronia Aubrey, a round, rosy woman, met them at the door. "Goodness, Kalli. I'm glad to see you, but—did I know you were coming? How is Harmonia? And where is Thalia?"

Charis and Kalli exchanged glances.

"I think we'd best go into the parlor, Mama," Kalli said.

Aunt Sophronia, after a searching look at Kalli, sent the younger children out to play in the back garden, then led them into the parlor.

It took only a few moments to acquaint Aunt Sophronia with the bare details—that Thalia had left Vauxhall gardens the night before with a young man and had not returned.

"And they mean to marry?" Kalli's mama asked, pushing a lock of hair back into a disheveled chignon. "But I do not understand this. Why not ask for our blessing? Why elope?"

"Thalia said Papa refused his consent," Kalli said.

"Refused?" Aunt Sophronia's forehead knit. "I know Harmonia expressed some concerns about the young man in her letters, but your father has never been able to refuse you children anything you were set on."

A dark thread knotted itself in Charis's stomach. Thalia had always talked of Mr. Darby as if she meant to marry him, and though Charis had been surprised by the elopement, she had not been shocked. But—

"Mr. Darby didn't come here to ask for Thalia's hand?" Charis asked.

"No, I'm certain he did not. He did not write either—Edward would have mentioned it to me." Aunt Sophronia shook her head. "I'm afraid I don't understand what any of this means. I do hope Thalia isn't in trouble."

Charis hoped so too.

CHAPTER TWENTY-FIVE

[Un]Compromising

(Thalia)

Thy vows are all broken,
And light is thy fame;
I hear thy name spoken,
And share in its shame.

—George Gordon, Lord Byron

Thalia slept most of the first night of her elopement through, her head pillowed on James's shoulder. It was a shallow sleep, interrupted many times by the rocking of the coach as it jostled across rough roads. A few times she woke to a soft snore, evidence that James slept too.

In the early morning, they stopped at a posting house for breakfast and to exchange their hired horses for a fresh pair. Thalia used the necessary room and splashed some water on her face, before walking along the green near the posting house. She rubbed her hands over her arms, chilled despite the light spencer she wore. Had Kalli discovered her note yet? Had they sent someone after her? She hoped they would not be so foolish—it would be a waste of time. She did not mean to go back.

James joined her, wrapping his arms around her from behind. She sank back into him, appreciating his warmth. He kissed her neck, a sensitive spot just below her ear, and a delicious thrill shocked through her.

"Any regrets?" he asked.

"Not a one," Thalia said, turning in the circle of his arms to kiss him.

James met her lips eagerly, and would have deepened the kiss, but Thalia drew back, abruptly conscious of how very public their location was.

In the carriage once more, James settled beside Thalia and began to tell her of the places he hoped to show her in Europe, particularly once he reached his majority and settled his debts. As he talked, he ran a bare finger lightly across her ungloved hand, over the ridges of her knuckles, in the indents between her fingers. Tiny pricks of heat flared in the wake of his touch.

"I should like to see Greece," Thalia said. "And Istanbul. Perhaps we could go as far as Egypt."

"Farther," James said. "We could go to India, or China. The whole world is ours." He pressed a kiss beside her ear, and when she shivered in reaction, he moved to her mouth. His kiss was warm, and intent, and when his tongue flicked along her lips, she opened her mouth to his.

For a moment, she lost herself in kissing, in the warmth that filled her. James caressed her jaw, then his hand slid along her neck, his thumb brushing the hollow at the base of her throat before running along her exposed collarbone. His hand drifted lower, tracing the edge of her bodice, his touch hot against the soft swell of her breasts above her stays.

Thalia caught her breath. She had never been touched so by a man before. And while she knew her marriage would entail more than kissing, had even tried to imagine what that might look like, her imagination hadn't prepared her for the reality—for the heat of his touch, the kick of excitement in her belly, and the rush of apprehension that followed both.

She wasn't ready for this. Not yet. When James's fingers went to the thin ribbon securing the front of her gown, she pulled back. "James, the driver—"

"In a closed carriage, who's to see us? And he won't hear anything above the rattle of the wheels." He moved to kiss her again, more gently this time, brushing his lips against hers. "It's all right," he murmured against her mouth. "You've nothing to fear from me. I promise you will enjoy this."

She pulled away again, this time moving to the seat opposite James. "Please," she said. "Not now. I'm not comfortable . . . the carriage . . ." She bit her lip, struggling to articulate the mix of feelings washing through her. She looked up at James, afraid she might have offended him.

But a slight smile curled about his lips. "I'd forgotten for a moment how innocent you are. I shan't tease you now." The intent light in his eyes promised, *Later.*

Thalia pulled a book of poetry from her traveling bag and began to read aloud, the words forming a fragile barrier between her and James, though she could not have said what she needed that barrier for. James leaned back against the squabs, relaxed, and Thalia read until her hands had stopped shaking—from surprise, she told herself—and her voice was hoarse.

As the long gold light of a spring evening filled the carriage, they pulled to a stop before some country inn, a plain, two-story edifice with whitewashed walls. Thalia did not know where they were, but she was grateful to be free of the rocking carriage, to be stretching her limbs. A serving boy took their luggage into the building, and James's driver led the carriage around back to the stables.

While James made arrangements with the innkeeper's wife, a maid led Thalia up to a room on the second floor, with a single window overlooking the road. The room was clean, if sparsely furnished: a double bed in the middle of the room under a white counterpane, with white linen curtains at the window, and a simple table beside the bed with a washbasin and small oval mirror hung above it.

Thalia went to the washbasin. Removing her bonnet, she set it on the table, and then began to remove some of the pins from her hair, still in place from Vauxhall, letting its weight tumble down her back. She sighed, then stretched and pinched her wan cheeks. Perhaps she could have supper brought to her room instead of venturing out again. Who knew that eloping could be such exhausting work?

Someone tapped at the door, and Thalia turned, ready to tell the maid that she didn't need anything. But it wasn't a maid who entered, it was James. Thalia flushed, her hand going to her unbound hair.

"James, you shouldn't—" She fell silent in some confusion. If

James was to be her husband, surely before long he would see her with her hair down.

"Shouldn't what?" he asked with some amusement. "Shouldn't be in the room we are to share?"

"Share?" Thalia echoed, her stomach jolting. "I thought—" She broke off again, trying to parse the strange feelings tumbling through her.

James came closer, still smiling. He lifted a lock of her hair from her shoulder and kissed the base of her neck, where the fabric of her dress gave way to skin. A shiver ran through her—and not entirely from pleasure.

"And why shouldn't we share a room? We've already run away together, and this is much more economical. I've told the innkeeper we're married, if it's appearances you're worried about."

"Of course," Thalia said. "Only—"

"Only it's not what you're used to," James said. "I understand. But everything will be splendid—you'll see. I love you, and you love me, and that's all that matters."

He was right, Thalia thought, biting her lip. Of course, it made sense to share a room when James's finances were so distressed. Then why did she feel so unsettled? James had caught her off guard, that was all. It was a lot to take in at once, the idea that they might be intimately connected *now*, when she had imagined that intimacy only at some unspecified day in the future, after their marriage. She could adjust her thinking, for James, but it might take more time than a single afternoon. Much as she loved him, she was not ready for such a tremendous step.

She squared her shoulders. Surely James would understand her feelings, if she could but explain them. "Only I did not expect to share a bed with you until we were married," she said.

James chuckled. He ran his thumb along her jawline, letting it rest at last on her lips. "Oh, my sweet Thalia. I fell in love with you for your mind and your exquisite body. Don't spoil it now by being conventional and missish. You must have understood from our conversation that I do not believe in marriage. Why should the law or the church make our attachment to one another more binding? If we love each other, that should be the only vow we need. We have no more reason to wait for intimacy."

Thalia stepped back, crossing her arms over her stomach. Was she missish and conventional? "I thought you were speaking of marriage when you asked me to commit my life to yours."

He still seemed amused. *Patronizing*, she thought, then tried to banish the word. James would not patronize her, not if he loved her. "Mary Godwin went away with Percy Shelley for love," he said.

"And Percy Shelley was already married," Thalia said. "And besides, he and Mary *were* married, after his first wife died." Only weeks after his pregnant first wife was found drowned, Thalia recalled from the papers. Much as she liked Shelley's poetry, she could not admire this aspect of his character.

James shook his head. "Marrying her only sullied something beautiful and pure—it was a pandering nod to convention, a sacrifice of self because of community judgment."

"Or perhaps because that commitment meant something to them," Thalia said, trying to keep her voice even. James would not respect her more for getting emotional. Their conversation at Vauxhall came back to her. She had mentioned marriage, and James had not corrected her. "Let us be clear then. When you asked me to run away with you, you did not mean to marry me? Did you even write to my father?"

"I don't mean to get leg-shackled, no. But I do intend to worship you with my body and endow you with whatever worldly goods I possess. A piece of paper, a few words said in a church before a God I don't believe in, won't change that."

He had not answered her question. "And my father?"

"This has nothing to do with your father," James said, impatience tingeing his voice. "This is about me and you."

James never wrote to my father. "And if I wanted to be married?" Her voice felt disconnected from her body. Through the window floated the sounds of a carriage arriving, a lark singing in a nearby bush.

"Don't be silly. Haven't I just said marriage doesn't change anything? We don't need society's approval to love each other. You're better than that, Thalia. Smarter." He stepped toward her, angling his head as if he meant to kiss her again, but Thalia moved away.

"James, this is . . . I need to think. I'm not sure I'm ready for . . ." She waved her hand at the bed. "For this."

"What is there to think about? Either you love me, or you do not."

Was it truly so simple? Was there something wrong with her, that she could not see her way forward so clearly? But James had lied to her—that, or he had deliberately misled her with his silences.

James rubbed his hands over his face. "I'm going to get a drink. I'll bring you one too. I hope by the time I've returned, you'll have come to your senses. You've disappointed me, Thalia. I thought you were different from the other society misses, but perhaps you're exactly the same."

He stalked from the room.

Thalia went back to the mirror. Shame burned through her, followed by a chill that seeped into her bones. Was she, after all, just being prudish? Mechanically, she ran a brush over her hair and struggled to think. Her thoughts seemed mired in molasses, sticky and sluggish.

She had envisioned a life with James where they might leave in scandal, but they could eventually return to society. But if they lived together without being married, they could not come back.

Oh, she knew the society James had introduced her to might not care particularly if they were not wed. But her family—her friends at home in the village—they would care. She did not think her parents would disown her, but she would never be welcomed at home like she had been, not when her scandalous reputation might still hurt her younger siblings. Her sisters especially.

Perhaps love was worth that sacrifice. As she had told Kalli, she should not stake her happiness on the feelings of others.

But—

Wasn't love supposed to be a give-and-take? A series of mutual compromises on behalf of the beloved? Thalia was being asked to give up her beliefs and expectations for the future, everyone she loved, even her own comfort. What was James giving up for her?

It struck her then, her hands gripping the edge of the wooden dressing table, that a man who truly loved her would care that she was not yet ready to be intimate. Would care that marriage meant something to her. Would not dismiss her concerns as conventional or missish. Would not lie to her to convince her to run away with him. Whatever James felt for her or thought he felt for her, it was not love.

Clarity shocked through her. She loved James—perhaps part of her always would—but she could not be with him. She could not stay and sleep with him when he had given her so little expectation of a return.

Thalia couldn't pin her hair up again without help, so she braided it into a single plait, then picked up her traveling bag from the bed. She had only a few small coins in her bag and a single pound note. It had not occurred to her that she might need to finance her own travel. With any luck, she'd have enough for a spot on the stagecoach as it came through on its way back to London. With a little more luck, she'd catch it before James noticed she was missing.

She put on her bonnet, crept down the stairs, and slipped out the front door into the yard.

CHAPTER TWENTY-SIX

Homecoming

(Kalli)

I love the man that can smile in trouble, that can gather strength from distress, and grow brave by reflection. 'Tis the business of little minds to shrink; but he whose heart is firm, and whose conscience approves his conduct, will pursue his principles unto death.

—*Thomas Paine, found in Kalliope Aubrey's commonplace book*

After breaking the news to Mama of Thalia's elopement, Kalli showed Charis to the spare room—there was no sense in sending her to Elphinstone manor when only a few servants were at the place, the rest having gone to the London house.

"Do you think Mr. Darby lied to Thalia about writing to your papa?" Charis asked her, walking across the room to the washbasin and splashing water on her face before lighting a candle.

Kalli sat down on the bed. "But why would he do that?"

Charis frowned. "I don't know."

A shiver passed through Kalli, raising the hairs on her arms. Something about this elopement wasn't settling right. Was it only her jealousy, that the elopement had clarified Adam's feelings for Thalia? Did a part of her still, secretly, shamefully, hope that Adam might return to her if Thalia's elopement proved successful? She shook herself. She shouldn't be thinking like that. Her only concern should be for Thalia's safety and happiness. Her own could wait.

Her stomach churned. She hated this waiting and not knowing. Kalli stood, clapping her hands as if she could dismiss her fears. "Do you need anything more? Something to eat?"

Charis shook her head, assuring her that she wanted only to lie down.

At the doorway, Kalli hesitated. She couldn't do anything for Thalia just then, but that wasn't true for Charis. "Do you want to talk?"

"About what?" Charis did not look at her but continued to stare at her own reflection in the mirror above the dressing table, tugging at a curl about her temple.

"Anything," Kalli said. "Mr. Leveson, perhaps?"

Charis turned back toward her, flashing a bright smile. Too bright. "There's nothing much to say. He was not who I thought he was, we have had a falling out, and I shall probably never speak with him again."

Kalli stepped back into the room, remembering again the sharp pang that shot through her when Adam announced he was going after Thalia. She didn't believe Charis, not for a moment, that their falling-out was unimportant. "If he hurt you—"

"He didn't hurt me." Charis sniffed.

Kalli took another step toward her cousin. "Earlier today, you held me in the carriage while I cried. If you need a good cry, I am here for you."

Charis shook her head again, the waves around her face bouncing. "I refuse to cry about Mr. Leveson," she said, even as a tear betrayed her by slipping down her cheek.

Kalli reached Charis and tugged her to sit beside her on the bed. "Very well then. Don't cry about Mr. Leveson. But do cry, if you want to. You might feel better."

"Did crying make you feel better?"

"As a matter of fact, it did rather."

A watery laugh escaped Charis. "Well then—" She broke off, her face crumpling, and buried her face in her hands.

Kalli put her arms around Charis, returning the hug her cousin had given her only a few hours earlier. She held her until Charis was wrung dry, until Charis broke free to crawl into bed, saying she wanted to sleep.

Kalli tucked the covers around Charis, whose eyelids were already drifting closed, and crept from the room, shutting the door gently behind her. In the hallway, she stood for a long moment.

Now what? There were hours to fill before they could expect to hear anything. Kalli wished for something to do, to keep herself from fretting about Thalia. To keep from thinking of Adam. To keep from feeling. But she'd left her embroidery and shellwork in London, in her rush to get home, and anyway such crafts might occupy her fingers, but they seldom occupied her mind.

It had helped to comfort Charis—perhaps Mama would have a task for her. Kalli wandered into the kitchen, where Mama was consulting with Cook and filling a basket with jellies and bread and a jar of soup. Kalli brightened. A basket generally meant a visit somewhere, which meant an opportunity to be useful. A memory surfaced of Adam, wan but smiling in a sickbed, but Kalli ruthlessly pushed it away.

"Whom is the basket for?" she asked.

"The Lambeths," Mama said. "Mrs. Lambeth just lost a baby and is feeling poorly. Her husband thought a visit from the vicar might cheer her. Would you like to go with your father?"

And so Kalli found herself once more traveling through the spring sunshine, this time on foot. The breeze carried with it a cool reminder that winter was not far past, but the sun was mild and warm, and she tipped back her head to feel its rays on her face.

Adam was lost to her, and Thalia might be in trouble, but there were still beautiful things and places in the world, and she was *home*. Her papa strode along the road beside her. Every familiar turn of the country lane, each burst of purple color where the violets had come back, even the dappled shadows across the road, lifted her spirits infinitesimally.

Papa glanced at her. "Are you well, my Kalliope-bell? I know you're worried about Thalia, we all are, but I can't help feeling something more is troubling you. Is it about your engagement?"

A wave of ice washed over her. Did they know that she had broken the engagement off? But how could they? She was not even certain Adam had received her letter.

Papa continued. "You must know that I like Adam a great deal, and I would be very pleased if you believed he would make you happy—but Kalli, you do not have to marry someone who will not make you happy simply because your aunt fears for your reputation. Marriage to the right person is a great joy, but in my business, I see too many unhappy marriages to want that for any of my children. Better to stay unmarried than be unequally yoked."

Her papa's kindness might undo her. Kalli blinked against a sudden stinging in her eyes, wondering how she had not yet exhausted her supply of tears. "You needn't worry on that account, Papa," she said carefully. "Before we left London, I wrote to Adam, telling him that I did not believe we would suit."

"Is that so?" Papa asked, studying her face.

She nodded, then looked away. Papa walked through much of life in a dreamlike haze, his thoughts clearly elsewhere, but he had a disconcerting habit of focusing sharply on one when one most wished he would not.

Papa reached out to take her hand and squeezed it. "I'm glad you're back, Kalliope-bell," he said. "I've missed you. You've got a home with us for as long as you want it."

Kalli sniffed and buried her face in her father's coat, hugging him tightly. "I missed you too, Papa. Thank you."

They walked hand in hand down the lane, until they reached the Lambeth house. The outside of the cottage was as neat as ever, with ivy growing up around whitewashed walls. But inside, everything was in shambles, dust gathering in corners and a doll and a solitary shoe scattered across the rug. Mr. Lambeth met them at the doorway with a strained smile. He gestured resignedly at the dirty hallway behind him. "I'm sorry about the mess. I've been trying, but I'm not as deft a hand as Rose, and Rose—well, you'll see."

A pair of children with white-blond hair sidled up behind their papa. The youngest—about two, Kalli guessed—stuck her thumb in her mouth and stared up at the guests with wide blue eyes.

Kalli handed the basket she carried to Mr. Lambeth, who set it on a table near the door. Then he led them down a side hall to a darkened room, where a woman lay on her side, unblinking. Kalli remembered Mrs. Lambeth as a pretty young woman. As a twelve-year-old just beginning to take notice of such things, Kalli had seen Mrs. Lambeth's wedding in a rose-strewn church as the epitome of romance. But Mrs. Lambeth now looked pale and washed-out, as though all the bloom of her namesake flower had leached from her.

The woman's eyes fell on Papa, and she smiled a little and struggled to sit up. "Vicar. Thank you for coming."

Papa settled into a seat beside the bed. "Your husband asked me to come. He's a good man, and worried about you."

Rose looked past Papa to her husband, who stood anxiously in the doorway beside Kalli, holding his children's hands. "The best of men. There aren't many what would try to mind the children or keep house for a sick wife."

Adam would, Kalli thought suddenly, surprised by a wrench of pain. She could see him so vividly in a scene like this—quiet, intense, listening. Looking to help. She shook herself. No. She wouldn't think of him.

Mrs. Lambeth closed her eyes and leaned back against her pillows. Tears leaked from her eyes, streams of silver in the darkened room. She whispered fiercely, "Sometimes I hate God for taking my baby. Sometimes I hate myself, that I could not bring her safely here." She opened her eyes. "Does that make me wicked?"

Papa shook his head. "No. You've had a great loss. It is all right to mourn. I'm here to mourn with you."

There was something private, almost sacred about this mother's grief: Kalli felt suddenly like an intruder. The youngest child broke away from her father and toddled to her mother, raising her arms to be lifted. But Mrs. Lambeth was far away, lost in her own thoughts, and didn't seem to see the toddler. Kalli hurried forward and scooped the child up in her own arms. She carried the girl from the room, pausing at the doorway to collect the older child as well, and took them both outside to play in the sunshine and let their mama begin the long process of healing.

As late afternoon turned to evening, she and the children ran in the garden, played hide-and-seek, and had a fairy tea served in leaf-cups on the grass. Kalli thought, sometimes, of the mother grieving in a darkened room and how there were sharper heartbreaks than losing a man one was coming to love. She thought of Thalia, of the children Thalia might have (or lose) somewhere in Europe, and hoped Thalia could come home before then. But mostly, she concentrated on the children and their bright faces and laughter, and something tight and knotted in her heart began to ease.

She might not have the life she had once dreamed of—a neat house and a husband of her own—but she could still have a good life here, with her parents, helping to raise her siblings and serving in the community she loved.

She could still be happy.

CHAPTER TWENTY-SEVEN

An Improper Observer

(Charis)

In the natural size the feet of the fly are so small, that nothing can be determined respecting them; and when highly magnified, such is the liability to error, that any person with a preconceived opinion becomes an improper observer of the appearances that are represented.

— *Sir Everard Home,*
Philosophical Transactions of the Royal Society *[Charis's note:* And have I not done this myself, my own preconceived opinions making me an improper observer, seeing only what I wanted to see?*]*

Charis woke early, to a trill of birdsong outside her window, and for a wild moment could not remember where she was. She had not heard songbirds over the roar of London traffic in months . . . Then recollection rushed in. She was home, or as good as. Much as she loved the library and greenhouses of Elphinstone manor, the cozier, noisier rooms of the Aubrey vicarage had always felt more homelike to her.

Charis pulled on an old dress, leaving the buttons undone in the back where she could not reach them, and draped a shawl around her shoulders to hide the gap. She put on her boots and crept from the room. None of the Aubreys seemed to be stirring. She let herself out the front door, and then out the gate leading onto the road. A few minutes' walking took her into a nearby thicket.

If the vicarage had been still and quiet, the woods were alive. Tiny songbirds—thrushes, warblers, chiffchaffs—tumbled through the air, flying from one branch to the next, singing as though the rising sun depended on their voices. Oh, how she had missed this. She didn't even mind the chill morning or the damp starting to seep through her boots.

For the better part of an hour, Charis tramped among the trees, keeping a mental tally of the birds and other matutinal wildlife. She didn't see any of the hummingbird hawk moths she intended to study come summer, though it was still early in the year for them. She did spot a wood warbler, a rare Oxfordshire bird she'd only seen a handful of times before, with its yellow-white belly, soft gray back and cap, and eye band. Such rare sightings always gave her the feeling of a pirate stumbling across someone else's buried hoard of treasure.

She wished, briefly, that Mr. Leveson were with her, that she could show him the best of the county birds and compare them with the avian life surrounding his estate. Then she remembered that they were no longer on speaking terms, and she did not want to speak to him anyway.

Birds and moths were safer. Less likely to disappoint or hurt, and much more pleasant to look at.

No, she reflected a moment later, incurably honest, even with herself. It would be a rare bird indeed that gave her greater pleasure to look at than Mr. Leveson, but she had ruined that friendship and would have to content herself with a lesser pleasure.

At length, Charis heard her name, distant and faint, and wondered if she'd imagined it. But when it came again, nearer at hand, she followed the sound until she found Kalli.

Kalli shook her head at Charis's appearance, fond exasperation printed on her face. "I thought we'd lost you again."

"Do you ever think that life would be much simpler as an animal?" Charis asked, ignoring Kalli's statement. "I am certain birds feel pain and joy, as we do, but the course of their life is straightforward. Rise with the sun, sing, mate when the impulse moves you, brood upon your eggs, raise chicks for a span of weeks, and move on. Human lives are so much more complicated."

"Do you fancy sitting upon a clutch of eggs? I'm sure we can find you some."

Charis swatted at Kalli, glad to see her cousin in a brighter mood. "You know full well what I meant. But one thing is certain: I don't mean to be distracted by romance again. I'm perfectly content being a cousin and a daughter, and I shall enjoy your children and Thalia's children, and fill my time with studies."

Kalli was quiet for a moment, scuffing her toes in the dust. "Is love only a distraction? Charis, I know how much your work means to you. I think you should study, and publish, as much as you like. But—life isn't only about work. Don't shut yourself off from love thinking that will protect you. It won't."

Charis knew Kalli meant well, that she was trying to ease what she must imagine of Charis's heartbreak. Still—"I said nothing about closing myself off from love. Did I not say I mean to be a good cousin and daughter? It's only romance I am done with."

"But Charis—you deserve love as much as any of us."

A hot anger rushed through Charis. She whirled on her cousin. "And you don't? How can you lecture me about love and romance when you won't even fight for your own happiness? You told me you loved Adam, but you gave up on *him*. I may have liked, even loved, Mr. Leveson, but he never wanted me."

Kalli flinched. "Charis—I . . ." She blinked hard, then drew in a sharp breath. "I'm sure that isn't true. I saw the way he looked at you."

Charis remembered the way Mr. Leveson had looked at her the last time they met, his face twisted with fury. "He liked a version of me that wasn't real. The real me, he despises." She straightened her shoulders, adjusting her shawl. "Anyway, I refuse to make myself smaller for anyone. They should love me as I am, or not at all."

"Most certainly," Kalli said, sliding her cold hand into Charis's. "I'm sorry if I upset you—I didn't mean to. I only want you to be happy. Please don't hate me."

Charis sighed and squeezed Kalli's hand. "I could never hate you. But please, let us speak of something—anything—else."

Kalli, obligingly, asked Charis about what she'd seen as she walked, and this topic carried them until they reached the vicarage.

The Aubreys were already gathered around the breakfast table, the two younger children squabbling over toast and Mr. Aubrey trying to read the newspaper while Mrs. Aubrey talked at him. The middle Aubrey child, fourteen-year-old Antheia, all long skinny limbs and big eyes, tried to look dignified and aloof, but lost her pretense as soon as she saw Kalli and Charis.

She sprang up from the table and ran toward Charis, brandishing something. "Charis! Only think, this came for you in the morning post."

Charis took the packet from Antheia—it was the newest issue of the *Philosophical Transactions*, with her letter. Ignoring the family, Charis flipped through the journal until she found her name and ran one finger across the lettering.

She had done it. She had published her first-ever scientific article—the first of many to come, she hoped. And yet—this article had cost her a very dear friendship. Was every achievement going to be so bittersweet? No. She would not let it. She would never again let her judgment be muddled by her feelings.

Kalli peered over her shoulder. "Oh! Charis—is that your essay? How brilliant you are."

"Thank you." She tried to sound pleased, but even she heard the flatness in her voice.

Kalli turned to look up at her. "What's the matter? I thought you'd be crowing this from the rooftops. It's what you've always wanted."

Charis stabbed a name on the page with her forefinger: *L.M.* "That's Mr. Leveson," she said softly. "It was his article that I—I didn't know."

"Who's Mr. Leveson?" Antheia asked.

Kalli said, "Oh. Oh, Charis."

"It's done now." Charis closed the journal, set it on the table by an empty plate, and slid into the chair. "Was there any other word with the journal?"

Aunt Sophronia nodded. "A note from your mother." She passed a square card down the table to Charis.

My dear Charis, this came for you just after you left.
Though I admit I don't understand one word in five,
I am happy for you. (I am also pleased you had the
foresight to omit your full name—not many gentlemen
want a bluestocking for their wife!) I wish we had
similarly happy news to share of Thalia, but Adam has
been unable so far to find their direction, though he
continues to search, and I continue to pray. God willing,
we will have better news soon.

She looked up. "Did you read this?"

Aunt Sophronia nodded. "Your mama enclosed it in a letter to me." She glanced at Kalli.

Good—then Charis wouldn't have to read it aloud. It stung, that her mother could not simply be happy for her success, though she knew Mama was doing her best to understand.

"I should go back to London," she said. She'd much rather stay here in the country, where she could immerse herself in her studies and avoid unpleasant encounters. But then, she knew how anxious Mama must be, waiting alone in London for news of Thalia, with only Papa to keep her company, and resolved to put aside her own feelings.

"What for?" Aunt Sophronia asked. "You can do nothing there, and your mama is too distracted to take you about to society events. You'd best remain here until this is settled."

"Mama will want me to comfort her," Charis said.

The older Aubreys exchanged a glance. Antheia giggled.

"What?" Charis demanded.

Kalli smiled at her. "Charis, dear, you are many wonderful things, but comforting is not one of them. You're about as comforting as a beetle."

"I like beetles!" Charis said, beginning to feel indignant.

"Of course you do," Aunt Sopronia said. "But when my sister is upset, she wants soft words and darkened rooms and a good novel, not to be fretted over. Your papa and her maid can care for her very well. Indeed, I believe Harmonia would prefer you to stay here, where you can be a help to me as we wait for news of Thalia."

"Oh," Charis said, her indignation fading as swiftly as it had begun. In her concern for her mama, she had forgotten how Aunt Sophronia must be feeling.

"And perhaps," Kalli said, more gently still, "your mama knows that being in town might be disagreeable for you just now."

Charis looked down at her plate. She would not think about Mr. Leveson. She would not—blast it. Now she was thinking of him.

Antheia brightened. "Is this about Mr. Leveson? Is he one of your beaux? Oh, how I should like to go to London and get myself a beau. Was it very wonderful?"

Kalli and Charis exchanged a grimace across the table. Luckily, they were spared any sort of response when Urania said, in tones of utmost loathing, "Oh, go soak your head, Antheia. No one wants to talk about *beaux*."

Whereupon Aunt Sophronia chastised her for language, Urania protested that Frederick said it all the time, Antheia said Urania was an ungrateful little addle plot, then Aunt Sophronia turned on her too, and general mayhem ensued.

Under cover of the distraction, Charis picked up the *Philosophical Transactions* and escaped to her room. Maybe reading the other articles would return her to the sensible attitude she usually cultivated, out of this agonizing insecurity, where she kept revisiting what might have been, had she acted differently.

CHAPTER TWENTY-EIGHT

A New Hope

(Thalia)

My muse plucked up my sentences and packed my words away.
And I—I failed to notice, for a month, a week, a day.
Till searching, found my tongue had stilled
And would not echo what I willed.
So I hunted in my heart till I found what I would say.

—Thalia Aubrey

The stable yard was a hive of activity—passengers alighting from a coach, a second carriage trying to maneuver around the first to reach the road, grooms rushing across the yard to reach the incoming horses. Thalia stood for a moment, uncertain. This was unlike her. Thalia was generally a woman who knew her own mind, knew what and where she meant to be. But just now she did not feel like herself: She felt small and vulnerable, a crab caught on the beach without its shell.

She drew up her chin, tightened her grip on her single bag, and plunged into the chaos. She tapped a nearby groom on the shoulder.

"Pardon me. Can you tell me where the stagecoach stops?"

The groom was patting down a horse and didn't even look at her. "Half a mile down the road, by the Lovely Crow."

He had not said which direction down the road.

"Which way?" Thalia asked.

He flung his arm out vaguely toward the southeast, and Thalia was loath to ask again as he was clearly disinclined to answer. She'd find someone else along the route to ask, if she needed to.

But it didn't come to that. She passed several businesses at the center of town—a milliner, grocery, bakery, and more—and the Lovely Crow was clearly marked, an impressive three-story inn with a sign displaying a black blob that she supposed was meant as a crow but looked more like a dying badger.

A few questions of a matron standing before the inn revealed that the London stagecoach was expected within the hour, though all the inside seats had been spoken for, by herself and her children. Thalia eyed the cluster of children—five, if she was counting correctly, though they were moving so much it was hard to be certain. Well, she could not ask a mother and her children to give way inside the stage, but that left only the positions atop or behind the stage.

Thalia eyed the horizon thoughtfully. It was not dark yet, but already the light was changing. Was she prepared to spend a cold spring night outside? It would seem she had little choice—James would likely come looking for her if she stayed, and in any case, she did not think her purse would stretch to cover a night at the inn in addition to the cost of the stage. At least an outside seat would be cheaper, she told herself. She'd have funds to feed herself as well.

Having decided, Thalia went into the parlor of the inn and

requested tea and cake. Thusly fortified, she whiled away a quarter hour. The tea and sugar calmed her nerves, making her feel less like an exposed crab and more like a girl whose world has been tipped sideways, but who is in the process of righting it.

When she returned to the yard, she was considerably dismayed to find that in addition to the matron's family, several men had joined the crowd waiting for the stage. A couple of them smelled strongly of gin.

"Waiting for the stage, miss?" one asked. He appeared to be about her father's age, with gray whiskers climbing down his cheeks to his throat.

His friend, younger by at least a decade, with reddish hair and a receding hairline, observed, "If you're riding topside, you'd best find something warmer to wear. It'll be cold, come night."

Thalia shivered at his tone. Or perhaps only at the fading light and growing chill.

The first man laughed. "I reckon we can keep you warm enough."

The matron shot her a disapproving look, as though Thalia had invited such comments, and Thalia walked away from the men, her hands shaking. Oh, how she wished Kalli were here. Or Charis, with her no-nonsense gruffness. She would even take her brother Frederick.

At least there would be others on the stage, she told herself. Those men could not harass her too greatly in front of witnesses. Could they? She would simply have to stay awake.

A light carriage, drawn by matching bay geldings, drew up in front of the inn. A young gentleman wearing a greatcoat and white-topped boots jumped down from the driver's seat, tossing the reins to the groom sitting beside him.

"I say, innkeeper!" The gentleman was already calling out as he ran toward the steps. "I'm parched. A glass of your finest—"

He broke off at the sight of Thalia, standing to one side of the yard.

"Miss Aubrey?"

She squinted at him, heart pounding. She had not expected to find anyone she knew here.

The young man drew nearer and swept off his top hat, revealing curling ginger hair, and she gasped. "Mr. Salisbury! What are you doing here?"

"I might ask you the same. I heard your sister was gone home. I thought surely you'd gone with her. What in blazes are you doing out here, alone?"

"Wait—Kalli has gone home? To Oxfordshire?" She must have taken their parents word of Thalia's elopement. "Are my aunt and uncle still in town?"

"Yes, I believe so. But dash it, you haven't answered my question."

She sighed. "A mistake. It's a long story. I'm on my way back to London."

He looked around the yard, as if looking for a carriage and groom. But the only carriage was his. His eyes lit on the crowd gathered for the stagecoach, and they widened almost comically. "But Miss Aubrey, you can't be thinking of taking the stage?"

"Why not? It's not as though I can afford a private carriage."

Mr. Salisbury paused, rubbing his chin. "Dash it. I cannot in conscience leave you here. I shall have to drive you back to London."

"But you've only just arrived!" And what was he doing here,

during the height of the Season? She'd thought he was bound to his sister and mother, as their escort.

"Can't be helped. You're in distress. I must assist you."

"I am capable of assisting myself."

"Of course," he agreed affably. "But only think—the stage! You'll be far more comfortable with me."

"And what of your reputation, when it's known that you spent the night driving me in a closed carriage?" The public stagecoach might be miserable, but there was no scandal attached to driving with so many other passengers. Even if Mr. Salisbury drove outside with his groom, as he'd done upon arrival, people would talk. And he could hardly like to sit outside the carriage all night.

"I'll hire the innkeeper's daughter. He's bound to have one that'll jump at the chance of seeing London. Besides, it's not my reputation that matters, it's yours. If you don't mind, why should I? What d'you say?"

She'd much rather drive the distance with Mr. Salisbury than sit, cold and cramped, atop the stagecoach for hours with drunken strangers. But she couldn't discompose him so. "You've other errands, I'm sure, that are more pressing."

He shook his head and smiled ruefully. "None pressing. Point of fact, I was sulking a bit. Let me do this for you—it will restore my esteem admirably."

"Sulking?" Thalia asked, beginning to feel amused.

"Your sister won't have me."

"She won't—" Thalia's mind churned slowly. "But she's engaged to Adam Hetherbridge." It seemed that she and Kalli were overdue for a long chat when Thalia returned home.

"And didn't seem happy above half about it," Mr. Salisbury said. "But that's neither here nor there. The lady says no, and here we are."

Thalia thought of the scandal that had forced Kalli and Adam into an engagement, of the scandal that would plague her, if even a hint of her failed elopement got out. Mr. Salisbury didn't appear to have heard anything yet, so perhaps Aunt Harmonia had managed to contain the gossip. Still, the man deserved a warning. "I should tell you now, that even if people do talk about me—about us—I don't mean to force you into marriage. You are quite safe."

A dimple appeared beside Mr. Salisbury's shapely mouth. "I am not certain any man is safe from you and your sister. At least your sister let me propose before dashing my hopes." His grin broadened, signaling that he was not in the least dashed by her words. "Does this mean you'll accept my escort to London?"

Had Kalli noticed the dimple? Thalia wondered. Kalli was quite susceptible to dimples.

"Yes, thank you," Thalia said, more briskly than she meant, on account of the dimple. "I'd be honored to accept your escort."

Mr. Salisbury insisted they have supper at the Lovely Crow—he refused to drive so far on an empty stomach. He ordered food for Thalia as well, though she demurred at first. But when the plate of mutton, potatoes and gravy, and creamed peas was set before Thalia in a private parlor, she found that she was starving, in spite of her earlier tea and cake. She set in with gusto and looked up a few minutes later to find Mr. Salisbury watching her with that dimpled smile of his.

"What is it? Have I food on my face?"

"No, only I like a woman who's not afraid to enjoy her food."

Thalia regarded him thoughtfully. "And you liked my sister. Why did you propose to her?"

"Who, knowing your sister, could fail to like her? She's warm-hearted and kind and funny." He assumed a mournful expression. At least, she thought it was assumed. "Alas, she did not feel the same about me."

Thalia set her fork down. "Liking and marrying are two different things. Of course, Kalli liked you. But I'm not certain she would have been happy with you. Or you with her."

"Oh? Do tell."

"You took her driving a week or so ago, yes? Someplace outside of London?"

He frowned. "What did she tell you?"

"Nothing much. Only that you'd gone farther than she expected. And much faster. Why did you do it?"

"I thought it would be an adventure, an escape from London."

Thalia took up her fork again and speared a piece of meat. "If you knew Kalli better, you'd know that she is at heart most content when she's close to home. Kalli likes to have fun, and some people mistake her sense of fun for a sense of adventure. But my sister isn't adventurous, Mr. Salisbury. She finds adventures wearisome."

"And you don't?"

"No. But we're not speaking of me. We're speaking of you and my sister. I think, if I am not mistaken, that you find adventures exhilarating? You're drawn to new things and new places."

Mr. Salisbury splayed out his hands upon the table. "You are correct."

"Imagine, then, being married to my sister. She wants to stay home, raise babies. You want to travel abroad. Your options then become leaving my sister behind, to grieve your absence—because Kalli is, for all her faults, quite loyal and affectionate. Or to drag her along with you, wondering all the time why she is miserable because she's too kind to tell you that she hates what you love."

Mr. Salisbury laughed and lifted his hands. "Enough. This ghastly vision is nearly enough to persuade me. Though perhaps I shall need to call on you in a week or two to remind me of my narrow escape."

Thalia laughed. "You are welcome to call, but no reminder will be needed, I am sure." Somehow, she did not think his heart had been as deeply engaged to Kalli as his pride. He'd recover soon enough.

So would she, for all that her heart felt small and bruised just now.

Somehow, Mr. Salisbury convinced the innkeeper to loan the eldest of his daughters (Mr. Salisbury was right—the man had three of them) to accompany Thalia. After helping Thalia and the red-cheeked girl into the carriage, Mr. Salisbury climbed up to the driver's seat beside his groom and set off.

"Lor' love me, what a fine carriage!" the girl said, eyes wide. Then she clapped her hands over her mouth. "Me mam said I was to behave and not to bother a lady like yourself. But you don't mind if I chatter a bit, do you? You have kind eyes."

Thalia smiled, exhaustion and relief washing over her at once. She was going home. She was leaving James behind. And the girl's chatter was friendly and warm. "I don't mind."

Miss Elsie King proceeded to talk for the next hour or more, with only minimal contributions from Thalia. She talked of her sisters and the happenings in town and the scandal at their inn when a fine lady had been found in bed with a fine gentleman who was *not* her husband, and the husband shot a hole through the plaster walls. "No one were hurt, though."

At last, even the innkeeper's daughter seemed affected by the rocking of the carriage. She yawned, trailed off a sentence or two, then closed her eyes. A moment later, she was snoring gently.

Despite her exhaustion, Thalia couldn't sleep. Her mind kept going over her last encounter with James, and then following that back further, trying to work out how she had so misread him. Perhaps her desires had been stronger than her sense—a dismal realization for one who prided herself on being guided by logic rather than emotion. She had not been at all logical where James was concerned, and look where that had gotten her.

The carriage stopped occasionally to change horses. Each time, Mr. Salisbury checked in on her, helping her alight when he saw she was awake, bringing her tea when needed.

"It's lucky we've a bit of a moon tonight," he said, "and good roads. We're making better time than I expected."

"I'm glad," Thalia said, wishing she had more precise words to tell him how grateful she was for his help, for the chance to sit in a darkened carriage and think, to let the night wash around her with a friendly caress. The night didn't judge her. Neither did Mr. Salisbury—an unlooked-for mercy.

It was mid-morning Friday when they finally pulled up in front of the Elphinstone town house. If the footman who answered her knock on the door was surprised to see her, he didn't show it. He let her and Mr. Salisbury in. The innkeeper's daughter hovered on the doorstep behind them, and the footman did raise his eyebrows at her.

"Would you take Miss King down to the kitchen and see that she's fed and given one of the maid's rooms for the day and has passage booked home for tomorrow on the mail coach?" Thalia asked. "I owe her a debt."

The footman nodded and led the innkeeper's daughter away.

Aunt Harmonia came tumbling down the stairs. "Oh, my dearest child! You're home!" She put her hands on either side of Thalia's face, studying her carefully. "You're not hurt? We have been so worried for you. How could you have frightened us like that?"

Thalia exhaled. "I am fine, only tired. I'm sorry to have worried you so—I made a foolish mistake, but I shall not do so again."

"Well, we shall talk more when you've rested." Aunt Harmonia patted Thalia's cheek and turned to her escort. "Dear Mr. Hetherbridge, th—" She broke off. "Mr. Salisbury? Whatever are you doing here?"

"I came upon your niece in some distress, ma'am, and had the honor of escorting her home."

"I was sure you must be Mr. Hetherbridge. He's been out looking for Thalia. I shall have to send him word. Oh! And to Sophronia— I'm sure she must be beside herself."

"Adam is looking for me?" Thalia asked, a curious lurch in her stomach. "I thought Kalli went home. He didn't go with her?"

"Oh, yes, she did. It is all a mess. I shall have to tell you—" Aunt Harmonia paused, eyeing Mr. Salisbury. "Oh, where are my manners? Do come in, Mr. Salisbury. Can I get you breakfast? Tea?"

Mr. Salisbury shook his head. "Thank you, but no. I'm afraid I'm rather in the way here. But I hope I might be allowed to call on you both in a day or two, when things have calmed down?"

"Yes, of course. Thank you," Thalia said, walking him to the door.

Before stepping out, Mr. Salisbury turned to her. "Courage, Miss Aubrey. Everything will turn out right enough." Then, whistling, he set off toward his carriage.

Thalia watched him for a moment, her throat prickling at his kindness.

"What a nice young man," Aunt Harmonia said, as Thalia returned to her. She tucked her arm into Thalia's and escorted her into the front salon, then sent a maid for some tea. "He would do very well for a bright young lady. I never did like that Mr. Darby fellow for you, and now that you've come to your senses, we can find someone much more suitable."

Thalia was not sure whether to laugh or cry. After two nights of minimal sleep, and the emotional upheaval she'd been through, her aunt's optimism was too much. "Oh, Aunt, I am done with men, I assure you."

"Perhaps he would do for Kalli, now she has turned down Mr. Hetherbridge? She sent him a note before she went home, calling off the engagement. He told me about it last evening, when he stopped by to update us on his search for you."

Thalia froze. Kalli had turned down Adam? Then why had she refused Mr. Salisbury too? What had happened to erase Kalli's fear of social ostracism and lead her to turn down not one, but two eligible offers? Oh, she needed to talk with her sister. And forestall her aunt. "Aunt, please, I beg of you, don't try to match Kalli just yet."

Once Thalia had drained her teacup, Aunt Harmonia allowed her to retreat to her room. Thalia had every intention of falling into her bed and sleeping for a se'nnight. But when she reached her room, something stopped her.

She cocked her head, trying to identify the feeling. It was something like an itch, deep in her gut. Only not so insistent.

Words. There were words bubbling up inside her. A poem, she was nearly sure of it, though the shape wasn't entirely clear in her head.

Her poetry writing had dwindled considerably after meeting James. She had tried once or twice after sharing her poetry with him, and every time she did so, she heard his voice in her head, telling her this word was not right, that image too trite. She had taken it as a sign that James's superior taste would guide her own talent to superior things, but what if it went deeper than that? What if she had allowed James to take over the role of critic in her head because it was easier that way? If she did not write at all, she could not write rubbish. She could not fail.

What she needed was not a critic, but a supporter. She had supported James in his ideas and fancies—but he had not once asked to see her poetry, and had only listened (begrudgingly, she now feared) to her poem when she begged it of him.

Well, she wouldn't give James that space in her head anymore.

He had been wrong about her, about what she wanted. Perhaps he was wrong about her poetry too.

Thalia sat down at her desk, facing a window. The morning was overcast, but she liked the gray clouds. They seemed fitting, somehow. Poetic. After all, a heroine should never return from an almost-scandal to sunny skies and a hero's welcome. Gray was more muted. Subtle. Perfect.

Thalia picked up her quill and began to write.

CHAPTER TWENTY-NINE

Since You Left Us

(Kalli)

To be sure a love match was the only thing for happiness, where the parties could any way afford it.

—*Maria Edgeworth,* Castle Rackrent, *found in Kalliope Aubrey's commonplace book*

"Kalliope," Mama said as Kalli tried to leave the breakfast room and her squabbling siblings. Charis had already escaped with her newly published article. There was something ominous in Mama's tone. Kalli's heart sank.

"Will you come into the parlor with me?"

Obediently, Kalli followed Mama into the more formal parlor, where they could shut the noise of the children away from them. Mama waited until Kalli had sat on the floral-print sofa and she had settled beside her before beginning.

"Harmonia sent me a note along with the letter for Charis. Can you imagine what that note said?"

Kalli looked away from Mama's somber expression and studied her hands. Either Aunt Harmonia blamed Kalli for not having suspected Thalia's elopement, or she had gotten wind of Kalli's broken engagement. Neither conversation would be pleasant.

"Adam told Harmonia you left him a note, ending your engagement." Mama put a finger under Kalli's chin and tipped her head up to look at her. Mama's eyes were serious and a little sad, and the kindness in her face made Kalli's throat tighten. "Why did you not tell me? What happened?"

Kalli was silent for a long moment. She wanted more than anything to throw the whole sad story on Mama, and let her mother make everything better. But perhaps Mama would say she was only being foolish? "Adam is in love with Thalia, and I care for him too much to go through with the engagement. I want him to be happy."

"Oh, Kalli." Mama cupped Kalli's face with her hands, and Kalli leaned into her mama's touch. She had missed this. "Did Adam tell you he loves Thalia?"

"No—but I know. He followed her around London, and he took off at once when he found Thalia had eloped."

"But Thalia did elope—with someone else," Mama said, a wry twist to her lips. "Even if Adam does care for her that way, Thalia does not love him. And you—do you love Adam?"

Kalli nodded.

"Does he know that?"

It did not matter if Adam knew what she felt. He didn't return her regard.

Mama sighed. "Kalliope. I have loved you since before you were born, and I have watched you grow into a smart, accomplished young lady. Your caring heart is one of your biggest strengths, but right now I think it may be holding you back. You care so much about the happiness of others—but what of your own happiness? You should not always be sacrificing yourself, particularly when that sacrifice has not been asked of you. Adam did not ask you to break the engagement—are you so sure you know what he wants?"

Kalli did not answer. Fragments of her conversation with Thalia before Vauxhall came back to her: *What if what I want makes other people unhappy?* And Thalia's answer: *You have to live your life, not other people's.*

Mama took her hand and squeezed it gently. Then she stood. "I must check on the children. But Kalliope, if you love that young man, don't give up on your own happiness without fighting for it."

The rest of the day dragged by with no news of Thalia. Kalli alternated between worry for her sister and her own tangled thoughts about Adam. She did not know for certain how he felt about Thalia or how he felt about her. Should she ask him? What was the worst that could happen? Several cringingly embarrassing scenarios occurred to her, and her courage began to flag.

The older Aubreys knocked about the vicarage in increasing anxiety and irritability, until Edward and Urania complained to Kalli that everyone was a grump, and she took them outside in the light rain to stomp through the mud.

The following morning, their third day in Oxfordshire, a note arrived by special courier to tell them that Thalia was found—that she was unharmed and unwed, and she was on her way home. Late that afternoon, Thalia herself arrived with Adam and Hannah.

As soon as the carriage wheels were heard outside the vicarage, Kalli rushed to the door, followed closely by Charis and Mama.

Adam alighted first, turning to hand Thalia down from the carriage, and Kalli stilled, her eyes drinking in Adam's familiar figure. She let Charis and Mama run past her, watched for a moment as they embraced Thalia and exclaimed over her. Adam looked above their heads to Kalli, light reflecting off his glasses. As soon as his gaze met hers, Kalli turned and fled back into the house, nearly stumbling over Antheia, who had emerged from her bedroom with her finger in the middle of a novel.

"What is it?" Antheia asked.

"Thalia's come back," Kalli managed, then darted to the safety of the room she shared with Thalia and flung herself on her bed. She had thought and thought and thought about what she might do when she saw Adam again, but now that he was here, it was all too much. Her heart felt as if it might beat free from her chest.

A few minutes later, Antheia called through the door, telling her that Mama had put together a luncheon. Kalli said she was not hungry, though her stomach gurgled.

Not long after that, someone knocked at the door. "Kalli?" It was Thalia.

"Go away," Kalli said, turning her face into her pillow. She wasn't ready to talk to Thalia either.

The door opened. She heard Thalia's footsteps across the rug, sensed rather than saw Thalia sit down on the bed facing hers.

"Are you angry at me?" Thalia asked. "Is that why you've been avoiding me?"

Kalli sighed. "I'm not angry."

"Hurt then?" Thalia moved from her own bed to sit beside Kalli, setting her hand on Kalli's shoulder. The bed gave beneath her weight, creaking softly.

Kalli started to deny that too, then stopped. She *had* been hurt by Thalia's disappearance, her indifference to how her elopement might affect her family. She would not deny that just to make Thalia's conscience easier.

Now Thalia sighed. "I never meant to hurt you—I thought that I was claiming my own happiness. But that future I thought I was claiming was just a mirage."

Kalli flipped back toward her sister, raising onto one elbow. "What happened? Did Mr. Darby hurt you?"

Pressing her lips together in thought, Thalia finally shook her head. "My heart and my dignity might be bruised, but Mr. Darby did not harm me. He simply revealed his true colors—that he liked me well enough for an affair, but he never meant to wed me."

Shocked, Kalli sat up and wrapped her arms around her sister. "Oh! Thalia, I am sorry." She tried to smile at Thalia, though her smile wobbled. "What a botch we have made of our Season between the three of us. A scandal, a failed elopement, and Charis has gravely offended Mr. Leveson."

"I would not have regretted the elopement if James had been as I thought him." Thalia returned the smile with a slight upward curve of her lips. "But I do not know how I came to be so stupid."

Kalli shook her head fiercely and hugged her sister again. "Not stupid. We all of us imagined Mr. Darby to be in love with you. And as you were not married and he was not married, and you are not the sort of girl to become a mistress, it was only logical to assume he meant marriage in running away with you."

"Logical!" Thalia laughed, but there was a bitter note in it. "Thank you, Kalli. You've restored some of my wounded dignity. I thought perhaps I had abandoned logic altogether. But I shall be more sensible about love in the future."

Kalli swallowed. *Be brave*, she told herself. "Do you mean Adam?"

"What has Adam to do with my being sensible?" Thalia asked, frowning. She lifted a dark curl away from Kalli's face. "Why did you call off your wedding? I thought you two were well matched."

Kalli pulled her knees up to her chest and curled her arms around them. "You did not. You were mad as anything when we got engaged."

Thalia reached out to Kalli again, dropping her hand when Kalli tipped her head to the side, avoiding her reach. "Oh, maybe at first, because I thought you were only using him to save your reputation. And because Adam had always been my particular friend."

"You were jealous," Kalli said.

"I was not—fine. Maybe a little. But only at first. Then I fell for James, and I began to see all the ways that you and Adam would suit. I even thought you were beginning to fancy him. Was I wrong? Is that why you called it off? It is certainly not because you wanted to marry Mr. Salisbury."

"Oh, Henry!" Kalli said, laughing a little helplessly. "How did you know about that?"

"He told me of his proposal himself. He's the one who found me when I had run away from James. Brought me back to London in his own carriage."

Kalli looked at her with wide eyes. "That is a story I should like to hear."

"Later," Thalia promised. "But you did not answer me. Was I wrong about your liking Adam?"

Kalli pressed her face into her knees. "No," she said, her voice muffled by the fabric of her skirt. "Not wrong."

Thalia ran a light hand along her sister's back. Kalli shivered. "Then why, dearest?"

"Because he loves *you*."

Thalia's hand stilled. "Why would you think that?"

"Because he always has. Everyone but you could see it." Kalli raised her face from her knees, blinking hard. "He went after you the minute he knew you were gone. He hardly spoke a word to me."

Thalia was silent for a long minute. "Is it possible," she said hesitantly, "that he went after me because I am *your* sister? Because my being in a scandal would hurt *you*?"

Kalli shook her head again. "I cannot believe it."

"Even if he did not do it entirely for you, he might have done it for the sake of our friendship. But we are only friends, Kalli, nothing more. We would not be a good match. I should forever be wanting more—new books, new places, new ideas. And you know Adam, like you, is happiest at home. He is too staid, and I am too unorthodox for him. We do not fit, as you do."

"Adam is not staid!" Kalli said, indignant. "He is comfortable and calm and deep."

Amusement lifted the corners of Thalia's lips. "That's what I said. Staid."

"But he doesn't love me." Kalli's voice was small.

"Strange that he spoke of little *but* you on the journey here then. I think you should talk to him. Suppose he does not love you? What have you to lose but your pride? And only think what you should gain if he does."

Thalia's words echoed what Kalli had already been thinking. She uncurled her legs and stood, her heart beating hard. She could not tell if it was in hope or terror.

Thalia murmured encouragingly.

"Very well," Kalli said, stretching. "But first I must eat something or I'm liable to cry all over his cravat and I should never live that down."

After a cold luncheon, Kalli went searching for Adam. He was not in the study with Papa, or in the parlor with Mama, Thalia, and Charis. She passed Antheia in the hallway, and her younger sister raised her eyebrows in an attempt to look arch. "Are you looking for Adam? He's in the garden."

Kalli blushed. Gathering her dignity and her courage, she thanked Antheia and then walked through the French doors leading to the lawn. She crossed the long stretch of grass to Mama's flower garden at the back. The roses that would be in rich profusion later in the spring had not yet budded, but the tulips were out, pink and red and white.

Adam was sitting on a bench in the sunlight, reading. His sandy hair fell about his ears, and Kalli itched to push it back. Adam nudged his glasses up with his forefinger and turned a page. Kalli's heart turned over. She wanted to memorize this moment, the way the sunlight brought out amber glints in his hair, the strong set of his shoulders, those long, thin hands that she loved.

She loved him.

And because she loved him, she would have to be brave.

She took a few steps forward. Adam did not seem to notice. It was not until she was right before him, her shadow falling across his book, that he looked up.

Behind his glasses, his eyes were astonishingly blue, nearly as clear as the sky overhead.

Kalli's pulse thrummed in her throat. "May I join you?" She indicated the bench, and he nodded.

"Please do."

Kalli sat beside him, carefully leaving a few inches of space between them.

"Thank you for looking for Thalia," she said.

Adam laughed a bit ruefully and rubbed his chin. He had shaved, Kalli noticed. His chin was smooth where earlier, after his arrival with Thalia, he had been covered with a fine golden stubble. Would his cheek be as soft as it looked? She curled her fingers in her lap.

"Much good it did me," he said. "I should have known Thalia could save herself."

"But you tried. That is the mark of a true friend." *Only a friend?* She caught her breath, waiting for his answer.

"Maybe. I scarcely thought—I saw your distress and your aunt's and I leaped into action. Having had more time to think, I believe I ought to have trusted Thalia more. If the elopement *had* been what she thought it was, what right did I have to stop her from pursuing what she wanted?" Adam looked away from Kalli, studying the garden beside him.

"You were trying to stop a scandal." Kalli hated the look on his face, the disappointment and air of self-mockery.

"Much Thalia cares for that."

"But she would not have been happy, and she's come home now. It's over, and Thalia is free. Do you . . ." She paused, nearly choking over her words. "Do you love her? I've released you from our engagement."

His head swung back around, his blue eyes meeting hers in a fierce blaze behind his glasses. "Do I love Thalia? Yes. As a friend. As a sister."

Oh. Kalli dropped her eyes to her lap. She could not seem to breathe properly.

"Is that why you broke off our engagement? Because you thought I was in love with Thalia? Or is there someone else?"

Had Thalia told him about Henry? Kalli forced herself to look up, meeting Adam's gaze. The light in his eyes made her cheeks warm. Hope fluttered in her chest. "There's no one else. Adam—I . . . there's something I need to tell you."

Adam waited, the tiniest of smiles curling his lips. He was good at waiting for her. Kalli wanted to kiss him there, right where the freckles clustered around the corner of his mouth.

"I love you, Adam Hetherbridge." The intensity of his expression was too much for her, and she looked out at the garden. "If you don't feel the same about me, I understand. I released you from our engagement. But I—I wanted you to know." She stole a cautious glance back.

Adam was still watching her, and the tenderness softening his face stole her breath away. "Kalliope Aubrey," he said, very softly, "there is no one else for me either."

His words hung between them for a long moment, before he bent his head toward her.

Kalli did not move, afraid to break whatever this curious spell was, and Adam kissed her.

The kiss was hesitant at first, only a bare skimming of lips against lips, asking a question. Kalli pressed forward, answering enthusiastically, deepening their contact. She untangled her hands and curled one of them into his hair, smiling a little as she heard his breath catch. Adam's lips were chilled from sitting outside in the cool spring air, but they warmed at Kalli's touch.

Adam cradled Kalli's head in his hands and broke away to trail kisses from her temple to her jawline before recapturing her mouth in a kiss. Then it was Kalli's turn to draw back, pressing a kiss to the corner of his lips like she had wanted to earlier. She traced the freckles on his cheek with one finger, as if she were mapping a constellation of stars, and then followed with her lips. Adam humored her for a while, before kissing her again.

Some minutes—hours?—later, they broke apart for air, grinning at each other. Kalli caught a flash from the house, as someone dropped a curtain down. She shook her head, more amused than ashamed, and wondered which of her sisters (or, heaven forbid, her parents) had been watching.

She threaded her fingers through Adam's, stroking her thumb across his. He brought their clasped hands to his lips and kissed the back of her hand.

"I love you, Kalli," he said. "It came over me so gradually I didn't quite realize how much until I got your letter. Do you know how that felt, after I'd spent the day fruitlessly trying to discover where Thalia had gone, to come home to a note like that? Such neat, prim lines, but each one like a stab wound."

"I'm sorry," Kalli said, but she was smiling. She would never have intentionally hurt Adam, but if that hurt meant he was here with her now, then she could not truly regret it.

"No, you're not," Adam said, correctly reading her expression. "Truth be told, I deserved it. I chafed against the engagement when I should have seen that I'd been given an unlooked-for gift. I let that ass Henry Salisbury take you driving because I was too stubborn to admit how I felt and told myself I didn't have a right to demand your affections. I thought I was letting you have the life you wanted."

"Is *that* why?" Kalli asked, considerably cheered by this admission. Adam had been *jealous*, not indifferent. "But you must know that the life I want involves you—I want to be with you, share your work, have your children . . ." Her cheeks burned with this admission, but Adam did not seem shocked. Instead, he tried to kiss her again, but she pushed him away. She needed to finish this thought. "Will you marry me, Adam Hetherbridge?"

"I thought you'd never ask," Adam said, and Kalli laughed.

This time, she kissed him, and when she pulled back, Adam's lips were delightfully pink, his breathing erratic. Kalli felt a curious mix of pride and affection: that *she* could have such an effect on this man she adored.

"We will have to wait some time," Adam said. "I cannot secure a living until I am twenty-four, more than three years from now, and you are not yet eighteen."

"I'm willing to wait, if it means I can be with you," Kalli said. She studied Adam's open, smiling, earnest face and her whole heart bloomed wide. "You said once that you didn't think I should kiss anyone else, so long as I was engaged to you."

Adam raised one eyebrow at her. "Are you disputing that claim?"

Kalli set her expression as prim as she could. "No sir. But since I don't intend to kiss anyone else, I rather think you should kiss me again."

Adam laughed and leaned in. Still smiling, Kalli met his kiss.

This, she thought, was happiness. Not some future possibility that she *could be,* but something that she was *now*. And with Adam, she hoped, *always*.

CHAPTER THIRTY

Know Your Own Happiness

(Charis)

According to this view with respect to hydrogene, it should follow that amongst other combustible bodies, those which require least heat for their combustion, ought to burn in more rarefied air than those that require more heat.

— *Sir Humphry Davy,* Philosophical Transactions of the Royal Society *[Charis's note: . . . Upon further reflection, perhaps I ought not to commit to writing what other thoughts on combustible bodies this prompts in me.]*

Smiling to herself, Charis set the letter from Kalli on her dressing table. The Aubrey sisters would not be coming back to London this Season: Kalli had decided to remain at home, near Adam, and the whispers about Thalia had not entirely died down. But Charis could not begrudge them. Kalli was happy, her words practically glowing across the page she'd written, and that was enough. Thalia had even begun writing poems again. She'd enclosed a copy of one with Kalli's letter, her wild scrawl a startling contrast to Kalli's neat print.

Charis's glance snagged on the small clock set on her dressing table. Goodness, was that the time? She'd be late. She started to rise, then caught sight of her hair in the mirror. Right. She'd come up to her room precisely to fix the unruly nest of her hair, only she'd been distracted by the letter and forgotten.

It wasn't that she thought one's appearance was a measure of their worth. She didn't. But she was going to the Thursday lecture of the Royal Society, and she could not bear it if anyone—most particularly a certain L.M.—read into her disheveled appearance some sign of her emotional distress. Or worse, her lack of fitness for their company.

She had debated not going. No one would fault her for it. (Most likely, no one outside her household would even care.) But the study of science was still what she wanted to do with her life. What she had always wanted to do. She could not let the possibility of an unpleasant encounter with Mr. Leveson deter her.

Papa graciously loaned her the use of the carriage and a groom, and her maid, Mary, attended with her. Charis held her breath as she entered the lecture hall, waiting for someone to deny her entrance without Mr. Leveson's protection, but though she caught some frowns, no one stopped her.

Sir Everard Home began lecturing on the passage of the ovum from the ovaries to the uterus in women, and Mary fell asleep almost at once, though Charis couldn't fathom how she could sleep through such engrossing information. Sir Everard Home recounted his discovery of an ovum, and though Charis was very sorry for the serving girl who had died to enable his discovery, she found the account fascinating. To think that science was only now beginning to understand a part of her own anatomy! To be sure, an understanding was not required for the part in question to function (or there would be a severe shortage of children in the world), but it was odd—and exhilarating—to find one's own body an object for scientific exploration.

Belatedly, Charis realized that several of the gentlemen near her were casting covert glances at her. Some were staring openly, eyebrows drawn together in disapproval.

Oh, dear. She thought she'd fixed her hair. But a not-so-subtle pat assured her that her hair was in order. Then why were they—Oh. Perhaps they thought female anatomy, particularly such intimate anatomy, was an indelicate lecture topic for a young lady? But how absurd. Surely if she *possessed* ovaries, she could listen to a lecture on them.

The drawings the lecturer displayed were rather fascinating too. Charis wished she could inspect them more closely, but when the speech finished and the room rose, she discovered that Mr. Leveson stood between her and the speaker.

Mr. Leveson's presence might not have prevented her from coming to the lecture, but her desire to avoid him was much stronger than her desire to see an ovum at close hand.

Charis turned around to find Mary had woken with the stirring crowd, and she tugged at Mary's arm to urge her out of her seat and out of the building. Mary protested. "Where's the fire, love? You needn't pull at me so."

At last they broke free of the crowd, and Charis's pumping heart began to slow. They slipped into the marbled hallway and made their way to the steps leading down to the road where their coachman should be waiting.

They were nearly to the coach when she heard her name. "Miss Elphinstone!"

Mr. Leveson.

She pretended not to hear him. Unfortunately, her maid was not so adept at ignoring nuisances. "Miss Elphinstone," Mary hissed, tugging at Charis's sleeve. "That gentleman is calling after you."

Charis kept moving.

"Miss Elphinstone!" Mr. Leveson called again.

Mary caught Charis's wrist, pulling her to a stop. Charis sighed and turned around.

Mr. Leveson stepped neatly down the stairs to join her. Their two weeks' separation had done nothing to render him less attractive, more was the pity, and her traitorous heart lurched as he drew near. A part of her wanted to lean in to his warmth, sniff his familiar sandalwood cologne, but she held herself rigid.

"Miss Elphinstone, I've been hoping to speak with you. May I escort you home?"

Charis cast a longing glance behind her at her father's coach. She'd rather walk home on her two hands.

"Please," he said.

Something about the simplicity of his plea touched her more than florid protestations could have. "Very well," she said, suspecting she would regret her acquiescence. "You can join me, I suppose."

"I'd prefer to deliver my message in private," he said, eyeing her maid. "My own carriage is not far from here, and my groom is discreet."

Charis didn't move.

"Please," he said again.

Charis sighed, and sent Mary home in her father's coach, telling her to inform Mama about the change in plans.

Mr. Leveson offered her his arm, and she took it out of habit, then wished she hadn't. At this proximity, his warmth radiated up her side and brought with it a flush of heat that had nothing to do with his own temperature and everything to do with hers. Drat it, why couldn't physical sensations be directed by intellect and not by bodily responses? If it were up to her, she would respond only when reason indicated it was called for. Though upon further reflection, she conceded that perhaps some activities—like kissing—would be much less pleasurable if they were purely rational.

"Did you enjoy the lecture?"

"I did," she said. "Though I admit I find it peculiar that there is still so much about our own bodies that we do not understand. How do the lungs know when to draw air, or the heart to contract? How is it that my eyes blink of their own volition, but I can also choose to open or close them at will?"

In her growing enthusiasm, she'd nearly forgotten who she spoke with. It was only as she saw a tiny smile starting at the corners of his mouth that she grew flustered and fell silent. Did he find her enthusiasm silly?

"I found the speaker rather pompous, myself," Mr. Leveson said, "but I'm glad you enjoyed it."

Mortification crept over Charis. Why had he insisted on escorting her home if he meant only to patronize her?

They reached his carriage, the brown and cream phaeton she'd grown so accustomed to. She thought, amused despite herself, that her current green walking gown did not suit it so well as the dress she'd worn the first time they went driving.

Mr. Leveson helped her into the carriage, then swung himself into the seat beside her and took up his reins. His groom, who had waited at the horses' heads, climbed into the tiger's seat behind the vehicle.

For a moment, neither spoke, as Mr. Leveson was occupied negotiating the traffic outside Somerset House, and Charis was busy trying not to panic. Her brain, helpfully, spun all kinds of scenarios in which this encounter could end disastrously. The least alarming option was a carriage accident that would set her free to walk home alone.

At last, Mr. Leveson said, "I read your article again."

Charis crossed her arms across her chest, wishing she could fold herself even smaller. "Oh?"

"It was good. Brilliant even. Had anyone but myself been the target, I might have enjoyed it."

So he had not enjoyed it. Why was he telling her this? No author cared to hear negative reviews of their own work. "Is this some form of torture to repay me for your own discomfort at the publication? If so, I must say it is not very gallant of you."

Mr. Leveson surprised her with a shout of laughter. "Oh, Miss Elphinstone, I have missed your frankness. No, I did not ask you here to berate you. I did say the article was brilliant. Let that be a salve to your wounded pride. Would you rather I lied and said I enjoyed something that showed so clearly the limits of my own thinking and pride?"

"Yes," she said, and he grinned at her. Her heart flipped over, an action she knew was physiologically impossible, but it *felt* just so. She promised herself—and her wayward heart—a severe reprimand when they were home. This kind of dysregulation simply would not do.

"I owe you an apology, not false compliments. You were right.

325

The only way for science to advance is for us to ask questions, and to put our own pride aside when it becomes clear we were mistaken. I was wrong. And I took it out on you rather than acknowledge my error. For that, I am sorry. We must have the truth, at any cost." He paused a beat, watching her, his eyes glimmering with humor. "Even if the cost is my own pride."

His smile tugged an answering smile from her. Oh, this was dangerous. *He* was dangerous. Every one of her good resolutions was abandoning her. But if he was going to own his mistake, she should own hers too. "Let us have the truth, yes. We shouldn't hide from it. But relationships—friendships—are important too. I ought to have told you of the article myself. And I should not have attacked a fellow scientist in such terms, even if I did not know the author. I let my own cleverness get away with me."

"Indeed. If you mean to abuse me in the future, please do so to my face."

Now it was Charis's turn to laugh. "Oh, you may be sure of that." She took a deep breath, tipping her head back so the sunlight slipped beneath the brim of her bonnet to warm her face. "Does this mean we can be friends again?"

Mr. Leveson did not answer at once, and Charis wished she had not spoken. A friendly professionalism was not the same as friendship, she knew that. Maybe professionalism was all he was willing to grant her, after what had passed. Her heart began to ache, as though someone had slid their hand beneath her breastbone and pressed on the organ.

"If that is what you wish, I should be happy to be your friend."

Charis forced herself to smile. This was what she wanted, was it not? So then why did the word *friend* on his lips seem so empty to her? She extended her gloved hand to Mr. Leveson, and he took it, keeping one hand on the reins. "Friends then."

She liked the feel of her hand in his so very much. Too much. She pulled her hand back and studied it in her lap. There was an ink spot on one finger of her glove that she had not noticed. Had Mr. Leveson seen it?

"Miss Elphinstone—Charis," Mr. Leveson said, drawing her gaze back to him. All the humor had gone out of his face, but there was a curious, almost tender look about his eyes. "You promised once never to lie to me."

Charis nodded. "And I have not."

"Then let me confess. I do not want your friendship."

Charis blinked once, twice. Though his words stung, she would not show him how much.

"I am far too selfish. I want you—all of you. Your time, your company, your thoughts—your heart. I want you to be my wife."

"What?" Charis asked. Surely she had misunderstood that last string of syllables.

"I want to marry you," he said. "If you'll have me. I'm given to understand that I can be proud, arrogant, and sometimes disagreeable. But I promise I am not inflexible, and I am trying to be less proud. And I do adore you, body, mind, and soul. Could you find it in your heart to accept me?"

"I beg your pardon," Charis said, "but—can you be serious? I know very well that I am not stupid, and you appear to find our conversation entertaining, but surely that is not sufficient grounds for marriage. How can you possibly *adore* me?"

"Perhaps I did not fully appreciate you on our first meeting, but I assure you that it has been some time that I have considered you one of the handsomest women I know. I would far rather be with you than with anyone else."

Charis's cheeks burned. He was too forthright to dissemble with her. Which could only mean that he meant exactly what he said. "Are you certain you wish to marry me?"

"As certain as I have been of anything. What else do I need to do to convince you?" A wicked gleam came into his eyes. "I kissed you once because you asked me to—may I kiss you again, because I *want* to?"

Charis nodded, not quite trusting herself to speak.

Mr. Leveson leaned across the seat and kissed her, never mind that he was driving, and anyone might see them. The kiss was brief, the barest pressure of lips on lips, but it promised future kisses in a way that sent pleasant shivers all the way through Charis. She rather thought she would need more samples of Mr. Leveson's kissing to determine quite why they had this effect on her. For scientific observation, of course. Only maybe when he was not driving, and they were not on a public street.

"Having kissed me twice—once very publicly—I'm afraid you've thoroughly compromised me, and I shall have no choice but to marry you," Mr. Leveson said.

She eyed him quizzically. "Haven't you rather compromised *me*? I shall make a terrible society wife, you know," she said, making one last effort to dissuade him. "I dress to please myself, I mean to have my own laboratory, and even should I have children, I won't give that up. I am a terrible hand at household management—Mama will not let me near the account books, because I inevitably turn them to different purposes—and I cannot promise I will ever be where I am supposed to be when I am supposed to be there."

"Is that all? I promise, I would endure far greater if it meant I could spend a lifetime with you. In any case, I've already warned you that you're getting a bad bargain in me."

"Not bad," she said, shaking her head and reaching out to take one of his hands. "Anyone should be lucky to have you."

"I don't care about anyone," he said, looking at her. "Just you. Would you be lucky to have me? That is really the only question that matters here. Do *you* want to marry me?"

Because Charis had promised she would never lie to him, she told the unvarnished truth. "I should like nothing better. I do love you, Mr. Leveson."

"And I do love you, Miss Elphinstone. But I think you had better call me Mark."

Epilogue

Charis Elphinstone was missing again.

This was not an unusual occurrence, but it *was* her wedding.

Kalli shifted uncomfortably on the wooden pew and caught her father's eye, where he stood to one side of the transept in his vestments. He raised his eyebrows and inclined his head subtly toward the entrance at the end of the nave. Kalli read his expression, she hoped accurately, as *Go determine what is happening.*

Mr. Leveson, standing near her father in a sober black coat and knee breeches, also watched her, though his expression was harder to read. Kalli turned to Adam, but he had seen the whole interchange and needed no interpretation. He squeezed her fingers gently. "Go," he whispered.

Such a small word, but it sent a pleasant shiver down Kalli's back anyway. They were only two months truly engaged, but she loved this security, that Adam was by her side, that he trusted her, that she could venture out into the world but always, always, return to him. Kalli returned his squeeze and stood.

From the pew behind Kalli, Mama leaned forward in her seat beside Thalia. "What's wrong? Where's Charis?"

Kalli shook her head. "I'm going to find out."

Frederick laughed beside Thalia. "Charis has got cold feet, I'll wager."

Thalia and Mama both glared at him, which only made Frederick laugh harder, shaking the blond curls that were so like Thalia's.

Edward asked, "Why should cold feet keep her from getting married? Is she sick?"

Mama shushed him as Kalli headed down the aisle, thinking. Uncle John would lead Charis up the nave when the ceremony began, so his absence was not unexpected, but Aunt Harmonia had not arrived yet either. Perhaps they were all of them simply late. Papa had chivied the Aubrey family out of the Elphinstone town house a good three-quarters of an hour early because he did not wish to be late to this ceremony, and they had arrived so early they had had to wait for another bridal party to vacate the church before they could take their seats inside. June was a busy month for weddings at St. George's.

Kalli made her way along the nave, past the small cluster of family and well-wishers. In addition to a handful of assorted aunts and cousins who had made the journey to London, Mr. Leveson had brought with him a few close friends. His mother and his sister had not been able to make the trip from India in time for the wedding, but Charis and Mr. Leveson meant to travel there for their bridal tour. Kalli tried to ignore the whispers as she passed. Surely Charis was only late.

She pushed open the doors onto the portico, the cool air of an overcast morning rushing to greet her. The Elphinstone carriage sat on the street before the church, and Uncle John and Aunt Harmonia were standing beside it, talking earnestly to someone still inside.

Kalli skipped down the stairs.

Aunt Harmonia turned toward her. "Oh, Kalli. Thank goodness. Can you persuade Charis to come out?"

Kalli peered through the open door of the carriage to where

Charis sat in one corner, hands clenched tight together. Creamy June roses were placed artfully in her pinned-up hair, and the ivory-colored gown with russet and gold embroidery had been fitted to exactness. She looked very pretty—and terrified.

Climbing into the carriage, Kalli took a seat beside her cousin. "Charis? Dearest? What's amiss?"

Charis looked at her, eyes wide. "What if I am dooming Mark to a lifetime of unhappiness?"

Kalli swallowed a laugh. It was clear to anyone with wits that Mr. Leveson doted on Charis. But laughing would not ease Charis's fears. "I think that is a decision only Mr. Leveson can make, and he has already made it."

"But what if I am terrible at marriage?"

"You are not a terrible friend, and friendship is, Mama tells me, a most important ingredient in marriage." There were other elements to marriage too, aspects that Kalli was becoming increasingly eager for. "Has Mr. Leveson kissed you?"

Charis nodded. It was hard to tell in the dark interior of the carriage, but Kalli thought she was blushing. A good sign. "And did you like it?"

Charis nodded again.

"Well then, you like Mr. Leveson and you like kissing him, and those both seem to bode well for future happiness. When you told him yes, you seemed to think so, at any rate. What kind of scientist would abandon her hypothesis without so much as testing it?"

Charis seemed much struck by this.

Aunt Harmonia sighed in audible relief as Kalli emerged from the carriage, Charis at her heels. Kalli darted back into the chapel ahead of them, to nod at her father and take her seat beside Adam again. Some of the tension in Mr. Leveson's face eased at her reappearance, and she smiled reassuringly at him. Taking Adam's hand in hers, Kalli sent up a silent prayer for the happiness of all of them: herself and Adam, Charis and Mr. Leveson, Thalia and the rest of her family.

Charis marched down the length of the church, her gloved hand resting lightly on her father's arm. It took everything in her not to clutch his arm as she had when she was a small child facing a night terror. Not that she was scared, precisely—oh, dash it, that's precisely what she was. She repeated Kalli's reassurances to herself as she walked, but that could not entirely dampen the fear that she was about to ruin Mark Leveson's life.

She did not remember the nave of the church being so long—St. George's was only a small, rather plain church that served the parish her parents' town house belonged to. Perhaps she'd entered some undiscovered scientific phenomenon that distorted both time and space. She'd wanted to be married at home, in Oxfordshire, with Uncle Edward as officiator, but Mama was determined on a society wedding. And then Mark had admitted that a London wedding would be easier for his friends and cousins to attend, so Charis agreed. As a concession, Mama had arranged with the local vicar for Uncle Edward to officiate.

Charis wished she'd stood firmer on her own wishes, as this church seemed suddenly unfamiliar and strange, though she'd attended almost weekly for the past four months. Even her body did not quite seem her own, magnificently corseted and accoutered as she was.

Then she and her father approached the front of the chapel, where she could see Mark more clearly. Mark smiled at her, but she could see the tension about his eyes betraying his anxiety.

He was as nervous as she was. At that realization, much of her fear sloughed off her, as though she'd come from a frosty winter's day to stand beside a fire. She returned Mark's smile.

Uncle Edward began reading from the Book of Common Prayer, the old familiar words washing over Charis. She'd heard this same ceremony many times before. But somehow they seemed new, personal in a way they never had been before. Charis stole a glance at Mark. He was looking at her with such an intense blaze of love and hope that her whole face grew warm. Uncle Edward asked the audience if any knew of impediments and was met with silence, so he went on.

He turned to Mark. "Mark Anand Leveson, wilt thou have this woman to be thy wedded wife? "

The moment of truth, Charis thought, catching her breath. If Mark did not want this, now was his chance to say no. But he did not hesitate; the confident glow in his face did not abate. "I will."

And then it was her turn to promise. "I will," she said, her voice sure and steady.

They exchanged the formal promises of the marriage vows, then Mark took the ring back from Uncle Edward and put it on Charis's ring finger. Holding it there, he repeated, in a voice scarce above a whisper, "With this ring I thee wed, with my body I thee worship, and with all my worldly goods I thee endow."

They knelt before Uncle Edward, who read the words of the prayer, before pronouncing them married. Everything that passed after that seemed hazy to Charis—the signing of their marriage lines, the collected well-wishes and kisses from guests.

She was married. She was Mrs. Leveson. She had not released Mark's hand after Uncle Edward joined their hands together, and she leaned in to whisper, "I only hope you shall not regret this."

He met her eyes. "Not a bit of it. And I have every intention of proving to you how much I shall *not* regret this as soon as we are alone."

Charis's entire body flushed. She began to think Kalli was right: She would enjoy the testing of this marriage hypothesis very much.

Thalia's mind wandered through the long recitation of the marriage vows. The words were old and rather poetic, but that was not enough to keep her attention, particularly as her stomach growled. And there was still that dull twinge of pain when she thought too much about the words: Once, she had imagined saying words very like these to James.

On the other side of Thalia, Edward and Urania struggled to sit still, and Frederick was attempting to tickle Antheia to make her laugh. Thalia poked him. "Stop it," she whispered. "You're not allowed to ruin Charis's wedding."

"Spoilsport," Frederick whispered back, but he stopped.

Thalia looked up at the beautiful stained-glass window above the altar. The glass didn't glow as it would when sunlight struck it, but it was lovely all the same. Her thoughts drifted again, from the pieces of colored glass to the hands that had made them, teasing new forms and shapes from molten sand. There was poetry in that somewhere . . .

And then she was gone, swimming in words inside her head and only half-conscious of the wedding around her until the company was standing, congratulating one another and buzzing with the general contentment of a job well done. Thalia kissed Charis's cheek as the new bride passed, then followed her mother to the portico of the church.

Mama was already going on about the breakfast she would set down for the guests at Aunt Harmonia's town house: the rolls and toast and ham and eggs and chocolate that would need to be hot and ready to serve as soon as everyone arrived. They were to leave at once, with Papa to follow later with Uncle John. Charis, of course, would come with her new husband.

The carriage had not yet arrived, so while Mama fretted about tasks still undone, Thalia continued composing her poem in her head. She didn't hear her name being called until Mama nudged her.

"Thalia! That gentleman wishes to speak with you."

Thalia blinked. Her eyes focused on a young man in a fitted blue coat, standing at the base of the stairs alongside the road, only a few feet away.

"Mr. Salisbury! What brings you here?" Surely he wasn't angling for some view of Kalli, at this late stage?

"Out on errands for my mother. Just passing by. And you?" He glanced up at the church behind her, at the wedding party just beginning to filter from the chapel and appeared to register the time of day and the fact that it was not a Sunday. "Oh! A wedding? Not yours, I trust?"

Thalia laughed. "The closest I have come to marriage this Season was that unfortunate situation you rescued me from."

"I admit, I'm rather pleased to hear that. Not—er, not your sister's?"

"No, not yet. Though Kalli is here with her betrothed. If you wait a moment, you might see her."

Mr. Salisbury tugged at his cravat, his first sign of discomfort. "Ah, as to that, I believe I'd rather trust you to convey my good wishes. Still a bit awkward, you know."

Thalia did know. She hadn't seen James, who'd made good on his escape to the continent, but she had seen his sister, Emma, at an event only two nights before with a chaperone, and both young women had made a concerted effort to avoid each other.

"Are you to be in London long?" he asked then.

"Perhaps a week or so, not long."

"Would you allow me to call on you, take you driving perhaps? I read that poem of yours, 'Cold Burns the Wind.' Rather pretty piece."

"You *read* it?" Thalia goggled at him. She had published her first work in a minor literary magazine only the week before, but she had not imagined above a dozen people outside her family had taken notice of it. Certainly not an aspiring dandy of Mr. Salisbury's stature.

He flashed a grin at her. "Don't be so surprised. I am a man of many talents and hidden depths."

"So I see." She returned his grin. "I should be delighted to go driving." A commotion behind her drew her attention; Charis and

Mr. Leveson had emerged at last from the church, with Kalli and Adam close behind.

Mr. Salisbury tipped his hat at the newlyweds, then at Kalli, who stared, wide-eyed, from him to Thalia. Thalia smothered a laugh as Mr. Salisbury strode off, then she climbed back up the stairs to join her sister and her cousin.

The London Season had not ended as any of them had planned. But improbable as the Season had been, it had been a season of possibility too. And what looked like an ending, wasn't. Not really.

The poet in Thalia believed that beginnings were birthed from endings as surely as spring followed winter. The realist in her knew life was not that simple: Relationships and trajectories began and ended and began again, meandering and transforming everywhere one looked.

But this—Thalia put one arm around Kalli's waist and one around Charis's, tugging them away from their respective partners for a tight, lavender-and-rose-scented hug.

This endured.

And the next chapter was theirs to write, however they chose.

AUTHOR'S NOTE

Before I began writing historical fiction, I was a fantasy writer, conjuring worlds that only existed in my mind. Writing a book about Regency-era England is, in many ways, a similar exercise in imagination.

I have loved Regency romances since I was eleven, the first time my mom put a Regency romance in my hands and said, "I think you might like this." But for all that I enjoy the pomp, glitter, ceremony, and romance, the much-older writer in me feels compelled to acknowledge how much of this world is a fantasy. A fun, escapist fantasy that many of us love—but a fantasy nonetheless. And while there's nothing wrong with enjoying that fantasy (I do!), it's also helpful to be aware of the reality.

The members of the *ton* were a relatively small fraction of British society, and the majority of people living in England worked for a living, many of them at poverty levels. According to the Napoleon Series, there were twenty-eight dukedoms in 1818 England ("The British Peerage in 1818"). Anyone with more than a glancing knowledge of Regency romance knows that there are many more dukes than that in Regency fiction, and most of them are young and dashing. Regency novels have always included an element of fantasy.

While I don't want to dismiss the pleasure of escapism (that's often why I read and write), I believe it's critical to remember what this escape is built upon. The very wealth that makes English high society fun to read about depended in large part on money earned from British colonial expansion, particularly in the British Raj and the Caribbean colonies. I made Mr. Leveson an Anglo-Indian to acknowledge this complex history. As historian Durba Ghosh has noted, it was not uncommon for Englishmen in India to take Indian wives and send their children back to Britain to be educated (from the BBC's *History Extra*, "Inspiring *Bridgerton*: the Real South Asian Women in Regency-era England"). According to historian William Dalrymple, in the late eighteenth century, nearly one in three British men in India left their wealth to Indian wives and children, although twenty years later such relationships had become more taboo ("Assimilation and Transculturation in Eighteenth-Century India," *Common Knowledge*, vol. 11, no. 3, Fall 2005). Author Tasha Suri has a fantastic Twitter thread from April 4, 2022, arguing that while readers can and should enjoy Regency fantasies (especially racially inclusive ones like the *Bridgerton* TV series), we also need books that explore the realities of BIPOC lives under colonization. While I am not qualified to write those books, I hope readers will search out those stories as well.

British colonialism also appears briefly in the book in the shape of the (in)famous Elgin Marbles that Thalia and Kalli go to see at the British Museum. In the early nineteenth century, Thomas Bruce, the seventh Earl of Elgin, had many of the marble sculptures from the Parthenon removed from Greece and brought back to Britain. In 1816, the British government purchased the sculptures from the debt-laden Elgin and placed them in the British Museum. Even at the time, this move was controversial, with many Englishmen (Lord Byron among them) decrying the looting of the Parthenon (Christopher Casey, "'Grecian Grandeurs and the Rude Wasting of Old Time': Britain, the Elgin Marbles, and Post-Revolutionary Hellenism," *Foundations*, vol. 3, no. 1, Fall 2008). In recent years, the government of Greece has petitioned for the return of the sculptures. In 2021, then-British prime minister Boris Johnson refused, claiming that Lord Elgin had acquired the sculptures through legal means of the time period. Later that same year, a UNESCO advisory board recommended Britain revisit this decision. At the time of this writing, the status of the Elgin Marbles remains unresolved.

One final note about historical accuracy: *The Philosophical Transactions of the Royal Society* is an old and respected scientific journal that did, in fact, print work by Caroline Herschel (along with occasional letters from women) in the late eighteenth and early nineteenth centuries. Although women were not generally allowed at the meetings, Margaret Cavendish was the first to attend in the seventeenth century. For the sake of the story, I have sped up the publication cycle of the journal, which at the time was published annually in January. (For more on women in the *Philosophical Transactions*, see "Women and the Royal Society" in Google Arts and Culture.)

ACKNOWLEDGMENTS

Every book may have its start in the mind of an author, but it takes a community to bring that book into the world.

My heartfelt thanks go out to the following:

My agent, Josh Adams, for believing in the book from the start; my editor, Janine O'Malley, for her enthusiasm and keen insights, and the fantastic team at Macmillan, including Melissa Warten, Asia Harden, Chandra Wohleber, Starr Baer, Lelia Mander, and Elizabeth Clark.

My writing group, for their constant encouragement: Helen Chuang Boswell-Taylor, Erin Shakespear Bishop, Tasha Seegmiller, and Elaine Vickers. Friends who offered early reads, excitement for the project, support, and/or advice: Cindy Baldwin, Joanna Barker, Ranee Clark, Shannon Cooley, Natalee Cooper, Sarah Eden, Jessica Springer Guernsey, Amanda Rawson Hill, Lisa Mangum, Melanie Jacobson, Emily Rittel-King, Jolene Perry, Shar Petersen, and Lydia Suen.

Charis Ellison, for letting me borrow her fabulous name. Julianne Donaldson, for organizing a magical Regency retreat that gave me an excuse to make and wear stays for the first time. The sensitivity readers who helped make this book more inclusive (any errors are obviously mine).

My family, especially my husband and kids—they know what they did.

And lastly, to readers—books don't truly exist until readers take them up and love them. I hope you enjoy this book as much as I've enjoyed writing it.